BRAVING THE EMERALD WASP

CONRAD BRASSO

ALSO BY CONRAD BRASSO

Hunting The Midnight Shark

Torching The Crimson Flag

Get notice of new releases and special deals by following the author at
http://www.bookbub.com/authors/conrad-brasso

Join the insiders updates list at www.conradbrasso.com for advance
access, insider information, and exclusive free bonuses!

BRAVING THE EMERALD WASP

By Conrad Brasso

Thanks, Steve, for all your help getting this sequel launched. Thanks Jeff for your insight into the process and for your encouragement and inspiration. Thank you to everyone who has bought, read, and reviewed this book. You are why I love to write. And thanks, Beautiful, for always being supportive.

The light shines in the darkness, and the darkness has not overcome it.

CHAPTER ONE

THE BACK STREET OF THE STRIP MALL IN KOREATOWN WAS POORLY lit; dark, in fact. But the man didn't hesitate at all. He flung himself into the alley in a desperate sprint, his phone lit up in his outstretched right hand, panic on his face. The beating sound of footsteps echoed off the walls as he ran. In the middle of it, he came to an overloaded dumpster piled high with putrid trash, the overflow spilling carelessly around it. He stopped, his chest heaving, his eyes darting wildly and then suddenly as he saw, deep groans of unspeakable sorrow rose from his soul and erupted uncontrollably out of his mouth.

She was dead! He was too late.

He dropped to his knees beside her and took in a gruesome sight he'd been dreading for ten years, a sight he'd relive in anguish for the rest of his life and wish over and over that he could erase. Her eyes in a once-beautiful face that now told the tale of merciless beatings stared up lifelessly. Her bruised arms spoke of torture, and her legs were twisted in a crooked, unnatural way. She'd been tossed into the foul-smelling refuse and left to die. Her hand was clutching her phone. It, too, was lit.

Connected to his. Her final words still burned in his ear, "I'm sorry, Jun, I don't think I'll make it."

He reached for her, stunned with grief, and clasped her body to his. Anguish began to wrack his body with waves of sobs and he pressed his warm cheek to her icy one.

"I'm the one who's sorry, Jee Hye," he whispered over and over. "I'm so sorry."

He couldn't remember how long he held her like that, maybe moments, maybe hours, but something in his brain broke through his living hell and made him aware again. He slowly reached for her phone—tears blurring his vision and flowing freely down his cheeks. *Why? Oh dear God, why did it have to end like this?*

The thing in his brain intruded again with increased urgency, and then he became instantly aware. A clicking noise had echoed through the alley. Danger suddenly screamed in his head. Without moving, he took in the details of his peripheral vision. Two barely-distinguishable figures were creeping towards him along the walls of the alley from the direction he'd come. Jun caught a brief glint of light from the guns in their hands. His heart begged him to stay. His brain told him to flee. But his legs were already moving, lifting him straight into another desperate sprint. A deadly flurry of bullets cracked into the night air around him, snapping past his head, embedding themselves in walls, and skipping off pavement. He spied a back door slightly ajar—dashed inside and slammed it shut. Korean barbeque was thick in the air as he leaned his shoulder against the heavy metal and fumbled with the deadbolt. Finally, he managed to slam the cylinder barrel into place, and darted down a hallway, through a kitchen and into the brightly lit dining area of Min's Korean Restaurant.

Patrons stared in surprise and a waiter yelped at him indignantly, but his ears were listening for something else as he crashed frantically through tables, knocking over chairs and charging towards the front entrance. Then he heard it—pounding on the back door. The deadbolt wouldn't last long.

He snatched a Lakers hoodie off the back of a customer's seat and burst through the front door out onto the street. Spotting a taxi, he jerked open the back-door yelling as he dove into the empty seat, "Go now! Go! *Bali bali!* Hurry!" Jun dug into his pocket and flung two one-hundred-dollar bills at the startled driver for added emphasis and then slammed the back door and dove to the floor. The two gunmen burst out of the eatery, guns still in hand, looking up and down the sidewalk. "Go!" he screamed in a desperate whisper. "Please! Get me out of here!" The taxi roared to life. The driver slammed into drive, and the car was off into the stream of traffic.

"Where to, mister?" the driver finally asked after they'd gone through a traffic light, turned a corner, and then another.

Jun sat up and looked cautiously around. He took off his shirt sticky from sweat and transferred blood. "Get over to Crenshaw Boulevard." He slipped into the hoodie and stuffed the shirt under the driver's seat. "Drive south for twenty minutes and drop me off. You keep the change."

The taxi driver nodded in relief. It was a good enough deal.

JUSTIN PARK WAS ENJOYING this moment. The wedding was over. It had been a classy affair on the grounds of a luxurious private residence overlooking Auckland's Waitemata Harbor. Everything had gone just as planned. The florist artfully created a beautiful ambiance; the photographer seemed to be in the right places at the right times; the officiant was genuine and professional, and the guests who had traveled to New Zealand for the lavish destination wedding were happy. Most importantly, Justin's fiancée was now his wife!

The night was everything he'd dreamed it would be. Turning, his eyes drank in the sight of his sleeping bride. Her dark hair framed a gorgeous face, still made-up. Her red lips were relaxed and full. His eyes wandered down to gaze in wonder at the curves of her body under the bedsheets. Just as he was debating whether he should kiss her awake for more love-making, his phone buzzed loudly. It came from the heap of clothes on the floor. He waited for the annoying sound to stop. Probably one of his groomsmen lost in the hotel. *Was his mother wanting to let them know how beautiful the ceremony had been?*

The buzzing started again. He couldn't believe he'd forgotten to mute it. He refused to get out of bed. Whatever it was could wait.

The third time, he began to worry that it might wake his sleeping bride. He slipped out of bed and hurriedly rummaged through his tuxedo pants. He looked at the front screen and didn't recognize the number.

"*Yobosayo?*" he answered in Korean.

"Justin?"

"Yeah."

"Jee Hye's dead."

Justin stood up straight.

"What? Who is this?"

"It's me, dude. Jun ... Park."

4

"Jun?"

"Oh my gosh – you're on your honeymoon! I'm so sorry! I forgot! I'm so sorry. I'm sorry, ... dude ... I'll ..."

"Jun? It's okay," Justin paused and took a deep breath. His cousin's voice sounded strange. Distant somehow and thick with grief. "What happened?"

"I ran into Jee Hye a few weeks ago at the Asian market. She was super excited to see me ... but ... it's a long story. She was in a lot of trouble. Her pimps were working her over." Jun paused. "I don't why, but I had to do something. I promised to get her out."

"Her pimps??"

"Yeah."

"Why didn't you tell me?"

"I should have. I know."

Justin sat down on the floor and leaned against a wall.

"When we met, and I'd made that promise, I put a tracking app on her phone. She knew about it. For the last ten days, I've been getting information, logging her movements, and planning her escape ... now she's dead!" Jun screamed into the phone.

"How do you know that?"

"She called me from her place. As we were talking, they broke into her apartment and dragged her out. She managed to keep her phone on. She'd snuck it into her pocket or something. I listened while they were beating her, yelling at her, and then they shot her. They executed her! I tracked down her position and rushed over there as fast as I could. It was too late!"

"Jun, did anyone see you?"

"They came after me, but I got away."

"What!? Jun! Are you kidding me? Did you get her phone?"

"Yes, but they can't track me. I disabled it completely and destroyed the power source. Figured you could reconstruct the drive maybe?"

Justin took another deep breath. "Yeah, probably can." There could be forces at work here that Jun knew nothing about. "Where are you now?"

"In a twenty-four hour Walmart on Crenshaw."

He checked his watch. It was 10:20 p.m. in Devonport, New Zealand. 2:20 a.m. on the West Coast of the United States.

"You'll need to kill time 'till I find someone to extract you. Walk around with a shopping cart. Make sure you have something to spray at a person if you should get attacked. Roach spray's good, or something flammable, even a small fire extinguisher. Try on lots of clothes – you can hide in changing rooms for a while. I'll text you the name and picture of a person who'll come get you. Don't interact with anyone else – especially if they approach you."

Justin's bride was stirring now.

"Thanks."

"Try to relax, okay? I'll figure something out. Jun, I feel so terrible about what's happened. Jee Hye was ... I ... I don't know what to say. Right now we've just got to get you out of there, okay?"

His bride sat up as the conversation ended. "Did you say *Jee Hye?*"

Justin looked at his gorgeous wife. Although she knew the kind of world he operated in, she'd still chosen to marry him. "She's dead, Bora. I don't know what happened, but that was Jun."

"Dead?"

"Tortured … then murdered."

"What? Why?? Tortured?"

"I don't know."

"Did she know something?"

"I don't know, babe. I just don't know. Right now, I need to figure out how to get Jun out of L.A."

"Is somebody after him, too?"

"Could be."

The young married couple looked at each other for a few seconds.

"What about Fox and Ashley?" asked Bora.

"What about them?"

"Weren't they flying back today?"

Kurt Middleton-Fox was a CIA agent. His close friend, Ashley, was a surgeon. They'd met and worked together with Justin once on a highly specialized team. Both had vacationed for a few days in order to attend the wedding in Auckland. Bora was right; they were already en route back to Virginia.

"I have their itinerary here if you want it," Bora was reaching for her own phone. "It's in my wedding emails."

She smiled sweetly at him as Justin stared over at her. *What a woman!*

"They have a three-hour layover at LAX. Then they fly nonstop to Dulles. As a matter of fact . . ." she pursed her beautiful red lips reading through her emails, "Honey, if they're not already in L.A. right now, they should be arriving any minute."

Just then, his phone rang. She was right . . . it was Fox.

"I know you miss me, Justin, but come on, man, focus on something else. It's your honeymoon!"

"Very funny. You got my text?"

"I did. What's up?"

"My cousin Jun called. His sister was just murdered in Los Angeles."

"What?" Fox exclaimed. "Seriously?"

Justin could hear the unasked questions.

"I don't really have many details but knowing him and from what he said, it was definitely not some random mugging. There seems to be some other element in play."

"You want us to put eyes on the scene?"

"No, the local police need to do their job. We can get those reports later. I was wondering if you could pick Jun up and take him with you."

"Of course."

"His tail sounds pretty hot. I'll send you his coordinates."

"Copy that. We'll just hop off and rearrange our flights later."

Bora mouthed something to Justin.

"My fiancé, I mean my wife, is already on it. She can book the three of you onto a 6:50 a.m. flight." He looked at his wife's mobile device as she held it out for him to read. "LAX to Baltimore, Maryland, with a short layover in Denver."

"You want us to take him to LaunchPad?" Fox asked, a little surprised. *LaunchPad* was their code name for a warehouse in Maryland – an off-the-grid location in a neighborhood just outside Baltimore where they sometimes ran a strategic black-ops command center. They kept a vehicle, and a comms and logistics setup there under tarps, and had enough tactical gear and weaponry stashed in secret hideaways to light up a small country. The risk of using it was always that they could attract attention and blow their valuable cover there. But Justin was willing to take that risk right now.

"I can't think of a safer place," Jun's cousin responded.

"That is true. It's safe enough, I guess. Will you meet us there?"

"I haven't talked with Bora about it yet, but I'll keep you posted."

"Copy that. We're walking out of the airport now. Ashley's already informed the airline that we would not make our connecting flight. They said it was too late to pull the luggage off, so our bags are headed to Dulles."

"Okay. We'll work on getting them sent to Baltimore."

"Thanks. We'll get a taxi. Send me those coordinates."

"Actually, Bora's booking you a rental. Go to Hertz."

"Copy that."

"Thanks, Fox."

"You're welcome. Go snuggle."

Justin hung up. He immediately forwarded the Walmart location to Fox, and then sent a series of texts to Jun. Finally, he looked up at his new wife to find her watching him studiously. She smiled.

"Is this what our life is like now?" Her tone was playful, teasing, and not unhappy. But her eyes were serious.

"Baby, I'm so sorry. I woke you up—you looked so peaceful. This has been such an amazing day," he paused. "And a great night. Sorry, it's..."

She brushed aside his apologies with a wave of her hand.

"That's okay, my handsome prince. But can you at least tell me more about Jun and Jee Hye?"

As Justin began relating what he knew of them to his bride, Fox and Ashley were already in a shuttle on their way to Hertz. They'd soon be headed to the Walmart nineteen miles from the airport.

Inside the store, Jun was trying to steady his heart. He tried not to imagine all the ways Jee Hye's killers might be tracking him right now. As discretely as he could, he put three cans of roach spray, a bottle of mace from the sporting goods area, a small fire extinguisher, some polo shirts and jeans of various sizes into his cart. His eyes kept darting back and forth, sizing up everyone he could see. He'd almost doused an innocent man in poison who had darted directly towards him. But as the guy ran, he called to his three-year-old daughter hiding right behind Jun.

"Zoë!"

Jun quickly dropped the can back into his cart and smiled weakly as the father scooped the toddler into his arms.

"You need to stay right by Daddy, okay? You understand me, Zoë?"

The girl nodded as if it would never happen again.

"Are you alright, Mister?"

Jun turned his head to focus on a high school kid restocking shelves. He had a skinny body with a round, boyish face, dark hair, and thick-rimmed glasses. The kid looked concerned. "You look kinda rough. You okay?"

"Oh, yes," Jun answered, forcing a smile. "I'm very fine. Great actually. This is my first full day out and about since a horrible car accident. I'm afraid there are still a few side effects."

"Oh! Okay." the young stock boy said, impressed. "That's a big deal. Getting out. Let me know if you need help with anything."

"Thanks." Jun's phone buzzed, and he looked down at the text message. It was a picture of Fox. He had a jaw that seemed cut from stone, lively blue eyes, and a surfer-cut to his blond hair. Hard to tell his size from the headshot, but his neck looked strong. His phone buzzed again. The second text also came from Justin. This picture was of a cute brunette with a pretty smile. She looked like she could be Latino or Middle Eastern.

The phone buzzed a third time.

Be in a checkout lane with two items at 3:48 a.m..

Male will checkout behind you. Female will wait in car.

He looked at the time on his phone. He still had twenty-seven long minutes.

CHAPTER TWO

Jasmine Stone was still reeling from everything she'd been through. Seven months ago, her family was attacked. She was abducted with her mother and brother, tortured, and almost trafficked as a sex slave. During that time, her brother had been murdered, her mother beaten, and she herself had come close to dying. Had it not been for the Herculean effort of her father and an elite group of very talented operatives, she would've most likely been killed in the most horrific of ways.

Their new normal wasn't normal at all. The Stone family was in hiding on Cape Elizabeth, Maine. Only three people knew where they were: David, the man who had raised Trey, her dad, from a young child; Leonard Stone, Trey's father, who usually went by *Leo*; and Ashley, the closest thing Jasmine had to a cousin, who'd also been raised by David. The family couldn't go into the open and risk being seen by a public camera, a random photo posted on social networks, or even more critically, a satellite. Maybe due to the isolation, the Stone's were having a hard time recovering from the emotional grief of losing their son and brother Koa. He'd been an amazing sibling to Jasmine and a great child who'd made his parents proud. They all missed him terribly.

"What will we all do now?" Jasmine wondered under her breath as she set the table for breakfast. Her long dark straight hair cascaded down the left side of her neck and her normally bright almond-shaped black eyes were clouded in thought and turbulence. *Will this lockdown ever end? Will I get to go to the mall with friends again or sit on the beach listening to music? What about a boyfriend – would that even be possible in the next few years?* Her lips tightened, and her eyebrows wrinkled as she reflected on her amazing father. *What will he do now? Can he even go back to the CIA?*

Agent Trey Stone was a very talented operative, not just because of his legendary photographic memory and natural survival instincts, but because of the many years of intense training and experience he'd undergone. The "Company" selected him for a specialized covert education at a secretive high school in Northern Japan. As a result, he was fluent in several languages, specifically skilled in individual assassination, creative in all aspects of fieldcraft and a top tier sniper. But having gone through so much turmoil with his family recently, the new acting director of the CIA, David Pearlman, was on the fence about him coming back to work for them. It's not that he didn't want him back. He did. But Trey himself was ambivalent. His fellow agents mostly assumed he would eventually return, but in his heart, Trey knew his life was forever changed. The path forward was still foggy to him.

Setting a plate on the table, where she knew her mother would sit, Jasmine noticed a muscle flexing in her inner forearm. From the time they'd hunkered down, she'd decided to use her time wisely. She worked out for several hours a day, grilled her dad about tactics in close-quarter combat, studied weaponry and ammo, and determined in her mind to be physically fit. Were she ever to get into danger again, she'd be ready to fight back. She looked at her hands, curiously. They already looked different. She'd not really noticed it before, but all the hard work was paying off. She'd always been model-thin. Now she was starting to look toned.

"We could go into protective custody," Jasmine mused aloud after her parents joined her at the table.

"Is that what you'd like?" asked Bao Zhen, Jasmine's mother, passing the orange juice.

Trey studied them both. His just-turned-seventeen daughter was so resilient. Despite all she'd been through and the evil she'd experienced, she still had that same positive outlook on life. More thoughtful, perhaps, but still positive. She refused to let what had happened affect her spirit. Her long dark hair framed an exotic face that reflected all her Moroccan, Chinese, and Caucasian heritage. When she flashed that full smile she'd gotten from her mother, it could melt hearts and weaken knees.

Jasmine cut up her bacon, put down her fork, and gave her father a quizzical look. "What are you thinking, Dad?"

"We're so blessed. I keep thinking of what my life would've been like, had you and mom not been found. I don't think I could've survived."

The Stone family had been told by their psychiatrist—a CIA-appointed expert who specialized with people coming out of brutally traumatizing events—to communicate at all times, even if it meant revisiting painful memories.

"Every time you speak things out, it helps to bring closure," Dr. Julian Messerman had suggested kindly, leaning forward in his chair and carefully looking at each family member. "Don't be afraid of where the conversation might go. Trust that the conclusion will be part of the healing process."

Jasmine looked at her mom, "Well, it's hard to imagine what it could've been like, thankfully, because we don't have to."

Trey nodded. "We could go into protective custody, Jazzy, you're right. That's an option."

"You don't sound very convinced it would be a good thing, Dad."

"Well . . ." Trey had obviously analyzed this option. "There are two challenges. First, I'm worried we'd still be found. There's a uniquely-trained group of very wicked people determined to find us. They have vast resources, including the sort that can penetrate law enforcement bureaucracies." Trey paused, "Second, I wouldn't be able to leave the family on missions and then return. The chances of being tracked or followed back home would increase with each mission. So, the only alternative is to give up on what I know I should do."

"Which is?" Bao Zhen asked carefully.

Her husband sat back holding a mug of black coffee and looked at his wife for a few moments before he answered. "I need to go after people involved in the trafficking of children. I'm not talking about the street-level thugs. I'm talking about high-rolling financiers, the movers, and shakers. I'm going after systems and networks of traffickers."

The way he said it told them everything. His mind was made up.

"How do you anticipate doing that, Dad?"

"When the timing's right, I'm going to call together the team. After that, we'll figure it out."

"When's the time right? What does that mean?"

"When the three of us are healed."

Bao Zhen tilted her head slightly to one side, "Trey, don't worry about us. The time is now."

"We'll see."

"Mother called in the middle of the night," she added softly.

"Is she okay? Why didn't you wake me?" Trey asked, sitting up straight. "What's going on?"

"I think she's fine. She wanted to call when she knew you and Jazzy would be asleep." Boa Zhen's voice faded away.

"Alright. Did she say why?"

"She's not going back to her work for the United Nations."

"Really? Why not?" Jasmine asked frowning.

"She seems to be done with governments and international bureaucracies."

Lin Lin Ma, Bao Zhen's mother, was a diplomatic translator for the nation of China in the United Nations. Her family history had been part of the reason Trey's family had been abducted. She'd gone through a lot of pain in her own life – especially with everything that had happened during the past months.

"Do you think she wants to live with us?"

"Maybe."

Trey looked at his wife. "What else, Honey?"

"She's moving out of her homes in New York City and Geneva."

"Two very meaningful places for her."

"Yes. Obviously, she doesn't feel safe in New York anymore. There may be people in the UN who don't have her best interest at heart. But giving up her home in Switzerland is a big deal. It's been part of her life for so long. In fact, it's been precious to all of us." Bao Zhen hesitated, then continued. "She was wondering if we could go there to help her."

Agent Stone knew why. Even though his mother-in-law was a Swiss citizen, officially, the Chinese would certainly want her to return to China. The sale and move would have to be done quickly and covertly.

"Does she have buyers lined up?"

"The sales have already gone through. She just needs to pack."

Trey thought carefully before he answered. "I suppose we could help her."

"Really?" Jasmine burst out, thrilled for an opportunity to get out of the house.

"We'd have to carefully plan everything. I'm sure David could help us. When was *Mama* thinking this should happen?"

"As soon as we'd be ready."

Trey's eyebrows shot up. "Is she in Switzerland already now?"

"No. She's been in New York signing paperwork with the buyer of her condo. But she's flying to Switzerland the day after tomorrow."

Trey was reading between the lines. "So, she wants us to travel with her."

Bao Zhen nodded and smiled slightly.

Trey and Bao Zhen had been married for eighteen years, but there were still times when Trey felt he was learning the art of indirect communication used in many Asian cultures – his wife's in particular. They'd met in Malaysia, where she'd been working for AIDing International, an NGO that specialized in helping orphans whose parents had died from AIDS. She was highly educated, articulate, and driven by a deep sense of right and wrong. Trey had discovered all of that while they were dating, but what had initially gotten his attention was her long black hair, slender body, naturally tanned skin and a perfect jawline that seemed to guide his eyes to her beautiful smile. He'd easily known, when they first met in a smoky jazz bar in Kuala Lumpur, that his life would never be the same again. He'd been dizzyingly attracted to her that night and still was today.

"So," Agent Stone deduced, "she's ending things in New York, flying to Switzerland, wants to move out of her house there, and is asking that we go with her."

His wife nodded.

"Then she'd like to move in with us."

"It sounds that way to me from our short phone conversation, Trey."

"We both know the Chinese are following her every move. Does she have some kind of extraction plan from Geneva?"

"We're it."

"Do you think they suspect anything?"

"I doubt it. I think they'd have expected her to sell her condo – given the shape it was in. Other than that, I wouldn't know."

Trey shifted his gaze to his daughter. "Well, what do you think, Jazzy?"

She shrugged contentedly and couldn't help but smile, "I like Switzerland. I'd love to spend more time there, especially with my grandmother."

CHAPTER THREE

RED DUST ROSE AND SWIRLED BEHIND THE ARMORED SUV AS THE scorching summer sun beat down on the narrow dirt road in New Delhi, India. Painted flat black, equipped with solid-state puncture-resistant tires, and its highly perfected engine roaring like a hungry lion, the heavy vehicle sent children and dogs scrambling to the side as it charged by. It was a fully intentional machine, meticulously built by Conquest Vehicle Incorporated and had no competition in its class. In fact, the Knight was its own class. Most armored carriers were upgraded with after-market protection packages, but CVI spent thousands of man-hours building theirs from the ground up with protection in mind. It was an intimidating beast of a vehicle, designed to drive through intense urban warfare environments, survive Improvised Explosive Devices known as IEDs, and even safely transport its primaries through missile strikes. It could travel on land, drive through rivers and climb the kind of rocky terrain that would defeat all but the most specialized off-road rock-climbers.

This particular CVI machine was transporting scum.

Dartanian Mayer was a regional director for the Chiu family. Most companies used the term regional to refer to a particular geographical area, the Chiu's used it to refer to different streams of family involvement in communities around the world. Ti Chiu, bearer of the family name, was sitting right next to Mayer. He too was a regional director, one who directed the region that dealt with computer-intervention – a polite term for criminal hacking. His group could hack into any Fortune 500 company and bleed their efficiency by cooking their books or doing something really nasty that would shut them down completely. He had a fifty-person team at his beck and call – ready to fulfill his every demand.

Ye-jin Yoon, another such regional director, was a respected politician in Busan, South Korea. Her husband had been a Chiu, but he died shortly after their marriage. Remaining single, she leveraged grief and pity to campaign on key principles that rang true with her constituency: creative solutions to old problems, moral leadership in immoral times; an office door that was open to the adoring public. In reality, she was a pawn – distributing money to keep the government from interfering with the Chiu family business, and her door was usually closed.

Mayer himself was a particularly low form of scum. But these days, his area of expertise was more highly valued by the Chiu syndicate than even Yoon's and Ti Chiu's. He was the regional director in charge of the buying and selling of children – a nasty trade that was already the bread and butter of the Chiu family. They had pulled out of drugs fifteen years before, quite relieved to get away from mucking around with competitive street values set by low-life dealers and product that could instantly implicate them in serious trouble whenever seized by authorities. Moving children was much more profitable.

Mayer, Chiu, and Yoon all rode in the heavily armed car. They'd just concluded three days of successful negotiations with the Chaudhuri crime family in New Delhi and were on their way to the airport. The basic framework of the deal was a straightforward trade: diamonds and bauxite interests for children, specifically girls. This was definitely the currency-of-the-future for that nation.

What the trio of regional directors didn't know was that they were being followed. As a matter of fact, they'd been followed from the day they'd landed in India. Conversations had been recorded, movements traced, drone footage cataloged, and anyone they met with was even now being carefully vetted.

"Sir? Um ... Sir?," the lady called, looking at Jun's cart and frowning. "You can only take five things at a time into the changing room."

Jun turned to her and observed her demeanor. She clearly didn't care what he thought about store policy. Looking down at the kaleidoscope of random clothes he'd snatched from the clearance rack, he surrendered. "Right. Okay. I'll take this and these." He snagged the five polo shirts he'd initially grabbed, and his aerosol can of roach spray from the pile in his cart.

"Oh, you can't take that with you."

"I'm blattariaphobic," he made up, using a Latin word and adding "phobic" on the end.

"Huh?"

"I have an acute fear of cockroaches."

"You have to leave the can in your cart."

"Can you guarantee there won't be a cockroach in the changing room?"

"No, but I guarantee that if you don't leave that can in the cart, I'll call security."

Jun sighed. "I'll leave it on your counter; if you hear me screaming, you'd better come running in, spraying."

"Changing room number three."

He had twenty more minutes to go.

"WHAT DO you think we should do?" Justin asked, looking at the ceiling with his bride cuddling up and placing her arm over his chest.

"I'm not sure."

"I guess the choice is to stay here in New Zealand and finish out our honeymoon ..."

"Or leave now, and make our way to Launch Pad?"

Justin nodded.

"The next flight out of Auckland would leave around 6:00 a.m." Bora thought for a moment, pursing her lips in a motion that had turned Justin on from the first time they'd met. "I think we should go."

"Why?"

"I just don't think we'd enjoy being here, knowing the team was converging at LaunchPad."

"I know I'd enjoy being here," Justin objected, grabbing her and pulling her up to be fully on top of him.

"Well – that's true," Bora agreed playfully nibbling on him and kissing him. Then she stopped and lovingly looked him in the eyes. "Actually, Justin, I think your cousin really needs you."

Her new husband nodded glumly, "You're probably right, Mrs. Park." He drew her head closer, and their bodies locked passionately. "Just not right away."

CHAPTER FOUR

"Absolutely not!"

"You're nervous. We'll be okay."

David stood up, leaned his head back, and cracked his neck. "Trey, moving your mother-in-law out of her house isn't rocket science. I could get a couple of guys to meet her in Geneva, sort through her stuff, help her pack, and even list her house. Let me make some calls."

"It's already been sold."

"Great! We'll just ship her stuff across the Atlantic. She can sort it all out here. Easy."

"It's not just the moving ..."

"Well then what is it?"

"It's that she's frail."

"So? I'm frail, too."

"She needs emotional support. She needs family around her. She needs closure."

"Did that psychiatrist Messerman tell you that?"

"No, David. Of course not. I'm saying it. Dr. Messerman doesn't know anything about this." Trey lowered his voice. "Listen, I know what it's like to have to say good-bye to a place – maybe for the last time."

"It's too dangerous."

Agent Stone knew that from a purely *security* standpoint, this wasn't a good idea. In fact, David was right, it was a bad idea. But the thing was, it was important to his wife and mother-in-law, and so it was important to him. He spoke with clarity and conviction this time. "David, we're doing this. We're leaving the day after tomorrow. Are you going to help us or not?"

David exhaled loudly. "I'll get back to you."

Trey hung up the phone and looked at his wife and daughter. "He was thrilled."

Jazzy giggled.

Boa Zhen raised her eyebrows, sardonically, "I could tell."

BOYD CARTER WAS AN EXTREMELY WELL-RESPECTED operator. In certain circles of the military, her name alone invoked all kinds of mythical stories. Yet few of her peers had ever actually met her. She'd been a member of the remarkable 5th Special Forces Group, 1st Battalion, Delta Company – an elite Tier 1 special operations force within the United States Armed Forces, located at Fort Bragg, North Carolina. They, of course, were armed with the very latest weapons-systems and equipment, trained in the best field and combat tactics of the world. Sometimes they were referred to as "Ghosts" for their ability to slip into situations and resolve them without even being detected. After working with Trey and his team to recover his family, Boyd had officially moved on from the Special Forces and was working on a new project.

The motor of her Honda XR650L roared and whined as she sped up and slowed down, dodging the crowds and trailing the black Knight carrying the trio of regional directors through the tight, crowded streets of New Delhi. She wore a full helmet over her bright red hair – black with dark glass – but it still didn't filter the cacophony of smells that assaulted her nostrils. This city was unique in that regard. As a matter of fact, the whole nation was unique in that regard. It's one of the best and worst things about India. Sometimes the overwhelming stench of feces, rotten food, decaying carcasses, stale cigarettes, and other trash was more oppressive than an army of roaches. At other times the symphony of rich, heady spices, bright aromatic flowers, and music from skilled players blessed the walker-by like a comforting Chinook wind in winter time.

Swerving around a cow, Boyd blasted through six tables of an outdoor café, causing a waiter to scream profanities and a taxi driver to stomp on his breaks as she cut him off accelerating back into the street. Her eyes were alert, and her hands quick as she maneuvered the competent machine. The semi-double-cradle steel frame flexed and surged like a horse about to spring over a fence as she yanked the bike into a rear wheelie and accelerated to avoid a dying dog shuffling through the middle of the road. His starving belly testified to the cruelty of karma. The front tire slammed back down onto the dirt road and she hunched over the handlebars, her eyes narrowing and her jaw clenching instinctively. A dust plume from the Knight was about a football field's length in front of her and providing a perfect smoke screen.

Boyd had done what many Westerners do when they get to India. She'd bought a motorbike for a few thousand dollars. In this case, it was an off-road machine with on-road capabilities. She'd ridden it fast and hard and would sell it upon leaving the country, easily getting her money back. It was much cheaper than renting a vehicle, and of course, the transactions were always cash and a handshake, no paper trail.

The black armored machine barreled ahead onto a wider, less crowded road. Boyd had anticipated this. And as she too reached the edge of Chawri Bazar, one of the most populous areas of the city on the way to the airport, she accelerated onto the highway behind a medium-sized truck, careful not to be spotted, gratefully leaving the insanity of the bazaar behind. This road had a few cameras that documented traffic patterns. Although their quality wasn't great, they'd pick up what was about to happen and most likely make for some great YouTube videos, if nothing else.

Boyd reached down to an old-school cell phone duct-taped to her gas tank. Keeping her head up, so as not to draw attention, her fingers felt the keys until they reached what she knew was the "redial" button. Her eyes hardened as she depressed the key.

The Knight vehicle suddenly lurched to the right, wildly crossed three lanes, and slammed into a concrete barrier with vicious force. Chunks of the wall sprayed everywhere. Cars and trucks on the highway swerved and squealed and screeched as they tried to avoid a collision. The huge black machine scraped along the wall like a sick drunk, its engine whining loudly, finally coming to a complete halt in a cloud of dust about three hundred yards later. The windows were splattered with red blood, and the interior was filled with smoke.

Boyd smirked as she roared past. The SUV had performed perfectly. There wasn't even a crack in the glass. "Not every blast comes from outside the vehicle," she murmured with grim satisfaction. Her painstaking covert work meticulously planting charges in the wee hours of the morning had paid off. At least, Mayer, Chiu, and Yoon would not be buying, enslaving, and selling children – but that wasn't the end game.

Buried in a maze of cubicles, Jennifer Wu would be particularly busy. From her bank's high-rise building, nested in Hong Kong, she would be keenly watching international money transfers like a hawk soaring over a field, eyeing unsuspecting mice. These three rolling heads would trigger a very interesting financial reaction. Their own money would swiftly move to the next in line – ensuring that there would be no break in their business of trading kids. Redirections and reallocations of funds from the Middle East would hurriedly take place as channels that used to bring money into these accounts would now be steering it to new accounts. Jennifer Wu would be tracking and recording every penny, centime, peso, and rupee.

Boyd kept driving for another twenty minutes when a computerized voice in her helmet caught her by surprise, "Incoming message."

She pulled off the highway, found the shade and cover of some trees, and brought her bike to a halt. This was unusual. She'd turned off her roaming function and thought she'd disabled the wireless receptor. Quickly unzipping her leather jacket, she reached into her inside pocket and slid out her phone. A red cross flashed in the upper left corner of her home screen. It was an emergency text message sent through an application Justin Park installed on her phone when they'd all been working together at LaunchPad to save Trey's family.

Converging. Find secure location. Dial in. LS

"Leonard Stone," Boyd muttered. She always enjoyed working with a talented team – for sure – but Agent Carter also really valued being out on her own, doing the type of thing she'd just done. If she responded, she knew it would most likely mean she'd be running with the pack again. At the same time, she'd grown to love the Stone family and the people they surrounded themselves with, a rare and elite group that she held in exceptionally high regard. Sitting on her bike, she took off her helmet and rubbed her face with her hand and took a deep breath. She needed to decide her next move.

The decision didn't take long. She thought about her immediate course of action and then decided this was as secure a location as anywhere in India. She wrote a text back and transmitted it using the same app. It was highly protected and impossible to trace.

HUA. ETA 24.

"Heard, understood and acknowledged," Boyd repeated to herself. "I'm guessing his area of convergence must be Launch-Pad." It was 1:00 p.m. now. She could be at the AOC in twenty-four hours.

Carter turned off her phone, slipped it into her jacket pocket, and zipped up. She put her helmet back on just as an ambulance raced by, sirens screaming. A familiar tingling began to rise in her as she fired up her bike. It was time to get the hell out of India.

CHAPTER FIVE

DAVID FELT THINGS WOULD BE SAFER IF THEY LEFT AT SOME ridiculously early morning hour. So, the private jet went wheels up from Baltimore at three in the morning and delivered the sleepy Stone family to Zurich in just under eight hours. By 4:30 p.m., they were reclining on the private seats of a luxurious first-class car on a Swiss train. The seats were facing each other and made of brain-tanned, full-grained nappe leather, that was soft and cool to the touch. The door to their cabin was shut to give the Stones both privacy and serenity during their three-hour trip from the Zurich airport to the Geneva station.

Trey looked out the train window at the beautiful Swiss countryside. The majestic Alps, adorned with snow caps, were footed with lush, dark-green forests and stolid granite cliffs. Deep valleys were lined with flashing blue streams and farms dotted the region in exact measure, boasting some of the most spoiled cows in the world. Each town flew by, giving train passengers a blaze of brightly colored homes and buildings.

Stone loved this nation. Not only was its beauty meticulously and proudly sculpted, but it had provided sanctuary for centuries of people. In the 1600s, the citizens of Geneva were encouraged to build extra stories on top of their homes and office buildings to provide housing for people displaced by injustice. The Swiss coined the term "refugee" at that time and offered asylum for thousands of people victimized by war. It was a young Swiss businessman, Jean Henry Dunant, appalled by the condition of the wounded soldiers in the 1859 battle-fields of Solferino, Italy, who laid the groundwork for the birth of the Red Cross. The name and the emblem of the movement bore the reversal of the Swiss national flag, to honor the country in which the compassion organization was founded. Switzerland had a long history of helping people. And even for his own family, it had provided a way for an abused, trafficked young Chinese girl to be generously helped. Rehabilitated, that girl would become a highly-educated and articulate UN woman and eventually find herself the mother-in-law of one of the most talented sniper-agents the CIA had trained.

"Thank you for coming with me," Lin Lin Ma said, taking Trey's hand in hers as if knowing that he was thinking of her.

"Of course, *Mama*," Stone answered, using the familiar Chinese word for mother-in-law.

"Can we stop in Lausanne for ice cream?" asked Jasmine, lifting her eyebrows hopefully. Their family had a history of sitting at Port Ouchy, on the side of Lake Geneva eating ice cream while gazing across the shimmering body of water to France.

"I'd thought about that, but we'll have to get the work done first." Trey looked at his wife. "We'll ride to Geneva and get to Mama's home tonight. Tomorrow, we'll begin the process of packing things. David organized a crew of people to help us."

"We may not need all that much help," Lin Lin spoke out gently.

Agent Stone waited for the explanation.

"I sold it furnished."

They all stared at her. "Really?" Jasmine asked, "You don't want to keep any of your beautiful things?"

"It's time to move on, Sweetie. Hopefully, the buyer will enjoy our house for years to come. If there's something specific you'd like to take back with you, just ask me. I'm sure it can be arranged."

Jazzy looked out the window as a train thundered past them. "Seasons change, I guess." She paused for a few minutes, and then she turned back to her grandmother. "I'm sure there will be something I'd like. Thank you."

"I'll let David know," Trey said. "He can send a smaller team to help clean the house. There's a covert moving company scheduled to arrive at midnight. We'll keep that scheduled. They can take whatever you decide to keep and roll out at 2:00 a.m. We'll need to travel back with only a carry-on." He turned to his daughter. "Mom and Mama are leaving around noon, via Turin, Italy. Their transportation has been prepared. They'll be driven from Geneva to Turin – stay there for the day – and then fly home via Paris."

"That's going to be fun," Lin Lin responded, smiling at her daughter.

Jasmine frowned. "What about us, Dad? What are we going to do?"

"Well, I'd thought maybe you and I could leave in the afternoon and stop by Mövenpick's for some ice cream."

"Really?" his daughter almost squealed, excitedly.

Trey smiled at her response, glad to see his plan was well-received. "You and I will spend some time in Lausanne, take the evening ferry from Ouchy to Évian, and then grab a train to Stuttgart. We'll spend a day there and then fly to Atlanta and home. It'll take a few days for all of us, but we should arrive back in Maryland around the same time."

"Why not fly back together, Trey?" Lin Lin asked, more out of curiosity, then anything else.

"David thinks that if there's any way we were identified coming here, then whoever would be looking for us would be looking for the same combination of people. By dividing up and leaving from different cities, we're improving our chances of staying under the radar."

"I think it's a great idea," Bao Zhen stated. "When was the last time we were in Paris together, mom?"

"It's been years, for sure."

"Sounds like therapy, quality time, and fun!"

The four were quiet now, looking out of the large window at the stunning scenery racing by. But Agent Stone had a profound sense they were all thinking of the same thing.

"Koa would've loved this trip," Bao Zhen murmured aloud.

Trey read the flash of sorrow on his wife's face. His son's brutal murder weighed heavily on his heart, too. He'd never forget those last moments– saying good-bye to his son in the hospital. His wife hadn't been given that opportunity. She'd been abducted, and her last memories of her son alive were hearing him scream as he was being beaten by their captors. She remembered so wanting to rip off her blindfold just to see him again, but her restraints had prohibited it.

"He would've – you're right," Trey nodded. "We'd all love for him to be here with us."

Jasmine stared out the window as quiet tears trickled down her cheeks. "I've wanted to talk about Koa, but I wasn't sure how to bring him up ... thanks, Mom."

"What do you miss most about him, Honey?" asked Trey.

"So much!" Her tears were flowing rapidly. "I miss his stupid jokes. I miss seeing him at breakfast with his hair sticking up in all directions. I miss the security I felt around him, knowing he was my big brother. I miss the girls swooning over him in school and confiding in me. But I guess most of all," she swallowed, "I miss his friendship, you know? We were so close."

"You were. He loved you very much and was so proud to have such a kind, smart, and beautiful sister." Now Trey was teary-eyed. He looked over to see his wife weeping.

Lin Lin, too, had tears rolling down her cheeks. "This is so depressing!"

As everyone looked at each other, they sniffed loudly and pulled back on the emotions. "Wow," Bao Zhen said meekly. "Isn't it amazing how grief comes in waves? One minute we're fine, talking about ice cream by the lake and shopping in Paris, the next minute we're all crying."

Jasmine agreed. "I'll be going through a day – just fine. Then all of a sudden, I'll think about something as stupid as his smelly high school football uniform. And it hits me – I'll never be at another high school football game to see my brother play."

"For me, it's the little things too," Bao Zhen admitted. "Like opening the fridge and seeing so much food in it. With Koa around, it disappeared faster than water evaporated. I remember going to the fridge to get dinner started, and the groceries I'd bought two days before were gone. Koa had already eaten them!"

Lin Lin began to chuckle.

"That kid sure could consume food!" Trey said, smiling. "Do you remember when we were at that Italian restaurant, and he asked the table next to us if they were done with their breadsticks and salad?"

All four of them were giggling and telling Koa-stories.

"I remember when he was supposed to meet up with that girl ... what was her name?" Bao Zhen asked.

"Hannah," Trey said chuckling – knowing what was coming.

"That's right! Hannah – the redhead from Australia!" Jasmine exclaimed, looking at her father. "I'd totally forgotten about her."

"Hannah ..." her mother continued. "He was supposed to pick her up for dinner but decided to stop by a restaurant first – to gobble down a pre-dinner meal," she said, laughing.

"Right," Trey reminisced. "He didn't want to eat like a pig later on the date, so he decided to grab food, first."

"He was thirty minutes late when he picked her up," squealed Jasmine, laughing so hard, "and stuffed full of fried chicken."

Time flew as they talked, laughed, and cried.

"Do you remember when he got his first job mowing lawns?" Trey asked Bao Zhen.

"I do," she grinned. "It was for that old crab, Mrs. MacCormaic."

"That's the one. She wanted him to use her electric lawnmower and her bright orange extension cord, remember? She'd just gotten them from her local hardware store and was so proud of her shiny new equipment. Within five minutes he'd rolled right over her cable and sliced it in half."

Jasmine laughed out loud, and Lin Lin Ma chuckled again, "I don't think I know this one. What did he do?"

"He'd never used an electric lawnmower before and wasn't paying attention to it. Chewed right through it with the blades."

"Oh my goodness! Was she upset?"

"She tapped into generations of Irish rage and chewed him out for fifteen minutes, spewing out every swear word that came to her mind."

"Really?"

"Yes!" Bao Zhen continued with a grin. "He promised her he could fix her cord, but she was dubious. I remember he came home almost in tears. But as he told the story, it was hard for me not to laugh."

"Why?"

"Well, there's this tiny, skinny, chain-smoking eighty-five-year-old, with a wig perched sideways on her head, berating a six-foot-tall fourteen-year-old football player. I don't think he'd ever heard those words before – especially not combined in the way she used them. And it was his very first paying job!"

Everyone was grinning.

"Did he fix it?" asked Lin Lin.

"He did," Trey answered. "He cut the cord cleanly, peeled back the cover, reattached the wiring, taped it up with electrician's tape, and went back to finish the mowing."

"That's so Koa."

"Sure is," Jasmine agreed. "He could fix anything."

The train began to slow down as they reached the Geneva city limits. In a few minutes, the car David had ordered would pick them up and drop them off at Lin Lin Ma's beautiful Swiss home.

CHAPTER SIX

"Excuse me, what are you doing?"

The man whirled around, his dark eyes showing his shock. His hand was reaching for the pistol in his holster.

"I wouldn't do that," Boyd warned. "You'll be dead in seconds." As she spoke the words, she snaked out a silver mini Glock from behind her back to help articulate her point and held it with her left hand.

"Is this your place?" the man asked, leaving his gun holstered.

"I'm just renting the room."

"I'm just cleaning."

"With no cleaning supplies. Are you alone?"

The man nodded, but as he did, a shadow darkened the doorway of the bathroom to Boyd's right.

"So, who are you?" she asked, pondering her next move.

"I'm with the police. We are investigating a robbery in this hotel," he answered, with the typical musical English that Indian's have in their accent.

"I've been gone all day."

"Do you have proof of where you've been?"

In a swift, decisive moment, she twisted forward, her legs flying up in a spectacular double kick that connected with his jaw as she landed on her right hand and then sprung up like a gymnast. She rotated to face the second *policeman*, her weapon pointed straight ahead of her. The element of surprise worked perfectly as the man in the door frame glared at the redhead. He was much bigger and stronger than the cheap-suit that had folded to the ground behind her, but he wasn't very quick.

Before he could make up his mind as to what to do, Boyd had closed the distance between them with violent grace and used her sudden momentum to plant her foot on the man's chest, knocking him backward into the bathroom. He stumbled and then straightened up, but the broad side of her gun caught the lower part of his jaw with surgical precision, and he was instantly out cold.

Agent Carter searched both men for identification and, to her surprise, it seemed that they were police after all. She yanked out some zip ties from her backpack and secured the men, making sure neither one could move, then sat on the edge of her bed. The hotel was a large sprawling structure with a massive luxurious pool in the middle of an elegant courtyard and the rooms all opening up into that area. Hers was on the ground level, as requested. She could go out her front door and immediately be among the hotel guests and workers or slip out her bathroom window and exit via a back alley. Her bag was always packed – that's just how she lived. She never knew when she'd have to grab-and-go. She was always ready. She picked up the hotel phone.

"Front desk."

"Yes, I have two handsome men in my room who claim to be police officers. I just wanted to check their story. They say they needed to look around."

"I'm sorry, Miss Henderson," the desk operator said, using the name Agent Carter had checked in with, "That's correct. We had a robbery earlier this morning, and the police are doing room searches. You should have a voicemail alerting you to their presence on our property if you weren't in your room when we called everyone."

Boyd looked at her phone and the little red light was indeed flashing – notifying her of a voicemail. "I apologize. I see the little red light flashing."

"No problem, Miss Henderson. Will there be anything else I can help you with today?"

"No. Thank you." Boyd hung up and grabbed her small backpack and her duffle bag. She walked into the bathroom, lifted the window, and checked the alley. Seeing that it was clear, she tossed her bags to the dusty gravel, gripped the top of the window frame, lifted her body and slid through. She closed the window behind her, shouldered her gear and sauntered past her motorcycle, realizing she wouldn't have time to sell this one. As she neared the end of the alley, a young man came walking around the corner towards her.

"Hey, kid. D'you want a bike?"

He looked at her, suspiciously.

She opened her hand, so he could see the keys. "I'm done with it."

"Does it not work?"

"It runs great."

"Is it stolen?"

She smiled. "No. But, I'm just about to catch a plane to Nepal to go hiking. Do you know how to ride?"

The young man nodded.

"It's more fuss to fly it to Nepal than just give it away."

A wide grin spread across his face. "Then, yes," he answered, bobbing his head from side to side. "I would like a bike. Very much."

Carter tossed him the keys and turned around to walk away.

"Thank you!" he shouted. "Really. Thank you!"

"Drive safely, okay?" Boyd added over her shoulder. As she reached the busy sidewalk, she heard the Honda roar to life and a happy shout from its new owner. *That kid's going to love that bike!* she thought, chuckling.

The taxi ride took over an hour, but Boyd used the time to book a flight from New Delhi to Baltimore. Her flight would leave at 7:00 p.m. that evening and put her in the air for eighteen hours with stopovers in Abu Dhabi and New York. Leaning back, she rolled her head around to stretch her neck and tried to relax a bit.

"Take me to Terminal 3, okay?"

"No problem."

The Indira Gandhi International Airport had storage lockers that were located in Terminal 3. It would cost about forty U.S. dollars to rent one for a year, and she needed a place to stow her guns, ammo, tactical gear, and grenades. Obviously taking those on a commercial flight was unwise. She chuckled a bit at the thought.

CHAPTER SEVEN

Time was up. Jun walked out of the changing room and handed the clothes to the clerk, muttering that nothing looked good on him. As he retrieved his can and cart, the lady feigned a concerned look.

"Did you see a roach in there?" she asked, snidely.

"It was your lucky day. You didn't have to save me with spray."

"Have a good night."

Jun dumped the fire extinguisher and a couple of the other items he'd collected. But he kept the roach spray in his hand. He meandered through the kitchen items, noticing there was a sale on copper-bottomed pots, and proceeded through the bedding section towards the front. As he emerged in the main aisle that led to the cash registers, a sudden movement to his left caught his attention. An olive-skinned man, possibly Middle-Eastern or Hispanic, was looking at shampoo in the hair product aisle. He was dressed in black – not unusual – but the type of clothes he wore was. His pants weren't dress pants, they looked more like tactical cargo pants. His long-sleeved shirt was tight-fitting, and his shoes looked to be black combat-issue. The man looked coldly at Justin's cousin.

Jun's heart skipped a beat as he decided to make it look like staring in that direction had been intentional. He walked towards the man and faced the shampoo.

"Head and Shoulders," he mumbled to himself. "Here it is."

The man said nothing.

Jun snagged a bottle and dropped it in his cart. As he began to walk away, he noticed the man had not taken any shampoo bottles off the shelf – or another hair product for that matter. He was actually leaving that section of the store and seemed to be interested in where Jun was going. At the same time, Jun noticed another man standing further down the aisle, in front of him with a fixed gaze on the cash register stations. He was dressed in the same kind of black combat gear. Now, another guy entered the store, and Jun saw he was wearing the same types of clothes. His hair looked messed up like he'd been wearing a hat – *a ski mask*, thought Jun, as he tightened his grip on the roach spray.

Fox and Ashley had just arrived and sat in their rented GMC Acadia. They were parked in the unloading and loading zone in front of the store with their parking lights on.

"I counted six," Fox noted, watching the last of the men in combat gear exit their black 2004 Suburban and walk into the super-store.

"Me too. I can't believe they parked where they did. That really irritates me."

"In the handicapped parking spot?"

"Yes. Those are for a purpose, you know. I don't think a parking spot for get-away vehicles is what the system was designed for."

Fox half-smiled. "I'm going in."

"Plan B?"

He nodded, getting out of the Acadia. "Keep the engine running in *drive* and the stereo off. Have the parking lights on and be ready to throw on the high-beam as we leave. A second or two of blinding light might make the difference between making it out or not."

"Okay," nodded Ashley. She'd not thought of those things. After all, she was a surgeon. Fox, on the other hand, was an operative. Different acquired skillsets.

As soon as he entered the store, Fox assessed the situation. One hostile posted by the cash registers, one further down the aisle straight ahead of him, another standing in the McDonald's area on the agent's right, and one walking towards him from far down on the left. Then he saw Jun slowly pushing a cart, dutifully carrying his can of aerosol protection. The two other men that Fox and Ashley had spotted must've penetrated further into the store.

"Welcome to WalMart," an elderly lady offered tiredly as he walked in, her grey hair and drained look telling him she'd rather be retired but couldn't manage without the income.

"Thank you, ma'am," Fox replied politely, taking a cart and looking straight ahead. "Crowded tonight?"

"No, sir," she said, smiling at the thought. "Not many people here at this hour. Don't tell anyone, but I kind of like it that way."

"Your secret's safe with me," he answered with a wink and pushed his cart forward. He could feel Jun watching him but didn't dare give away that they were connected. The hostile eyeing the cash registers and the one in McDonald's were observing Fox carefully. He stopped the cart between him and the man on his right and bent down to tie his shoes. This way, the cart screened him from the hostile in McDonald's and the guy watching the cash registers couldn't see over a magazine rack. He hoped Jun wouldn't cash out – and he didn't.

Jun had seen Fox come in and desperately watched him for some kind of clue, but the big agent had talked politely to the WalMart greeter, moved forward, and bent down, disappearing from view. With his roach spray still in his hand, Jun pushed his cart towards McDonald's but looked to his left as if interested in a clearance rack of women's athletic wear. He stopped the cart to look more carefully. As he did, Fox got up and pushed his cart past Jun, staring straight ahead.

"On my six," he whispered.

Jun heard him, picked a yellow and blue UCLA sweatshirt from off the rack, placed it into his cart, and casually fell into stride behind the big blond. Apparently unwittingly, the two men started a whole caravan of nonchalant-looking people – all dressed in black and appearing to be mildly interested in whatever product was around them, following each other at distances of ten to twenty paces.

Fox moved slowly enough to let Jun follow at a distance, but fast enough so that he wouldn't have to stop. He walked to the elbow-end of the aisle and turned left, heading towards the electronics section and hunting supplies. The only disadvantage of coming from the airport was that he didn't have a gun. As a matter of fact, he didn't even have scissors or a pocket knife. He'd left the latter with an appreciative airport security agent in Auckland who would, no doubt, add it to his extensive collection. The big agent arrived at his destination and turned right to go down an aisle in the outdoors section. He snagged some rubber mallets from off a rack next to some camping pegs and ripped the protective plastic off them. Just as he finished, Jun turned into the same aisle, and their eyes met.

"Lawn and Garden. When we get there, take off running. Sprint into the parking lot to a white GMC Acadia. Open the passenger door – leave it open – and get in the back. I'll be right behind you."

"Now?"

"Now!"

Two men in black combat gear had stepped into the aisle entrance – one at each end. Jun's face paled as he looked past Fox. Then, his eyes widened as a mallet whistled past him, inches from his head. It'd been thrown with such force that when it impacted the chest of the man behind him, he could hear the ribs splintering. With a roar, the man behind Fox whipped out a razor-sharp Suarez Fighting Knife and charged the agent.

"Go!" yelled Fox.

Jun spun around and leaped over the man on the floor who had been behind him. He could hear the gurgling gasping sound of a collapsing lung as he sprinted away. Just as he reached the entrance to Lawn and Garden, he was forced to slow down and wait for the automatic double glass doors to open. A hostile was running towards him from his left – he could hear the steps getting closer. Jun raced through the doorway, searching desperately for something he could use as a combat weapon. The doors closed behind him as he ran down an aisle on his right, grabbing a gardening trowel. The doors opened again. His pursuer had arrived.

Jun ducked into the next aisle and stopped. He could see through the shelves to where the hostile was standing – just inside the Lawn and Garden doorway.

"What am I doing with a trowel?" he wondered, looking down at his hand. Sweat formed on his face.

The hostile was starting to move. He was walking down the aisle adjacent and parallel to his. The shelving was about six feet deep, and the two were almost directly across from each other. Bags of mulch were stacked on Jun's side and bags of grass seed on the hostile's side. Jun moved towards the shelf, very slowly, but as he did, he saw the hostile stop.

Jee Hye's brother knew he'd been spotted.

At that moment, a number of things happened at the same time. Jun saw the hostile bend down slightly and peer through the shelving, directly into a continuous spray of roach-killing liquid. As he screamed profanities, the interior doors of the store swooshed open again, and Fox went sprinting by. Suddenly the store alarm started screaming.

"Fox!" he yelled, dropping his trowel and spray.

The big agent whirled towards him. "Run!"

The two men dashed for the exit while a huge garage-style door began to creak, and squeal shut – an automated response to the alarm.

Fox got there first and knelt down, planting himself under the closing door and pushed against it with his shoulder as Jun arrived and dive-rolled underneath.

A white GMC Acadia careened into the area and did a U-turn of sorts. The trunk of the vehicle was up, and the two men leaped into the rear cargo area, colliding into each other. Fox reached up and slammed the hatch-door closed as Ashley floored the accelerator. The American-made SUV sprang forward and raced through the parking lot with Fox and Jun gripping the headrests of the captain's seats in front of them.

"Stop immediately!" yelled a WalMart security guard from his golf cart, the orange light flashing angrily from the roof. He was directly in their way.

"Right," Ashley snickered, swerving to her left to miss him and then abruptly veering to her right, avoiding a light pole. Her high beams were on, the radio was off, and the Acadia was in *drive*.

"Where's their Suburban?" Fox yelled over the screeching tires and the straining axle.

The brunette smirked. "You don't think I was jus' sittin' around, do you?" She glanced in her side mirror. "I let the air out of one of their tires. Can you believe they didn't leave a driver?"

Fox shook his head in admiration. "Nice play!"

Ashley turned off her high beam and slowed down to a normal pace when police cars became visible in her rearview mirror. Like ants to honey, they all poured into the WalMart parking lot – red and blue flashes lighting up the night sky. "Should we switch vehicles?"

Fox was climbing out of the back and slipping into the front passenger seat. "No. Let's just ditch this somewhere and catch a cab. We don't wanna get caught in a stolen vehicle."

Jun tumbled into the seat, behind Fox. "I'm Jun, by the way."

Ashley turned to look at him. "I'm Ashley. This is Fox."

"Nice to meet you both. Thanks for coming to get me."

"Those guys weren't Asian," Fox noted.

"No." responded Jun, suddenly a little perplexed.

"I would have thought they'd be Asian."

"Yeah, that'd make sense."

"I don't really know what's going on here, Jun. Why don't you fill us in?"

Jun briefed them on how he'd found his sister and that she'd been caught up in a high-end prostitution ring. He told them how he'd been making plans to get her out and what had happened earlier that night.

"So, did you meet her pimps?"

"No. I was just tracking her movements."

"Do you know who was running her?"

"I don't know anyone, specifically. That was going to be the next conversation I had with her."

Sensing that something wasn't adding up, Ashley turned to Fox and asked, "What is it?"

"Well, the guys in Walmart were Middle Easterners. I'd bet my career on it."

"Mossad?"

"No, they weren't Israeli. Besides, they weren't professional enough to be Mossad." The agent twisted in his seat, so he could see Jun. "In Koreatown, the guys chasing you. Were they Korean or Middle Eastern?"

Jun thought hard. It had been very dark. He pictured the glint of a gun he'd seen in the alley, then he replayed what happened in his mind. As he got to the part where he was in the taxi looking back into Min's Korean Restaurant, he froze the picture. The tables were tossed, there were angry guests, the waitress was scared, a manager was picking up a phone, and the hostiles were crashing through the room as the taxi sped off. He remembered seeing one of the men looking at the taxi. He had black fatigues on. He had a black ski mask on. But his eyes … he was not Korean.

"They weren't Korean," he said, a little shocked with the realization.

"I think we need to go back to Walmart," declared Fox.

"No way," Ashley stated flatly.

"We need to find out who those guys are."

"Did you kill any of them?"

"One has a collapsing lung, and the other has his own combat knife embedded in his thigh." He paused. "I may or may not have crushed his jaw with a rubber mallet," Fox reported. "Sorry, that didn't really answer your question. No. They both have a shot at staying alive."

"What about you?" she asked, looking in the rearview mirror at Jun.

"My guy got a face full of roach spray."

Fox's face broke into a grin. "You were holding that can like you were the *Crocodile Hunter* of roaches."

Ashley chuckled, then Fox sobered up and said, "But seriously, Jun. Good work. It probably saved your life."

"Thanks."

"So, there you go," Ashley said firmly. "The police will be crawling all over that place, looking for the two of you. If you ask me, we'll just have to identify these guys some other way." She turned the SUV down a dark street to the right and parked under a tree.

"That's not going to work, Ash. I need to know who this squad is, how they connect to Jun's sister, and who they work for."

"Our instructions were to safely deliver Jun."

"You're right. That's still the most important objective, but it can be your orders now. Call a cab. Get to the airport and get him to LP. I'll stay here to snoop around a little."

Jun felt like a child in the awkward presence of tetchy parents.

Ashley sulked, "I know you're right. It's just that ..."

Fox reached over to gently take her hand in his, "Don't worry. I'll be careful. And you'll both be fine without me. I know that for sure."

"Okay." She looked back at Jun in the rearview mirror. "You ready?"

Jun nodded.

They got out of the SUV, and Ashley pulled up an app on her phone to order a car to a block away from their location. Fox dug through his backpack – carry-on luggage from the plane – and pulled out an extra t-shirt, jeans, his wallet, and a red baseball cap. He changed and stuck his old clothes back into the pack.

"Here," the big agent said to Jun, handing it over to him as he stuck on his cap. "When you get to the airport, go to the men's restroom and dump the clothes I was wearing. If you can, spill a lot of mustard on them or something – so it's obvious as to why you'd have thrown them away. They're less likely to draw attention that way. Before you go through security, make sure to wear a brightly colored t-shirt, so you don't fit the description of an All-Points Bulletin. I'm positive there's an APB out on all of us by now."

Fox fist-bumped Jun, gave Ashley a quick hug, hopped into the SUV and saluted as he roared off.

CHAPTER EIGHT

CASEY BAKER'S WHITE EARBUDS WERE ALMOST IMBEDDED INTO her eardrums, and her head bopped back and forth with whatever she was listening to. Her coach looked at her, amused, and pushed the button to recline his leather seat into an almost flat position. "This is definitely the way to travel," he thought as he rested his head and looked through the oversized windows of the chartered Boeing Business Jet. Although the BBJ was a 737-800 that normally accommodated over one hundred and fifty passengers, this particular version had been modified to transport exactly sixty-two passengers.

Casey's soccer team was representing the United States in an international tournament for twelve to thirteen-year-old girls hosted in Gaborone, Botswana. Before they would make the trip to southern Africa, however, they would stop in Munich, Germany, to pick up one of their competing teams as a gesture of friendliness. The spectacular white plane and the well-intended goodwill gesture had been George Baker's idea. Casey's grandfather was in the elite club of the ex-presidents of the United States. He'd been a strong leader loved by everyone and known particularly for his ability to build consensus. Her father, on the other hand, steered clear of politics and started a little software company which, over time, had become very lucrative. Algostar as it was called, specialized in writing, and implementing algorithms for anyone who needed one. Whether it was thousands of strings long and serving the needs of a Wall Street firm responsible for the security of the World Trade Center, or just a small company needing a specific formula for maximizing efficiency, Ted Baker's company served a diverse, well-funded, clientele. When George had texted Ted his idea of chartering a luxury plane for transporting Casey's team and picking up another team along the way in Europe – the son agreed it would be a great way to go.

The whole tournament had benevolence at its heart. The international organizing committee determined that the world should learn more about Botswana's emerging economy. One of the most sparsely populated nations on the planet, it had once also been the poorest. But over time, with clear representative leadership and a consistent record of uninterrupted elections, it had transformed itself into a fast-growing economy which boasted the highest Human Development Index score of continental Sub-Saharan Africa. True, an international tournament would be a challenge for the organizers in Gaborone. But everyone understood the opportunity for goodwill and more importantly, for financial investment in the future of an African nation with a lot of things going right for it at present.

To qualify the national teams, there'd been a handful of rigorous loser-go-home tournaments played in selected countries. The winning teams kept advancing and eventually, after the championship game, a group of players—all-stars of sorts—were selected and extended invitations to Africa. Each team was allowed to bring twenty players, two coaches, two medical specialists, a publicist, four parents, and two security personnel. The Secret Service of the United States objected to the granddaughter of an ex-president traveling to southern Africa with such scant security, but Ted argued that it was exactly what his daughter needed, and George was satisfied.

Now, relaxing on the plane, Coach Murray closed his eyes and imagined his team winning again and again – first in Africa and then in all sorts of exotic global locations. It was a soothing way to fade into a deep sleep.

LIN LIN MA'S house was just the way Jasmine had remembered it. There was a sophistication to her grandmother's interior designs that always garnered admiration. From the outside, her place had a classic, yet modest, Swiss appeal. The neighborhood was at the center of an area that included several local villages. Over time, the homes built in the 15th century had been razed, and larger estates had gone up. Hers was now surrounded by homes of like value – all boasting proximity to downtown Geneva and minutes to the golf course at Cologny. The outside had pale yellow stucco walls with crisp mauve wooden shutters. The roofline was high with steep sloping forest-green clay shingles, and both ends of the home were anchored with large chimneys. Gracing her property with privacy were the striking pine trees and generous greenery characteristic of the region. From inside, all the window views were of soothing forestry.

The interior included beautiful reception rooms and numerous bedrooms that enhanced the unique character of the home. A master suite presented a spiral staircase leading to a private rooftop terrace with breathtaking views of Lake Geneva and the

French Alps. There was a clean, modern chef's kitchen, with the latest in gas appliances, and refined gray Carrara marble floors throughout the home, selected for its classic quality and style long before Carrara marble was a thing for Millennial designers. The basement featured a luxurious tasting room, complete with an extensive wine cellar as well as an indoor playground for children. Adding to the allure was a distinctly Chinese combination of color and artistry. Stuffy red leather seating drew the color from the shutters inside the home, Chandeliers, normally decorated with crystals had been swapped for antique lanterns. Large yellow and red dragons were displayed on awe-inspiring hand-painted murals. But despite all of its lavish sophistication, Lin Lin's home was warm and inviting and insatiably interesting.

"Welcome back to Geneva," Ms. Ma said graciously as she opened the front door and held it for her granddaughter, daughter, and son-in-law.

"Thanks, Mom," Bao Zhen responded, pecking her on the cheeks and walking in.

The driver followed, carrying their suitcases into the foyer.

"Do you know where to take the bags?" Trey asked him as he turned on some lights.

The young man nodded, "Oui Monsieur."

"Come, let's open a bottle of wine and relax," Lin Lin said. "We can talk about our plan of action."

They settled down in the living room, which overlooked the fabulous backyard – treed with walnut, beech, and mountain spruce. A tall, thick, green Hornbeam bush ran the entire perimeter of her property and furnished the opportunity for hidden security cameras to quietly protect the property. The sun had set, and dusk was deepening quickly. Trey poured wine into three glasses and tossed his daughter a bottle of Evian spring water.

"This home has been such a safe place for us, hasn't it?" Bao Zhen commented, thoughtfully with a hint of sadness in her voice.

"It has," her mother agreed. "It's taken me a while to find peace in my heart about moving on. Ultimately, I think the money will be better spent on your family." She waited for a moment. "I'm giving it all to you."

Trey looked at her – touched with the offer. "Wow, Mama, that's very generous of you."

"Of course, there are strings attached."

"Of course."

"Did Bao Zhen tell you that I'd like to move in with you?"

"She did. And we'd love it."

"Thank you, Trey," Lin Lin Ma responded, with genuine gratitude. "It's an interesting time in life – when a parent begins to depend on the kindness of her children. But I hope I won't be a burden to you. If I am, I can always find my own place close to wherever you'll be."

"I'll keep that in mind," Agent Stone said, smiling at Lin Lin. "But you'll never be a burden – I know that." He raised his glass in a toast. "To moving out, moving in and moving on."

"Well said, Dad." Jazzy laughed, raising her plastic bottle while the rest clinked their glasses.

"HEY, COACH."

Neil Murray stirred, groaned, and forced his eyes open.

"Food's coming."

He blinked the sleep from his eyes and focused on the face in front of him. Shelly Brown was a constant ball of energy. Her long black hair was usually in a high ponytail, her face always playfully about to break into a smile. She had long toned limbs that screamed athlete – even at age thirteen. As team captain, goalkeeper, and general on-and-off-the-field team-motivator, she walked with a self-assurance that was magnetic.

"I figured you wouldn't want to miss it."

"Thanks, Shell. Is everyone awake?"

"Everyone but the security guard guys. I figured I'd let them sleep. The flight attendant says we're ninety minutes from Germany."

Murray moved his seat into the upright position and stood up to stretch. "What's for breakfast?"

"Well, it's around 6:30 p.m. in Germany and 1:30 p.m. on our East Coast. So, a lot of us are having dinner. But seriously, I think they'll make whatever you want … just what you would expect from the staff on this plane. It's pretty amazing, isn't it?"

"It is. I've never been on anything like it."

"Me neither."

Coach Murray and Shelly Brown had that in common. They were the only two from the soccer team who had not been born into wealth and opulence. Murray's parents had passed away a few years ago; his dad first, and his mom a few months later. His father had been a school bus mechanic and always loved knowing that his work kept children safe. His mom had been an ICU nurse for over thirty years. Shelly had no idea who her father was. She'd been raised an only child by a single mom who worked several different jobs to keep food on the table. Her mom saw to it that her daughter would be in quality sports and music programs after school.

"Hi, Coach."

Neil looked up as another one of his players approached him and Shelly. "Hi, Abril – did you sleep okay?"

"Like a baby."

He looked down the aisle of the plane and saw all the girls chatting excitedly in their seats, standing up and stretching, or walking to the restrooms in the back. The flight attendant was moving his direction, taking food orders.

"Have you been to Germany before, Coach?"

"No. I'd love to get out of the airport and see the country. I've heard it's beautiful. Maybe on the way back we can do that."

"I wanna meet Phillip Lamm."

Murray grinned. Abril Fuentes was a defender, just like the legendary World Cup winner from Germany, and he was her favorite soccer player – something a person would find out within minutes of meeting her. She was short in stature but fast as lightening and completely unafraid to slide into an oncoming forward to knock the ball out from under her feet before doubling her body in half with a hard tackle. She rarely fouled, winning the ball consistently, but with force. Off the field, she was friendly and approachable, despite the fact that her father was the founder and CEO of Nocturno, the most successful chain of high-end night clubs in the world. Her mother had been a model in Guadalajara, before meeting her dad at a fundraising event for saving street kids in Mexico City. Felipe and Priscilla had gotten married in Atlanta but now lived in a sprawling home on swanky Croatan Beach in Virginia Beach, Virginia.

"What can I get you for breakfast, Mr. Murray?"

He looked at the flight attendant, "Orange juice, water, scrambled eggs and wheat toast with butter."

"I'll have it ready in a few minutes."

"Thank you."

"Ladies and gentlemen," a resonant voice floated through the speakers in the ceiling, "This is Captain Luttrell speaking. We're just over sixty minutes from beginning our descent and will be on the ground in Germany for forty-five minutes. That'll give us time to welcome our new passengers, bring on a fresh crew, and refuel the aircraft. Then, you'll be on your way to Botswana."

The girls all cheered excitedly. Although many had traveled for family vacations and a few for a semester abroad, there was always something quite exciting about the kind of journey they were on. The buzz in the air was tangible.

BOYD CARTER WAS on a plane too – in economy class, near the back. She'd carefully wiped down all her gear, put on a moderate disguise, and used some fake ID to rent a storage locker. She didn't know when she'd be back to retrieve her gear. If not before the twelve months expired, it's discovery would doubtless cause some alarm, but should there be an investigation, it would lead nowhere. Boyd looked out of her window as the plane took off, reflecting on all that had just taken place in

India. "It's funny how when you take off, you think about where you've been and when you start to land you think about what's coming up," she reflected. With that bit of wisdom, Agent Carter settled into her seat, pulled out her Kindle reader, and looked for something interesting to read.

CHAPTER NINE

ASHLEY AND JUN HAD STOPPED BY A TWENTY-FOUR-HOUR TARGET store in Culver City on their way to LAX to dispose of Fox's clothes and to buy some new ones for themselves. They'd checked through airport security and were waiting in the gate area for their 8:35 a.m. flight to Baltimore that would arrive at 4:33 p.m. Eastern Standard Time.

"Other than these clothes, I have nothing with me," Jun commented.

"I'll go shopping with you."

"I hate shopping."

"Then, I'll go shopping for you!" Ashley answered happily.

Jun smiled. "We could go together, but I'm an in-and-out shopper."

"You should've picked up everything at Walmart while you were waiting for us," quipped the surgeon, starting to feel a little less anxious now that they were surrounded by the familiar buzz of airport activity.

"You never gave me a chance to check out." The two of them chuckled at the thought. Jun stretched his arms and then got a little more serious. "So, where are you taking me?"

"I can't tell you anything about it. But you'll be safe."

"Will Justin and Bora be there?"

"Knowing them, I'm sure they'll want to be in on the action."

"I feel so bad for ruining their honeymoon."

"I doubt they see it that way, Jun." She watched a mother trying to appease her loudly, unhappy two-year-old. Then Ashley leaned sideways in her seat, to look at the Korean-American.

"Tell me more about your sister."

"We grew up in a fairly upscale family but not because we had actual money. When my father committed suicide, we found that everything we owned had been bought on credit or leveraged against multiple mortgages and bank loans. My mom couldn't handle the truth and ended up sinking into a deep depression. She'd hardly ever leave the house and rarely even come out of her room." He paused, remembering, "My sister and I fended for ourselves."

"How old were you?"

"Thirteen."

"How old are you now?"

"Twenty-two."

"Are you the oldest?" asked Ashley.

"Yes. Jee Hye is ... was three years younger than me. There were only the two of us. I don't know what it is about Korean culture, but being the oldest carries a lot of responsibility that wasn't really mine to carry. We always take it on as some kind of duty. Of course, in my situation, if I hadn't shouldered it, nobody would have."

"So, your sister was ten when you lost your father?"

"Yeah – she found him in the car. He'd plugged the tailpipe, run the engine all night in the garage and checked out. The next morning, she heard the car running and made the shocking discovery. It drastically altered her life – but not for the better."

"That's horrible, Jun! Really terrible. She must've been utterly traumatized!"

"It was pretty bad. Over the next two years, I worked at a restaurant bussing tables. Jee Hye kind of did her own thing. I'd try to stay connected with her, but between school and work, I just didn't have much time, you know? Looking back, I should have asked someone for help. But, honestly, I didn't know whom to trust."

"What about Justin?"

"Justin's great. He would call me every other week and check on me. But I lied to him. I guess I was too embarrassed to tell him what was really going on." He paused, watching a family with young kids get organized in the seats across from them. The waiting room was beginning to fill up. "Of course, we got evicted from our house because the bank seized our place. They also took our SUV and everything else they could get their hands on. When I got older, I applied for low-income housing, and we got accepted. We could afford the rent because I'd gotten promoted from busboy to waiter and was able to scrape together enough cash." Jun waved back at the five-year-old boy sitting in a chair across from them. "We qualified for food stamps, which kept food on the table, but my mom changed from being depressed to being depressed and addicted to alcohol. So, I had to hide my cash in the backyard to keep her from stealing it."

"Wow."

He unscrewed the lid from a bottle of water and took a long drink before continuing. "Soon after that, I found out that my sister hadn't been attending school. She'd just gone through the motions. I tried to talk to her about it, but she just shut down, you know?"

"Yeah, I do ..." Ashley responded, "I can see why. She had nobody to talk to, really. No girl, anyway, and no mom."

"Exactly. So, every time we talked, we'd fight. I'd get all 'older brother' on her, and she'd just end up crying, but not talking – and not changing." Jun sat in silence for a few minutes. "Occasionally, she'd be gone for weeks at a time. I'd get so worried. I didn't know whether to report her to the police or not." His lip was quivering.

"I can't imagine what that must have been like. Plus, you were probably still feeling the loss of your dad."

"It was hard, you know? He sucked as a father, but at least when he was alive, there was hope that someday we'd all get along, that maybe one day in the future he'd have time for his kids."

Ashley nodded understandingly.

"Anyway," continued Jun, wiping a straying tear. "One day, I went through her room while she was gone. I thought I'd search for some clues as to what she was up to. As I was rifling through her mattress, I found a small incision. When I stuck my arm into it, I pulled out rolls of cash. It was a lot: over eighty-five thousand dollars!"

"Are you kidding me? Eighty-five grand? Wow!" The pretty brunette thought for a minute. "Drugs?"

"Prostitution."

"Oh, no!" Ashley sank back as her hand covered her mouth.

"I made a tactical error. But I didn't know what else to do. I told Mom. She freaked out. And when Jee Hye finally got home, Mom had drained a bottle of Jack and went crazy on my sister. She threw a vase at her and proceeded to pick up anything she found lying around to launch in her direction – scissors, books, a lamp, the remote. The whole time she was calling her a lousy whore and cussing her out! When Mom tried to whack her with a chair, I intervened. Still, she went on and on. Finally, she ordered my sister to leave. I pleaded with Mom – telling her that it wasn't the right action to take. I told her that if Jee Hye was at home at least, she'd be safe. But mom screamed that she didn't want to live with this slut of a daughter."

"Wow, Jun!"

"I told my sister that I'd get us a place. I pretty much figured mom needed to face her own demons and fend for herself. My sister and I could live on our own and survive. But then Jee Hye said something I'll never forget."

Ashley turned to look at him

He was barely holding himself together. "Jun, I never wanted to become such a bad person. Stay away from me, okay?"

"That must have been so hard to hear!" the surgeon said, softly.

"It was." Jun nodded. "I'd never seen her as a bad person. She was just my beautiful sister, who made some bad choices. You know, the kind of decisions that others might've made had they been in her position. When she left, I found a note she wrote me where she apologized and begged me not to look for her."

It was time to get on the plane. As their boarding group was called, Ashley gave young Mr. Park a long therapeutic side-hug. "That took courage – you sharing your background with me."

"I feel kind of relieved."

"You're with a tight crew now. I think this will be very good for you," she said, slipping her arm into Jun's.

The young man wiped tears from his eyes and pulled out his boarding pass from his pocket.

"I THINK we've made the right decision, Justin," Bora said, looking lovingly at her husband. They'd checked out of their hotel, grabbed some espressos and croissants from a nearby French bakery, and arrived at the airport in Auckland. Now they were standing sleepily in line at the ticket counter. Although they were ending their honeymoon early, they'd promised each other to resume it sometime in the next two years.

"Excuse me, are you the Parks?" an Air New Zealand agent asked as he approached them.

"Yes," answered Justin.

"Could you follow me please?"

"Is something wrong?"

"Please. Right this way," he held his right arm out politely, but his voice was firm.

Justin and Bora looked at each other, nervously.

"Let's follow him," Bora said, picking up her suitcase and carry-on bag. Justin did the same as they ducked under the queue rope.

The ANZ agent led them out from the ticketing area, past security, and through a set of thick glass doors into a room that had a markedly private feel to it. The walls and carpet had the dark blue and green décor of Air New Zealand's colors. There were some plush leather couches surrounding an onyx coffee table that held tea and cookies. To their left, was an elegant quartz counter with an ANZ employee typing into her computer. The relaxing music of a string quartet floated through the air.

"These are the Parks," announced the agent as he led them to her.

The lady behind the counter looked up. "Ah, the Parks – right – thank you, Gordon."

The man left the room with a nod.

"So, you are Mr. and Mrs. Justin and Bora Park?"

The newlyweds nodded as Justin produced their passports.

"Well, you don't have to go through the regular ticket line. You can leave your passports and bags here, and head to our executive VIP Lounge."

"I'm confused," Justin said, crinkling his eyebrows.

"Oh, I'm sorry – of course you are. I have a note here from a Mr. Leonard Stone?" She handed an envelope to him.

"What does it say?" asked Bora as her husband ripped it open.

Too bad, you had to end your honeymoon early. Enjoy your upgrade.

"Oh!" said Justin, looking at the agent. "I thought we were in trouble. You got us good."

69

The agent smiled sweetly. "Congratulations! You've been upgraded to our international first-class cabin. Go to our lounge, take hot showers if you'd like, help yourself to our gourmet breakfast, and relax. We will make sure your bags get loaded, process your passports through customs, bring them up to you, and let you know when it's time to board."

Bora squeezed Justin's hand excitedly. "How awesome is this?! I've never flown international first-class before."

"Me neither," he responded, unable to keep the big smile from spreading across his face.

They thanked the agent and headed off to enjoy the luxurious ANZ VIP Lounge.

"I WONDER who designed these crummy seats," grumbled Boyd as she twisted her back and stretched her tight spine, trying not to think about the more than thirteen hours left to go. "Sorry," she apologized as she accidentally elbowed the lady beside her.

CHAPTER TEN

CASEY, SHELLY, AND ABRIL WERE THE THREE GIRLS CLOSEST IN relationship to the coach. They'd known him the longest. He'd coached them from the time they were seven years old in a yearly soccer camp for kids in Williamsburg, Virginia. The other all-star girls had been recent arrivals – flying into Washington D.C. for two weeks of practice before launching out together to Botswana. Although everyone naturally thought they'd been picked for their skill and hard work, most of the picking was in fact due to politics. All of the parents, except for Shelly's, had made significant donations to the non-profit American Youth Soccer Organization. Everyone involved would vigorously deny any impropriety, but one had to wonder how nineteen out of the twenty girls were from very prominent families. Of course, nobody *was* wondering, and as far as the girls were concerned, they'd earned the right to be where they were. Coach Murray made sure they knew that.

The plane touched down, taxied along the runway to a ramp for private jets and came to a gentle stop. The girls were buzzing with excitement.

"Alright, listen up team," Coach Murray ordered from the front of the plane.

"We're all getting off the plane, but you can leave your personal belongings here, including your ID and money. We won't be in the open airport. There won't be anything to buy. What you do need to take with you are the gifts we're going to exchange with our friends from Germany, okay?" he raised his eyebrows, nodding. "Got that? So, take the jersey you're going to exchange, the little American flag, the gift from your region of the States and the pink whistles. You should have four gifts in your gift bag."

"What if we can't find it?" someone asked from the back.

Coach Murray tilted his head to the side. "Really, Amber?"

"Kidding, Coach." All the girls laughed as Coach Murray rolled his eyes.

"Okay, listen," he said. "We are going to disembark, do the protocol ceremony, pair up with your German buddy and then as we re-board, you're going to escort her to her seat. You all know their seat assignments, right?"

"Yes, Coach!" the girls answered in unison, causing a few more giggles.

"It is 8:00 p.m. We're going to take about an hour for the protocol, refueling and a change of crew. Then we'll re-board and take off for Botswana. I understand we'll arrive there around 8:30 a.m."

At that very moment, the plane door opened, and a tall, very blond man came onto the plane. He had a young-looking face with smooth tanned skin and a smile that beautifully showed off his perfect teeth. The girls on the plane were instantly smitten. His ocean-blue eyes danced around the interior of the plane until they landed on the American skipper.

"Coach Murray?"

"Yes?"

"I'm Coach Hans Schmidt."

Murray advanced up the plane, and the two coaches shook hands warmly.

"*Herzlich willkommen.* Welcome to Germany."

"Thank you. It's wonderful to be here. We're excited to get to know you better and have a great international experience."

"So are we. Are you ready to deplane?"

"We are," Murray responded graciously, "Let's go, girls!"

The coaches turned around to get off the plane, followed by the two security agents, Coach Murray's assistant coach, the girls, the four parents, and the two medical personnel. As they passed the cockpit, they thanked the pilots and flight attendant who, of course, wished them the best of luck.

IN THE CONFERENCE room of LaunchPad, Leonard Stone was sitting with his life-long friend David Hirsch. The two had met as students at Cornell University where Hirsch had specialized in what he called a social major – with a little English Literature on the side. Lenny, on the other hand, graduated two years before Hirsch, was ushered through high levels of national security and floated into the Pacific Ocean on a clandestine U.S. Navy submarine. From there, the talented twenty-one-year-old had helped coordinate strategic offenses and create sophisticated codes for inter-military coordination between the United States and her allies. Unbeknownst to Lenny, his girlfriend had given birth to a son and died a short time later of Rocky Mountain spotted fever. David, being a loyal friend, adopted the boy and took him back to Philadelphia where he had an old courthouse building that he was transforming into part luxury loft and what was to become an iconic cigar bar. Hirsch still owned the bar. Through the decades it had become a backroom for unofficial political deals and compromises, a place where business contracts were negotiated, and sophisticated intellectuals philosophized over quality scotch.

When the war was over, and Lenny was back on American soil, his friend finally told him about his boy, Trey. It was in that following year that the elder Stone legally adopted his own son.

LaunchPad was an off-grid location arranged by Trey Stone two years earlier when he had brought together a covert group of high-level operatives to help find his abducted family. The formerly vacant warehouse at Middle River, Maryland, used to serve the Glenn L. Martin Company before it became Martin Marietta and later Lockheed Martin. It was on Chesapeake Park Plaza, right next to Martin State Airport across the water from Kingston Point Park. Back in the day, rocket scientists had test-fired their experimental advanced missile configurations through an underwater tunnel extending into the bay. Although Trey's family was now safe, the decision had been made to keep LaunchPad intact. After all, it was fully furnished with the latest technological devices and loaded with high-end tactical gear and equipment. Although the CIA was aware of its existence, their particular location had never been officially recorded, and the small group of operatives working from there were careful to keep it that way.

The interior of the building had an almost courtyard feel. In the middle was a group of computers and hanging flat screens that formed a makeshift office area. Along the far wall were six small rooms furnished with bunk beds and Jack and Jill bathrooms; a break room with overstuffed chairs and couches; a small snack room housing a round table and four chairs; and two rooms that had been set up as holding rooms with reinforced walls and doors. Off to the right, were two other rooms that had thick insulated walls and extensive electronic surveillance – interrogation rooms. An open kitchen was on the left side of the warehouse with a refectory table and a dozen chairs.

Just beyond the kitchen, in the far-left corner, was a workshop area with lockers, wooden crates and a workbench. In it's opposite corner was a small medical clinic – something Ashley had overseen. And between the workshop area and the clinic was a large glass-enclosed, completely sound-proofed conference room. The table, which comfortably seated fourteen, was made from state-of-the-art glass which also acted as a multifunctional touch-screen and had been specifically set up by their technical guru, Saara Tuuri. She was a tall blonde-haired Finn who was usually sitting at one of the computers in the office area and working on upgrading the security protocols for a software program she had designed that would allow her to hack into drones and borrow their surveillance footage.

Saara had been with the CIA for a decade. She'd specialized in coordinating satellite imaging, data flow, information management, and covert digital actions. Discovering a Chinese spy satellite and overseeing its destruction, had made her a legend in her field. The math that it took to guide a launched missile from a submarine off the coast of Kauai to a direct hit on the spacecraft was astonishing. One physics professor at MIT later compared it to standing in Philadelphia and hitting a moving golf ball in Pittsburgh with a pea shooter. At LaunchPad, Tuuri had programmed and synchronized most of the gadgets used by the team. In addition to her technological talents, Saara was a doctor, although she hadn't practiced for quite some time. For several years, she'd worked covertly in a Middle East hospital that had treated terrorists and had been able to glean valuable information for the Company in its ongoing war against Islamic intimidators.

Today, Saara was busy on the computers while the two elderly gentlemen were sipping coffee and talking in the glass-walled conference room.

"How's the family doing in Switzerland?" Leo asked his friend as he sat back in his chair, munching on a chocolate chip cookie.

David Hirsch leaned back, too, his hands cupping the back of his head. "Fine, I guess. They arrived safely. The only camera that picked them up was outside a restroom in the Zurich airport."

"Could you see a face?"

"Bao Zhen's. But Saara went back and fixed the footage. You'd never know it, now."

"Ashley's on her way with Justin's cousin, Jun. They'll be arriving here in about seven hours."

David nodded. "Boyd's on her way back, too. She'll get here around 5:00 a.m. tomorrow."

The two men sipped their black coffees in silence.

"Do we converge everyone?" the elder Stone then asked.

"I think we're moving towards concurrency, not necessarily convergence."

"Everything happening at the same time."

"But not in the same location."

Leo reached for another cookie, "Saara's updating our security, but she's also working on figuring out why Jee Hye was such a hot target."

"How?"

"With the Company's database, cross-referencing the clients that Jee Hye worked for. She's running facial recognition software to see if we can trace places she might've been, and researching who else was in the area at the same time."

"We need to get into Jee Hye's apartment."

Trey Stone's father nodded as he stood up and stretched. Then he leaned on the table with both arms and looked right at his old friend. "When we know the truth, do we tell Jun about his sister?"

David pondered the question as he reached in his coat pocket to pull out a cigar, "Let's meet the guy, first. I think I've got a plan for him."

ASHLEY STIRRED the cream and sugar into her English Breakfast Tea. "So, the note from your sister asked you to stay away from her. Is that what you did?"

"Not by choice. I searched all over Los Angeles for her: I took her picture to the police, I showed it to former and current hookers, I grilled pimps, I even tried to access her phone company's records, but to no avail."

"Did you tell Justin?"

"No," the young man said sadly. "Maybe I should've."

Ashley thought about that for a moment. "Does he know the truth now?"

"Parts of it."

"So, then what happened?"

"I moved out of Mom's place and told her to pull it together – which she didn't do. When I found my own place, I was hoping that Jee Hye would join me. Five long years went by. I was so worried about her. For the first few years, I'd spend almost all of my spare time trying to track her down. I realized that it wasn't healthy for me anymore. So, I tried to move on. Then, out of the blue, I ran into her as I was buying groceries at an Asian market in Koreatown."

"Wow!" Ashley said, shaking her head.

"It was pretty incredible!"

"How did she react?"

"We both cried and hugged each other. She kept holding my hands and staring into my face – like it was a dream too good to be true."

"Amazing."

"She looked quite different, though. Kind of sad and maybe a little hard, but still super beautiful."

"What else do you remember about that initial reunion?"

"She wore clothes that must've cost her thousands of dollars. Just her Givenchy crocodile handbag alone, I knew was over fifteen grand." Jun shifted in his chair and stared out of the airplane window at the white clouds below. "I knew it was just a dream. That it wouldn't last. It was too good to be true."

"Why?"

"Well, we went out for dinner and chatted about things in our childhood ... it was great. It turned out we never lost our sibling connection? You know? We always loved each other. For the first time ever, she thanked me for standing up for her and being the only person that really cared."

Ashley got the sense something sad was coming up.

"After dinner is when she told me that she wasn't just a street girl. She was a high-end call girl of some sort. She would fly all over the world at people's beck and call. But it gets worse. The truth was, she was being abused over and over and over." Jun turned to his new friend. "I got the sense then that she wanted out but didn't know how it would ever happen. Jee Hye was convinced that her clients would kill her first. She never said that, exactly, but I knew it." He turned back to the window. "That's when I determined to help her somehow."

"Did you exchange contact information?"

"Yes. We texted back and forth a few times. Two months later she told me about her place in Santa Monica and wanted to meet me there. But the day before that was supposed to happen, is when she called."

"You mean *the* call. The one that started all of this."

"Yeah. That call."

Trey's niece stared into her empty cup, her thoughts swirling. *My God, Jee Hye. What on earth were you into?*

CHAPTER ELEVEN

TRAFFIC FELL INTO ITS DAWN RHYTHM AS THE EARLY MORNING sun peaked over the horizon of Greater Los Angeles. Fox was in the Walmart parking lot trying to figure out how to get information about the people who had murdered Jee Hye and chased Jun. Looking to his left, he spotted the pudgy security guard who'd been furiously driving the little golf cart. He'd attempted to chase them down when they were escaping from the parking lot in the Acadia. The protector-of-the-super-store was sitting at a picnic table in an employee smoking area next to thick bushes. They created a barrier of sorts between the giant store and whatever was beside it. The blue and red flashing lights from the cop cars in the parking lot were reflecting off the young man's face as he stared straight ahead and blew out a cloud of smoke.

"This must be the smokers lounge," Fox said with a grin before innocently querying, "Hey, can I borrow a cig, dude?"

The security guard looked up, not saying anything, and handed the giant agent two black Davidoff cigarettes.

"Nice!" the big agent said, looking at them. "Sorry, I wouldn't have asked if I had known you smoked the expensive stuff."

"No problem."

"What's going on over there? Did the store get robbed or something?"

"Hell if I know, man. It was like something out of a movie. Guys dressed in black, chasing down some dude who had his exit planned, I guess. He got away."

"Guys dressed in black?"

"Yeah."

Fox flicked the ashes off the end of the cigarette. "Where do you even get these, bro? They're really nice."

"My cousin owns a tobacco shop."

"Wow. Nice hookup." He looked up at the sky and back into the parking lot as a group of SUV's pulled in. They had yellow markings in big block letters on the side of their vehicles. The FBI was here. "Were they commandoes or something?"

"No idea, man. All I know is I'm probably going to get my ass fired. But what was I supposed to do, right?"

"Were they armed?"

"I think so – it just all happened so fast. Those punks didn't even speak English."

Fox tried to act nonchalant. "Chinese?"

"Naw ... Arabic. At least, that's what someone said."

Fox turned to look at the security guard; he was probably in his early twenties. "Was this a terrorist attack?"

The young man stood up and walked over to his cart. "I guess so. I never thought of it that way." He reached into the front compartment and pulled out a fresh pack of cigs, packed it, and ripped the plastic seal and perforated tin foil covering off. Then he opened it up – tossing the trash into a garbage bin close by. He flipped one more Fox's way. "But you're probably right, man. I think we were just hit by a terrorist attack."

Fox nodded empathetically.

"I mean, I wasn't involved, you know?" the guard stated again defensively and sitting back down. "I was just out cruising in the parking lot when I noticed a group of guys walking into the store. They looked intense – pretty organized, you know what I mean?"

The big agent lit his second cigarette, making sure his new friend was as comfortable as possible with his presence.

"I thought it was a little strange you know – them being dressed up in fatigues and all. So, I waited for a while to see if anyone else would arrive, but the coast seemed clear. I drove right up onto the sidewalk and got out of my cart. Next thing I know, all hell broke loose." His hands started to shake a little as his cigarette sprung to life. "The door of the Garden Center started closing, and a white GMC Acadia came flying onto the scene – I don't even know where it came from. Some guy jumped into the back. I couldn't really see it from my angle, you know? Next thing I know, the tires were squealing, and the thing tore out of here."

"You're kidding me," Fox stated with appropriate shock. "That's crazy, dude!"

"I tried to chase them, but you know …"

Fox nodded, looking at the security golf cart. "Not much of a race, huh?"

"Yeah. No chance," the kid nodded, angrily. He stubbed the butt into the ash tray's sand. "I ran inside through the cart door to see what was going on but didn't get very far."

It was then that Fox noticed a nasty black and blue bulge on the parietal ridge of the security guard's head. "Someone knocked you down?"

The young man nodded. "I ran into something. I don't know what it was. A baseball bat or something. They got me pretty good. When I got up, the police had arrived."

"You should put some ice on that."

"Good idea." The guy gingerly touched the bump on his head. "I told them my story and got the hell out of there. But they told me I couldn't leave the property."

Fox put his hand on the young man's shoulder as he stood up. "You did everything you could. I mean, you're not equipped to fight those kinds of guys. I doubt you'll get fired, dude."

"I hope not."

Fox thanked the kid for the cigs, crossed the side access road of the superstore and slowly made his way to the front of the Walmart – sticking to the shadows. He was just wondering how he could harness more intel when a black Cadillac Escalade pulled up to the main doors of the giant store. Its windows were tinted darker than state laws allowed, and it positioned itself directly in front of a police vehicle parking against the curb. Fox stopped in the shadows created by the concrete awning and a giant cement pillar, pretending to listen on his cell phone while situating himself for a better look. The driver's side opened, and a tall, thin man with a dark neatly trimmed beard and a black bowler hat stepped out. His distinguishing hooked nose supported round wire-rimmed glasses, and he walked with a gait that projected complete control. Fox would've recognized him anywhere. They'd served in Qatar together. It was Mohammad Al Serwabi – a Middle East Operative for the Company.

"What on earth is Serwabi doing here?" Fox wondered. "And what capacity was he operating under?" One thing was for sure, Fox needed to get out of the area before the MEO saw him. Pretending to end his phone conversation, he turned his back on the store and headed out into the parking lot. The white Acadia was about a mile away. Fox would just leave it there. It was high time to catch a cab, board a plane, and get to LaunchPad.

PROTOCOL IS LARGELY a foreign concept in the United States, but Coach Murray had been well-briefed on the importance of gift-giving, hospitality, and open-heartedness. The ceremony went smoothly, and the bond of goodwill had been created with grace. He looked down at the German Flag in his hands and thought about the nation's history. Certainly, it had been a remarkable achievement – rebuilding a nation torn to shreds by an idiotic hate-filled Austrian dictator. Not only had the German people reconstructed their economy from scratch, but after that, they'd even absorbed the East into the West and become a pillar of the European Union. Consistently they produced some of the world's best driving machines, inspired by innovative engineering, had an economy that blossomed, and currently were redefining the game of soccer.

Now, as the plane elegantly reached climbing altitude, the girls were continuing the friendliness with their new acquaintances

– some standing in the wide aisle and others kneeling in their seats, backs facing the front, as they included the girls behind them. Parents, too, were talking with each other, giving way to occasional laughter.

A male flight attendant was making his way up the aisle, taking drink orders or selections from the *carte de nuit*. He had thick black eyebrows that matched a neatly trimmed goatee, naturally-tanned skin, and a broad white-toothed smile that beamed as he took each order. It was clear that under his impeccably ironed Corneliani shirt was the kind of sculpted body that took a great deal of energy to maintain. There was a trace of exotic accent to his English that was hard to pinpoint.

Coach Hans Schmidt looked across the aisle at his American counterpart just as Coach Murray turned to look at him.

"Was this the flight crew that brought you to Germany?"

"No. The pilots told me we'd be getting a completely fresh crew."

"He seems to be a hit with the girls."

The American chuckled, "That's the kind of smile that wins friends and influences people."

Both coaches laughed.

"What's it been like for you, coaching these young girls?" Hans asked.

"I've been coaching girls' soccer for a long time now. I actually look forward to every season. But this team is a little unique."

"In what way?"

"I guess it's a combination of things. Of course, they're all exceptionally skilled for their age. They truly love to play the game, be competitive, and enjoy working out. Sometimes it's a bit challenging."

"As a coach?"

"As a manager."

The blond German understood and smiled. "Managing egos is one of the trickiest tasks."

"Right. And managing the parents' egos is even trickier!" The two coaches laughed together, and Murray continued. "Our team is mostly made up of socially privileged young ladies."

"Ours too. We have a club system in German football. It produces magnificent players, of course, but it's not designed for the Euro-less."

Both coaches re-counted their ups and downs of overseeing a national team at this junior level. It was the common denominator for all the guests on the plane and was an obvious point of bonding. Parents could relate to each other, players shared common emotions and experiences, and even the security guards were talking quietly near the back of the air-limousine as they traded stories.

THE STONE FAMILY had accomplished its mission. Everything had been identified and labeled: there were things to throw out, things that were part of the sales agreement that stayed, and a few things that would meet them back on the East Coast. The covert moving company, along with a group of people David had organized, would be arriving soon. They'd bag and dispose of all the trash then load up the "save" items. When that was completed, they'd all clean the house.

"I hate moving." Lin Lin announced as they sat down to take a break.

Trey agreed. "It's the fact that everything needs to be touched and decided on. Whether it's a receipt that you find behind your dresser, the book on your bookshelves, the sentimental items like photos, CDs or movies, they all need to be thought about."

"I'm tired of making decisions."

"If in doubt, throw it out. That's usually been my motto."

Ms. Ma smiled at her son-in-law, "I like that."

"Dad," Jasmine spoke up. "What's a covert moving company?"

"They specialize in moving people out quickly and quietly. Maybe it's because a wife needs to leave suddenly with her children to escape an abusive relationship or people who need to leave a neighborhood filling up with crime, or someone involved in a witness relocation program. Whatever the reason, sometimes people need to move without rippling the water. These companies get it done."

"How can they move people so quickly?"

"It's all in the preparation. Some companies will secretly spend a week inside the home before the actual move out day, packing everything up, and even prepping the furniture. If it's too dangerous to actually pack anything in advance, they will do a complete inventory. Then, like in our case, they arrive with a small army that can do everything noiselessly and with precision. I've heard of homes where everything was moved out in less than twenty minutes."

Just as he said that, the door chimes sounded. Their movers had come.

"HAVE you decided on what you'd like for breakfast?"

"Does the mushroom omelet really use nine wild mushrooms from six continents?" Bora asked, reading the ANZ menu aloud.

"It certainly does. If you flip to page seven of Kia Ora, our inflight magazine, you can read about who hand-picks them and how they end up on your breakfast plate."

"I will," the young bride answered with a smile. "And I'll taste every mushroom, too."

Justin duplicated the order and added orange mimosas for both of them.

CHAPTER TWELVE

It was 2:04 a.m. when the chartered Boeing Business Jet 737-800 made a sudden sweeping turn. Few people noticed. They were asleep in various positions, stuffed with food and dreaming of soccer greatness. But Jason Kennedy noticed. It was his job to recognize any change, however slight. He was one of two personally selected security guards for the American team. Born in Ozark, Arkansas, he grew up hunting wild boar, white-tailed deer, and elk with his dad on the other side of the Arkansas River. When he was eighteen, he left home to serve God and country, not necessarily in that order, and then found his way into being recruited by a private security firm that the government contracted to protect VIPs. He was dependable, talented, and brighter than most.

Kennedy sat up in his seat, blinking away the sleep and poked the security guard next to him. "Something just happened."

His battle buddy tried to fight away grogginess. Miles Howell was selected for this job on the same merit as Jason. Although he'd never had the military experience, he cut his teeth on the legendary training of the United States' Secret Service and put in twenty years of spotless work. At age fifty-two, he'd just retired when he got the call to escort this team to Botswana. He was hired for the job because of the field experience and street smarts he brought to the partnership.

"Something's happened," Kennedy repeated. "Wake up!"

"What thing?"

"You have an analog compass?"

"Hold on."

Kennedy's eyes narrowed as he lifted the window shield next to him and stared into the dark night sky.

"Here it is," Howell said, shielding the digital glow with his hand as he glanced down. "We're headed East." He snapped the cover back on the compass and slowly moved his body to his left, so he could continue talking without drawing attention. Although the cabin had been darkened, he wasn't taking any chances.

Kennedy leaned right, his elbow on his armrest, and showed his partner the face of his phone. "Here's the flight path we should be on. South – almost all the way."

"Do you know where we are now?"

"Yeah," Jason answered, tapping his phone's screen to open up a GPS app. "I didn't think this could be right, but I guess it is." Taking a quick glance at it to make sure it was on, he turned it towards Miles.

"Shit."

As if on cue, the plane's nose lurched downward. Kennedy felt his stomach flip as gravity disappeared. The jetliner had plunged into a nose dive! Screams pierced through the air from every direction!

Howell twisted around to look at his German counterparts across the aisle. A flash of moonlight lit their lifeless faces and spirit-less eyes. Dark sticky liquid oozed out of their sliced throats. His hand darted to his hip holster. It was empty.

JUN WATCHED the mountains of Colorado tumble away as the plane climbed its way to a cruising altitude.

Stifling a yawn, Ashley shifted into a more comfortable position. She wanted to continue a snooze that had gotten interrupted by their forty-seven-minute Denver layover. "I wonder how Fox is doing?" she thought. "Has he identified the guys at Walmart?"

She leaned her seat back and started to doze off.

NOT EVERYONE HAD BEEN seat-belted when the plane plunged downward. Abril Fuentes' body lurched upward, plastered against the ceiling above her. Amber let out a long shriek, locked her arms straight out in front of her, and shut her eyes. Shelly Brown, always the optimist, was terrified. Life memories began to flood her mind in a weird super-slow motion. Casey Baker, the ex-President's granddaughter, started breathing quick breaths, exhibiting a panic attack.

"They took my gun!" Howell leaned and hissed to his seat partner.

Kennedy's face paled as he realized his piece was gone too. He looked out of the window and saw the wing on his side bent up, looking like it was about to snap off.

Their bodies were straining against their seatbelts, as the aircraft groaned and creaked like a thousand fingernails scraping on a chalkboard. Miles strained to get his neck and head to face forward. The force of the plummet made it almost impossible as the plane chased gravity. He freeze-framed what he saw: the cabin was in chaos; dishes and backpacks were flying through the air; unsecured handbags and soccer balls were floating in weightlessness ; people were clinging to each other – as if holding on to life itself.

Coach Murray knew it was the end. He'd led a pretty good life, but even with that thought, anxiety was wrapping itself around his heart like a boa constrictor. He gasped for breath and wanted to scream, but no sound came. The plane continued to groan deafeningly. Then, it leveled unexpectedly and banked steeply. Murray's stomach felt like it had been pulled out onto the floor.

Hans Schmidt was puking all over himself.

Without warning, the force of gravity violently shifted as the pilots of the giant machine fought to control the flight path. The enormous beast rose and paused in the air before shaking like a violent earthquake. It was clear that they were entering a defining moment. A sharp, putrid smell was permeating the cabin. Jason Kennedy wondered whether it was coming from the airplane or the people. He noticed the flight attendants were seat-belted into their seats. Their eerily placid faces sent chills through his rugged body.

CHAPTER THIRTEEN

SAARA TUURI AND DAVID HIRSCH HAD GONE TO THEIR RESPECTIVE bedrooms at LaunchPad to get some rest. Although it was late in the morning, the team had been up most of the night trying to button down the situation in California. Allies had been contacted and cleanups were in play, but the connection to Jee Hye was remaining strictly in-house.

Leonard was on the phone. "Sorry, Fox. I know you wanted to get back here, but you're the wolf on the ground. We need you there."

"Copy that. I'll see what I can find out."

"I'm sending her address to you now. Ashley got it for us."

"I need a kit, sir."

"Justin has a Company contact in L.A. who's already put one together for you," Trey's father responded. "Get to The Ambrose Hotel in Santa Monica and look for a white Honda Pilot on the northwest edge of the parking lot with license plate number two bravo tango whiskey niner four two. Key fob will be in a magnet box in the driver's side front wheel well. Everything you'll need will be in the navy-blue duffle bag in the back."

"Copy that. Fox out."

The big blond agent pulled up Google Maps and saw that traffic was thinning out after the morning rush. It was slightly better than he'd expected and it would only take about forty-seven minutes to get to The Ambrose. From there, Jee Hye's apartment was a ten-minute drive. He leaned forward and gave the taxi driver new instructions.

LEONARD STONE WAS SITTING BACK in his chair, reading the information on his tablet that Saara had compiled about the Middle East Operative, Serwabi. He looked up when he heard one of the bedroom doors open. It was David standing in the doorway with a phone in his hand. His face looked pale.

"Leo," Stone's old friend's voice was thin and unsteady. "Something's happened."

A SUDDEN SPAT of turbulence woke Ashley with a start. She sat up, gathered her long auburn hair, moved it over her right shoulder, and rubbed her eyes. Stretching her arms up in the air as far as she could, she turned her back to the left and to the right.

"I guess I'm not going to be able to sleep anymore," she told Jun reluctantly, "We've got forty-five minutes left."

Jun turned towards her. "It's one of those flights. Sudden noises and dips kept me awake too." He looked back out the window. "I don't know much about you, Ashley. What's your story? How'd you and Fox meet? Are you two dating?"

Ashley chuckled and then looked across the aisle at three college kids who were playing games on their tablets and then turned back to Jun. The questions were kind of personal and intrusive, but he'd been so transparent with her, she knew she should open up, too. "Well, no. Not exactly. I was engaged to someone a few years back, but he died." She pondered silently for a moment, then added, "I think I'm ready to start dating again though. If he's interested, Fox would be first in line for sure. I like him a lot."

"I'm sure he's interested."

She smiled at the way Jun said that. "Maybe when this is all over . . ." She surrendered her empty cup to a flight attendant walking by. "We met when my uncle's family was kidnapped. I was just working at a golf course . . . you know, getting my head together after my fiancé died. I don't really know exactly what Fox was doing before that. I know he'd been with the Navy Seals in some capacity. But we were both recruited into the group that worked to find them and bring them back."

"Were you successful?"

Ashley turned away. Her voice was suddenly distant.

"You know, I can't talk about that. No offense. It was a really hard time for me."

Jun looked out the window.

"I've had to work through a lot of grief in my life," she went on, not wanting him to feel cut off. "My parents and grandparents were killed in a car crash. It was my uncle, David, who raised me."

"I thought you said your uncle's name was Trey."

"I'm sorry," Ashley turned in his direction. "It's confusing. Trey's more like my older brother, but I call him uncle."

Jun was clearly puzzled.

"David was my mom's brother and is my real uncle. But, because he raised me from when I was five, I actually see him more as my father. I call him 'Dad.' His best friend, Leonard, had a son whose name is Trey. But, because he's ten years older than me, I call him Uncle."

"I get it now," Jun said, nodding still fairly confused. "So, what do you call Trey's father?"

"Leo's more like a grandfather to me even though he's the same age as David. He's always the one who would buy me random presents and spoil me when I would visit. When I think about him, I'm sure he's just what my grandfather would've been like."

THE YOUNG MARRIED couple was busy choosing a topping for their ice cream sundaes. There were so many options. From the heated Ghirardelli chocolate or caramel sauce to an assortment of roasted macadamia nuts and tropical fruit, one thing was certain, Bailey's would need to be liberally poured over the top of it all.

"Can we fly like this all the time?" Bora asked her husband, cheekily.

"You'd better finish law school, first, counselor."

"Duly noted."

Justin was eating his dessert, but jotting things down on a little pad of yellow paper at the same time.

"What are you working on?"

"Homework," he grinned. "I'm outlining the weapons cache contents at LaunchPad, as best I can remember it all. If I know Leo and David, we'll be hitting the ground running. I want to make sure we have all the essentials to gear up when the time comes. I'm also listing the people on the team and reminding myself of their preferences. That way I can reference this list if I have to."

"You're such a boy scout! Always prepared."

Justin grinned, "And I'm sure you love that about me."

"Actually, I do."

FEW PLACES on the planet are as beautiful as Switzerland in the spring and early summer. The deep blue sky frames the pristine Alps in breathtaking splendor. Cheery crocuses and primroses dot the fields. Later, impatiens of every color will flood the scene as geraniums, petunias and calla lilies show off in stately fashion. Bluethroats, warblers, finches, and firecrests all chirp happily along the forest trails. People, too, seem to be more relaxed in the Swiss summers. The uber-wealthy pull out their custom Maseratis, Ferraris, Lamborghinis and Porsche Spyders to cruise around the Lake Geneva waterfront. Many store-owners close up their shops and leave for family summers in the high Alps. Others go hiking or cliff-climbing. Some take sail-boats out on the lakes. And the ever-important tourists will be dutifully drained of cash while enjoying their own vacations.

Movers had come and gone, so Lin Lin and Bao Zhen were on their way home via Turin and Paris. Trey and Jasmine had finished a glorious time along the Ouchy shore and were watching tourists who waiting to board the ferry from Lausanne to Evian, France. Although appearing relaxed, Trey was constantly on the lookout for danger. His keen sense of vulnerabilities and his raw talent for scanning every scene and projecting scenarios kept him alert.

"Do you think we'll ever be back here again, Dad?" asked his seventeen-year-old, wistfully.

Trey thought for a moment. "I don't know, Honey. With Mama leaving the area, we won't have as much reason to return. But we do love it here, don't we?"

"I really do, Dad. I hope I can be back here someday."

The ferry was a simple vessel with two decks. There were rows of seats upstairs and downstairs. But the real treat was to hang out along the taffrail, feeling the twilight breeze blowing gently and witnessing the stars starting their night glitter one by one. Jasmine made her way to the bow. It was her favorite place to stand. Trey stood next to her as she leaned over to gaze at the sparkling night water of Lac Leman. Her eyes twinkled with satisfaction. She started humming softly to herself. Lights from smaller sailboats bobbed up and down, their owners doing some night fishing or partying with friends. The engines began to purr, slowly converting their rotational motion into thrust, and the wide boat propeller started its powerful churn. The thirty-five-minute crossing was underway.

Father and daughter were soaking in the moment when Trey drew in his breath sharply and tightened his grip on the railing. His eyebrows furrowed as he systematically accessed his memory bank to remember where he'd seen this person.

The man was roughly 5'11, solidly built with square shoulders, defined biceps, and black hair, drawn back into a ponytail. He was sporting a black polo shirt, dark jeans and sunglasses propped on his head. His sharp facial features could easily be Native American, possibly from the Lakota tribe. Trey concentrated a little harder. He'd seen him in a coffee shop at the Zurich airport. At that time, he'd had on shady gray skinny jeans, a navy-blue polo and had purchased a coffee with a bagel. Agent Stone recalled spotting him a second time when he was getting off the train in Geneva and heading for baggage claim. He'd worn a green T-shirt with khaki cargo pants and shouldered a camo backpack. Those two sightings were justifiable. Many people commuted from Zurich to Geneva. But what were the odds of the very same guy being in Switzerland on a ferry-boat to France? About 8,435,544,455.03444 to one, Trey concluded.

It was time for a decision.

The ferry was big enough to find a place for a private conversation but too small to put a guy out of commission without causing a commotion. Agent Stone stared straight out across the water, barely making out the shadowy shores of the lake. David had insisted they carry no cell phones and nothing that had a hackable GPS. But in a situation like this, Trey wished there was some way of sending a message. He'd just decided to take some kind of action, when an attractive Asian lady came to the front of the bow, nudging up beside Jasmine looking to get a better view of the distant Evian. Fishing her phone from her purse, she began to take pictures, checking each one to see if anything was visible in the night sky.

Trey understood. There was an interception underway somewhere. He casually glanced back at the man who had been following them. He was gone.

Trey touched his daughter's elbow, holding it firmly.

"Jazzy."

His daughter turned towards him.

"I'm going to the restroom."

"Is something wrong, Dad?"

"No, Honey. Everything's fine. Let's just keep chatting."

With Michiko Imada there, he knew his daughter was in very safe hands. But why was she on this ferry? And who was Ponytail?

"Wait a minute," Jasmine responded quietly, "I know your voice and I've seen that look."

Trey turned and again looked out across the water. "Whatever you do, Jazzy, just keep looking at me and then across the lake like we're discussing something completely unimportant. Do not turn to look at the person next to you for any reason and don't talk with her."

Her gaze was fixed on him. Then, she started to chuckle and pretend to talk.

"Good. Keep focused on me," Trey muttered quietly. "Michiko is standing next to you."

"She's the one taking touristy pictures?" Jasmine asked in a low voice as she threw back her head and laughed.

Trey was proud of how she'd noticed that.

"Are we in trouble, Dad?" In spite of the laugh, fear had already spread across his beautiful daughter's face.

They both looked out across the water, and Trey put his arm around her shoulders. They both smiled and gazed across the water. "No," he responded firmly and reassuringly. "Nothing like that. If we were in trouble, Michi would never have let us board this boat. My thinking is that someone needs to pass me a message of some kind. So, she's going to wait here close to you. Don't give any sign that you know her. That means, no eye contact at all and no conversation unless she initiates it. Turn slightly to me."

Jasmine did.

"I'm going to walk around a bit, and I'll be back within ten minutes."

"Okay, Dad," Jazzy muttered, tossing her hair back and calming down. "How did she find us?"

"I have no idea, Honey."

"Why is she here, beside me?"

"I'm sure we'll find out."

Agent Imada, or Michi, as she was called by those who knew her best, had gone to the same Company boarding school as Trey. They'd first met at that top-secret location in Japan. She had been a child then, but Trey remembered her well. She'd spoken seven languages fluently and had a sharp mind for sciences. Since then, she'd become a disguise specialist who could easily draw attention to herself, or go completely unnoticed, depending on what was needed. But, her true talent as a spy lay in her ability to graciously put people at ease while learning almost everything about them. Like most field agents, she could defend herself extremely well and Trey had always warned people that she was "certifiably crazy" as a mixed martial artist. Recently, she'd been a major help in saving Trey's life when his family had been taken.

All kinds of thoughts went through Agent Stone's mind as he left to walk through the boat and find the man with the ponytail. "Were the people who wanted him dead, close by? Were his wife and mother-in-law safe? Had something happened to his father or David? Was LaunchPad in trouble?"

In Trey's line of work, caution usually meant you stayed alive longer. As long as it didn't turn into paranoia. His mind was spinning with ideas as he arrived at the indoor part of the main floor of the ferry. Ponytail was nowhere to be found. Trey glanced into the sitting area, but only a few people were there, and half of them were dozing. He found the stairs, but just as he reached the top step, a stocky, muscular man with a Marine's haircut, came around the corner and rudely shoved him aside to descend the staircase.

"Get out of my way!" he growled as he pushed past Agent Stone. In a flash, he'd slipped a piece of paper into Trey's hand and bounded down the steps.

It had all happened so quickly that even Trey was surprised. "Now Bruce was here, too? How'd they gotten to Switzerland so quickly?" he wondered.

"Jerk!" Trey shouted after the disappearing hulk, to keep up the ruse. "Watch where you're going!"

Agent Bruce Locke was one of the Company's best-kept secrets. He was an ex-Marine who had met Trey on a mission in Colombia where they'd almost shot each other's head off. Since then, they'd become inseparable for years. In the past few months, however, when Trey's family was in relocation, he'd had no contact with Locke or anyone else from LaunchPad, other than David and Leonard. In just that moment, Trey realized how much he missed his friend.

Bruce had short blond hair that made no secret of his military background. His piercing blue eyes were steady as he seemed to look through the walls of your soul. He was old-school in a lot of ways, though technologically he was as current as anyone. Fox once described Bruce to a colleague as, "the kind of guy who would rather blow up an old car in a stone quarry at night than take the time to clean it up and sell it."

Trey found the men's restroom, checked to see that it was empty and quickly bolted the door behind him. Carefully he unfolded the tiny piece of paper and immediately recognized Bruce's precise handwriting.

Green. Whiskey is scarlet. Friends stick together.

The first word spoke to his specific situation: his family was safe. Yellow, would have meant that actionable intelligence had put hostiles in the area of his loved ones. Red, would have indicated that there was credible and imminent danger of some sort. But his family was green.

The second phrase referred directly to President George Baker, the former President of the United States, and Bruce knew that Trey would recall Baker's codename. Intelligence organizations have secret words to identify every President as well as each member of his family. Good ones are created to be easily pronounced and readily understood by anyone who transmits or receives voice messages, regardless of their native language. If need be, these words could change over time for security purposes, but often they'll stick throughout the President's season in office. President Baker had been Whiskey, and scarlet meant that he was in distress.

The last sentence indicated that Bruce and Michi wanted Trey and Jasmine to leave the boat with them. Trey looked at his watch. The ferry shuttle would reach France in just six minutes.

CHAPTER FOURTEEN

COACH MURRAY WAS JUST AS CONFUSED AS EVERYONE ELSE. A moment ago he'd thought for sure they were all going to die, but the plane had landed as if dropping out of the sky. It had slammed down on what felt like an unpaved runway. An acrid stench hung in the air, oxygen masks dangled from random places on the airplane, and he felt a sharp burning pain in his abs. Lifting his shirt and gently peeling back the top of his pants, he saw red skin-burns and deep bruising. "Seatbelt," he muttered to himself.

"What's going on?" the German coach wanted to know, wiping the puke from his mouth.

"No idea," the American answered as the plane jerked unexpectedly and began taxiing forward. The cabin was eerily quiet with the occasional sniff and wimper. People were terrified.

Jason Kennedy looked at his partner. "What do we do?"

"I have nothing on me," Miles Howell responded, shaking his head. "No gun. No knife. Nothing. Someone must've stolen them while we were sleeping. Were we sedated?"

"That would explain my pounding headache. I'm going to sneak forward. See if I can take down one of the flight attendants."

"How?"

"I'll figure it out."

"Don't do it. This isn't the time for heroics."

"It's exactly the time for heroics," Kennedy mumbled to himself while he unbuckled his seat belt and slid quietly to the ground. He gave a quick nod to Howell and then began to belly-crawl along the right edge of the aisle. In a flash, the flight attendant with the million-dollar smile jumped out of his rear-facing seat, drew a weapon, and shot Jason Kennedy in the head.

Screeches of panic pierced the air! Parents started screaming their outrage at the flight attendant. Girls wailed hysterically as blood fountained from the crown of the guard's skull.

Coach Murray sat up, unsure as to what had just happened. Another shot rang out. It had been fired into the ceiling.

"Everyone shut up!" the flight attendant roared; his million-dollar smile replaced by a wicked sneer. "Stay in your seats!" He waved his gun around, randomly pointing directly at specific people.

Suddenly, blackness covered the plane like a funeral shroud. They'd taxied into a darkened hangar.

TREY CAREFULLY TORE the paper into tiny shreds and flushed the pieces down the toilet. He found his way back to his daughter, sauntering up to her as if there was nothing unusual.

"Hi Dad," Jasmine said, forcing a smile. "It's still so beautiful out here. I can't decide whether to look across the lake or up at the magical night sky."

Trey put his arm around his daughter, and they gazed up into the stars together. "I see what you mean, Sweetie. It's breathtaking." He looked down to where the water was splashing as the boat cut through the lake and muttered quickly. "Jasmine, we're going to get off the boat. We'll go with Bruce and Michi. Something's going on. Not with our family; Mom and Mama are fine. But for some reason, Bruce wants us to go with them."

He felt his daughter tense up.

"Jazzy, listen," Trey reassured quietly, "We're going to be just fine. I promise."

"I'm not scared, Dad. My body's just reacting with adrenalin," she muttered, "I've been training so hard over these past months for a moment just like this."

"Not really," he countered, "You've been training for a moment like when you were kidnapped. You've been trained defensively. This is not like that."

"Whatever, Dad," she said, as she looked up at the stars again, grinning. "I'm kind of excited."

Trey shook his head. She was the mirror of her father. In a low whisper, he gave instructions, "Our standard protocol for this situation is that you'll walk off first, spot Bruce, and go directly to him. He'll probably have a vehicle ready. Michi will be behind you."

"What about you?"

"I'll get there, too. There's something I need to take care of first. Tell them to wait for me."

The boat engaged its thrusters and began pulling up to the dock, triggering a scurry of activity. Messenger lines were tossed onto the pier, so the dock workers could pull up the ropes and tie them to the iron horn cleats as passengers hurriedly gathered their belongings and began making their way to the exit door. Bruce was one of the first in line, sporting a light gray Kangal Squad beanie with a matching long-sleeved tee. Jasmine made her way to the back of the line of people waiting for the gates of the boat to open, allowing passengers to walk down the short gangplank onto the shores of France. Others filed in behind her and she turned slightly, to say something to her father, but he was already gone. She noticed Michi, about fifteen people back, searching for him too.

Jasmine Stone almost hesitated. Yet, she knew she needed to do exactly what her father had told her to do. So, she moved forward slowly to the rhythm of the debarking passengers.

Trey had deftly ducked out of the forming line, satisfied that Michi hadn't noticed. He made his way to the shadowy corner under the staircase in position. As the people started deboarding the boat, a figure could be seen quietly descending the flight of stairs. Agent Stone waited until the man with a black ponytail was about to step off the last step. With a fluid motion that only comes from years of experience and practice, he darted out, grabbed the Native American's wrist with one arm, while simultaneously punching his elbow with his opposing fist. Trey continued to twist the man's wrist and arm, and two seconds later had dragged him under the stairs. Then he slammed his body and face against the wall.

"One sound and I'll slit your throat," Stone hissed.

The man in the black polo protested, "You're breaking my arm!"

Trey tweaked the arm a little tighter. He used his other hand to grab the man's ponytail and shove his face into the wall, almost busting the guy's cheekbone.

"What do you want?"

"When these passengers are off the boat, you and I are going to have a short, conversation. You're going to tell me why you're following me. Then I'm going to walk away, leaving you maimed or dead."

"Trey," the man panted. "Bruce, Michi, and I are working together."

Agent Stone had been just one twist from snapping the young man's arm. "Prove it."

"Michi told me that you used to lay by a lake together when you were in a private boarding school overseas, and swap stories. She loved those summer nights. Bruce told me that when he met you, he tried to kill you, but his gun jammed."

Trey held him for a few more seconds and then relaxed his hold. "Bruce's gun didn't jam. I was quicker on the draw then he was and he got scared."

The Native American turned, shaking his arm out. "Shit, man! You almost broke my arm! I'm going to have a bruise on my face, too."

"What's your name?"

"Tatanka Ptecila."

"Little Bull?"

The young man's jaw dropped. "You actually speak my language?"

"I wish," Trey responded. "Several years ago, I read about the Lakota tribe when I was interested in Native American history. For some reason, your name stuck with me."

"I heard about your memory; still, I'm surprised," Ponytail responded. "I was born in Wyoming, but as you know, my people came from the Black Hills of South Dakota."

Trey nodded, "Do I call you Tatanka for short?"

"My friends made an even shorter name. Just 'Tank.'"

"Good to meet you, Tank. We should probably get off before this boat sails back to Switzerland."

Tank patted Trey on the back with the sore arm as they turned to leave. "I'm glad we're on the same side," he said ruefully, rubbing his cheek with the other hand.

Most of the passengers had dispersed into the town of Evian or hooked up with waiting friends. As Trey and Tank made their way down the gangplank, Agent Stone spotted Bruce's gray beanie. He was standing in front of the Hôtel Alizé Evian and next to a black Lincoln Navigator, with heavily tinted windows. As they approached, Trey noticed the green license plates with orange lettering and the number six – a U.S. Embassy vehicle.

"Nice ride."

"They dropped it off for us. Leather seats." Bruce opened the back door. "I see you and Tank met."

"Sheesh did we ever! I'm just happy to be alive," Tank responded, as he scrambled into the far captain's chair in the middle row with Trey following behind.

Bruce settled into the driver's seat and closed the door. He didn't turn around but started up the engine. They roared off through the roundabout and past the Hilton Evian Les Bains.

Nobody spoke until Agent Locke had pulled into a dark parking area under some trees and shut off the engine. Rotating in his seat, he stared at Trey.

"Man, it's good to see you!"

"For sure, Bruce. I had the same thought when I almost knocked you down the stairs."

Locke chuckled. "I was afraid you were going to collapse from fright when I came around the corner."

Trey laughed.

"Some things never change," Michi said, grinning. "You two need to get your stories straight."

"It was so hard, standing next to you and not giving you a big hug," Jasmine squealed, from the third row. She threw her arms around Michi beside her. "I've missed you so much!"

"I've missed all of you, too," Agent Imada responded warmly.

Trey had a big smile now. "Not having any contact with the people at LaunchPad has been ridiculously hard. We talked about all of you often. We're all doing well. But, how did you get here so quickly?"

"We've always been close," Bruce admitted. "David wanted us to never be more than a five-minute drive away." He turned to Tank. "You were made?"

Trey responded first. "I saw him in Zurich and then again in Geneva. When he popped up tonight, I knew it wasn't a coincidence. So, before I connected with you and Michi, I decided to introduce myself."

"Trey was breaking my arm," Tank related, "but I told him about Michi's memory of the lake and then how you two met."

"You remember, right Bruce?" Trey chimed in. "That time you saw me and shook so hard with fright, you couldn't squeeze off a round."

"Never heard that version," Agent Locke responded with a grin.

Tank continued, "Anyway, I'm still alive and have both arms."

Everyone chuckled, but Trey sobered up. "I'm guessing you didn't just want to give us a ride to Stuttgart."

Bruce tipped his head at Jasmine.

"It's okay," Trey said, reading his friend's mind. "Anything I receive about this op, she can know, too. She's been getting a lot of training these last few months."

"Okay. I'm good with that if you are."

Jasmine squeezed Michi's hand. Her facial expression reflected how proud she was at that moment. Her father was trusting her with sensitive information!

"Leo contacted me about an hour before you boarded the boat to Evian. David had just gotten off the phone with Whiskey."

"Baker?"

Bruce nodded, "Apparently, his granddaughter was on a private plane with her soccer team and one from Germany – some kind of goodwill thing – they were supposed to go to Botswana for an international tournament. About sixteen hours ago, the plane went off the radar. It totally disappeared. They've been trying everything to figure out what's been going on. We'll get more details from Saara in a few minutes. They want us to find her and bring her home."

"What do you mean? It just disappeared off the radar?"

"Vanished."

"Sixteen hours ago?"

"Apparently. They've all been spending a lot of time and energy drawing blanks."

"Where was the plane located when this happened?"

"It pinged properly … Stuttgart, Venice, San Marino, Rome, Naples, and Catania. Then there's a signal from Malta, and just before it reached the North African line, it evaporated."

Trey frowned. Wheels began to shift gears in his head. "It shouldn't have pinged in Malta."

"No. By then they should have been flying over southern Greece."

"So, they went off course."

"Slightly."

Michi spoke up. "We have a working theory, Trey, but you're not going to like it."

"Maybe we should bring in Saara now," Bruce suggested.

Agent Imada nodded as Tank reached into his backpack to pull out a tablet. In a few minutes, Saara Turri's face came up on the screen. There was no doubt about her Scandinavian features and blonde hair. Even in her early fifties, she was keeping the gray at bay. Her blue eyes sparkled as she recognized Agent Stone and his daughter.

"Hello, Trey!" she exclaimed in her musical Finnish voice. "How lovely to see you. And you, too, Jasmine!"

"Saara, you look great," Agent Stone responded. "You're still at LaunchPad, I see?"

"I am," she responded, smiling and nodding. "Your father has kept me very busy. I've been updating protocols, retooling our secure communications software, tracking a developing situation in Los Angeles, and now piecing together a plane disappearing in thin air."

"Trey – Jasmine!" It was David and Leonard coming up behind her.

Trey and his daughter responded together at exactly the same time, "Hi!"

They'd been communicating some in the last few months, but this was the first time Trey and Jasmine had seen Leo and David since they had been hidden. Trey struggled with his emotions. Jasmine teared right up and began to sniffle loudly.

"We've missed you terribly. It's so good to see all of you ," Leonard stated with a certain wistfulness in his voice.

"We've missed you too," Jasmine responded, wiping her eyes and nose with the back of her wrist.

Everyone kept smiling at each other, trying to pull themselves together.

Trey finally, cleared his throat, "So there's a plane missing …"

"Yes," Leo answered. "A privately chartered Boeing Business Jet. It went off the radar. We need to find it."

"Isn't the Company and the very impressive United States military, Secret Service, FBI and NSA already swarming with intelligence and force. Why were you contacted?"

"Whiskey is adamant that he wants us, in addition to whatever official government efforts are being made. He has a notion that in the end, only a small group of people operating outside an official government capacity can get out in front of this.

"What about a private security firm?"

"We're it."

Trey sat back to let this sink in. "Yeah, Dad, that's not really what we're about."

"What do you mean?"

"Didn't we agree that if we ever reconvened LaunchPad, it was going to be about bringing child traffickers to justice? We were going to expose systems and networks, lay the financials bare, and take down movers and shakers. I'm not sure how a search and rescue assignment taps into our mission statement."

Leo leaned forward in his chair. "There are forty twelve to thirteen-year-old girls on that plane. Almost all of them are from very affluent families in the United States and Germany. I don't want to jump to any conclusions, but we all know how these things often end. My gut tells me this is exactly in line with our mission statement. The bastards behind this have gone to a lot of trouble." He sat back, and everyone sensed the resolve on his face. "Trey, we've been asked to help. We need to."

"Maybe the plane just malfunctioned or blew up?"

"Saara?" Leo asked, implying that she should take over at this point.

"When Whiskey called us, he gave us some information that only a few people are privy to. Casey Baker, his grand-daughter, had been outfitted with a chip in her right shoulder. The technology isn't quite like in the movies. It doesn't just send out a homing beacon all the time. There simply isn't enough energy in the chip to keep it powered up for very long because it's not a rechargeable system." She paused, to throw a picture on the screen that showed the exact kind of embedded transponder the girl was wearing. "She can dig her fingernails into it and activate the power. Once it starts transmitting, it's programmed to stay on for three minutes and then shut down to save energy. She can do that about twenty times. After that, the power will have run out, and the device will have died. She's already triggered it twice. The first time was in Germany, for a test. She texted her grandfather before trying it, and he texted her back that it worked. The second time was about three hours ago."

"So, she's probably alive," Jasmine stated, relieved. "Where is she?"

Saara paused and pulled up a map onto the screen. "Libya."

The gravity of the situation was obvious. Trey looked at Bruce. "Libya? That's like Iraq and Syria."

David came on. "Yes, Trey, you're right. No commercial jet from the United States or any of her allies can fly over those nations."

"What about private jets?"

"Some can, of course. But definitely not this one. It was supposed to fly over southern Greece, down over Egypt and Sudan, and then right down the gut of Central Africa, south to Botswana."

Saara had switched maps on the screen. It showed the exact flight path David was referring to.

"I'm assuming that our military can't waltz into Libya for an extraction?" Bruce asked.

"That's correct," David answered. "As a matter of fact, even a tactical spec ops team from a private firm would draw attention, especially if it left from American soil. The only viable solution is to use a very small operational unit. We must find out what's going on."

Saara continued, "So, our working theory is that the plane went off the radar right after it pinged from Malta. It flew straight south into Libya. But here's a problem, Trey. I was able to unofficially link into a few Company satellites that have eyes on the region. As you can see, it looks like there's some kind of activity. It's night, though, and it's hard to make out what we're looking at."

She put the grainy images up on the screen.

"Please excuse my chicken scratches. I kind of drew on this one to show what could be a runway and maybe a plane. It's a guess, at best." She pulled up another picture onto the screen, but this one had yellow markings on it where she had traced a possible runway and plane. "These yellow circles are where it looked like there were lights of some sort. Maybe they're runway lights. Maybe they're lights from a plane."

"Uh-huh, I see it," Trey confirmed. "I can see why you're unsure, but it looks like you might have identified them. So, what's the problem?"

"This shot is from the next morning," Saara went on, pulling up an image that had been shot from a secretive CIA satellite armed with an industry-blowing 350-megapixel camera lens. It had been snapped in the bright daylight of a cloudless morning and was fascinatingly crystal clear. There was nothing in the image but miles and miles of bright, sparkling, undisturbed sand.

"Where's the runway?" asked Tank in the silence. "Where's the plane?"

CHAPTER FIFTEEN

FOX SECURED HIS KIT AND AS USUAL, JUSTIN HAD COVERED everything, even when working through a friend. There was an extensive lock-pick set with an assortment of rakes, twin and triple peaks, different sizes of hooks, various tension wrenches in differing widths, comb flat bars, and a Sandman – master crafted by the illustrious Las Vegas lock-pick, Dr. Dennison. With Fox's large hands, his weapon of choice was a custom-designed Fusion Tactical pistol. Its six-inch slide was impressive to look at, but he was less concerned with the impression it made than the extra weight up front – it stabilized his accuracy when he used it in close combat. He pulled it out and slipped it behind his back, knowing that his shirt would cover it up when he untucked it. A snug ankle holster held a little Walther PPS 9mm – a gun many people had forgotten about, but Fox found it to be one of the most dependable, steady, and well-performing single-stack compact firearms he'd ever used.

Justin Park knew that despite his large frame, Fox was an agile CIA-certified blade specialist. He set him up with an impressive four-blade knife set. The cold steel Tiger Clawed Karambit was perfect for close-quarters combat, the titanium German Neck Knife was something that most people wouldn't find when they did a quick body search, the Gerber Guardian Back-Up Tanto Boot Knife was comfortably strapped onto the leg opposite his pistol. And the more traditional five-inch Carbon Steel Sawback Blade from the Ontario Knife Company slid into a sheath sewn into his right jeans pocket.

Back in Fox's hometown, outside of Akron, Ohio, he was a legend of sorts for always winning the Fall Protestant Church Picnic Knife-throwing Contests at Quail Hollow Park. He'd won his first trophy at age seven and continued his championship run every subsequent year until he left to serve his country. All kinds of stories circulated back at home about things he did in the military with his knives and hardly any of them had merit, although people sure liked to think they did. To them, he'd reached legend status.

In addition to the weaponry, Justin had included an assortment of zip ties, a roll of black duct tape, basic first aid tools and meds, a small digital camera and a mini-tablet. Fox found a little earpiece that he presumed would link him with LaunchPad. It was rechargeable and whoever put the kit together included various numbers of USB chargers. He also noticed a small black round cylinder – about the size of a fat cigar. It was a video camera that he could strap to his head, shoulders, or waist using a stretchy Velcro-type of material invented by some Company brains. There were a few changes of clothes, some protein bars, a money clip with a thousand dollars in various denominations, and a spare set of car keys. Fox found that last addition amusing. Justin must have thought it would be good for the big agent to be prepared for a quick extract: he could leave the Honda Pilot's engine running while he'd get into a building and still lock the doors with the extra key clicker, so nobody could steal it.

Kurt Middleton-Fox had already been thinking about how to access Jee Hye's building. Most likely it would have a doorman and state-of-the-art video surveillance. These people were trained as if they were protecting expired milk but usually projected an attitude of defending the president. Fox knew that there was one weakness among doormen worldwide. They'd do almost anything for a generous tip. He'd added a stop at a flower store on his GPS and purchased a ridiculously large beautiful bouquet. As he pulled in front of her building and parked, he noticed a doorman standing just outside the main entrance, just as he'd expected.

"Hi," Fox said cheerfully as he bounded up the stairs to the front door.

The doorman looked to be about nineteen. He was two thirds the height of the giant agent, and courteous, but not overly friendly. "Can I help you?"

"I'm just here to see my girlfriend in 1204."

"She can come down to meet you. I'll call her."

"That's okay. I'd like to just go right up."

"Either she comes down, or you leave those right here. I'll let her know you stopped by."

"Or, I could leave these with you," Fox said, handing the doorman two crisp $100 bills, "and surprise her."

The doorman looked at the c-notes in his hand. "I bet she loves being surprised," he smirked as he opened the door for Fox. "What's in your duffle bag?"

"More surprises," the agent answered with a grin as he hurried through the door into a large contemporary lobby. He entered the glass elevators, and as they went up, he looked down on the expansive courtyard.

Jee Hye's apartment complex was one of those ultra-modern social experiments where people lived a lifestyle of community steeped in environmental sensitivities. An odd number of square-shaped pools were surrounded by brightly-colored stuffy couches that were placed in strategic places by a highly-paid Parisian decorator. Large bowls of gas-fed fires and giant stainless-steel grills provided an experience for the young executive class to make them feel important, rich, and connected. Her specific pad was designed with a simple two-bedroom/two-bathroom layout on the top floor of the building, and as Fox got closer, he was surprised to see her door was cracked open. Pausing to listen, he slipped his hand under his shirt, behind his back.

JUN AND ASHLEY had the cab drop them off on Beech Drive. When the taxi was long out of view, they leisurely walked down an alley that ran perpendicular to a small park.

"You know where we are, right?"

Ashley thought about joking but decided they were both too tired. "Yes. Let's just pretend we're not in a hurry and are enjoying an early-evening walk."

When they got to the end of the alley, they took a road to the right and walked for a few minutes until they came to a chain-link fence.

"We can walk all the way around the property and let ourselves in by the gate, or we can jump over this fence and be there in a few minutes. Which would you prefer?"

Jun looked at her. "Is that even a question? Over the fence."

They stalled until a small white pickup truck had passed them and there was nobody else around. Then Ashley dug the toes of her shoes into the diamond-shaped squares and pulled herself up and over the fence. Jun did the same, and soon they were walking through a row of neutrally colored deserted ware-houses. At one point, the young surgeon paused in front of an unassuming dented door and pounded on it six times. She waited for ten seconds and then pounded on it five times. After another ten seconds, she was just about to pound on it four times, when the door unlocked with a click. Yanking it open, she quickly pulled Jun inside. The door closed behind them and a long poorly lit corridor extended in front of them. The walls were made of a dark brown tin, and the floor was the kind of polished hard linoleum tiling that clacked loudly when you walked on it. At the far end, was another door. Just as the two were approaching, it swung open, and Leonard Stone was standing there with his arms wide open.

"Ashley!"

"Leo!" she cried as she sunk herself into his hug. "It's so good to be back."

When they pulled back, he looked at her kindly, "You've certainly had an exciting twenty-four hours." He turned to Jun, "And you must be Justin's cousin."

"Yes, sir."

"Welcome to LaunchPad, Jun."

"Thank you, sir," shaking Dr. Stone's hand.

"I haven't told him anything about what we do here," Ashley stated. "I didn't feel comfortable talking about it in public."

"Well, you can find out about it now," Leo said. "Ashley, why don't you take a few minutes to show him around? When you're done, grab some food and join us in the conference room. I'll introduce Jun to David and Saara. We're about to link up with Fox and take a tour of Jee Hye's apartment."

Jun was stunned. "Jee Hye's apartment?"

Stone nodded. "We located it and sent Fox to check it out."

"Come on, Jun," Ashley said, tugging on his sleeve, "I'll give you a quick tour and then we can join them."

He nodded and tried to focus on the impressive warehouse. Dominating the middle of the large space, was a make-shift command center. Suspended from the beams running along the high ceiling were six fifty-five-inch flat screens. Cables from the office area were gathered into a thick, flexible, black Material Handling Hose, which ran to a handful of Honda generators, humming quietly in a corner closet.

"Do those supply electricity for the whole place?" he asked.

"They can, if need be, but we supplement them with completely off-grid solar panels. Something Saara and David installed about a month ago."

She showed him the bunk rooms, bathrooms, interrogation facilities, Justin's workshop area, her medical clinic, and ended the tour in the kitchen where they grabbed some sandwiches, veggies, and a few drinks from the fridge. Ashley led the way to the conference room just as Fox powered up his camera and pulled out his pistol.

COACH MURRAY'S heart was pounding like a set of Fijian drums, and he had no control over his shaking body. His throat was parched, and his tongue was sticking to the roof of his mouth. He was terrified! When he was a teenager, he'd often wondered what he would do in a truly dangerous situation. His current response wasn't exactly what he'd envisioned. "I've got to pull myself together. The girls will need to see a leader who's not afraid," he told himself.

He tried not to think about the gun-waving flight attendant, the dead security agent next to him or the screaming passengers. Instead, he tried to concentrate on how he might be able to calm the girls down. It had to start by regaining control of his own emotions.

Miles Howell looked grim. He wasn't some donut-eating mall cop. He was hired for this mission because he'd stared death in the face dozens of times. Whether by luck, skill, or divine providence, he was a ruthless survivor. He locked down his anger at Kennedy for leaving him alone and being so uncharacteristically stupid under pressure. Howell determined to stay focused.

In the row in front of him and to his left, were the Jacksons. Their daughter, Savannah, was a striker. He could see her, up near the front. She was curled up in a ball, crying. He was looking at her parents just as Mr. Jackson turned wildly in his seat to stare at him. Howell made a downward motion with the palm of his hand. They needed to remain calm. He looked to his right and saw the other American parents – Amber's mom and dad. Both of them were huddled on the floor, hiding behind the seats in front of them and holding each other.

Howell thought back to when he'd crawled out from a hole in Afghanistan after an IED had blown up the two Humvee's in front of him. He'd prayed a prayer that many a soldier prayed – some who made it and some who didn't. Then, he emerged from the smoke and dust and killed seventeen Taliban terrorists who were closing in on their location, rescued two fellow Army Rangers who'd gotten pinned behind enemy lines, and somehow helped them survive in the hot zone until extraction. Somewhere in his mom's house were a bunch of awards given to him for bravery. He appreciated what they represented. But they were hidden out of sight because it was just too painful to recall the stories behind them. He would never understand the mystery of why some people lived while others died.

Howell observed the two sets of German parents in front of him. They were all exhibiting symptoms of shock: drenched in sweat, breathing irregularly, pale, nauseous, and a visibly dazed state. He remembered what a doctor told him one time. "If untreated, shock could become fatal."

The already ominous silence continued to spread throughout the plane. He recognized the poison; he could smell it in the air like the pungent smell of rotten eggs in vinegar. It was abject fear. He flexed his jaw and looked back at the Jacksons. He was not going to give in to terror. Not now. Not ever. Miles Howell had cheated death before. He'd cheat the damn thing again.

The flight attendant was joined by others, and a piece of the puzzle came together. The pilot and his co-pilot flanked him, with sinister glares on their faces. Three other flight attendants emerged from the front. Apparently, this new flight crew was part of the entire plot. Howell began to profile them in his head.

"We will not hesitate to kill you," the pilot snarled, his English thickened with a heavy Arab accent. Howell guessed it was an African Arabic of some sort. "If anyone tries to escape or disobey orders, we will shoot you." As he was speaking, the lights of the warehouse began to turn on, creating an unnatural pale bluish light.

"There will be two bins by the door of the plane," the pilot continued. "All of your electronic devices will go into the white bin." He looked around at everyone. "That means mobile phones, cameras, flashlights, music players of any kind, hairdryers, curling irons, or anything electronic. If we find out later that you were trying to sneak something past us, you'll be killed." His point was made with his forefinger and thumb, mimicking a shooting gun. "In the red bin, place all of your jewelry. This includes watches, wedding rings, earrings, necklaces, bracelets, nose rings, navel piercings, toe rings – any kind of decorative item you have on you."

The only female flight attendant stepped forward. Her eyes were black and flashed with anger and a lifetime of penned-up aggression. Howell hadn't noticed her in the plane before. He guessed she'd been working in the galley or flying jump seat with the pilots. "Your luggage in the cargo bay is being unloaded and will be lined up against the wall of the hanger. You will replace whatever was in your carry-ons with three changes of clothes from your suitcases." Her English had a decidedly East London bent, but something told him she'd not grown up in Europe. "If anyone needs to go to the toilet, there is a bathroom in the hanger. You will not have another opportunity for quite a while. When you have your carry-on bag packed, raise your hand. We will inspect it. Your suitcases and the rest of your belongings will stay here." She paused as her eyes darted back and forth, watching the passengers. "We'll be leaving this building in exactly twenty minutes. Whoever is not ready on time will be shot."

Howell looked at his watch, quickly took it off his wrist, and disassembled it. He pocketed the metal case back. It was sharp enough along the edges to cut a rope. Then, he carefully placed the big hand in the upper corner of his inner lip. It was something he could pick cuffs with. He slid the glass face into his sock, knowing he could start a fire with it if he needed to use it as a magnifying glass in the bright sunlight. Behind the links of the wristband was a long thin metal sheaf. He slipped it under his foot, between a Dr. Scholl's insert and the insole of his shoe. Finally, with his fingernail, he pried out the battery. Underneath was a small black magnetic transponder. He ran his thumbnail along its edge until he felt a notch. Pressing into it, he felt a slight release as it depressed. It was activated. Unlike Casey Baker's chip, he would not turn his on and off. Hers was designed to conserve battery; his was designed to send a locator signal for the next five hours. He might've recently retired from the Secret Service, but they'd given him a few special items for this particular trip.

Everyone scrambled to get their clothes packed and take a bathroom break. Nobody talked. Coach Murray would nod or wink whenever he got the chance, trying to boost morale. The German coach, too, had pulled himself together. He was gently encouraging his players to hurry and do exactly as they'd been told.

Miles Howell had turned in his electronics and had his backpack inspected. Now he walked over and stood under the nose of the plane to talk to the pilot.

"What's your name?" the aviator asked.

Miles looked him over before answering. The man was fairly tall, maybe around six feet four inches, with a thin mustache. His rugged face looked like it had once been attacked with severe acne. The agent guessed he was in his late fifties or early sixties. His eyes were decidedly very green. He had an angular nose that stuck out noticeably – not necessarily in an ugly way – just noticeably. Dressed in a solid black suit with a white shirt and a green tie that drew out his eye color, he could have been a business person on a banking trip to Zurich. Howell concluded that this man was smart and carried himself with a confidence that exuded authority.

The Secret Service agent answered truthfully, "Miles Howell."

"Howell." The pilot thought for a moment. "Your friend is dead, is he not?"

"Yes."

"He was stupid."

"It's a fine line," Miles nodded, slowly, "between being stupid and being brave."

"He should not have made a move down the aisle. That was stupid."

Howell noticed the pilot's hands. They were absurdly strong looking. There were scars that looked like he'd been bladed while fighting. This man was not an airline pilot. He was a ruthless and experienced warrior.

Coach Murray had joined them and now queried the pilot. "And what is your name, sir?"

The warrior seemed amused at Neil Murray's direct question masked in Southern charm – a culture where "sir" and "ma'am" are commonly used. "My name, Mr. Murray sir, is Sa'im Kashif Zafar, a name that means nothing to you," he stated honestly. "If we were in my country, people's knees would start to weaken or they would start wailing at the sound of my name. They often start apologizing for things I didn't even know they'd done. Some, defecate themselves. Others would crawl up to me and kiss my ring." He looked around at all the other adults who had gathered. "They would react this way … not out of respect, but out of fear." His green eyes gleamed with a bit of crazy. "In many nations, I'm simply known as The Lynx."

"Like the snake, huh?"

The pilot fixed his stare on the coach.

Howell worried about the German couples. On the outside, they seemed to be holding together, but he could read their faces. The two team doctors had been thoughtful and kind – but now they, too, were terrified. Briefly, he reflected on what it would be like to study so faithfully in medical school and fight hard to save lives, only to come across a group like this – terrorists who had absolutely no respect for life.

The Lynx was speaking again. "We have no use for any of you. The girls, on the other hand, are very valuable." His voice took on a low, sinister tone. "Keep this in mind. Killing you would relieve me of having to drag you along with us. Just give me a reason, and I'll do it quickly."

"What is it that you want?" Mr. Jackson suddenly burst out. "Do you know who we are? We can help you. Please, just let us all go. If you want money – no problem. You want fame? We have connections to the media. Please … please …" he started to break down, sobbing. "What do you want?"

The female flight attendant walked up and whispered something in Sa'im Kashif Zafar's ear.

The pilot nodded and clapped his hands together, "We're ready to go! Everything is on schedule."

As he spoke, a loud screeching noise of metal grinding against metal filled the warehouse. Just fifteen feet in front of them, a gigantic square of the concrete floor began to lift up and slowly slide backward. Coach Murray's head spun to the right, and he noticed that the entire mid-section of the floor was on a wheel mechanism of some sort. As the concrete slid backward, it exposed a giant hole. The American stepped forward.

"Yes! Look." Zafar encouraged everyone.

Almost everyone advanced and stood at the edge of where the floor had been. They were looking down about one hundred and fifty feet. At the bottom of the enormous cavity were some vehicles. From up top, they looked like white school buses or trucks.

"You're all seeing something almost nobody has seen. Isn't it remarkable?" There was pride in The Lynx's voice. "Many legends have been told about this place; authors have written mysteries – guessing that it exists. Mystics have seen it in the dark spirit world. But my father helped build it. It is Muammar Gaddafi's smuggling tunnel. From this very place, he moved millions of American dollars and spread them around to his friends. Thousands of tons of gold have passed from here to his secret vaults. Young girls and little boys that he gathered from all over the world, passed through here secretly on their way to be loved by many of our own leaders in the Muslim world." He sneered, "For some, it's been a tremendous aid in transporting resources. For others, unfortunately, it was the tunnel to their death. For me, personally, it has always been our Emerald Wasp," he ended dramatically. "Now, pick up your bag and follow!"

CHAPTER SIXTEEN

Fox stood outside Jee Hye's door. He could hear noise coming from inside, and it sounded like the place was getting tossed. Pushing the door open a few more inches, he tried to peek around but wasn't getting the angle. He took off his cigar-shaped head cam and carefully moved it to the edge of the door.

Saara Turri's voice gave him the intel he needed. "He's not anywhere in the picture."

"Roger that."

Fox quickly repositioned the camera on his head and slipped around the door, gun in position. He quietly closed the door behind him. Whoever was throwing stuff around wasn't too concerned about noise. He'd left the door open, too, so the giant agent assumed this person was in a hurry to get in and out.

The layout of Jee Hye's pad was exactly as Saara had predicted from studying the building schematics. The front door had opened up directly into a formal dining and living room. Straight ahead of him, through the living room, was a set of sliding glass doors that led to a balcony with a little storage closet on the right. To his left was an open-concept kitchen and the master bedroom. On his right, was the second bedroom with a large walk-in closet and a full bath that was accessible from the living area. Before he followed the noises to his right, he decided he'd better clear the left side of the apartment. Quickly he crouch-ran through the area, making sure he was ready to shoot anything that moved. Everything looked like a hurricane had hit. Each drawer had been pulled and dumped. The bed had been flipped. The mattress had been sliced open. The closet contents had been scattered everywhere. Water was leaking onto the floor from the bathroom where the toilet had been pulled off its moorings. Even in the kitchen – everything had been torn apart. Fox returned to the living room just as Leo came on the comms.

"Fox, wait. There's no sense in jumping him. Let's just wait and see if the guy finds what he was looking for. Obviously, he hasn't found it yet."

"Copy that."

Fox darted across the room so that he was waiting against the wall of the second bedroom. As soon as the invader came out, he would be walking right past him. The noise this guy was making reflected his boorish search job. A true professional would be able to search a place without bringing any attention to himself. Drawers were being flung across the room; the sliding closet doors were being kicked down. There was a sudden ripping sound, and unexpectedly everything stopped.

"I think this is what we're looking for," a guy said.

A female voice concurred. "That's it alright. What's in the wooden box?"

There were a few seconds of silence as they opened whatever box they'd found.

"Holy mother of Mary!" the first voice exclaimed, stunned.

"I can't believe this."

"That's a lot of cash."

"Five hundred thousand dollars? And that doesn't include the diamonds."

"Holy moly."

Having two people made it a lot more complicated. If they walked out, one after another, Fox would surprise the first one, but the second one would have time to strike. Or if the first one walked by him and he surprised the second one, the first one would have a chance. Just because they weren't professionals at searching a place, didn't mean they weren't dangerous as fighters. It would be better to keep them contained in the bedroom, he decided. He crept to the corner of the doorway and then spun into the room; his gun was pointed directly at the couple.

"What the hell? Who are you?" the man demanded angrily.

Fox growled back, "Get flat on your stomachs, both of you."

The girl dropped to the ground. The man glared at the large agent. "Look, I don't know who you are, but if you think ..."

He was interrupted by a blur of motion and then sudden burning pain. Fox's left hand had soundlessly whipped his smallest knife out of his belt and pitched it directly into the man's left thigh.

"Ahhh!" he screamed.

"You'll live," Fox assured him, using his right hand to keep the gun trained on them. "On the ground or I'll upgrade to a bigger knife and throw it a little higher up."

The man lay down, awkwardly keeping his left leg off the ground, trying to avoid pushing the knife in deeper. Fox sprang over and grabbed the girl's right wrist and the guy's left wrist and zip-tied them tightly together. Then he yanked them up into a sitting position and pulled his knife out of the guy's leg. Blood started to ooze out.

"Dammit, that hurts!" They both looked scared. Amateurs. "Where's the box?" the big agent barked.

Fox grabbed their ankles and zip-tied them, as well.

"On the bed," the girl finally answered, starting to cry.

Fox saw a cedar box almost twice the size of a shoebox, laying on the guest bed. He walked over, picked it up, and pried it open. Inside were fifty neat rolls of one-hundred-dollar bills. Some loose diamonds lay scattered on the bottom. He returned to the couple and stood tall.

"Amateur hour," he breathed.

"No doubt," Leo responded in Fox's earpiece.

Reaching down, Fox enclosed his considerably large-sized hands around the top of their arms, just under their shoulders. Picking them both up, he plopped them onto the bed. He pulled up a wooden chair from a small computer desk and sat down close to them, looking right into their faces.

"Give me what you really came here for."

The woman looked at the man, flustered.

"I don't know what you're talking about," the guy answered, his wobbly voice betraying him.

"You came into this apartment, tossed the place like a couple of high school crackheads. Then you found what you were looking for. I bet you're not able to keep any of this, right? Did you already get paid?

"Yeah," the girl confessed.

"Shut up, Meagan!" the guy warned.

"I mean, you see all this cash, the diamonds, and the other thing. And what was he going to pay you, a thousand dollars?"

"A few hundred."

"Meagan, seriously, shut up!"

"A few hundred?" Fox said, feigning shock. "While he pockets all of this?" he asked, looking at the cedar box under his left arm. "What else did he want you to get?"

"It's none of your business!" the guy spat out.

Fox paused, looking at the ground. When he slowly looked up at the guy, his eyes were icy cold, and his voice was low and menacing.

"Actually, it literally *is* my business." For added effect, he pulled his biggest knife out of the sheath in his pocket.

"Look, we're just doing what we got paid to do, okay?" the girl whined.

"By whom?"

"I don't know. He was about as tall as you but real skinny. Dark hair. Kind of creeped me out. He had a hat on and a long-hooked nose, you know? Little round glasses. Beard."

"That's a pretty good description, sounds like you might've made it up," Fox snarled.

"I'm a journalism major."

"You kids are in college?"

She nodded. The male student stared straight ahead. Fox noticed his hands were shaking.

"How'd you get in?" Fox asked.

"The guy gave us a key."

"He had a key? He gave you a key?"

"Yup."

"Meagan, please. For the love of all the saints. Shut up."

"Screw you, Adam. I'll talk if I want to."

Fox held out his hand. "Give it to me."

"He's got it," the woman said, jutting her chin out at the guy.

"Meagan, you're getting us both killed."

Fox stared at the guy, flexing his massive jaw. He flicked his thumb across the knife's razor-thin edge – checking it.

"Adam. That's your name. Am I going to have to search you?"

The kid caved in. "It's tucked in the front of my pants, under my shirt."

Fox reached forward, jerked the guy's shirt up and dislodged a black book. "Is this everything?"

"Yeah," Adam confessed. "That's it."

"How did you two meet this tall, skinny, creepy guy?"

"He walked into the bar last night and asked us if we wanted to make some money."

"Which bar?"

"The Irish Craic."

"What did he tell you to look for?"

"A black book with hand-written stuff in it. He guaranteed it would be here. He said we might have to spend a few hours trying to find it. We watched a YouTube video on how to search a person's place."

"What were you going to do with this stuff?"

"We were supposed to turn everything over to him tonight at the bar."

"When?"

"Same time as when we met him."

"He told us that if we stole anything or didn't show up, he'd hunt us down and kill us," Meagan said pointedly. Then wistfully added, "I was hoping we could keep the wooden box and see if he'd bring it up. If he did, we'd give it to him. If he didn't, we'd be rich."

"Geez, Meagan. Why're you telling him everything?"

Fox looked at their glum faces. Their lottery ticket was only worth a few hundred dollars and not the hundreds of thousands they'd been hoping for.

"So, where'd you find it?"

"It was in the box spring under the mattress. The wooden box was on top of it."

"This tall, skinny, creepy guy ... did you see what he was driving?" Fox asked.

"Yeah. Nice ride," Adam answered. "It was a black Escalade. Pretty new."

CHAPTER SEVENTEEN

BOYD CARTER WOKE UP AND CHECKED HER PHONE. SHE HAD three more hours to go before she landed in Maryland. Standing up and stepping into the aisle, she took a moment to stretch in a very systematic and compact routine. These long trips were brutal, even on her well-trained body. She wasn't part of the Israeli Defense Forces, but she was an expert in Krav Maga, a form of hand-to-hand fighting that was created for and perfected by the IDF's special units and reconnaissance brigades. Its seeds lay in street-fighting skills generated by the renowned Hungarian-Israeli martial artist Imi Lichtenfeld. He'd built his method by mixing his training as a boxer and a wrestler to defend his Jewish neighborhood against Eastern European fascist gangs. The modern version mixes aikido, judo, boxing, tae kwon do and wrestling, along with real-world fight scenarios. It's exceptionally efficient, brutal, and famous for neutralizing threats through aggressively attacking and defending at the same time. Like many systems of martial arts, levels are identified by various colors of belts – black being the highest. Boyd Carter was a black belt by the time she was fifteen. She'd pioneered various additions to the training that made her a lethal killing machine. Although she was a legend in the operator community of the American military, rumors of her abilities had also permeated the ranks of the Mossad and the halls of Shin Bet.

Boyd decided to slip to the back of the plane to do some vertical pushups, deep knee-bends, and dynamic stretching. Not only would it pass the time, but it would get her blood flowing and keep her flexible.

———

MEANWHILE, Lin Lin Ma and her daughter were walking into the Charles Du Gaulle airport. They'd thoroughly enjoyed Paris, but it was time for them to say *au revoir* and head back to the United States.

"Do you think this will be your last time in Europe?" Bao Zhen asked her mother.

"I hope not, my dear. Europe will always be special to me. Someday I would like to leisurely revisit some of the great museums of the continent. But, I might never return to Switzerland. Somehow, leaving there the day before yesterday just felt like the end of an era." She paused, reflecting. "I didn't really expect that. It felt so final."

"Switzerland has been a nation for healing and restoration for so many. I suppose that when that process is complete, people move on."

"I guess you're right. Anyway, I'm really looking forward to living with your family and being free from the pressures of my old responsibilities."

The two stepped forward. It was their turn at the United Airlines ticket counter.

———————

"Look, we're no strangers to corruption in the Central Intelligence Agency. It has more people living double lives than The Actor's Studio. I just have a hard time believing that Serwabi would be in all of this." Leo was pacing around in the conference room. David was sitting cross-legged, toying with a pen. Fox's face was spread across Saara's tablet and perched on a stand at the end of the table.

"I'm with you, sir," Fox agreed

"I reached out to some Company contacts," David said. "They don't know him very well, but there weren't any red flags. He's still actively running ops on the books."

"Speaking of books, what's in the black book?" Dr. Stone asked.

"It's all in Korean. I paged through it and videoed it with my phone." Fox looked puzzled. "I uploaded the file to Saara. Did she not give it to you?"

"She's asleep. So are Jun and Ashley."

"I see," Fox responded, relieved. "So, Jun and Ashley arrived?"

"They did. And they're fine. When they get up, we'll put Jun on the Korean text. Hopefully, he can translate it for us. If not, Justin and Bora will be landing soon. I'm sure they can do it."

"They're skipping their honeymoon?" Fox asked, a little surprised.

"Postponing for a while."

"I see. How should I proceed?"

Trey's father was a military strategist and on the crew at LaunchPad for just that reason. He saw minute details, the big picture, and everything in between. "We've looked at that bar ... The Irish Craic. It's the perfect place for something like this. Taller buildings all around it and all great places to set up. They'd have a clear line of sight to watch who goes in and out or to be positioned for sniper fire. Getting in would be no problem; getting out would be completely unpredictable."

"Why don't I just make a call to the bartender?"

"You read my mind. Leave a message that suggests an alternate meeting place, right?"

"Exactly."

David shifted in his seat and sat forward. "Why don't you just call Serwabi yourself? You say you know him personally?"

"He'd remember me."

"So, I'll get his number. Call him and tell him to meet you here."

"You want me to bring one of the premier Middle East Operatives from the CIA to LaunchPad? We aren't even sure of his agenda."

Leo obviously agreed with Fox. He looked at David like he was out of his mind.

"Seriously?"

"Why not? Let's pick him up in Baltimore, stick a hood on his head, and bring him here."

Trey's father tried to see the benefit of David's suggestion, but couldn't.

"Look," David continued, "Right now, you're on the West Coast by yourself, Fox. Granted, you're worth a whole team, but still, there's only so much one guy can tactically do on his own." David looked down at his pen as he kept toying with it, "You can't get close to Serwabi because he'll make you – so that complicates things." He looked up at the camera. "The only other people involved in this are two college kids who could also identify you if they had to. It's only a matter of time before the APB from Walmart catches up to you. Then it'll be a mess to clean up. Let's get you back here, draw him over, and we'll get him to talk, one way or another."

"So, you think I've wrapped things up with Jee Hye?"

"I think you've tagged the bullseye by securing that black book. The rest is minutia that local law enforcement can pursue."

Leonard Stone stopped pacing and sat down beside his friend. "The good thing about this scenario is that you don't have to waste the whole day waiting for tonight's meeting at the bar. Head for the airport now. Park your car there. We'll get someone to take care of it. David will send you the ticket info and Serwabi's contact number. Don't reach out until just before you take off. I don't want him making a move on you."

"You have the contents of the wooden box with you?" asked David.

"Yes, sir," answered Fox, starting up the Honda Pilot.

"Great. If he knows about it, it'll motivate him to chase you. Return to base."

NEIL HOWELL WAS WONDERING how he could kill Sa'im Kashif Zafar. The pilot was pure evil. His whole crew was wicked.

They'd followed Zafar to a large freight elevator, ridden it down fourteen stories into the belly of the cavern, and stood before an enclosed glass grow-lab of some sort. It was bursting with greenery but that wasn't what turned Howell's stomach. The enclosure was also filled with bright blue Emerald Wasps in various stages of reproduction.

"Just look at them," the pilot said with great admiration. "Aren't they beautiful?"

Several of the girls began crying, again. Others just stared. The parents and their daughters clung to each other in a desperate group hug. Coach Murray and Coach Schmidt were standing with the doctors. The other two male flight attendants were armed with Chinese-made assault rifles that originally made their entrance when the United Kingdom transferred sovereign authority of Hong Kong to the People's Republic of China. The QBZ-95's were deadly accurate and fired small-caliber, high-velocity, copper-alloy-jacketed hardened steel-core bullets.

"Laila, come here, *Habibi*. Tell these people what's happening in there."

"The Blue Jeweled Wasp or Emerald Wasp, as its sometimes referred to, is considered to be one of the evilest creatures on the planet," the female flight attendant stepped forward to explain. Her dark eyes looked like black saucers in the dim light of the cavern. As she spoke, the lights of the warehouse clicked off, causing everyone to jump. The only light now was the purplish glow from inside the glass lab.

"But, they aren't evil. They're stunning in their beauty. They begin their reproduction by attracting the large dark-brown American Cockroach. Watch what happens to this one," she said, pointing to one of the wasps engaging with a roach.

What happened next could only be described as one of the most furious and fiercest fights in the insect world. After minutes of no-holds-barred combat, and in a micro-second of opportunity, the wasp injected a paralyzing venom into the thoracic ganglia of the roach with incredible precision, reversibly freezing the legs of its victims.

"The momentary loss of kinesis in the roach," Laila explained, "sets up a second venomous attack directly into the portion of the roach's brain that controls its escape reflex. The roach desperately starts to clean itself, thinking the attack is on its shell, but as the minutes go by, it begins to become sluggish and slips into a coma."

The group followed what was happening, with ghastly fascination. Wasting no time, the demonic wasp chewed off half of each of the roach's antennae and consumed them. "It knows the perfect amount of poison and is now pruning its victim," the woman continued with glistening eyes. "The wasp is thirsty from the battle, so it draws from the liquid in the roach's receptors to nourish itself."

The giant roach was too large to be carried, so the wasp locked its jaw on what was left from the roach's antennae and used it as a leash to drag it to its burrow which it had built for this moment. Once inside, it lay a single white egg on the roach's chest, about two millimeters in length. As soon as the egg was out, the wasp began to seal off any access to the burrow with rocks and pebbles, carefully making an escape for the cockroach impossible. Its mission complete, it flew away.

"In three days, this egg will hatch," Laila informed them. "And then, in one of the most beautiful moments in nature, it will begin to feed off the live cockroach. It will bury itself deep into its body. For five days, the larva carefully eats its way into the abdomen. Then, in perfect order – making sure the roach will remain alive – the maggot will consume the roach's internal organs one by one."

One of the girls started throwing up. Laila ignored the slight commotion it caused.

"When the roach is almost dead, the larva forms a cocoon inside its body and, after a short while, a wasp emerges from the roach's cadaver and breaks out of the burrow as a fully-developed adult Emerald Wasp."

"Amazing, isn't it?" Zafar asked, giddy with excitement. "These wasps go on to live for several months, mate in less than a minute and then successfully parasitize several dozen roaches."

Howell had his eye one of the doctors – the American one. He was growing more and more agitated.

The pilot lowered his voice, "All of you are a part of the system I call the American Cockroach. We are the beautiful Emerald Wasps," he said motioning to his crew. "We have been embedding ourselves into mighty America, feeding off your internal organs, and now we will multiply when the life is finally sucked out of your bodies."

"Hell, no!" yelled the frantic doctor, springing forward towards Laila.

Instantly one of the Chinese weapons discharged. A trail of high-velocity copper-alloy-jacketed hardened steel-cored bullets split his ribs, tore through his heart and lungs, and trickled through his chest. He fell to the ground, his eyes wide in surprise, anger and finally frustration.The girls all shrieked in shock.

"What is wrong with you?" the German physician yelled. "Who in the hell do you think you are?!"

The pilot hadn't even flinched. But now everyone screamed at him along with the doctor. He threw his arms in the air and yelled at the top of his voice, "*Takbir!*" and the crazy returned to his green eyes.

The other three terrorists responded with loud shouts of praise, "*Allah Akbar! Allah Akbar! Allah Akbar!*" Their voices echoed back and forth off the cave walls in a weird rhythm to the buzzing sound from the purple glass lab.

CHAPTER EIGHTEEN

"I'm not doing it, Dad," Trey told his father in no uncertain terms.

"We've got no choice, Son. She needs to come back here."

"I'm not letting her travel alone. This should've been thought through."

"I didn't think you'd be tentative about it."

Leo's son sat back down in his chair. He was alone in a small conference room at the American Embassy in Geneva.

"Look, Trey, we can organize an armed guard to travel with Jasmine and escort her right into Bao Zhen's waiting arms at the airport in Baltimore."

Trey didn't think it would be this hard. His fatherly instinct was overpowering every logical cell in his brain, and he knew it. But after what had happened to his family, he wasn't ready to be separated from his daughter again. They'd been together every day since she'd been rescued. He couldn't bring himself to send her on a flight alone or with a guard of people he'd never vetted.

"Sorry, Dad. I know it's not logical. But I just can't do it."

Leo's eyes darted down from the tablet camera to look into his son's eyes on the screen. He could see the struggle and concern. Most of all, he could see the love of a father for his daughter.

"What's the alternative, Trey?" David asked, putting his face next to Leo's.

"Either Bruce, Michi and Tank take care of this while I fly back with Jasmine …"

"Or?"

"She comes with me."

Neither of the elderly men liked that idea, but they could tell Trey's mind was set.

Leonard Stone broke the ice. "Trey, should she go with you, there would be times when she'd be an asset, times when she'd be in the way, but worse than that, times when she'd be a liability."

"I know, Dad."

"Don't you think you should ask Bao Zhen about this?"

"Probably. But we don't have time. We're already way behind on this whole thing. She's just started an eight-hour flight from Paris to D.C., and we need to leave Switzerland as soon as possible. I'm not leaving Jasmine here, Dad. I just can't. I don't trust a single living soul with her other than the people working at LaunchPad. That's it."

"I get it, Kid," David said. "I do."

"When you leave, put someone with her at all times," Leo instructed. "We'll send Boyd to meet up with you."

Trey nodded. "Okay."

There were a few minutes of silence as the weight of it all sunk in.

"So, we've got the plan, Son. Why don't you let the others in?"

Trey nodded and opened the door. Tank was standing outside, ready to intercept anyone who might've tried to interrupt the meeting that had been taking place. Agent Stone acknowledged him with a nod and said, "Get everyone in here for a quick briefing."

JUSTIN AND BORA were a little disappointed when the captain explained that their flight was ending. Eighteen hours of sitting in international first class would spoil anyone for returning to normal life.

"How much time do we have in New York?" Justin asked, returning his fully reclined bed back into a sitting position.

"Forty-seven minutes."

He did the math, "So we should be at LaunchPad in less than three hours."

"Right. David said he'd chopper us in ... so it won't be long at all."

Justin pulled out his little pad of yellow paper and began to read it all again.

"Relax, Honey. You're the best at what you do. You'll be ready when the time comes."

He inhaled and exhaled slowly, "You're right," he said, returning the pad of paper to his backpack on the floor in front of his feet.

He sat back gazing at Bora's face. She was so attractive! His heartbeat sped up just looking her over. His eyes returned to her face, seeing that she was watching him, curiously. "I love the way a little crease forms at the end of your lips when you smile," he confessed.

His wife grinned and reached over to stroke his right ear. "Thank you, my Handsome Prince. I love you, too."

Justin sat up suddenly. "Oh! I just thought of one more thing," he said, reaching back down for his yellow pad.

Fox KEPT the call short and to the point. He used the same code names they'd used in the Middle East when he said, "Daylight, this is Razor."

Serwabi was clearly shocked. "What? Really? How did you get this number?"

"I intercepted something black. It's got a leather cover. The Korean writing in it is pretty. Almost artistic."

There were a few seconds of silence.

"How did you get your hands on that?" the CIA's MEO asked.

"I went and got it. Next time don't use some college punks."

"You're in town?"

Fox didn't answer.

"Razor, there's more going on here then you realize. You're risking a lot of lives."

"I just sent you a text."

More silence as Serwabi checked his phone.

N39°10.54' / W76°40.14' You have six hours.

The big blond agent had sent him satellite coordinates, and it didn't take the Middle East Operative long to figure them out. "What are you now, Jason Bourne? Come on. What is this? You want me at Baltimore airport?"

Fox had already hung up and was showing his boarding pass to the gate agent.

CHAPTER NINETEEN

NOT ONLY WERE THE EMERALD WASPS DEEPLY DISTURBING, BUT the presentation was very convincing. There was a moment during the propaganda when Coach Murray realized his life, as he'd known it, was over. The adults would most likely be killed one at a time. He was just a simple soccer coach, but he'd watched the news at night. He'd seen these kinds of people slice into the necks of journalists, drag Americans to their death behind stolen Humvees, shoot large groups of Christians on the beach and drive suicide trucks into packed crowds. It was the girls he was most worried about. They were so young. Just a few days ago, their lives were bright, exciting, and full of adventure. He looked at Casey Baker, the granddaughter of one of America's favorite presidents. Even in the doorway of this abyss, she was a born leader. She wasn't one of the girls shivering in the chilly air. She'd obviously worked through something in her mind and stood resolute. Not defiant, just resolute. He was sure her grandfather had told her narratives of battling evil people in the world. She may not have experienced any of this before, but the American coach got the feeling that she wasn't completely shocked by it.

He noted the parents. *Am I the only adult not wetting my pants?*

Murray scanned the group as the flight attendant with black hair, and shadowy eyes kept ranting about death to America – and not just the nation, but the ideal. Then he saw Miles Howell. The Ranger's face was like granite, and he was menacingly staring Laila down. It was obvious to the coach that this warrior had been in dark situations before – maybe even eviler than this one if that was possible. Just as he was about to turn away, Howell slowly looked in his direction and gave Murray an ever so slight nod.

Okay. He's not in shock. Thank God. He's in the opposite of shock…

The coach looked at Schmidt. His German counterpart didn't look entirely out of it, either. After puking on the plane in panic, it seemed he was now coming to grips with the reality of the situation. He was just staring at the ground in front of his feet.

"Thank you, Laila, my princess," the terrorist concluded. He turned to look at everyone with a sick triumphant arrogance. "Treasures. That's what you are, dear girls. We are ready to load up. Follow me. Keep in your minds that if anyone tries anything stupid – like that doctor – you will be shot."

The girls were to walk two-by-two; the adults were to walk in single file. The Lynx led the way down half a flight of stairs. As his foot touched the first step, a set of dim orange lights along the left wall lit up a platform of some sort. At that moment Murray realized the white things he thought were buses, were three cargo cars for a train. The sides had been cut down almost all the way, and reinforcement posts had been added to support the ceilings. He glanced at the front of their line and saw some sort of converted semi-truck on track-wheels.

"Hold your hands out in front of you and face the wall!" It was the first time one of the men holding the Chinese-made guns had spoken. Howell was surprised that the guy's accent betrayed a decidedly British influence.

Everyone complied. Laila walked down the line of people, snugly zip-tying their hands together with heavy industrial-strength ties. Their luggage was then taken and loaded into the third car, along with some other items from the plane.

"The Americans will follow me," ordered the man with the gun as he stepped into the first car, behind the engine, "Sit on the floor in rows of five people and face the back of the train."

Laila addressed the Germans as the other man with a gun slipped into the second car and stood at the front. "You will board the next car and sit the same way."

Coach Murray led the Americans into the first car, noticing that Howell had snuck in line right behind him.

———

TRUE TO HIS WORD, David met Justin and Bora at the airport in Baltimore and choppered them directly to LaunchPad, landing the sleek grey and black ACH 130 at Martin State Airport to avoid attracting undue attention. At the helipad, they grabbed an electric golf cart for the quick ride over to the warehouse. The happy couple, still in their honeymoon glow, told David all about their wedding, the phone call with Jun, and their luxurious flight from Auckland. David updated them on what Jun and Ashley were doing and briefed them on Fox's work in Los Angeles.

"Dr. Stone, thank you for your generous gift to us," Justin said to Leonard as they opened the nondescript warehouse door and entered the secret base of operations.

"You're welcome," Trey's dad smiled broadly. "Did they take good care of you?"

"They spoiled us," Bora answered, giving him a big hug. "I've never flown like that before. Thank you so much."

"Saara!" Justin exclaimed as they stepped into the large war room and the tall Finnish blond emerged from her sleeping quarters. "It's so great to see you again."

"Welcome back, you two. Sorry I couldn't come to the wedding."

"No problem. It was so nice! We really appreciated the champagne you ordered to our room. Thank you. That was very thoughtful of you."

"You're welcome. I'm glad you enjoyed it, but we're really glad you're back," she responded, giving them both hugs.

"Ashley just left to pick up Boyd and Fox at the Baltimore airport. They'll be arriving about twenty minutes apart from each other. Jun is still sleeping," Leo explained. "I think we'd better just leave him in his room. He's completely exhausted in every capacity."

"I bet he is," Justin agreed. "David briefed us while we were on the helicopter. Where's the black book? We're ready to jump right in."

"Are you sure?" Leonard Stone asked, a little surprised.

Justin smiled. "We had a very restful flight. I'm ready."

"Me too – if there's anything I can do," added Bora, grinning.

"Alright then," Leo said, glad to have the help. "Why don't the two of you go into the conference room and look at it. Saara already prepped the video for you on the LED table-screen – just touch it to play and pause. We're all eager to find out what's in it. When you're done with that, I'll need to talk some things over with you, Justin. We're going to need some serious kits prepared on the Navy's sixth fleet."

He turned to Bora, "Saara is going to meet with you and run you through some testing. They're not the kind of tests you can fail, but they'll identify your strengths and give us some ideas of where you'd work best on our team. How does that sound?"

"Great!" Bora answered excitedly. "I love those kinds of tests, actually."

Justin was already on his way to the conference room.

FOR A MOMENT, Trey's wife had tried to access the internet, but then she realized that it would never work as they were flying over the Atlantic Ocean. It was just as well. Lin Ma and Bao Zhen Stone ended up chatting, as mothers and daughters do. Had she succeeded in logging on, she would've pulled up a message from her husband and spent the rest of the flight fretting. As it was, she didn't worry until eight hours later when their plane touched down in America.

CHAPTER TWENTY

THE SIXTH FLEET OF THE UNITED STATES NAVY HAS HAD ITS headquarters in Naples, Italy since the days of WWII. Officially, its mission modern is to conduct Maritime Operations and Theater Security Operations in order to promote safekeeping and constancy in Europe and Africa. It works with various interagency organizations and international security institutions to promote teamwork and trust. Unofficially, it facilitates intricate undercover work in the modern world. Almost all of the United States' naval activity involving countries along the Mediterranean are performed by this talented and very active cluster. Whether it was the U.S. intermediation in Lebanon, in 1958; the clash with the U.S.S.R. during the Yom Kippur War of 1973 and the ensuing decongesting of the Suez Canal afterward; multiple confrontations with Libya during the 1980s or the preservation of task forces in the Adriatic during the Yugoslavian wars of the 1990s, this battle group was certainly not for the faint of heart. And of course, there is the ever-present need to keep tabs on North African piracy, a mission for the U.S. Navy that dates all the way back to the Barbary Pirates of the early 19th century. Some people mistakenly think that

America's struggle against Islamic piracy, abduction, and human trafficking began at 9/11. The U.S. Navy and especially the Sixth Fleet could disabuse them of that notion.

Nestled into this remarkable fleet, is the Mediterranean Amphibious Ready Group known as MARG. Although the full extent of their makeup is known only to select top brass, it includes three amphibious assault ships, a very talented expeditionary strike group, and various types of landing craft. From these vessels, the U.S. Marine Corps ground forces can seamlessly move from water to land for surprise attacks, emergency rescues, or less stressful humanitarian interventions. Once ashore, MARG logistically supports the ground forces until the objective of the landing has been accomplished and all the Marines are safely back on board.

Trey, Jasmine, Bruce, Michi, and Tank had flown from Switzerland to Italy. They were now catching up on sleep aboard the USS Bataan – one of MARG's amphibious threats in the WASP Class of assault ships – the largest amphibious airfare vessels in the world. This ship can carry more than 1300 people, a full-strength Marine Expeditionary Unit, five M1 Abrams battle tanks, sixty-eight trucks, eight M198 howitzers, twenty-five Assault Amphibious Vehicles, and a full complement of over nine different kinds of impressive air machines from the Sikorsky SH-60 Seahawk helicopter, to the famous AV-8B Harrier II attack aircraft. In addition to its billions of dollars' worth of fighting equipment, each ship in this class has a hospital with sixty-four patient beds and six operating rooms. They can also set up an additional 536 beds in case an overflow casualty ward is needed.

Despite all their equipment, David had pulled some serious strings and requested that a CIA Sikorsky UH-60 Blackhawk be added to the ship. Although the military around the world uses the Sikorsky and several were already onboard the USS Bataan, none were quite like this one. It was completely outfitted with the latest in stealth technologies, making it virtually undetectable to sound and radar, even with its engines upgraded to include a variable-pitch pusher propeller at the aft end of the fuselage to provide forward thrust when needed. With the combination of being difficult to detect and its ability to move very quickly, it was one of the most valuable assets in the CIA's arsenal of flying machines. This particular one carried a crew of six, instead of four, adding extra seating for a second team of gunners. It had been resting under camo netting on a CIA yacht off the coast of Croatia, but with David's contacts and President Baker's influence, the Company had flown it over to the USS Bataan where it was quietly assigned to a very elite and secret group of Marines.

FOX COULDN'T BELIEVE what he had just seen. He'd stood up in the economy class cabin to go to the restroom. But while returning to his seat, he spotted a familiar face at the back of the plane. The guy had auburn hair, a roundish face with a slight pug nose, and was wearing a dark red USC sweatshirt. He'd added a black baseball cap since Fox had seen him last and pulled it down to cover his forehead. Sound asleep, he didn't notice that he'd been made. It was Adam, from Jee Hye's apartment.

The big agent sat back in his Economy Plus aisle seat and wondered how on earth the kid had boarded his plane. It couldn't have been a coincidence. He must have followed him to the airport. Fox was kicking himself for just walking out of Jee Hye's apartment and not securing them better before he left. He'd figured that a knife wound in the kid's leg would be effective enough. He pondered what to do as the plane began its descent into Baltimore. His first impulse was to walk back there and break the kid's face, but he figured that might be too traumatic and would probably get recorded and uploaded to social media from half a dozen phones. Instant viral notoriety wasn't what he was after. Waiting until people deplaned wasn't a viable option either. His best course of action was to pretend he hadn't spotted him and then just draw him into something.

The aircraft touched down gently and Fox thought about Ashley. He remembered the first time he'd met her at the Lake Wright Golf Course when Trey had stopped to talk to her. Kurt Middleton-Fox had been very new to the team and sitting in the passenger's seat of Agent Stone's vehicle. He remembered her leaving her clubs at the range and walking over to them. Her auburn hair was pulled back and up in a high ponytail, held in place by a white hairband. Her smooth skin had shown off her tan against a peach polo shirt and her white mini skirt. He remembered her beautiful long legs and glistening full lips. But most of all, he'd never forgotten her smile as she had come walking towards them. He'd been at a complete loss for words. Even now, Fox couldn't remember a single thing he'd said. He was really looking forward to seeing her again. A scowl came to his face as he looked out the window at the flagman. Instead of being able to focus on Ashley, he'd have to deal with this punk Adam. The kid was obviously more than he had seemed and Fox was furious with himself for being taken in. He mulled over the likelihood that Adam was, in fact, one of Serwabi's agents. If he was legitimately a CIA asset, Fox had to treat him carefully.

The plane eased up to the gate and gently jerked to a stop. The ramp rats scurried to place blocks behind the tires, start unloading the luggage, hook up the refueling hose, and work as hard as they could to get the plane back out in time. Fox grabbed his duffle bag, unfortunately, minus the weapons he'd had to leave back in the Honda Pilot, and headed off the plane towards the baggage claim.

Behind him, Adam grabbed his satchel and hurried up the ramp as fast as his limp would allow. He wanted to make sure he wouldn't lose sight of the big blond agent, three hundred feet ahead of him.

Fox stopped at a rack of neck pillows and picked one up to check their price, making Adam pause and look around awkwardly, unsure of how to follow the standing agent without appearing obvious. Carefully returning the cushion to the rack, Fox resumed heading toward the baggage claim.

He started down the escalators when all of a sudden, he spotted Ashley. Trey's "niece" was even more beautiful than the last time he'd seen her; he was sure of it! Simply dressed in an orange and blue paisley summer dress with big black boots and a denim jacket, she was nothing short of gorgeous. Her hair hung down her back, and when she saw him, she flashed that smile he'd never forgotten. He waved at her, forgetting his tail for just a second, then quickly lowered his arm and shook his head at her, making some motions in front of his chest with his fingers. She realized something wasn't quite right. Not being a well-trained double agent, she wasn't picking up his signal. It was then that Fox saw the person beside her was Boyd Carter!

Boyd, too, saw something wrong and instinctively, backed away from Ashley; she pretended she didn't know the big blond agent nor the surgeon. Out of the corner of her eye, she saw Fox sign the letters USC in front of his chest. Seconds later, they saw the man wearing a maroon sweatshirt with matching yellow letters.

Boyd began walking around the carrousel, away from all the action, thinking she would flank the group and get a read on what Fox wanted her to do. Just as she was rounding the big metal baggage machine, a side door to a storage closet door burst open right in front of her. Three men in black combat fatigues rushed out.

Boyd raced after them. Four more people in fatigues were standing outside on the sidewalk with weapons hanging from the end of their arms along the sides of their legs. They'd all fixed their gazes on Fox.

"Ashley, car!" Carter yelled as she tripped the last person in the group in front of her and slammed his head into the ground, knocking him out. "Pull it up in front!"

Ashley raced outside to the parking garage across the street and spotted their vehicle. They'd parked in a twenty-minute parking spot that was close to passenger pickup. By this point, the twenty passengers who were waiting for their bags started shrieking and scattering like a startled kit of pigeons.

Fox saw what had happened and noticed the four men in black combat fatigues were coming in from outside. "They have weapons!" he yelled.

"I don't!" replied Carter.

"Neither do I!"

The two in front of her were obviously surprised that the big agent was not alone and twisted around to see who he had been talking to.

Everything seemed to slip into slow motion as Fox launched himself into the air, threw his body into a horizontal flying log, and knocked down three out of the four attackers from the outside. They were so shocked that two of them lost their weapons in the air. As they were hitting the ground, Fox caught one of their guns by the barrel and smashed the butt of it into the face of the attacker nearest him. The man crumpled.

Carter's Krav Maga training was now in full gear as she kicked one guy in the groin with brutal force while simultaneously jamming her palm into the other hostile's throat. His windpipe shattered. She rotated around to the first guy, and before he could react, she viciously whipped her ankle into his nose. She could hear his nasal passage caving in and his cheekbones breaking. Still in complete control of her balance, she whirled around to the guy who was suffocating. Grabbing his neck, she stretched it out, allowing air to flow again and then lay him on the floor.

"If you don't move and keep trying to breathe, you'll live. Consider it your lucky day."

Fox had delivered such a solid punch to his second attacker's chest that he'd snapped a few of his ribs. The man started gasping for air, trying not to pass out. The big agent spun around just in time to see Boyd spring on to the shoulders of one of his remaining two hostiles. She wrapped her legs around him, under his arms, thrust her body backward with such force it caused him to literally twist around. As he fell, his head crashed into the side of the baggage carousel with the full force of his own body weight. He wasn't dead, but he'd certainly wake up with a headache and probably a cracked skull.

"Boyd, get USC. Bring him with us."

Boyd sprang to her feet just in time to see Adam disappear into a men's restroom at the far end of the baggage claim area. She tore after him with the speed of a bloodhound after a rabbit.

The fourth man was now facing Fox mano a mano. He was stupid enough to whip out a knife.

"You didn't read my file," Fox stated flatly.

"We'll see, big boy." The man hissed out the words, just enough for Fox to detect a Middle Eastern accent.

"*Shukran*, bud," the big agent said, thanking him in Arabic. "I didn't bring any of my own knives." When Fox was going through Seal training, he'd learned the hard way not to whip out a weapon unless he was sure the other person wouldn't be able to overpower him and use it against him. Apparently, this guy missed that class.

The man lunged forward like a cat on its prey. His right arm came swinging through in a perfect arc as the blade flashed in the fluorescent lights. The large agent bent backward with impressive flexibility and let the knife sail by harmlessly. The hostile followed it up with a high kick to the back of Fox's head, but the large agent blocked it with his elbow. Almost simultaneously, the man's knife hand was back, just missing Fox's throat by less than an inch. The agent's left hand followed the blade and snagged the hostile's right wrist. Twisting it backward in a practiced motion that ended with a vicious rip, Fox heard the ligaments breaking as he'd expected, like over-stretched rubber bands.

The man screamed in pain as the agent's right foot came crashing down on the side of the Arab's knee. It flexed sideways in an unnatural fold but didn't break. The man was fit. Fox would give him that. Just as the assailant started focusing past the pain to take another swipe, Fox's right hand came flying through the air in a devastating roundhouse, connecting with the hostile's jaw. It broke, and the man crumpled to the ground, unconscious, his knife falling out of his limp hand. Fox picked it up and took off running. He reached the men's room just as Boyd came out, dragging an unconscious Adam behind her.

"Let me take him."

"I won't stop you," Boyd smirked. "I have his phone, too."

"Saara will love digging into that," Fox said as he grabbed Adam and swung him over his left shoulder.

"Follow me!"

The pair of them hustled out one of the glass exit doors and across the street just as airport security flooded the baggage claim area and police pulled up to the curb outside with their lights flashing. Sirens wailed in the distance, meaning more cavalry was on its way. The entire episode had lasted less than a minute, but Fox was worried about cameras. They needed to get out of there fast.

Boyd had grabbed a baseball cap from somewhere and held the brim of it down, concealing her face. She also screamed in feigned fright. "There are more in the men's room! They have guns and hostages!" She jogged along and continued to shout to the police who were getting out of their cars. "They're wearing black and yelling about bombs or something."

The police drained into the airport, their adrenaline in high gear, as the two agents converged on the waiting Audi A5. The trunk was open as were the doors.

Boyd jumped into the back seat as Fox tossed Adam into the trunk and slammed it shut. He hurried around to the passenger's side and jumped in the seat.

"Maybe I should start charging for these high-pressure getaways," Ashley commented, grinning.

"You're getting good at them. We might even hire you," Fox answered with a smirk noticing that the stereo was off and the high beams were on, even though the dawn light would've offset the glare.

They sped out of the airport just as more police cars were motoring to the scene.

As they were about to get on the Maryland 295 North, Fox said, "Ashley, don't get on the freeway yet. Let's find a place to pull over and have a conversation with the kid."

They drove around for a few minutes until they discovered an undeveloped cul-de-sac. It was unkempt and had large trees and thick foliage hanging into the asphalt area. The enveloping weeds were just taller than the car, and the whole area reeked of urine and stale beer. Ashley pulled the Audi under some low-hanging branches, making sure they wouldn't scratch her car. She turned the engine off and Fox hopped out to pop the trunk.

CHAPTER TWENTY-ONE

THE GROUP AT LAUNCHPAD WAS GATHERING IN THE CONFERENCE room to hear what Justin and Bora had to say.

"Were you able to translate it?" Leo asked, sitting down and trying not to appear overly excited.

"Every word," Justin replied. "It's what you'd expect … at first."

David poured himself a glass of water and leaned forward, "Expect from what?"

"A little black book," Bora said. "She kept track of every single person she escorted. Sometimes she has names, sometimes she has descriptions, most entries include the times they met and the places they went to … what they did … that sort of thing."

"Wow. That's incredible. Anything interesting?"

"They're all Arabs. They all paid a lot of money."

"Thousands?"

"Tens of thousands."

"Is Serwabi on the list?" Leo asked.

"No. But he shows up later in the book."

"In what capacity?"

"Well, let me put it context. First, the book is astonishing. She was not just beautiful, but highly intelligent," Justin answered. "If you open it up from the front, it's the little black book stuff. But if you open it up from the back, it's more like her personal journal. It took us a while to figure it out because Fox had just recorded it page by page. When we got to the end, we realized it was the first page of the second half, going backward. So, we took digital images of each page and re-arranged the second half properly."

Bora swept the photos from her tablet to the LED table-screen. "So, this is the first half. You can see that she kept all the account numbers every time there was a money transfer."

"They didn't just pay cash each time?" Saara enquired, a little surprised.

"Most of them did, but if you see here, for instance, a Mohammad Seif Nazari paid $75,000 and did it as a wire transfer from a bank in Kuala Lumpur, Malaysia. She kept the account number."

"Was that just for one night?"

"No," answered Justin. "She spent at least three days with her clients. In Nazari's case, she spent ten days with him. I actually found a file in our databases and pulled up this picture of them together. They were at an embassy ball at the Ritz-Carlton in Moscow." He sent it to the LED tabletop.

"She is simply one of the most beautiful people I've ever seen," Saara commented.

"I agree," Bora added. "She was stunning and apparently worth the money, for whatever reason. Many of these clients were repeat clients, and there were around ten of them who would hire her for at least two weeks."

"I wonder what happened," David mulled. "How did she end up dead in an alley?"

Leo nodded. "We need to find out." He turned to Justin's wife, "Bora, when we're done here, could you send all the names in that book to Jennifer Wu in Hong Kong? Saara has her contact information."

"Yes, sir."

"Now … the second half," Justin said. "If the first half is the pot of gold, the second half is pure platinum."

FOX SLAPPED Adam across the face a few times, trying to wake the kid up. Finally, his eyes began to flutter and eventually opened wide in recognition and fear. The large agent picked him up out of the trunk and shook him like a rag doll. Then he propped him up against the car.

"Adam, Adam, Adam. What are you doing here, Adam?" Fox asked.

"I don't know where here is."

"We're in Paris."

"Seriously?"

"No. We're in Maryland."

"Oh, okay," the university student said with relief.

Fox looked at him and then pulled out the knife he'd lifted from the hostile at the airport.

"Oh, geez. Please. Put that away, bro," whined the kid.

"Why should I put it away?"

"You don't understand."

Fox took his giant hand and wrapped it around Adam's throat. The kid began to choke and cough, his face starting to turn purple from a lack of oxygen. He opened his mouth as wide as possible, trying to get air.

"Are you going to tell me the truth, Adam?"

The kid's eyes were bugging out as he tried to nod.

Fox let him go and kneed him in the thigh, where one of his throwing knives had been, just a few hours before. The college student doubled over, coughing and sputtering, inhaling large amounts of stinky air.

"What don't I understand?" Fox asked as Boyd Carter came out to hear the answer. Ashley stayed in the driver's seat in case she needed to fire up the engine for another getaway. She glanced down to make sure the stereo hadn't turned on by accident.

"Oh, God," the student said, seeing Boyd. "Don't kill me."

Carter reached inside the trunk and began to dig through Adam's satchel. She found his wallet and opened it up just as the kid sat down on the asphalt, against the back tire of the Audi.

He pulled his knees up against his chest. "You know my father."

Fox could see he wasn't lying. "I know your father?!"

"Yeah. I mean, you know of him."

Boyd held up Adam's driver's license. "Adam Talek Serwabi."

Fox picked the kid up and sat him on the hood of the car, so he could look at him eye to eye. "Serwabi? Daylight? Your father is Mohammad Al Serwabi?"

Adam nodded and glanced at the watch on Fox's wrist. "He'll be in Baltimore in thirty-five minutes."

Fox turned to Boyd, and they exchanged a *What the hell is going on?* look.

SHELLY BROWN WAS TERRIFIED. Her normal positive, contagious energy was completely dissolved. The train was speeding along at an alarmingly fast pace only inches away from rock walls flying by on either side. Every few minutes, there was an abrupt jolt as the cargo cars shifted in a turn. Shelly shrieked fearfully along with all the others.

All she could think about was her single mother. Did mom know what was happening to her child, yet? She'd been so excited that her daughter had gotten this opportunity. Precious memories began to take over as if her mind were a large movie screen. She was with her mom at the post office, picking up an application for her passport. She'd never had one before, so she had to get her photo taken at a local FedEx Store. When they saw the result, they started laughing uncontrollably. Her eyes were wide, and her mouth was open as if in mid-conversation. She thought of how they'd said good-bye. Her mom was desperately trying to hold back the tears. Both were struggling so hard to be brave, but when Shelly burst out crying and saying, "I love you, Mom! I'll miss you so much!" her mother lost it, too. They hugged forever. At that moment, she realized something that had never occurred to her before. Her mother loved her so much that she would actually miss her daughter's presence while she was gone. The strong, tall, athletic goalkeeper balled up in a fetal position. Now the tears flowed down in torrents.

Miles Howell saw her, but he remained focused in thought. He knew that everything going on now was just an experience – a horrific one – but just an uncontrollable point in time. What he needed to get ready for, was that moment he prayed was coming that he could control. If his life testified to anything, it was to his ability to alter circumstances by seizing a tiny moment to reverse a situation. He began to replay the plane-landing in his mind for what must have been the hundredth time. The Lynx had purposefully caused the jet to nose-dive, and it wasn't just to land as soon as possible. It was a smart move. It had set the tone by terrifying all the passengers. Clearly, they'd landed in one of the most dangerous regions on the planet; it was the hottest up-and-coming training ground for terrorists. But, where in Libya were they heading?

CHAPTER TWENTY-TWO

PRESIDENT GEORGE BAKER HAD BEEN OUT OF OFFICE FOR ALMOST a decade. Still, he was as popular now as he'd been the day his second term had ended. Popular that is, with everyone but his son.

Their relationship had been rough even before he'd taken his first oath of office as governor of Colorado. Although he'd never admitted to it to Teddy, he understood his boy's disdain for politics. The machine tore at family relationships like an unrelenting lion, determined to devour them. The media was that lion's jaw, incessantly lying and pitting people against each other. Young Ted Baker had been forced to accept the relentless attack because his father, who'd had a good run in business, insisted that being a public servant was to be his legacy contribution to the greater good. As his son saw it, the public was incapable of goodness. They were selfish, arrogant, boastful, hostile, and hate-filled. They didn't deserve his father, nor were they worthy of his family's sacrifice.

"Ted, damn it. Let me help."

"You chartered the plane, Dad," the younger Baker said into his phone. "But it was my idea to send them with minimal security. It's my ass on the line. I'll take care of it like a big boy."

"Nobody gives a damn about your reputation at this point, Son," President Baker retorted. "We need to get those girls back. From both countries. You can't write an algorithm to solve this. You have no idea about how to get this done on your own. I'm calling you as a courtesy. You want to help? Then let's put our heads together. If not, just stay out of my way."

The silence was heavy. Ted knew his father was right. Lots of money wasn't going to solve the problem. He looked at his tablet. Miles Howell's transponder had been activated south of Benghazi. It briefly started moving eastward before being lost. It was time he told his father.

"I know where they are, Dad."

He could hear the President slam a door and knew exactly where he was, too. Anytime there had been acute tension, his father retreated to his cigar room, slammed the door, poured himself a whiskey and, if he was on the phone, ended that conversation. Next, he would light up a Gurkha, probably the Black Dragon, and think. He could hear the liquid therapy being poured into a tumbler now and pictured his father in his stuffy Italian-crafted leather chair.

"What in the hell do you mean exactly, you *know* where they are?" his father growled.

Ted quickly realized his father had misunderstood him. It was a classic example of how much they mistrusted each other.

"All I meant is that I had the security outfitted with transponders. The one on Miles Howell kicked on about three hours ago."

"Is it still on?"

"No. It moved a bit and then went off. He's probably in an area where there's no reception."

George Baker was trying not to go ballistic. Instead, he chose, to take a light sip. "When were you going to tell me, Theodore Randall Baker?"

"Now."

"Ted," President Baker finally stated, "Both of us have been working behind each other's back it seems. How soon can you make it to Colorado?"

"You actually reached me on my jet. I'll be landing in Telluride in about thirty-five minutes and will take a chopper to you."

George Baker hung up, emptied his glass of Oban single malt and set it down on his sculpted walnut end table with much more force than usual.

Before he could light his cigar, he had more phone calls to make. He paged his Secret Service detail and told them to get him the phone number of each of the parents on both teams. It was time to be the bearer of bad news. He certainly didn't want anyone else to do it.

I'd better pour myself another, first.

"WE'VE read everything Jee Hye wrote, and I'll walk you through the sections. If you have any questions, just stop me, okay?"

Everyone nodded.

Justin continued, "When she first started keeping this journal, it seemed to be a real outlet for her. She didn't appear to have many people she could talk to. Nobody, actually. She felt horrible about how she'd walked away from Jun – a lot of guilt about that. It appears she was pretty devastated by the things her mother had called her. She was furious at her father for having screwed the family over the way that he had."

Bora interjected. "We're not too sure what that's all about, but Jun could fill us in later, I guess."

"I know the general points. You're right about everything," Ashley remarked. "Jun's father made them think they had money, but it was all a mirage. He committed suicide, and Jee Hye was the one who found his body. It turned out they were in debt past their eyeballs."

"That's awful!" Saara responded, completely shocked.

"Their mother fell off the deep end into a terrible depression which led to alcohol, so Jun, a teenager, tried to take on all the responsibilities. Jee Hye got into prostitution, and when her mom found out, she kicked her out of the house. It's a horrible story. Maybe that's part of her beauty," the surgeon said, bringing Jee Hye's picture up on her tablet. "Her features are mesmerizingly svelte, but her eyes … there's so much sorrow there."

"I'm amazed that Jun's here with us," Bora commented. "We've got a real opportunity to be family to him."

Everyone agreed. Justin picked up where he'd left off.

"As she experienced the hardships of a call girl, the journal changes in tone," he paused to bring up the correlating journal pages onto the LED table. "What used to be her raw voice – full of deep emotions– changes into just a sad reporting of the facts.

She names specific people and goes into explicit detail of what they made her do. Much of it is so grotesque involving little boys and girls, trafficked in from around the world! It's just unbelievable!"

Justin paused to drink some water, "That reminds me. Have any of you ever heard of some guy called The Lynx?"

Leonard Stone and David Hirsch gave each other an intense look.

Hirsch spoke first. "Yes, we know of The Lynx, Justin. Why do you ask?"

"Jee Hye had many horrible experiences with him. He is a full-on child, trafficker. One of the most feared people in that business. Ruthless. It's a good thing Jun is still sleeping. He tortured her in sexual ways that aren't human. If he were in the States, he'd go to the supermax prison in Colorado. But he's too smart for that. He stays in nations that don't protect children. Mostly Arab ones. Just reading some of these parts of her book made me want to puke."

"I'm sorry," his bride confessed. "I had to walk away ... I just couldn't ..."

Leo and David could sense their cumulative temperatures rising.

"It's just that she seemed to be such a beautiful person ..." Bora continued with her eyes moistening. "She didn't deserve this kind of treatment."

Leonard spoke, "Bora, these things are very difficult to deal with. Should you ever want to work on a different part of the project, just let us know. There are many ways you can help."

"Thank you, Dr. Stone. But as sickening as it is, I have to say, it's made me so much more determined to see this through to the end."

Everyone understood her sentiments, more than she realized. Her husband picked up where he'd left off, as Bora leaned against him.

"One of the worst stories is with this freak, the one called The Lynx. They were in Cairo for a gathering of Arab leaders who are involved in clean energy projects. She was supposed to be escorting some Sheikh named Ahmed something or other. I couldn't find information on him outside of her book, but I didn't have much time to check him out. Here's his name," Justin threw it onto the LED table screen. "Ahmed Al Hammad." He leaned back in his chair. "From what I gather, the Sheikh ended up dead somehow, and The Lynx met Jee Hye. He took her back to his Imperial Suite at the Mena House Oberoi and grotesquely raped her. Then, he invited a group of five older freaky Arab men, like himself, to continue. She indicates there were some other men there, too. Not sure who, though. After that, the freak brought in fifteen twelve-year-old boys and girls from China." He sensed his new wife was still struggling. "Well, whatever you think you could imagine, it was ten times worse."

Everyone was feeling deeply disturbed and disgusted. At the same time, they were oddly galvanized. This was the core of their mission. They'd formed as a team to stand against exactly this kind of evil. They knew they were uniquely gifted to avenge Jee Hye and the many others who had been and were even now being so appallingly abused.

"So, here's where Serwabi comes in," Justin stated, breaking people's thoughts.

Leo looked at David and back at Justin, "He was one of them?"

"No. He was in the same hotel. Saara was able to obtain their guest log."

Justin slid the hotel records onto their tablets. "Four days after she'd gone through hell, she finally emerged from her hotel room," Bora added. "From what we could tell, it was her first time in Egypt."

"So, she went to the Pyramids?" David guessed.

Bora nodded. "Yes. What every tourist wants to see, right? It was a guided expedition organized by the hotel. They kept records of all the passports from each guest that went. Check it out."

Leo looked at the photo that glided across his tablet. "Mohammad Al Serwabi. He went with her? You two have done outstanding work in a very short time."

"It's mostly Bora," Justin admitted with admiration. "She's the researcher extraordinaire."

Leo agreed, "I think we've found one of your talents, Bora. Anything else?"

"Yes. One more thing," she answered. "Apparently, during that terrible night of hell, as she was lying on the floor wishing she were dead, she overheard a conversation. It was a scheme being put together by The Lynx and the men he'd brought in to rape her and the children. There was some kind of plot that involved Russians and Chinese. She recorded in her journal and told Serwabi about it at the Pyramids that day."

"She must've met Serwabi before," Leo pondered.

"Other than meeting him at the Pyramids, she doesn't mention him in her black book, but it certainly seems like she told him a lot for a first-time encounter."

CHAPTER TWENTY-THREE

"I HOPE FOR YOUR SAKE, THAT YOUR FATHER DOESN'T DEVIATE from the plan," Fox said as he turned in his seat to look back at Adam.

The college kid was sweating as though he were in a sauna.

As soon as Serwabi's plane had touched down, he'd sent a text to his son, wondering how his tracking of Fox was progressing. His son replied that he was being held at knifepoint and that his father had exactly twenty-three minutes to meet them alone in the parking lot of the movie theater off Winterson Road. He was to walk up to the vehicle, open the back door on the passenger's side, and sit down.

The Audi was again parked under a large tree, this time at the furthest parking spot from the movie theater entrance, and Ashley had the engine running. Fox was in the back with his knife touching Adam's rib cage. Boyd had scampered up the tree directly over Ashley's car. In a more perfect setup, they would've had Trey hidden on a roof to provide sniper cover, Bruce in an optimal location to cut off an escape, and Adam wouldn't have been on location at all. But it was the best they could come up with. They didn't want to give Serwabi time to organize any kind of counter-play.

A green taxi pulled up to the theater's front entrance and dropped off a tall thin man with a hooked nose and round-rimmed silver glasses. Fox recognized the MEO's familiar profile and his trademark stride as he purposefully strode towards the Audi. Adam tightened up, wondering if he should spring out of the car.

"You might make it away before I cut out your kidney, kid, but Boyd would break your neck and shoot your dad without much effort." Fox hissed, reading Adam's mind. "Put your head down and don't look up until I tell you to."

Serwabi stood in front of the Audi, staring.

Ashley and Fox stared back.

The tall thin operative walked slowly to the back door, and as he reached for the handle, Boyd plunged out of the tree to deliver a stunning blow to the back of his head. His face hit the frame of the car before he tottered backward. She swept his legs out from under him and lowered him to the pavement.

Boyd's hands quickly zip-tied the Serwabi's wrists, elbows, knees, and ankles.

Fox climbed out, "You can raise your head and get out of the car."

Adam looked around and spotted his dad. "Did you kill him?"

Boyd shook her head. "How'd you get your plane ticket, kid?"

"I used my credit card," he said as he got out of the car and sat down on the curb, visibly shaken with the whole ordeal. "Dad said he'd pay me back."

Ashley turned the car off, got out and handed Adam's satchel back to him, but not before snapping a photo of his driver's license with her phone. Fox lifted the MEO into the back seat where his son had been. Then, the big agent sat down beside the kid on the curb, behind the Audi. "Here's a C-note for dinner and the cab ride back to the airport. Buy a plane ticket home. Your father will reimburse you for that, too."

"I'm going with my dad," Adam protested.

"Look, son," said Fox. "There's no way you're coming with us. Period. Either take my offer, or we're just going to leave you here with nothing, including your satchel."

Tears glistened in Adam's eyes. "Are you going to murder my father?"

Fox shook his head. "We're going to take him to a place where he'll have to explain some stuff. Answer questions. That sort of thing."

"Okay Adam," Ashley chimed in, "You did your part. Now go home. I'm sure your dad will contact you soon."

"Screw all of you. What happened to the money and diamonds we found?"

Fox helped the kid up. "You mean the ones you stole out of our friend's apartment?"

Adam Serwabi glared at him. "Can't you at least give me a piece of the action?"

"The piece I'd like to give you is a decade in jail for trashing her place and stealing her stuff."

"Whatever. You're the one who walked out with it all."

"Have you decided what you're going to do?" Boyd asked, sensing that Fox was about to blow a gasket.

"I'll get on a plane, I guess."

Ashley had gotten back into the Audi and started the engine.

"Good choice," Fox said as he got into the car. "Make sure you get your leg looked at properly. It looks like your bandage needs to be changed."

Boyd climbed into the passenger's seat beside Ashley and rolled down her window. "I'm glad I didn't have to send you to the hospital, kid. If you ever try something this stupid again and I'm around, I will. Even if I'm not around. I'll find out, and I'll find you."

Adam stood up and gave a limp wave as the Audi drove off. He could see his father's head flopping against Fox's shoulder as the car turned sharply out of the theater parking lot.

MICHIKO IMADA GROANED QUIETLY, stretched and glanced up at Jasmine's bunk. It was already empty. She got up, took a quick shower, changed into a set of Navy fatigues and a t-shirt, and headed out of the room. Jogging up some stairs, she found Bruce and Trey sitting in a small lounge area designed for guests of the Captain. They were all outfitted in similar Navy gear, obviously to help them fit in and keep a low profile on the ship. She greeted them with a short bow and sat down.

"Thank you very much," she said as Bruce handed her a freshly brewed cup of coffee.

Locke smiled, "Would you like some fruit or a toasted bagel?"

"Both, please," she responded. "Trey, where's Jasmine?"

"Gazing at the ocean. It's her favorite thing to do. Of course, I'm sure it gets more exciting when the Harriers start landing and good-looking squid start hitting the deck," he smirked, referring to the navy personnel.

"Maybe I should go stand beside her," Trey joked.

Michi chuckled. "She'd love that, I'm sure."

Bruce laughed and then said, "I'm guessing she'll be back soon. She'll be getting hungry."

THE DRIVE from the movie theater to LaunchPad took less than thirty minutes and just as the group in the conference room was taking a break from going through Jee Hye's black book, Ashley burst through the door of the warehouse and held it open for Boyd. A few seconds later, Fox came in, carrying a Middle East Operative from the Central Intelligence Agency over his shoulder. Blindfolded and still groggy, Serwabi was quite unresponsive to his environment. Fox took him straight to Interrogation Room 1 and secured him to a chair and zip-tied his knees. He re-tightened an extra t-shirt that Boyd had put over Zerwabi's head to blindfold him and made sure that the Middle East Operator was still unconscious. As Fox left, he made sure the door was shut securely, guaranteeing that it would be sound-proof to ouside noise.

Everyone had emptied the conference room to greet the incoming group. They couldn't believe how quickly things were happening. It was good meeting up again.

"Do I still call you Bora, or are you going by Mrs. Park?" Boyd teased, giving the young bride a big hug.

"I was glad you were chaperoning!" Justin told her. "I was worried Fox and Ashley would elope!"

Fox had just walked up to the group and grabbed him playfully, putting him in a headlock. "Now that you're married, you've got all the relationship advice, huh?"

Leo and David were visibly relieved to have this group together and back at LaunchPad.

"Take time to get settled," Trey's dad was encouraging them. "But not for long. We're in the middle of stuff. Come join us whenever you're ready."

"I'm ready to rumble, sir," Fox responded, letting go of Justin.

David looked at him carefully. "You don't need to rest?"

"Later."

Hirsch didn't argue. "Then get to the interrogation room, wake up the package and talk to him. Leonard will join you."

Fox left the group and returned to where he'd secured the MEO. He was sitting in a solid steel chair flanked by a solid steel table. The big blond agent cut the zip ties off the MEO's knees, but quickly re-tied his individual ankles to the chair legs and secured his hands to cuffs bolted into the tabletop. Then he slapped the CIA operative in the face a few times.

"You don't know who you're messing with," Serwabi mumbled, slowly coming to.

Fox ripped Boyd's shirt off his eyes. Blinking in the bright lights, the captured man drew in a sharp breath.

"Razor!"

"Daylight."

"What the hell are you into?"

Fox didn't answer. He saw Leo approaching and opened the door for him.

"Where's my son?" Serwabi demanded angrily, becoming fully awake.

"He's bleeding like a stuck pig in the interrogation room next door," Leonard Stone answered. His fury was like molten lava, about to erupt. "I can't figure out if he's innocent, or just well-trained. He's put up with a lot, though. I guess he's learned a lot from you, eh? But ... I'll be honest. He doesn't have much left."

"To hell with you!" the MEO screamed.

Leonard got very close to the right ear of the zip-tied agent. "Mohammad Al Serwabi, if you answer us quickly and truthfully, your son will live. If you don't, he'll stay lying on the floor, gasping like a fish out of water. His life is in your hands. He's hoping his father gives a damn. Me? I don't really care."

Serwabi glared.

"Deal?" Fox asked, looking at his watch. "Your son has about seven minutes, give or take a few, but I'm no medical expert."

"What do you want?" the MEO snarled.

Sitting down, Leo looked him in the eyes. "I want to know about Jee Hye. Why did you kill her?"

Serwabi looked confused, "Kill her? You're idiots! I was trying to save her!"

Fox and Leo kept their eyes focused on the CIA's MEO, reading every micro move.

"We thought we had the murderer in a back alley of Koreatown in Los Angeles. But the bastard got away. I tracked him to a

Walmart off Crenshaw. Then he actually took out some of my guys." Suddenly a light turned on in Serwabi's head. "What the hell? Razor!!"

Fox didn't talk. His ocean blue eyes were boring a hole into the MEO.

"It was you, wasn't it? You're the one who went into Jee Hye's apartment to steal her black book from my kids. Adam had the sense to follow you all the way to Baltimore. Is that where we are?" He glared at Fox. "It was you who took out my men at the airport!"

"Tell me more about your men. You have a private little army?" Leo asked.

"It's classified."

"I'll bet you a new Escalade that my security clearance is higher than yours. Declassify it."

Serwabi couldn't stop glaring at Fox.

"How did you know about Jee Hye's black book?" asked Leo, completely unfazed and changing tact.

"We'd been tracking a prick by the name of Sa'im Kashif Zafar. He's bad news. He's been on the top three of Whiteboard."

Neither man responded, but they knew. The CIA's official list that's published in conjunction with the FBI, NSA, DHS and a host of other three-lettered organizations is mostly for the media. The unofficial list – a list that never makes the light of day – is a list that only the Company's top agents know about. It's called Whiteboard. When someone from that list disappears, their name gets wiped off a whiteboard hanging in a small room that's attached to the Director's office. It's known as the CIA's War Room. Agents send no communications to each other referencing it. No book will ever be written about the assassin who took the person out. And the media would never know it had happened, or at least that it was a CIA hit.

"When Muammar Gaddafi got taken out, there was a dogfight to get his gold. Thousands and thousands of tons of it."

"Everyone knows that," Leo snarled.

"And everyone knew that's why we took Gaddafi out. The United States is in so much debt that we needed the gold. Imagine that!"

Fox and Leo didn't flinch.

"Well, the USA got to it first. The night he was assassinated, we were already in place. We loaded the loot onto a C-5 Galaxy, protected it with jets, radar, subs, and drones, and got the hell out of there. It's safely locked up in Colorado." Serwabi twisted uncomfortably in his chair. "Get me some water, please?"

"No," Fox replied coldly.

Trey's father shook his head and stood up. "My wife made dinner and hates it when I'm late."

"Screw you."

Fox delivered a lightning strike to Serwabi's face. "Show some respect, Daylight. You don't realize who you're talking to."

The MEO groaned as blood oozed from his split lip. He couldn't put his hands to his face, so he put his forehead on the table, looking at his zip-tied ankles. Blood dripped onto the floor from his mouth.

"You're telling us about gold in Libya?" Fox asked, angrily. "Didn't we ask why you killed Jee Hye, Serwabi? Your son has about three minutes left."

"Listen!" The Middle East Operative spit out as he lifted his head. He glared at Leonard, then at Fox, "The reason we got away with the gold and didn't get blown out of the sky by the Russians and the Chinese was that they were interested in something even more lucrative. A nation like ours wasn't willing to go after it. Not then, anyway." He paused. "The Russians and the Chinese only cared about Gaddafi's smuggling enterprise: children, drugs, women, weapons, and money from around the world, more than any other individual enterprise on the planet. They wanted to take Gaddafi's place as the Emperor of Grand Central Station."

Mohamad Al Serwabi stared at Leonard. "You know I'm right, don't you? I don't know who you are, but you've been around a long time. I can tell." He took a deep breath, exhaling as he continued. "Believe it or not, the Chinese and the Russians lost both races. They lost the race for the gold. And a certifiably demonic emissary of the Muslim Brotherhood won the race for the smuggling operation. He destroyed their armies, and with some help from friends in Europe, he stole the secret funding they were going to allocate to their Libya project. They don't call him The Lynx for nothing. He's a deadly hunter and smarter than all of us."

MICHI WAS JUST SITTING down to eat when Tank entered the lounge, out of breath. "Hey, Trey. I just got a text from Justin. Your dad wants all of us to link up in ten. There've been some developments."

"Okay," Agent Stone responded. "Can you go find Jazzy? Let's meet in my cabin – there's an adjoining room with a table and chairs. It's probably secure."

Trey waited for Michi to finish eating. Bruce went on ahead to set up his computer and establish a test link with Justin.

Tank found Jasmine watching the action on the ship's deck. "Your dad wanted me to come get you – we're about to link up with LaunchPad."

Jasmine hesitated, "Do you think I should stay here on the USS Bataan? My dad wanted me to think about it. What do you think?"

"Why wouldn't you?"

"Because even though this is the United States Navy, there could still be someone here who'd want to hurt me."

"Is that how you're going to live the rest of your life?"

"What do you mean?"

"There might be someone … somewhere … somehow … who wants to hurt you or your family?"

Trey's daughter looked back towards the deck as one of the impressive Harriers landed gently, right on its mark. "I don't know. It's not normal to think that way, I guess."

Tank watched the action for a little bit. Then he said, "If you come with us to where we're going, I guarantee there'll be people who would want to hurt you. Very soon, we'll be coming up against pure evil. You can bet on it. In my opinion, you need to think about whether you're really ready to face all that again."

A gentle breeze swept her long dark hair across her face. She lifted her head and looked across the ocean. "That's good, Tank. I don't really know whether I am prepared or not. I had thought I was." Her hand brushed across her face, clearing it. "But that's exactly what I have to do – think about it some more."

"In the meantime, can we get to your dad's cabin before he snaps my arm off, for real this time?"

She grinned. "Yeah, okay."

COACH MURRAY HAD PUT his hand into the air. Howell turned his head to watch through the darkness. It took a while, but the guy with the gun finally responded.

"What you want?" he asked with broken English.

"Even you probably need to pee by now," the coach said. "Please. We're all hungry and thirsty. We need to go to the bathroom. How much further are we going?"

The man glared back, reached inside the front of his shirt, and pulled out a throat mic. Speaking Arabic, he must have received the answer.

"We break soon and then keep going."

Through the darkness Howell, too, could see that he'd used his throat mic and suddenly he had a discouraging revelation. The throat mic was most likely for a closed network that was connected to the train's truck-engine. He'd turned his transmitter on too early. There was no way his device would work this deep underground. At the time he'd turned it on, he had no idea they'd be down more than a hundred feet beneath the earth's surface. By now, the battery would be dead.

As the train continued to speed along, most of the girls were lying on the floor, too tired, too hungry, too emotionally drained to respond to its jerks and shifts anymore. Some had defecated themselves. Both sets of parents were sitting silently on the cold floor.

Although she wouldn't tell her husband now, Mrs. Jackson blamed him for all of this. She'd never felt that a trip to Africa was a good idea for her thirteen-year-old daughter. Had this tournament been held in London or Paris – or even in an Oriental country like Singapore, she would've been agreeable. But Botswana was something she'd not been comfortable with. She hadn't even known where it was when she'd first heard the name. She thought it was in Mexico somewhere. The emotions were constantly hardening in her. When the plane did its controlled fall from the sky, she'd been terrified. Then when Jason Kennedy was shot, she'd become completely petrified. It was the first time she'd seen somebody die in real life. It was totally different from the movies. Not only did the blood spurting out of his head haunt her for hours, but the unnatural sounds that came from the cavities of his body was something she would never forget. There were smells that she knew her nose would always recall. And his eyes. The vacancy was immediate. His spirit had fled a gurgling shell of flesh.

Mrs. Jackson remembered being horrified at her daughter having to witness all of this. She desperately wanted to protect her, somehow, but couldn't. Then, the shock gave way to indignation. What right did these people have anyway? How dare The Lynx treat people with such contempt and coldness? And that awful wasp display. That was ghastly. Creepy! She had seen everything happening but somehow felt as if she wasn't at all in her own body. She was somehow outside it, experiencing some twisted nightmare like the ones she had had in college when she was tripping on acid.

Sitting next to her husband, her anger had morphed into rage. What kind of a useless man had she married? He seemed as lost as she was. His Harvard Law degree? His leadership of the New Hampshire Democrat Party? His connections, influence, and money? What did it all amount to? A great big zero! And what was that Howell guy doing? Wasn't he supposed to be their protector? She wondered how much he was being paid. *Too much!* That's for sure. She resolved that she would most certainly demand money. Not just a refund. They'd file a lawsuit! Lots of them actually. Maybe there was an upside to evil, after all! Lucrative book deals. Talk shows. Good Morning America interviews, awards, movie deals ... the fastest way to wealth and fame in America.

The train started shaking and the wheels started shrieking as the brakes were being applied. Fountains of sparks lit up the tunnel walls in an eerie orangy glow. Everyone's hearts began to quiver too, wondering what new horror lay ahead.

CHAPTER TWENTY-FOUR

"Hello. Testing. Hello." Justin's voice came in loud and clear, before the video appeared, showing the conference room.

"You're coming through great, Justin," Bruce answered. "Hold on a minute. I'm going to hook up this HDMI cable, so we can see your face on a 54-inch flat-screen."

"If I'd known, I'd have brushed my teeth," Justin responded.

"Right? No time to primp."

"I'll work on bringing in Whiskey and Maverick," Justin chuckled.

Bruce paused and popped his face in front of the camera. "Did you say that you're bringing in Whisky *and* his son?"

"Roger that."

"Together?"

"Roger."

"Are they in the same room?"

Justin paused and stuck his head in front of his camera, too. "Is that unusual?"

Bruce shrugged and found where to plug in the cable on the television. "Maybe you should've sent Boyd to Telluride, instead of bringing her home."

He heard a familiar laugh. "I heard that," Boyd said. "You're right. I hope they don't kill each other."

Trey and Michi walked in and waved to the camera, just as Justin and Boyd's face came up on the screen.

"Hey, you two," Agent Carter greeted them.

"Boyd!" Michi exclaimed, happily. "You made it back safely!"

"Yeah. I came back, but half the *ohana* is gone."

Trey had a big smile. Every once in a while, Boyd Carter would let her Hawaiian roots slip out. She grew up on the Big Island of Hawaii and had spent her youth surfing, spearfishing, and pig hunting. "I knew you'd make it back in time to get in the mix, though."

She grinned back. "You know it, brah. I couldn't stay away."

"The connection is working fine," Bruce cut in, speaking to Justin. "But I have an extra camera here. I'm going to hook it up to the TV instead of using the laptop's camera."

"Copy that," Justin answered.

Bruce got to work while Tank and Jasmine filed in and greeted everyone. David and Leo had just sat down in the conference room, nodding to everyone. Suddenly the screen in Trey's sitting room split, and President Baker and his son's faces came on.

"Can everyone hear us okay?" Justin called out.

Trey gave a nod.

The President responded, "Yes, great. Thank you." He cleared his throat and smiled. "Leonard, it is great to see you, my old friend."

"Same here, George. You know David, of course."

"Yes, yes, David ... it's good to see you, too," the President's eyebrow's shot up as he peered into his screen. "Trey? Is that you?"

"Yes, sir."

"Thank God!" The president said turning to face his son, "This is my son, Ted, whom most of you know."

Everyone greeted the younger Baker while trying to mask their surprise at seeing them together.

"So," Ted began, "Where are you located? I just pinged you, and it said your ISP is in Northern Ireland."

Saara walked in, trying to hide a smirk on her face as she heard his question. Their location was masked, of course, and it changed every few seconds. If he pinged them now it was likely they'd appear to be in Australia or Canada. Nobody answered. Ted realized he wasn't going to find out. At least, not yet.

"Mr. President," David spoke up, breaking the awkward moment. "Just so you know, everyone here has been cleared by the Department of Defense for Top Secret clearance and the Company has issued an SCI clearance for all of us. I realize Mr. Baker Jr. has a vested interest in our success, so I think we can all agree that he be here."

Everyone nodded as Ted responded, "Thanks, David. It's a formality, but an important one. I appreciate you putting that on the record."

"In addition," David continued, "By circumstances, Jasmine Stone is also sitting in with us. If it's okay with everyone, I think we should extend the same courtesy to her."

"Agreed," answered the President as Jasmine tried not to blush with excitement.

Leo picked it up from there, "Thank you, everyone. Mr. President, our team is in the Mediterranean at the moment, onboard the USS Bataan. They're about sixty minutes from landing in Libya."

"Where?" asked Ted.

"Benghazi is the logical spot. It's our Company's station, and it holds all of the critical data for the Middle East, including our assets. I figured that might be helpful."

President Baker leaned left and looked down, "Ted has something."

The younger Baker looked directly into the camera. "When we set all of this up, there were a few things I did to help bolster security. I outfitted the security detail with steady-report transponders and injected one into Casey, too. Hers is intermittent ... I think you know about that one."

Saara was putting up images of these types of devices onto the LED table in the conference room. They appeared simultaneously on the tablets of the team on the ship. Justin jotted down details on his little yellow pad of paper.

Ted continued, "From what we can tell, they've left ground zero and are headed east." He leaned forward and tapped a few keys on the President's laptop. "Watch this." He pulled up a locator map with an orange dot and a yellow dot inside a green outline of the plane. "We're looking at the orange transponder for Miles Howell. I believe he turned it on when the plane had landed, and he realized they were in trouble. For our purposes, I also put a yellow dot in the place where Casey turned on her transponder. It stayed on for three minutes and is virtually in the same location."

"Where is this?" Michi asked. "I don't see any defining names."

"You're right. We're not getting much to delineate the positioning. This is in the desert area of Qaminis, forty miles south of Benghazi."

Saara quickly sent a map of the area to everyone's tablets. It looked like her satalite imagery projections on where the plane had landed were right on point.

"Ted continued. "Watch what happens. Casey's three minutes were up, and her transmitter shut off. But Howell moves around slowly – probably walking, then he stops. My guess is that he is sitting or standing. But then, here ..." The orange dot took off very quickly and vanished.

"What the heck?" Bruce asked.

"Whoa," said Justin. "Did they get into a vehicle of some sort?"

Saara shook her head. "There are no roads there," she said with her musical Finnish emphasis on her English. "We've looked at the satellite footage."

Ted nodded. "I have too, and you're right. There are no roads in that part of the desert."

The President leaned forward. "There's one possible scenario."

Nobody said anything.

"As you know, I get all the CIA briefings, even though I'm out of office. Every President who has served gets the same thing. Usually, it's consistent with the types of briefings we dealt with when we were in office. But a few months ago, I started tracking some chatter regarding a person called The Lynx."

THE UNDERGROUND TRAIN had stopped for a short break. People were climbing down onto the dark tracks in groups of two, carefully watched by Laila, to relieve themselves. When they were all back in their places, the lady with the flashing black eyes and The Lynx went through the cars passing out sandwiches and drinks. Coach Murray recognized it as food from the plane.

After they'd finished eating, the train began to move, again. Howell estimated the break had taken about forty-five minutes.

WITH THE BROAD STROKES COVERED, Theodore Baker disconnected the video link, leaving LaunchPad and the group onboard the USS Bataan to figure out the details of their plan. "What do you think, Dad?"

"Leonard Stone is the best damn strategist alive. His son is one of the CIA's most elite operators, and he's built himself a hell of a crew." Baker paused to light up his cigar with cedar matches and then sat back, looking his son full in the face. "I remember reading reports about Boyd Carter that would make me thank God she was American." His eyes got a distant look in them as if remembering a story. Ted didn't interrupt. This was probably the most civil conversation he'd had with his father in twenty-five years.

"There were a few phone calls I received in the Oval Office that I will never forget. One was the time your mom called to let me hear the results of her cancer testing. That was the worst call. Another shocking one was on the day the Chief Justice of the Supreme Court was shot. That was a terrible day." He paused for a few seconds, "Then there was the day that the Prime Minister of Israel called and asked for help. It was another one I'll never forget."

"I didn't know the Israelis had asked you for help."

"It was a strict man-to-man conversation and completely off the record. One of their top Mossad agents was in trouble. As you know, the agents of the Israeli Intelligence Community are involved in collecting intel, performing covert ops, and countering terrorism. But they also help bring Jewish people back to Israel from nations in which they're no longer appreciated."

Whiskey lingered for a long draw on his cigar. "One of those nations is Argentina. Lots of ex-Nazis are hiding out there. Some places are still very dangerous for Jews. Anyway, I got that call. The Mossad chief said that one of their agents had been captured and was being held in some camp close to Villa Maio, just south of Bahía Blanca. I was surprised he'd called me. Like you said, those guys bleed blue and white and pride themselves on doing it all themselves. Israel first. So, this was different. I told him I'd see what we could do."

President Baker poured his son a drink and topped his off. "I made some calls. We saw that Agent Boyd Carter was down there, doing something for the Company. At that time, nobody had heard of her, but she'd come well-recommended, so we contacted her and relayed the situation. We asked her to scout out the territory and then meet the team we were sending to get the Mossad agent out of there. By the time the team arrived, a few hours later, the camp was cleared, and Carter was waiting with the Israeli for extraction."

"Wow!" Ted responded.

"By cleared, I mean that she had taken out eleven highly trained Argentinian operatives, bound up seven more and set fire to most of their buildings. She'd even taken the time to collect all the hard drives from their computers."

Baker's son was incredulous. "By herself?"

"In her debriefing, she went through exactly how she'd done it." President Baker watched his ash fall off the end of his cigar into his Venetian marble tray. "Genius. Pure genius. Plus, a hell of a lot of talent and skill."

Ted smirked. He'd heard his dad's lecture many times. *Talent* is what God gave you. *Skill* comes from a *hell of a lot of hard work and practice.* "So, what happened to that agent?"

"The Mossad guy? We put him on an Israeli freighter, and he eventually found his way home. It took its toll though. After that, Carter left the CIA and joined Delta Company."

"Because of all the deaths?"

"No. Because of the political fallout afterward. The Argentinean government was outraged that we hadn't briefed them about our plan and included them."

"Why didn't you call them?"

"They couldn't be trusted with knowing my age, never mind issues of national defense."

Ted knew the corruption among the top leaders in that area of the world was legendary. He'd seen it in the business world, too. It hadn't reached the level of Chinese duplicity, but it was well on its way.

"Dad, I think I should go to Libya."

"What the hell for? What on earth would you do there? Casey would be fatherless as soon as your feet touched the ground."

"But, I feel helpless." Ted stood up. "It's not a feeling I'm used to."

President Baker finished his cigar and placed the butt in his tray. "I've called all the parents."

"You what?!"

"I called all the parents."

Theodore looked away, irritated.

"It had to be me, Ted."

The younger Baker turned back to his father. "How'd they respond?"

"The Americans are flying in tonight."

"Flying in to where?"

"Here. To Telluride."

Ted thought about that for a moment. He realized that his blood was simmering but not boiling. In the past, he would have blown up! He would have been bitter and vindictive. Something was changing in him.

"What are you going to do with them?"

"We're going to video conference the German parents into everything. We'll give them all a complete NBS update. No Bull Shit." President Baker stood up and walked over to his panoramic cigar-room window that overlooked thousands of acres of forested Colorado mountains. "Then, we're going to load them all up and fly to Rome. I don't know where all this will go down, but Rome is less than three hours from almost anywhere over there. Secret Service has organized all the bookings at the Waldorf Astoria. I'll be recommending that all the German parents meet there too." He turned back to his son. "I think you and Helen should come along. You're much better at managing people then you are at covert ops, son."

Ted nodded, "Of course. So, who's paying for all of this?"

The President took a second to brace himself for his son's guaranteed explosion. He knew he would scream and yell like a three-year-old. George just hoped that in his rage, he wouldn't smash the Craig Nichols koa wood whale sculpture on his right. That thing was worth a small fortune besides being completely irreplaceable. He stared out the window before answering Ted's question quietly, "You are."

There was a moment of silence before Ted answered.

"Okay, dad. I guess that's only fair. You made the calls. I'll foot the bill." It came as a complete surprise. Father and son stood together now watching an elk herd meander through the meadows. "Is Boyd Carter still that dangerous?"

"From what I've heard, she's better than she ever was, son. Better than ever."

CHAPTER TWENTY-FIVE

JUN HAD AWAKENED, SO BORA WAS BRINGING HIM UP TO DATE ON a few things while he sat down to eat some waffles, scrambled eggs and fruit. She tried to spare the ugly details, knowing that Jun would want to read the black book himself, later.

"Okay, we have a lot of work to do," Leonard Stone reminded them all, pouring himself a cup of coffee and sitting down at the conference room table. "How's everybody doing energy-wise?"

"We're good at this end," Bruce responded, looking into the camera. "We've had five hours of sleep just before this meeting."

"Great. Then let's get started."

"Dad, before you do that, can you fill us in on Serwabi? I noticed you never mentioned him in our meeting with Whiskey."

"Fox? What were your impressions?" asked Leo. "You know him a little better than any of us."

The big blond agent leaned forward, "He's hard to read. Always has been. If we take what he told us at face value, the first time he met Jee Hye was at a club in Los Angeles. Then he ran into her a few other times, never as a client, but working on her as an asset. He flew to Cairo to be near her when she interacted with some important Arab leaders that were gathering there." Fox blushed slightly as Ashley placed a plate of fruit in front of him. Then he saw that she was serving everyone else, too. "Thank you," he mumbled. "One of those leaders was Sa'im Kashif Zafar – The Lynx. A few days later, Jee Hye decided to get all touristy and Serwabi purposefully crossed paths with her at the Sphynx and the Pyramids. She journaled about the meeting in a Pyramid and wrote that they'd gone down a long narrow passageway leading to the main tomb. On the way, apparently, they had a brief conversation. It was there she told Serwabi that she'd overheard a plan The Lynx was presenting to a few men in his suite."

"What had they talked about?" asked Michi.

"She didn't hear the whole thing, but she heard them mention Russians and Chinese. She distinctly heard a name that she recognized. Baker. Jee Hye wrote it in her journal with the impression something really big was going down involving President Baker."

"There's something else," Leonard said, putting down his coffee cup and picking up a pad of paper to look at some notes he'd been taking. "Serwabi said that The Lynx had taken over Gaddafi's smuggling operations. That he had beaten the Chinese and Russians."

"That makes sense," Bora added, pulling up her tablet. "When President Baker saw Howell's little dot move quickly and disappear, he guessed that they might've been hauled off on an underground train system of some sort. That would certainly be a smart way to traffic their goods. Maybe The Lynx took over that network if there actually is one."

"What do you think, Dr. Stone?" asked Michi.

Leonard looked at David and back at the camera. "It's a very real possibility. Although nobody in the West could ever prove it, there were lots of rumors coming from our Benghazi desk about a network of train tunnels that were facilitating a tidal wave of black-market products. Goods from the West came through Libya and went into the Middle East. Stuff from Africa went through Libya, too, and stuff from the East went through Turkey and across the Mediterranean into Libya. If the rumors are true, Gaddafi sat at the top of one of the most powerful food chains in the world."

Trey spoke up. "Getting back to Serwabi, why was he after Jee Hye's black book? How did he know about it?"

"He says she'd told him about it before they exited the Pyramid," answered Fox. "Serwabi claims that he didn't kill her but was trying to protect her."

"Do you believe him?" asked Bruce.

"We don't have any reason not to. He's a decorated Middle East Operative. I've heard of him before. Nothing bad," David answered.

Fox spoke again, "He says that the men in Koreatown, the guys at Walmart, and all the men I took out at the airport ... as well as the odd one that Carter took out, were all his men."

Boyd, sitting across from Fox, chuckled. "What Fox meant to say was, 'the many guys Boyd took out to save his tail ...'"

Trey and Bruce snickered. They often ribbed each other the same way.

Fox continued, "He wouldn't tell us what they do for him, what the mission is exactly ... or who sanctioned it. I don't know.

That's a lot of armed men to have under you. If he's telling the truth, I'll apologize for laying out his guys later."

"So, what have you done with him now?" wondered Bruce.

"I put a cot in the interrogation room," David replied. "We've secured him to his bed. Justin put an ankle bracelet on him. It lets us know where he is at all times – just in case he tries to get free. We're not treating him as a hostile, but we're not overly hospitable either. We can't afford to give him too much leeway until we figure all of this out."

"If he's lying?" Tank proposed.

"It would be because he's deeply involved," Leo finished.

"I agree. Listen to your gut."

"If anybody needs to excuse themselves to take a quick break, go ahead. We're going to keep right on going," David stated. "How are the kits for Trey's team, Justin?"

"Great. They're all ready."

"Who did you work with on our end?" Trey asked.

Saara answered, "We have a few Company guys on board over there."

"CIA? On the USS Bataan?" asked Michi, a little surprised.

"After 9/11, we put people on a few different ships. They appear to be military, but they're coordinating some black sites. I corresponded with some of them when I was undercover at the hospital in Amman. A few of them on the USS Bataan are actually Coast Guard, officially."

"Saara gave me their contact info and my specifications," Justin explained. "They worked with the Navy and the Marines on board to put together your kits. You'll have everything you'll need. They'll contact you when you're ready to go."

"Justin, you always amaze me," Boyd admitted, looking over at him. "Here I thought being married would distract you."

A few people giggled.

"He's very focused," Bora insisted, suddenly blushing after she said it.

Now they all had to laugh. "I'm sure he is," Bruce intoned, "very focused."

When they'd all simmered down, Leo took charge. "Saara had sent the plan to all of your tablets. So, pull it up while I summarize," he waited for a few seconds for them to access the right information. "Trey, Bruce, and Tank will land at 31.627125, 20.067760. That's just Southeast of Qaminis, exactly one mile from the plane's last known location due east."

"Roger that," Bruce answered.

"You're on your own from there. Go find them. Bring them all back. The Priority Objective in this mission is to recover Casey Baker. She's officially why we're involved. Of course, we want to get everyone else back. That's our Second Objective. Third and Fourth, we want to put down The Lynx and blow his operations to all to hell. Are we clear?"

"Copy that," replied Trey and the others.

"By the way," commented David, "If you do find a tunnel, either wire it up if you can and blast it to rubble as you're leaving or get the USS Bataan to bunker-bust it when you're safely out of harm's way."

"Copy that, wilco," Bruce replied.

"Michi and Jasmine, you'll be standing by." Leo waited for a moment and proceeded, looking directly into the camera. "Jazzy, I understand you don't want to be left on the ship."

Jasmine Stone nodded, sure she was going to be told what to do, like a little girl.

"I'm going to respect that. I hope I don't live to regret it. I'm not looking forward to seeing your mother and grandmother in a few hours to inform them of where you are."

"Thanks, Grandpa!" Jasmine exclaimed.

"Well, thank me in person a few days from now, okay?"

"I will," she said with determination.

"Alright. Michi, you and Jasmine need to be ready for whatever's next. We'll coordinate with you as we go. Justin prepared kits for the two of you, too. I want you to spend any downtime, reviewing protocols and equipment with Jasmine, so she'll know exactly what she has, and when and how to use it."

"Yes, sir," Michi answered. "Good idea."

"Fox and Boyd," he said, turning to face them. "You're going to Egypt. You'll be there in less than seven hours, using a Company jet. Unless new information comes while you're in the air, plan to start at the hotel in Cairo where Jee Hye had been, and follow up on the older male Arab guests that were there at the same time as The Lynx and Jee Hye." He looked at Justin, "Have you given them the wardrobe they'll need to move in high-money circles?"

"Yes, sir. I've got different types of wardrobes for everyone on the team. We started putting that together a few months ago. There are hijabs and burkas, as well."

Leonard Stone's countenance darkened, and his voice grew cold. "We're going in now to have another conversation with Mr. Serwabi. We are going to find every single one of those Arab leaders who raped Jee Hye and those children."

CHAPTER TWENTY-SIX

Leonard Stone looked at Fox. "Can you come with me to talk with Jun about something, please?"

"Sure," Fox replied, following Leo out of the conference room.

Saara headed over to the office section to work on coordinating the comms for the Libya team. She liked working there because she could have several computers going at the same time and make use of the large flat screens that were suspended from the ceiling. Finishing some notes on his note pad, Justin slipped out of the conference room to prepare kits for Fox and Boyd. Ashley went to check on Serwabi, so he'd be alert and ready for the next set of interrogations. Bora stayed in the conference room to pull the names out of Jee Hye's black book and send them to Jennifer Wu in Hong Kong. David Hirsch was the only other person in the conference room. He had just called *David's* to make sure that his cigar bar in Philly was still operating smoothly in his absence. It was. He had reliable management who'd been with him for decades. His next call was to a USMC contact he had on the USS Bataan. He wanted to go over the landing details for Trey's crew and make sure everything was covered. His personal Rolodex knew no bounds, and it seemed each contact had stories of how David had helped them out. He was well-loved, and everyone who knew him deeply appreciated the *get it done* attitude that kept him rolling when others would have gotten bogged down.

Finished with washing dishes, Jun was wondering what to do next, when Fox and Leo motioned for him to follow them into the smaller sitting room between the bedrooms at the far end of the warehouse. Fox opened the conversation.

"Jun, you remember Dr. Stone – I think you met last night."

"Of course," Jun responded. "Thank you so much for everything you've done."

"You're welcome. Please … have a seat," Leo said, motioning to one of the four wooden chairs sitting around a small round table. When they were all seated, Dr. Stone continued. "Jun, I don't know you very well. What were you doing for a living when you called Justin about Jee Hye?"

"I was working as a waiter during the day and a bartender at night."

"That's a lot of hard work. I don't mean to pry, but I'm going to get right to the point. How did you make ends meet? Did you survive, financially?"

"I got by month-to-month."

"I guess you've figured us out a little bit."

"Not quite, but it seems like you guys are with the NSA or CIA or something."

"We're none of that, really. We're just a group that's gotten together to work on some projects in various places around the world. In the process, we've gotten to become pretty close."

Jun waited for more details, but Leo wasn't going to give any.

"So, you worked in a restaurant and tended bar?"

"Yes, sir."

Leonard looked through the doorway at David Hirsch, who had moved to the kitchen table and was talking on his phone. "Did you know that guy over there, David, owns a cigar bar and restaurant in Philadelphia? It's an intriguing place."

"Really? He does? Intriguing, how?"

"It used to be an old courthouse, built in 1797. But in 1923 it was abandoned for some new facilities with the modern conveniences of the time, like indoor plumbing. When David bought it, he put a few years of blood, sweat, and tears into it and now it's been an icon for decades. If you want to be successful in the *city of brotherly love* and move any significant projects forward you need to know about *David's*. Government leaders roll through there, a couple of Philadelphia Eagles' players, the odd celebrity, a few mafia guys who may be sitting next to the Chief of Police … it's quite a crowd. I've seen two politicians who hated each other, meet for cigars and whiskey in *David's*. When they walked out, they'd gotten some deals done and shook hands."

"Wow."

"Have you been to college?"

"I've been working my way through a degree online."

"Good for you. In what field?"

"It's a Business Management degree."

Fox smiled to himself, knowing that Leo already knew all of these answers. Trey's dad would never have brought him to

LaunchPad had he not researched every single crevice of Jun's life. He knew that Dr. Stone was baiting and catching; the close was right around the corner. He wondered what the offer was going to be.

"You enjoy studying?"

"Yes, sir. I like it a lot. I'd been thinking about quitting my day job, so I could focus on my degree more."

"When were you planning to do that?"

"Just before all this happened." Jun was trying to push down his sadness. But Leo had noticed it.

Just then, Ashley popped her head around the corner of the door. Fox motioned her in.

"See Jun, I think you might need a break," Leo stated.

"Would you like to meet later today?"

Trey's dad smiled. "No. I mean you probably need a break in life. Could I lay out a scenario for you?"

Jun nodded, slightly confused.

"Son, you need to get out of Los Angeles. That's clear. There's nothing there for you, anyway. It could be, although we don't know yet, that the people who were after you there might still be looking for you. So, here's what I'd like to do for you."

Justin's cousin nodded.

"I have a friend who is willing to pay for some movers to get all your stuff out of your place in California and move it to Philadelphia. Philly's not far from here. About a two-hour drive, at the most. David has a nice house there, but nobody's living in it right now. So, he'd appreciate having someone to house-sit for a while. I've been thinking you'd be the perfect person."

Jun stared at him, dumbfounded.

Leo kept going, "You could live there rent-free for now, work on your degree during the day, and bartend at *David's* at night. I've already talked to Hirsch about it, and he's good with the plan if you are. He said he'd double whatever you were making in California. He'd also want you to drive his old Toyota 4x4 pickup. It needs to be driven, or it's going to fall apart."

Justin's cousin was speechless.

"I've been thinking about something else, too. When you were flying over here with Ashley, David and I came up with this plan for you. We talked to a few of the folks here and decided we're going to pay for that online degree."

This time, Jun couldn't stop the tears. They flowed freely down his face, and with them, the sorrows and fears he'd been struggling with for many years. Soon, his sobs became loud and uncontrollable. Ashley walked over to put her arms around him.

"I told you, you were running with a pretty good crew now, Jun," she whispered into his ear. "They actually care about you. We all do."

David walked in and quickly understood what had happened. He folded his arms and leaned against the doorframe, waiting for Jee Hye's brother to process the wave of emotions he was experiencing. Finally, Jun's sobs subsided. He looked up and saw Hirsch there.

"Is this really happening to me?" he asked. "I've never had a place to live in or a job where I wasn't busting my ass to make it all work financially. Nobody's ever cared about my life since my father died. And he was kind of a fraud."

"How old were you when that happened?" David asked.

"Thirteen."

"Come over here, kid."

Jun got up and went over.

"This is the key to my house," Leo's old friend said. "My day manager's name is Rocco. He'll meet you and give you instructions. You'll like him. He doesn't know about LaunchPad, so don't bring it up. But he's a good guy. He knows I travel a lot on business and also knows not to ask me questions about it. Take a few days off to get situated and then head over to my bar. He'll train you. You can start working at night whenever you're ready." He looked at Jun and then pulled him in for a long fatherly hug. "I don't know if Leo told you, but I've already gotten your stuff in California packed and shipped. It should get to my place in about ten days."

"I won't let you down, sir," Jun said, blinking away the tears. "I'll do my very best."

"What're you talking about? I'm the one who's not going to let you down," David responded.

"TELL ME ABOUT TANK," Trey asked Bruce when everyone else had left.

"He's a good guy. Doesn't have your sniper skills or Michi's field experience, but he's fine in hand-to-hand and good with a weapon. I tested him at eighty-five percent, the way that you and I have tested each other."

"Okay. Why did my dad put him on our team?"

"There're a few things that make him special. The first is his uncanny ability to track people. He's got an awareness that can't

215

be taught. It's inherited in his case, I guess. He just knows how to find people. It's stronger than intuition or a gut feeling. I've come to respect that spidey sense of his. I also contacted a few people I trust who have worked with him in the field. They each said something similar to *If he's tracking someone, depend on his call.*"

"That explains it. We'll likely need that. What else?"

"He's got Michi's ability to blend in unnoticed."

"I noticed him."

"You're exceptional, Trey. Most people don't have a photographic memory and years of top-level spycraft training. When you saw him was he ever looking at you?"

Trey thought for a few seconds. "No."

"Was he sticking out at all?"

"No."

"Was anyone looking at him?"

"No."

"Trust me. He blends in. And I'll tell you this. He can look Middle Eastern if he wants to – that can't hurt us, right?"

"True."

"Saara's been working to get him up to speed on how we're going to communicate in the field. He's been learning how our particular gadget-interfaces work. She pointed out that he's a really quick learner."

"Are we making the right call with my daughter?"

Bruce shrugged and shook his head. "I'm not a father, Trey. I don't know. I can tell you this, though. Whatever decision you make, think about the worst-case scenario. Could you live with it? Then think about the best-case scenario and ask yourself the same thing."

"That doesn't help me."

"Well, then, how about this? She's with us now. Can't do anything about that. Would you rather have her with Michiko Imada or waiting here on the boat with a bunch of lonely, bored squids?"

Trey rolled his eyes.

"Should I tell Michi to never let Jazzy out of her sight?" Bruce asked with a smirk.

"Thanks for adding to my stress."

"What are friends for?"

A HAND-SELECTED GROUP from the United States Marine Corps' 22nd Marine Expeditionary Unit aboard the USS Bataan was gathering in the mess hall. The 22nd MEU's full multi-mission force was commanded by a Marine Corps Colonel by the name of Mitchell T. Strobe. It included an Aviation Combat Element, the Marine Medium Tilt Rotor Squadron 263; a Logistics Combat Element, Combat Logistics Battalion 22; a Ground Combat Element, Battalion Landing Team, 2nd Battalion, 2nd Marine Regiment; and of course the Command Element. Everyone involved from top to bottom had been relentlessly and meticulously trained as only the U.S. Navy can do, to provide an immediate and effective response to any hostile environment or crisis.

"I just want to review this with you, Agent Stone."

Trey nodded, surprised that Col. Strobe himself was on the flight deck with the team. "Thank you, Colonel, sir. That's great."

"We were going to insert a team ahead of you to secure the LZ, but we've been ordered to slim down and keep ground troops to a minimum."

Trey recognized his dad's advice. Leo knew his son didn't like a large team – there were too many variables. He was the CIA's top sniper, after all, and was used to a very low profile.

"We'll chopper you in with the CIA's stealth aircraft, on loan from your Company, and drop you all off. Five Marines will watch your back while you take a look around."

"Thank you, sir," Trey said. "I thought our chopper can take nine people. Why five Marines and not six?"

"One of the seats was removed to carry some kind of drone, I guess. Your man, Justin, had it built to his exact specifications."

Trey smiled. "He knows what he's doing."

The Sikorsky UH-60 Blackhawk had lifted from where it was being stored and was coming around the side of the ship, getting ready to descend on the landing platform for pick-up.

The Colonel raised his voice to compensate for the noise. "Once you're at ground zero, I want a sitrep within the first fifteen minutes. Tell us how long you intend to remain on the ground and if there's anything you need from us."

"Roger that, Colonel. Thank you!" Trey hollered back, saluting Strobe.

Michi and Jasmine came running out on the flight deck. Trey's daughter threw her arms around him. "I love you, Dad. We'll see you soon, okay?"

Trey looked over Jasmine's head intensely at Michi. "You take care of her, okay?"

Tank grabbed Trey's elbow. "Come on, let's go!" Then he turned around. "Wait, where's Bruce?"

Just then Bruce Locke burst through the door, in full combat gear, shaking his head at Trey. He ran up and put his mouth close to Agent Stone's ear. "Your dad just called!" he shouted above the thumping of the rotary blades. "Change in plans! They've just picked up a new signal from Casey Baker's transponder!"

MILES HOWELL HAD FINALLY FALLEN asleep, emotionally, and physically depleted. Coach Murray was wide awake checking out the train car in the dim light. *How long had they been on this God-forsaken train?* Casey Baker was laying down on her side, sound asleep. Tossing fitfully, Shelly Brown was unable to find a comfortable position. Amber Taylor, next to her, was groaning and murmuring unintelligibly in her sleep. Most of the other girls were sleeping or dozing. He caught Mr. Jackson's eye and nodded encouragingly, but only got an angry scowl in return.

Murray turned his head a little further to see the gunman. He was sitting against the wall staring at Abril Fuentes in a way that sent chills of disgust down the coach's spine.

All at once, the brakes on the wheels started squealing as showers of sparks flew behind them lighting up the tunnel as they had before. The train started jerking to a slowdown. Most of the girls woke up, panicking.

"I'm so scared!" Murray heard a girl behind him.

Howell was fully awake now. "What's going on?"

"I don't know," Murray whispered. "We're slowing down."

Suddenly, the walls along the sides of the train disappeared and gave way to a large, flat, concrete platform. It extended for hundreds of feet on either side of the train, into the darkness.

The cars came to a jerky stop, and Laila stepped out from where she'd been, in the modified semi-truck. "We'll be here for several hours. If you need to go the restroom, you may go two at a time, over there," she pointed to a door that was barely visible in the wall to her left. "After that, I suggest you sleep. You'll need it."

The pilot, Sa'im Kashif Zafar – The Lynx, appeared beside her. Even in the dim light, they could see his sinister grin. "Laila and I will relieve the guards, so they can get rest. If any of you try to escape, we'll shoot you."

Casey Baker stood up. "I have to go to the restroom."

Laila jerked her head towards the wall door.

Whiskey's granddaughter stood up gingerly. Her muscles were sore, and her body dehydrated. She looked at Shelly. "Come with me," she whispered urgently.

The two girls stumbled out of the train and made their way to the giant cave's wall on their right. For a moment, Casey felt a breeze on her face and looked up. She couldn't really tell, but it seemed like this cave was different, somehow.

CHAPTER TWENTY-SEVEN

PRESIDENT BAKER'S SPRAWLING THOUSAND-ACRE ESTATE IN THE Colorado Rockies could only be described as awe-inspiring. It included four guest homes in addition to the main house – all anchored on a wooded hillside overlooking a pristine private mountain lake that was surrounded by a breath-taking vista of peaks. Some visitors would drive up a twelve-mile winding gravel switchback road lined with pines and aspens. Passing through all the extensive forestry, they'd reach the pass into the valley and be struck by the raw beauty of sheer granite cliffs opening into sprawling meadows. Most visitors though flew in via helicopter to land on one of three helipads located in a secluded glade near the lake. The main building's bold exterior of natural gray stone and oak columns was exceptionally well-designed. Somehow the whole place communicated stability and peace.

Ted now understood why his father had concluded he was the only person who could call together the parents. The meeting was full of chaotic fury, wild accusations, and panicky hysterics from a cluster of very wealthy and entitled individuals used to getting their way who naturally thought that money could solve everything. Only his father had the skill and stature that was needed in this situation, obtained during his time as the alpha male in Washington DC's most iconic residence. He calmly weathered the storm and managed, in the end, to bring order to the meeting and instill some sense of trust.

With all the parents duly informed, the Germans disengaged from the video call to be read into what was next on their end. Ted took over in Telluride. "I've chartered four private jets to take us to Rome. As you heard, when the President called you, we've booked forty rooms and suites at the Waldorf for us as well as the German parents. We will cover all the costs of your transportation and accommodations. You, or your insurance companies, will be responsible for any other expenses incurred. If your missing daughter has siblings that you want to take along to Rome, we'll pay their airfare and hotel as well. If there is anyone else you wish to bring who is not part of your immediate family, we ask that you cover that cost yourself. This includes nannies, butlers, physical trainers, personal assistants, and anyone else you might need during this time." He looked down at his notes. "We're already setting up a comms room that will be in live 24-hour contact with the Secret Service. They will keep us fully abreast of everything going on in real-time. The room will be open twenty-four hours a day. There will also be a team of crisis counselors there. Any time you have a question or an idea, or you just need someone to talk to please know, the people in that room are there for you."

The group filed out of where they'd been meeting to make their preparations for the trip to Rome as quickly as possible. All, except for one. Monica Brown, Shelly's mother. She stayed in her seat, unmoving. Ted's wife nodded at him, as he and the President slipped out of the room.

Helen Baker had been in the fashion industry since childhood. She'd been a runway model for an astounding twenty years, after which she'd started her own clothing line, famous for its redesign of women's coats. Her beauty was of the sort that never faded, rather, like a fine wine, it only improved with age. Tall, slim, and gracious, she could stun on the red carpet, yet be warmly personal and approachable in private. She put her long blond hair up in a quick bun and walked over to sit beside Shelly's mom.

"It's a lot to take in, I know," she said, gently.

Monica nodded. "I'm so scared."

"Of what could happen to Shelly?"

"You know her name?"

"Of course, I do," Ted's wife said. "I've been praying for all of our girls even before this started happening."

"What scares me the most is ..."

Helen put her hand on Monica's. "Honey, I understand. Could I show you something?" She looked at the doorway. One of the president's Secret Service detail had a manila folder in his hand. She nodded for him to approach.

Handing it to her, he said, "Here you go, ma'am."

"Thank you," Helen replied. She turned to Monica, "We've looked into how we could somehow help you during this time, Monica. You've been working three jobs to provide for your daughter, haven't you?"

"Everything's just so expensive. It hasn't been easy. But I'm not one to complain. She's worth it, you know. I hope you get to meet her. She's a wonderful girl. I'm so proud of her. You know? She just amazes me all the time at how open-hearted she is and how free of bitterness she is. I don't think she's even capable of holding a grudge. She's that good-natured." She looked down at her hands in her lap. "All I've wanted was for her to have a different life from mine."

Helen withdrew her hand from Monica's and opened the folder. "We've contacted your employers to explain that you'd be gone for a while. Two of them weren't very understanding, and I'm afraid they don't want to keep your position open for you. The third, your broker-in-charge in the real estate office, was really great. We couldn't go into detail, of course, but he guaranteed that you would always have a desk waiting for you there. We looked into your financials and made a list of all your bills and debts. Does this look like we've covered everything?"

Shelly's mom was stunned. She looked it over and nodded. "I'm sorry you had to see how much credit card debt I have. There've been so many unexpected expenses – especially this whole tournament. I didn't want to tell anyone that I couldn't afford to let her go to Botswana. We raised almost half of it with car washes, babysitting and cleaning houses on my day off, but ..."

"Listen, Monica. I don't want you to feel awkward about this. We just want to help, and we don't want you to have to deal with any of this other stuff at this time. I've made arrangements to pay off your credit cards and loans, and we've paid your rent and other monthlies ahead for the next three months. Honestly, hon, it's the very least we can do, and we're very glad to do it."

Monica Brown was done in. She started sobbing.

Helen was tearing up, too. "Honey, it's been a hard road for you. But do you know that your daughter is my daughter's favorite person in all the world?"

Shelly's mom shook her head and started to tremble uncontrollably.

"It's true. My daughter said that your daughter is authentic, dependable, and friendly to everyone. Those are great compliments, coming from a teenager, especially from my girl, trust me."

Surprised, Monica wiped away her tears with the back of her hands. "Really? She said that?"

Helen nodded. "So, let's get you to Rome, okay? You ride with us. I know you didn't come prepared for all this but just don't worry about any of it. I need to get your sizes, and I'll make some calls on the way there so that we can have things waiting for us in Italy. I'm doing the same for myself. I didn't have time to pack." She smiled genuinely, "If I'm already buying clothes for myself, it's absolutely no trouble at all to get some for you, too!"

"Oh my gosh. Oh really. I just don't even know what to say." Monica said, standing up, and straightening out her slacks.

"Oh, one more thing. Here are three thousand Euros for the expenses over there. If you need more, please let me know."

"That's way too much."

"Don't be shy about asking me if you need more. I insist."

"COLONEL, COULD YOU FOLLOW ME PLEASE?" Trey shouted, tugging at Strobe's elbow and throwing him a salute when he turned. Stone, Bruce, and the highest-ranking Marine on the ship slipped inside a steel hallway and closed the door on the noise from the flight deck.

Bruce handed Trey the phone. "I've already heard his idea. In my opinion, it's the right call, but you need to decide."

Trey put it on speakerphone so that the Colonel could hear it too.

"I'm guessing this is you, Dad. You're on speaker with Bruce and Colonel Strobe."

"Trey," Leonard answered. "You're right. It's me. You're on speakerphone here, too. Justin, David, and Saara are with me."

"Copy that."

"Son, Shelly Baker's transponder indicates they've stopped a little less than four miles from the Egyptian border."

Trey's heart dropped. Going into Libya was one thing. It would be like a shootout in the old Wild West. If they were compromised, he wouldn't be too worried about the implications in the United States or on the world stage. But Egypt was another story. The diplomatic community would be outraged, the United Nations would have seizures of allergic reactions, the entire Arab world would be foaming at the mouth in outrage at any covert interference by the U.S. in their region. Trey already knew the answer but asked anyway.

"Are you sending Boyd and Fox over there?"

"Negative. They wouldn't get there in time."

"What are you suggesting."

"Send Michi and Jasmine on their own to investigate the plane. You, Bruce and Tank go to the Egyptian border."

"Jazzy stays with me."

"Trey, it's important to find out where the plane landed, but the real action will be at the border. It's not a good idea for my grand-daughter to be there. You know, Jasmine will be safe with Michi."

Trey looked at Bruce. He was nodding.

"Sir, if I may?" Colonel Strobe asked.

"Go ahead,"

"My team will be landing with your daughter and Agent Imada. I know Michi is well-trained. But she'll also have some great people at her side. My best. We won't let anything happen to either of them."

Trey's mind was made up. He looked at Bruce as he said, "Okay, Dad. I need to pursue our primary objective. Bruce and Tank will go with me. Jazzy goes with Michi."

The team at LaunchPad were agreeing.

"Okay," David said, relieved that Trey was entrusting Jasmine to someone other than himself. It wasn't just a healthy step, but it was also critical to the success of the mission.

"Trey," Saara added, "I'll send you the coordinates for Casey's transponder. I don't know how much battery power she has left, but if she signals again, you'll all see it on your smartwatches. The face will light up red. The coordinates will be scrolling at the bottom. If you're on comms, I'll also verbally confirm that you received the alert."

"Roger that. Thank you, everyone."

"Good luck, Son," Leo said, before hanging up.

"Colonel," Trey said, turning to Strobe. "We'll need to get a team of three to the coordinates Saara's sending me."

"No problem, Agent Stone. Whatever you need."

The three men stepped back out on the flight deck. Trey pulled his daughter aside for an intense conversation followed by a long hug. Bruce went over to Michi and explained what was going on.

CHAPTER TWENTY-EIGHT

FOR A FEW MOMENTS, THE CONFERENCE ROOM WAS SILENT.

"They'll be okay, Leonard," David said, reaching over and putting his hand on his old friend's shoulder.

"I thought my grandson would be okay, too. But ... he's dead."

"He didn't have the USS Bataan off the coast."

"No. No, he didn't." Leo stood up. "I'm sorry everybody. That was tough. I'll take a break."

"Of course," Saara said. "If something comes up, we'll find you."

Leo headed for the door and then stopped. He turned around, "Fox and I were going to question Serwabi. Can you do it, David?"

Hirsch nodded, standing up. "Of course. Go get some rest."

Trey's dad left the room and slowly made his way to his sleeping quarters.

"I was just checking the kits for Trey's team, Michi and Jasmine," Justin announced. "If you don't mind, I'm going to slip out and call our contact on the USS Bataan. With the change in plans, there are a few adjustments I'd like to make."

"Go ahead," Saara said. "I'm updating their security protocols. Then I am going to see if there are any nearby UAVs or other systems we can secure for tactical overwatch."

"Great idea," Justin replied, following David out of the room. "Boyd, can you come with me to look things over?"

"Of course," Boyd answered. Even though she was almost a decade older than Justin, she had gained tremendous respect for him during the Stone family rescue mission. He'd surprised her with his uncanny ability to know exactly what each kit should contain. It was like he was able to project himself ahead of the action, anticipate each operative's unique abilities, and assess the situations they'd find themselves in.

Bora was sitting alone in the office area. She'd just sent off the names from Jee Hye's black book to Jennifer Wu in Hong Kong. Ashley came over and sat down beside her.

"Is Serwabi ready for us?" Fox asked, walking up.

"He's awake and ready," Ashley answered, smiling. "I just checked on him."

"Great, thanks."

David turned to Fox as they walked off. "You know she likes you."

"Yeah. We're taking it slow."

"We or you?"

Fox shrugged.

"Because you need to take the lead."

Fox suddenly felt like he was being schooled by his father.

David stopped to look up at him, "Fox, do you want to ask me something?"

The large agent was completely caught off guard.

"Let me tell you something, big guy. Ashley is beautiful. She's a smart girl. A very talented surgeon. But in her heart … you know … she has lots of love to give, and she needs to be loved. If you don't make a move, someone else will."

"Who?"

"Nobody here, but she has a life outside of LaunchPad, you know."

Fox was facing David but looked back at Ashley. "You think she's ready? She seems unsure. Maybe getting over her fiancé's death is still something she needs to keep working through."

"You're totally misreading her hesitation, kid. She's unsure because you seem unsure. It's up to you to show her that she's ready."

Fox thought about that for a few seconds. "I guess I needed your advice to help me think that through."

"You needed someone who loves her to help you think that through."

Fox smiled. "David, I really do want to get serious when this is all done. Is that okay with you?"

"My man!" exclaimed Hirsch. "Greenlight on Operation Ashley." Then he smiled and kept walking. "You've got my blessing, Kurt Middleton-Fox. Now let's get this Serwabi-guy to spill his guts. Hopefully, not literally."

Fox nodded but needed to bring closure to their conversation. "David?"

Hirsch stopped.

"Before we go in there, I just wanted to say, *thanks!*"

"You are welcome. Whatever else happens on this mission, your objective is to stay alive, okay?"

"Roger. Wilco."

THE SIKORSKY UH-60 Blackhawk had been gone for forty-five minutes. Trey, Bruce, and Tank couldn't afford to think about it. They were methodically prepping for a landing by the Egyptian border in twenty minutes.

"I'm looking over this kit-list from Justin," Tank said as he checked his gear. "He's great! I have a note here to let you guys know that I've got the emergency survival pack."

Trey nodded, suiting up in body armor and checking the batteries in his sniper scopes. "Copy that."

"I've got a note here to let you both know I've got the DON vision system," Bruce reported, as he checked it out and tested the power. "This one is fantastic. It combines visual data with infrared and feeds from the UAV's overhead – super helpful. Also, Saara messaged me that she found an Israeli class III drone for overwatch."

"That's great news," Trey said as he checked to make sure all his mags were loaded. "Has anyone heard how we're going to get there?"

"It's going to be a combination of things. Another chopper and then a Jeep."

"Seriously?" Tank asked, surprised.

"That's what they said. They're going to throw us into a Chinook that they've modified with full authority digital engine control. We'll have to do a mid-air refuel, but it'll take us within ten miles of our target. Then they'll drop us off with a special Jeep."

"I'll ask the obvious question," Trey said grinning. "What's special about it?"

"It's bulletproof, mostly. So, with the added weight, it only gets fifteen miles to the gallon. But they've built in two extra fuel tanks, so we'll be fine. Tires are solid-state, so we won't get any flats. It's painted with stealth technology and loaded with comms, but the most beautiful part is the Wolfe technology."

Tank turned around. "Really? It has Wolfe?"

Bruce nodded.

"Awesome," agreed Trey.

"That's okay, Trey. It just came out. Wouldn't really be something you'd have stayed on top of," his friend smirked, "I don't think it was even on your Sniper Magazine app."

Tank chuckled. "It turns out there is something you don't know, huh Agent Stone?"

Trey retorted, "Well, if it wasn't on my app, then I probably wouldn't need it."

"You'll love this, actually," Tank resumed, excitedly. "Peter Heinrich Wolfe invented a guidance system that can lead us in real-time, across any terrain and consider all the mitigating factors."

He had Trey's immediate attention. "Say, for example, that we have this Jeep, so we enter all the pertinent information – our total weight, wheel type, engine specs, and anything else the Jeep might be outfitted with. Then, we enter where we are and where we need to go. This technology leads us, identifies threats, takes us on the fastest route, and even provides thermal imaging data."

Trey looked impressed after all.

"So basically," Bruce stated, "it will take us over brooks, through forests, on roads sometimes, and eventually, to the exact target coordinates on the fastest and safest route."

"But …" Agent Stone said.

"But what?"

"I'm just waiting for the *but*. There's always a downside."

"Well, sometimes inclement weather can affect it."

"And …"

Tank sighed. "And … I guess … if somebody was really good … they could intercept our signal and track us … or even worse – they could guide us to the wrong place."

"Almost impossible, though. Someone would have to know exactly what we're doing and where we are," Bruce added defensively.

The wheels were spinning in Trey's head. He turned to Tank and said, "Get in touch with Saara and let her know that we're going to use the Thermal Dynamic Real-Time Wolfe Anatomy Tracking System 4.0."

Bruce and Tank both spun around in surprise.

Agent Stone grinned, "You can't add the wheel-type in 3.0, right?"

Tank rolled his eyes.

"Had you guys fooled, didn't I?" Trey said, chuckling. "It wasn't in my sniper app, but I'd read about it a few weeks ago. You forget that I've been in hiding for months and bored out of my mind. Saara hooked up limited internet access behind a web of firewalls and VPNs. I took full advantage to stay current."

Bruce shook his head, "You always amaze me, my friend."

"What did you want me to tell Saara?" Tank asked Trey.

"I think you guys nailed the weaknesses; those are the same things I wondered about when I was reading the article. Ask Saara to piggyback a counter-hacking program onto the Wolfe software. We need to know right away if someone is snooping. Also, see if that drone she's getting can provide some kind of backup in case we do run into bad weather. Maybe, if she uses our target coordinates, she can set climatological parameters and design an automated decision aid."

"Copy that," Tank responded. His respect for Agent Stone, as well as for Saara Tuuri, mushroomed.

SERWABI WAS SECURELY, but not uncomfortably, chained to his cot. The carbon steel links were long enough for him to lay down or sit at the table in the room. He started whining the moment David and Fox entered. "I'm going to sue you if you don't release me immediately."

David smiled, "I'll put that in my report to POTUS. I'll put it right next to the part where you told us it was your men in the alley with Jee Hye chasing Jun with loaded guns and that your people brought illegal weapons into BWI. All those reports will look really nice together."

Serwabi glared at Hirsch. "I don't think I know who you are."

"I'm that guy who makes things disappear. The whole Walmart thing? Never happened. Video footage? What video footage? For reasons of national security. Although, of course, we kept a full and very complete version of everything for our own archives. Your guys will probably take a little vacation to Cuba – except for the ones who are still lying in hospitals trying to live. People with lots of questions will sit them into a wet, dark cell in Guantanamo, to get some answers from them. And we've got really nice footage of you at Walmart. You look pretty directly involved. In charge, actually."

"So, you're a cleaner."

"Sometimes I clean things up, other times I make them messier. But one thing's for sure. I never get snowed. You know what I mean?"

"Not really."

"I can spot a liar as well as anyone on this planet," David said, sitting down. "Better than most in fact. And you're a pretty good one, liar that is. But you know, something you said, made me laugh. I've watched your tape. Let's see here," he said, looking down at his tablet while Fox closed the door behind him and stood against the wall staring intensely at Serwabi. Hirsch tapped the *play* icon and faced the tablet so Serwabi could see it.

The MEO watched himself talking to Leo and Fox earlier, saying, "The reason we got away with the gold and didn't get blown out of the sky by the Russians and the Chinese was that they were interested in something even more lucrative. A nation like ours wasn't willing to go after it. Not then, anyway."

David tapped the icon to pause the video. "That was good, right? The Russians ... the Chinese ..." He touched the screen again, and it kept playing Serwabi's statement.

"The Russians and the Chinese only cared about Gaddafi's smuggling enterprise: children, drugs, women, weapons, and money from around the world, more than any other individual enterprise on the planet. They wanted to take Gaddafi's place as the Emperor of Grand Central Station."

David turned the tablet off. He just stared at Serwabi, as if waiting for the punchline from a joke.

Finally, the MEO broke the silence. "You think I'm lying?"

Hirsch reached back and gave the tablet to Fox. "The Russians?" Leo's old friend said, his eyebrows arched in mockery. "The Chinese." He leaned over the table, and his look changed to ice. "You're talking about one and a half billion people. Stop playing us like idiots. The Lynx didn't beat out a quarter of our globe's population. He beat out a few individuals."

Serwabi's face had a definite scowl, now.

David's face turned to ice, "I want those names, Mohammad Al Serwabi," he growled, his gravelly voice slightly louder than a whisper. "Which Chinese? Which Russians? Who, specifically?"

The Middle East Operative's face paled. He feebly attempted to play his only card in the game.

"Did my son make it?"

David completely ignored him and sat back in his chair. "Let me tell you what I think," he said, biting his lower lip as if he were thinking deeply. "I think that you were a diligent operator overseas for the United States Military. Fox here, remembers you. Don't know if you remember him."

"I do."

"Well, that's nice. So, you both have fond memories of each other," David said, faking a big smile. "But after leaving the desert and getting back to the United States, you were faced with a decision that a lot of people in these positions face. *Should you stay in the military? Should you retire and start a consulting company? Maybe you should go into private defense work.* Then Sam Walker came along."

Serwabi showed surprise. "You know Mr. Walker?"

Leonard Stone had actually trained the legendary recruiter for the CIA, but Hirsch didn't tell the MEO that, he just kept going. "I know everybody, Serwabi. But here's the thing." David sat forward, "Someone else recruited you too, right? I'll bet it was Abdullah Abdallah Whatever-the-hell-his-name-is. He recruited you to the dark side, didn't he? I think you've walked a very thin line … and pretty successfully, too. But I'm sure you had your moments. Confusion. That happens sometimes. You don't know where your real loyalties would lie if you'd have to choose." David leaned in closer. "Then … a gorgeous, barely legal, or was she even legal at the time? Maybe not. We'll find out. But this beautiful Korean-American girl threatened to upset your tightrope. She wasn't just attractive, she was dangerously smart. The kind of smarts that can cause problems for people like you. She was that rare blend of book-smarts and street-smarts. Jee Hye wasn't some crackhead dimwit. She worked for her abusive clients, sure, but she kept detailed records – and those records have something in them that threatened to expose you."

David leaned back now, reading every single micro-expression in the face across from him. "You know what, Serwabi? Eventually, we'll find out what that is. You're right to be scared. Let me tell you something. The fact that you cared more about her little black book than saving Jee Hye's life is what guides us now. I don't give a damn if you yourself pulled the trigger or not, and I think you did. Her blood is on your hands. Your men weren't trying to protect her that night in the alley. You needed that little black book."

Sweat was popping out of the MEO's forehead.

Fox stepped forward and braced his arms on the table while still standing.

"If you're not who you've said you are. Well, today is your Titanic. You've already hit the iceberg and now you are starting to sink." David stood slowly. "You can't stop it. It's happening. This is your meltdown, your fiasco, your personal disaster. You know those nights of fear when you tossed and turned all night because you couldn't fight that thought? *What if it all starts coming down? Where will the hit come from?*" David's rage was focused and real. "We're that nightmare you knew was coming. You've had one foot on the dock and one foot in a slow-moving boat. And the water that you see as you realize you're spreading too far? It's not water. It's red hot lava. And you're about to fall into it."

Serwabi wasn't as shaken as David thought he would be. It ticked Leo's friend off. Abruptly he stood, opened the door, and walked out. Fox was right behind him.

"What about my son?" the MEO screamed, as the door slammed.

David marched straight to the smaller lounge area, motioning for Fox to follow. Bora and Ashley just stared. They'd never seen Hirsch this angry, before.

Fox sat down in a lounge chair, while David plopped into a couch right across from him.

"I've got to calm down," David admitted quietly.

Fox chuckled. "Not in that interrogation room, you don't. That was fantastic."

"I'm not so sure."

"Why not?"

"He should've been more nervous."

"He was sweating."

"So was I. He's confident."

"In what?" asked Fox.

"I'm not sure. Either he's covered by higher-ups inside the Beltway, or he's got something else going on that we haven't connected yet."

"One thing's for sure. He really is after that black book." Fox arched his eybrows. "Why didn't you press him for those names? Shouldn't we just hammer away at him or employ intensive methods to get him to talk?"

"We could. But he's very good. It's rare to meet someone like him. He's an ace. If he does have friends in high places, we have to tread very carefully. Right now, we need to let fear do its work. Either way, he only needs one thing to start talking."

"A way out?"

"Exactly. We'll give him one. We're not like our enemy, Fox. We won't kill his children. We won't burn down his home and slaughter his relatives like these traffickers did to Trey's family and many others. We'll give him one chance to do the right thing. If he really is the person I think he is, he'll cough up those names or declassify whatever he needs to. But, if he's not that guy," David paused, "if he's a guy who loves darkness rather than light, we'll send him to the abyss where he can greet the devil he's been serving in person."

CHAPTER TWENTY-NINE

THE CIA BLACKHAWK COULD BARELY BE SEEN AGAINST THE starry, moonless, night sky. It nestled down surrounded by desert sand dunes near the coordinates of where the private plane had landed. The Marines exited first, setting up a safe perimeter. They motioned for Jasmine and Michi to follow them. As they fanned out to explore, the back-cargo door of the large black helicopter opened and a sizeable wooden crate slid out on a dolly with large tires at each corner. One of the pilots hopped out to place Justin's drone on top. Then he climbed back into the Blackhawk and closed it up.

"Returning to safe zone."

"Copy that," acknowledged a Marine on the ground.

The Sikorsky lifted up, hesitated and then leaned to the right as it left the area. In just a few minutes, the place was dead quiet. The team crept through the sand, looking for evidence of something man-made.

At last, one of the Marines said, "Ma'am, I've got something."

Michi looked over and saw a flashing green pencil light. She hurried over to the spot and muffled her shock. The sand dune closest to the Marine was covered in sand, but when she touched it, the surface was hard as granite.

"What is it?"

The Marine led her around the large hill, to the back. A giant sand-covered warehouse door was cleverly hidden under a large canopy, concealed in sand and completely invisible to the satellites. "This is the entrance," he pointed out.

"It's genius," Michi had to admit. "Can we break in?"

"I wouldn't, ma'am. It could trigger an alarm. We'll get a Sawzall and cut into the door, but we'll sweep the structure, first."

"Okay," Michi said, watching a few Marines pull out their gadgets to get to work.

Jasmine was setting up comms and running a test link with Saara, back at LaunchPad.

"Jazz to Saara, how copy?"

"We've got both of you five by five on audio," the Finnish tech-guru confirmed. "But negative on visual; have you hooked up your helmet cams?"

"We have," Jasmine answered.

"Okay, then. And they're powered on?"

"Yes. They have a flashing green light."

"That means the problem is at my end," Saara said. "Hold on just a minute."

One of the Marines approached Michi, "Ma'am, there's no evidence of an alarm system on the door. However, we're picking up indications of a video camera inside. It's not transmitting anything, so our tech says it's passive. My thinking is that it's probably aimed at this door and continuously recording. Every few hours, it probably erases the footage and starts recording again, or it could be downloading the recorded data to a hard-wired drive."

"So, you don't think someone's watching in real-time."

"Correct."

Agent Imada thought for a minute and then said, "Cut two panels. One hole that's small enough for me to crawl through. It's so dark that it will barely be noticeable if I cover the camera for a few minutes. That's better than blinding it with a laser. On the left side of the door, we'll cut a large panel big enough for all the others to slip in with their gear and that crate," she said, pointing to the large box on wheels. "As soon as we're in, the team outside can replace the panels, and I'll uncover the camera. It needs to happen in less than thirty seconds."

"Yes, ma'am. Stay here with Jasmine and give us a few minutes. We'll get everything ready."

"Great," she said, giving the Marine a short bow.

He left her to let the others know the plan.

"Jasmine, can you reboot your cameras?" Saara asked.

"Okay," Trey's daughter answered, unsure of how to correctly answer in military-speak. She reached over and snapped Michi's camera off of its clip, rebooted it and replaced it. Then she did the same with hers.

Justin had arranged for their kits to be in a black duffle bag that could also be used as a backpack if needed. The compartments inside didn't allow things to slide around if the bag went vertical. Trey's daughter shouldered her backpack and knelt down, ready for whatever was next. The Marines had already screwed handles to the outside of the large door where the panels were going to be created, making it easy to pick them up, move them to the side, and then set them back into place when the teams and equipment had passed through.

A pair of Marines pulled the small panel off, and Michi slipped inside. They quickly replaced the board. She crept to the right and squatted down to touch her right temple and activate her night-vision goggles. Twenty feet in front of her was the tail of the Boeing Business Jet BBJ 737-800. Her heart started pounding. They'd solved the mystery of the disappearing plane!

Moving slowly, she looked around and spotted the video camera on the right side of the wall, above her head. One of the Marines had given her a black tee, and she carefully threw it over the camera.

"Jazzy, you're clear."

"Okay, copy," answered Trey's daughter, excitedly.

The Force Recon Marines pulled off the large panel on the left side of the door. Two of them came inside and squatted down, searching for hostiles, weapons ready. Then, they waved in the large wooden crate, Jasmine, and two more Marines. With everyone inside, they scurried to the nose of the plane, out of the view of the camera. The panel was quickly replaced, and Michi cautiously pulled the shirt down, off the camera. She moved along the right wall to join the others under the nose.

"We've got eyes on the bird," she whispered. The cheers she could hear from back at LaunchPad brought a grin to her face. Michi tapped the Marine closest to her. "Let's check out the plane. The rest of you prepare the gear."

"Copy that."

As they entered the business jet, Michi almost threw up. The stench was completely unexpected.

"I smell a body," she notified the LaunchPad crew.

"Be careful, Michi," Leo cautioned. He'd been awakened again for the moment.

Saara came on comms, sounding relieved. "The reboot worked. We've got visuals now."

"Copy that," Michi answered. "Good timing."

The Force Recon Marine went to his left and checked the cockpit. "We have a dead pilot," he announced.

Michi waited for him to return to the cabin, then broke right. He went left. They slowly advanced up the aisles. Suddenly Agent Imada recoiled in horror. She was staring at another corpse; this one was horribly disfigured with a face that was unrecognizable because of the gunshot wound. "I have another body," she said. "It looks like a security detail." She wrinkled her nose and reached down to take his wrist. Removing her head cam with her other hand, she pointed it at the victim's fingers, holding them completely still.

"Thanks. We got the snapshot and can clean it up a bit," Saara confirmed. "It's good enough for prints."

"Copy that," Michi answered, letting the arm fall to the ground and reattaching her camera onto her helmet.

The two continued down their respective aisles.

"Do you see all of this?" she asked, looking at the hanging oxygen masks, torn seats, and scattered debris.

"Yes," Leo answered. "Both your camera and Jasmine's are on our flat screens in the office, and we were able to brighten up the resolution. I don't think I've ever seen an interior of a plane so destroyed. It must have been a terrifying ordeal, whatever happened."

"Two more bodies, ma'am," the Marine announced.

Agent Imada took pictures of their faces and fingers; she was sure they were the two German guards.

Michi and the Marine agreed that the plane was clear. They exited back down the stairs and were relieved to get into fresher air, even if it was in the warehouse.

"That plane was cursed," Michi muttered.

"Ma'am, this way."

Agent Imada followed the Marine to the back of the warehouse where a door to a large freight elevator was being held open. It was loaded with the team, the wooden crate, and the drone. Jasmine stood outside, waiting for Michi to confirm getting on.

"Where does this go?" Imada asked.

"Pretty far down, ma'am," answered a Marine from the back of the elevator. "It leads to the railroad tracks, alright. But ... it's kind of creepy, to be honest. A few of us cleared the area while you were on the plane."

Michi nodded, following Jasmine onto the large elevator. "LP, we're going to decend into the tunnel system. I'm sure we'll lose comms when we start moving through it and I'm not sure what or who we'll run into. I'm initiating go EMCON until we go clear."

Saara understood the need for communications silence. "Copy that. We'll be standing by."

The freight elevator began to descend, rattling and clanking loudly. Jasmine couldn't decide which was freakier, the sudden noises it was making or the creepy echoes off the limestone and quartz walls.

CHAPTER THIRTY

JENNIFER WU OFFICED IN HONG KONG AND WAS HIP, SOLICITOUS, brainy, and communicative. She had a broad endearing smile and a strong British accent which is why Trey called her Asian Lara Croft. Known for an uncanny ability to follow money trails, Jennifer was highly paid by HSBC Bank but still seemed to find time in her busy schedule to help friends. Her sister had dated one of Trey's best buddies from college, but their calamitous break-up hadn't strained the relationship too badly for Jennifer and Trey. If there was one thing that did sometimes irk Agent Stone, it was the inevitable imprint of arrogance the Ivy League had left on her personality. That aside, she was definitely good at what she did.

Bora and Ashley were eating a light lunch when Jennifer called. Saara, Boyd, and Justin were in their respective rooms, sleeping, but Leo was available and went to fetch David and Fox. Jun joined them in the conference room, and they called Ms. Wu back on video.

"Jennifer, thanks so much for doing this," Leo said, getting the conversation going.

"You're welcome, Dr. Stone."

"I think you know David, Fox, and Ashley. This is Jun. Have you met Bora? She's the one who contacted you and sent you the list of names. Bora just got married to Justin."

"That's right! Justin's married now," Wu exclaimed, flashing a genuine smile. "Congratulations, Bora."

"Thank you," the new wife replied happily.

"What do you have for us, Jennifer?" asked David.

"The names you sent were remarkable," Wu responded. "It was like reading a Who's Who of Arab high society. From the royal family in Saudi Arabia, all the way to heads of Islamic crime syndicates. I'm sending the complete report of what I found to Saara, but I'll just highlight two important ones." She took a moment to bring up a photo onto her screen. "This is Fawwaz Ahmaadi." Then she paused to bring another picture up beside the first one. "And this is Ghalib Ahmaadi."

"Same guy?" asked Ashley.

"Identical twins."

Leo studied their faces. They were dressed in tailor-made suits, had neatly cropped hair with full black beards. But their eyes caught his attention. They were as black as polished onyx and flashed a projection of implacable superiority. Something about them seemed familiar.

"You may recognize Fawwaz. He owns a football franchise in England and is worth hundreds of millions of pounds."

"I did recognize him," Trey's dad acknowledged, glad she'd triggered his memory. "There's a story about his background if I remember correctly."

"Impressive, Dr. Stone. You're right. They're actually Palestinian born. The brothers were separated at birth to save them from Jewish oppression. Fawwaz grew up in England and Ghalib in Russia. But they reunited at Oxford and have worked together since."

Both Leonard and David brushed aside her ignorance of the realities in Israel, a predictable bias borne of her half-million-dollar Princeton education.

"It took me a while to trace their flow of money, but eventually everything added up," continued Jennifer. "I can explain it. I'll use a hundred dollars as an example. Let's say that they acquire something on the black market for a hundred dollars. They would never get paid a hundred right away, but over time the money makes its way to an account in the Caymans and then back out, via a lending institution in Croatia, fifteen through an account in Malaysia, fifty makes its way through various accounts in Istanbul and Greece. The rest lands up going to Russia. Eventually, it ends up in their Ahmaadi Foundation in London. One hundred cleverly sanitized dollars that is. The numbers add up."

"You're able to trace all of that?" Jun asked incredulously.

Jennifer nodded.

"What is the Ahmaadi Foundation?" Ashley asked, furrowing her eyebrows.

"Their mission, according to their website, is to *turn concepts into achievement by creatively realizing innovative solutions for global challenges.* They have projects that address issues of Arab immigration; they work to broaden understanding of Arab culture on Western college campuses; they're *dedicated to helping the Palestinian cause in the Middle East* ... things like that."

"So Fawwaz manages their foundation, too?" asked Bora, already looking it up on her tablet.

"No. He's focused on European football. His brother, Ghalib, is deeply involved. He …" Jennifer took a second to find a little yellow piece of paper. "He's the Manager of External Affairs and also the Operations Specialist for the Foundation."

David burst out with a chuckle. "Is it just me, or do those titles mean absolutely nothing?"

"It's not just you," Leo nodded. "Let's just say they give him a broad range of motion."

"Were they both on Jee Hye's list?" asked Fox.

"Just Fawwaz," Wu answered.

"He hired her?"

"Four times. Six days, each time."

"Okay. There must be more besides being on her list and having a family foundation," Leo stated, knowing Jennifer. "Give us the meat, Jennifer."

"The Lynx has done business with them," she stated, nodding.

"What kind of business," asked David.

"Well, this is the murky part. I was able to trace him through some financial coincidences. For instance, they would have a big fundraiser for the foundation on the island of Ibiza, and it would just so happen that Sa'im Kashif Zafar would be staying at the same hotel."

"He'd check in with his own name?" Bora asked, surprised.

"No. But I 've got his known aliases. I can send them to you if you'd like."

Bora nodded, "Thanks. I'll check them against the list I'm putting together."

"How often do these coincidences happen?" asked Hirsch.

"Thirteen times. As far as direct money exchanging hands from one to the other, I can't find any trace of that." She sat forward and tapped at her computer. In seconds a document came up on the LED table screen in the conference room, marked, *Classified*. "I found out that his name is listed as a *contributor* to the foundation, though."

"What's a *contributor*?" Justin's wife asked. "Shouldn't it read donor?"

"My thoughts exactly, Bora," Jennifer responded. "Dr. Stone, if I were you, I'd try to find out how these guys met. As far as I can tell, they go back at least a decade. It's not a money trail. It's something else. I guess I'd look into those fundraisers. Maybe there's video footage you could get your hands on? It would be a good place to start." She bit her top lip as if trying to decide whether or not to continue.

David's phone vibrated. He'd gotten a text message from Jennifer.

Is everyone cleared? Who is Jun?

"Oh, Jun," David remarked. "Are you packed and ready to go?"

"Yes, sir."

"Okay, then. So sorry, Jennifer, Jun needs to go to Philadelphia right now. I have to see him off, but I'll be right back."

Justin's cousin and David slipped out of the meeting.

"Rocco is looking forward to meeting you," David said, acting as if his text message had been from his bar manager in Philly.

"But before you head north, I need you to go south. Just a quick assignment."

"Okay, what am I doing?"

David explained it to him carefully and then clapped him on the back. "You're going to do great, Kid. Enjoy settling in. We'll keep you posted on developments as they unfold, okay? Call or text me anytime."

Jun nodded. He went to get his backpack.

"Sorry about that," Trey's father said to Jennifer as David and Jun were talking, just outside the conference room. "You can keep going."

"No problem, Dr. Stone," Wu said. "There is one other connection to this foundation that I think you need to know." She pulled some documents onto the screen. "One of the regular donors to the foundation is The Red Flag Commerce and Development Company."

Leo started. "You're sure?"

"Very."

Trey's father looked at Ashley, seeing the name register on her face, too. Red Flag, as it was nicknamed among the LaunchPad team, was a Chinese company that had helped finance the abduction of Trey's family and the attempt to traffic Jasmine Stone. They were in bed with the Russian mob, the Chinese Triads, and a host of black-matter, but operated legitimately, on the surface as a shipping company.

David walked back in and looked at Jennifer's documentation on the video screen. He just shook his head.

"That's all I have for now," said Jennifer. "I hope that helps. Let me know if there's anything else you need."

"You've helped a lot," David acknowledged as everyone else voiced their thanks. They disconnected the call.

"I'll fill you in on who they are, Bora," Leo said. "But it looks like our researcher extraordinaire would like to say something."

She blushed at the compliment and smiled. Then she said, "I was just sitting here thinking ... soccer ... the foundation ... and then I thought about all the articles I've read about how trafficking skyrockets during the World Cup. Look at what I just found," she said, flinging what was on her tablet screen onto the LED table. "It turns out that Fawwaz Ahmaadi is part of the FIFA Congress, the supreme body that governs international soccer."

The conference room fell silent.

"So, you have a guy who owns a multi-million-dollar soccer franchise and serves on FIFA's governing body, ensuring that the organization turns a blind eye to human trafficking during their events. You have his brother, who leads a foundation that raises a lot of money for who knows what ... and is tied to The Lynx."

"Was FIFA involved in organizing the soccer tournament in Botswana?" Bora asked.

Nobody knew the answer.

David turned to Leo. "I think I need to have a convo with Serwabi again. You wanna come?"

"No. We can all eavesdrop from here. Ashley, can you get some food together for Mr. Mohammad Al Serwabi? Let's feed him and then grill him." He hesitated, "Grill him with questions, I mean."

THE GIRLS WERE SHIVERING in the night cold. The train had been at a stand-still for several hours, and they had no blankets or heaters. Howell realized The Lynx and company were waiting for something, and just as he was wondering what it could be, an ear-piercing scream filled the air! It came from the car with the German girls. Suddenly, a gunshot rang out, echoing against the cave walls and what was one scream was now everyone on the German team shrieking in anger and fear.

Howell watched as Green-Eyes dragged a body from the train car behind theirs onto the platform and then pulled it over to the cave wall. Laila was yelling, too, now, at the guard who had been the flight attendant with the pearly whites and smooth skin. She was raging! The Lynx walked over and swatted the guard on the side of the head.

One woman in the German car was wailing, uncontrollably.

"My guess is that the flight attendant was trying to molest one of the girls," Murray whispered. "When the German chaperone tried to intervene, he got shot."

Howell nodded. He'd thought the same thing. The dead man's wife was probably the one screaming. And The Lynx wasn't going to let one of his men touch these girls – they were high-grade product and not to be sampled.

As she calmed down, Laila's head jerked around to stare at Howell and Murray, sitting on the floor of their train car. It seemed she knew they'd been talking.

The good-looking guard with the evil heart was being re-assigned and was walking with The Lynx. Apparently, the green-eyed freak wanted to keep a closer eye on him. The guard that had been positioned in Howell's car was transferred to the German car. And Laila left the platform and came to the American car to take his place. Howell just stared straight ahead. Her intense dark eyes were like lasers burning into his back.

CHAPTER THIRTY-ONE

THE ELEVATOR DOOR OPENED INTO THICK DARKNESS. IT WAS THE kind of blackness that can only be found in a large cave with no light from any source. Jasmine was still getting used to the greenish glow of night-vision goggles. She couldn't decide if it would be eerier to go without them and use a flashlight, or not. But since nobody else was using theirs, she wanted to fit in.

"The railroad is this way, ma'am," said the Marine who had cleared the area. He led Michi and Jasmine while the rest of the team rolled the crate forward, with the drone still perched on top.

They walked through a long wide tunnel and then turned the corner. Jasmine let out a short shriek. "Oh my God!" she screamed, trying to get a hold of herself.

It was the purplish glow emanating from the growing-lab for the emerald wasps.

Michi was frozen in place. Her silenced Sig Sauer P229 Enhanced Elite pistol was drawn and pointed to the far wall of the cavern. It took less than a second, but one of the Marines took notice and followed her line of sight. Someone was sitting against the far wall.

"Identify yourself!" he said loudly, drawing his weapon. The ghostly buzzing of the wasps was on-going in the background, and the air smelled and tasted earthy and musty.

All the Marines had whipped around by now and were training their weapons on the sitting human form. Michi fired off one round, purposefully hitting sixteen inches above the person's head. Neither the noise nor the crumbling debris from the cave's wall caused him to flinch.

One of the Marines broke right and was sneakily approaching the figure. As he got closer, he stopped, peering into the darkness.

"He's dead," he called out a few seconds later.

Everyone relaxed. "I'm sorry, ma'am," said the Marine who'd told Michi that they'd cleared the area. "I didn't see him when we came down earlier."

"I'm sure these freaky bugs distracted you," answered Michi, "but we can't have any mistakes. We have to be perfect."

"Yes, ma'am."

"When we leave, make sure you have someone on watch down here."

"Yes, ma'am. We'll cover our six."

Agent Imada walked over to the corpse and recognized the face from the photos she'd studied. "It's probably too dark for you to see, but he's one of the doctors."

The Velcro ripped as she pulled the camera off her helmet and captured the doctor's face and fingers. She turned to the

Marine, "Take my camera upstairs and stand there for three minutes. That should be enough time for this footage to automatically upload. Then come right back down and give it to me."

"Yes, Ma'am," he replied, taking the camera. He hustled off in the direction of the elevator as Michi joined the rest of the team.

The Marines had unpacked the large wooden crate revealing an interesting vehicle. It was a four-wheeled Yamaha Banshee – or at least that was what it had been in a previous life. This one had large rail wheels in place of black tires and sat lower on the frame than the original vehicle. Its six-speed transmission, manual clutch, and the two-stroke twin-cylinder engine had all been left in place. However, it had two extra gas tanks on each side that contained ethanol-free petrol. The seat stabilization system would allow for navigating the railroad tracks at a very high rate of speed. On the front of the modified ATV was a black box with a small saucer resembling a mini satellite dish of some sort.

"Ma'am," the lead Marine asked, "the guys are wondering what this is."

Michi smiled. "It's an invention from back in the office and some talented people on board your ship built it to our specifications. We should be able to cruise anywhere from forty to eighty miles per hour, depending on the hills and bends. The wheels have a magnetic force we can activate to keep us stuck to the track. This black box here is our drone guidance system. It's preprogrammed to keep the drone exactly four feet above us and one hundred and fifty feet ahead of us." She pulled out her tablet from her backpack and clipped it to the black box, so she could see it while driving. Then, she took the drone and handed it to Jasmine as Trey's daughter sat down on the back seat and adjusted her backpack. "This bad puppy," Michi said, pointing at the drone, "is a modified Autel Robotics X-star Premium Quadcopter. We've added some battery packs, so it'll stay on for several hours, and we hacked the GPS navigation to adjust some things." Clearly, she was making an impression. "But the real treasures are the dual cameras. One is filming in crystal clear video, using an HD camera. The other uses thermal imaging with a radiometric upgrade. Both of the cameras can be detached and used as additional intelligence-gathering with our headgear."

The Marines were stunned.

"So, basically, you're going to fly this drone ahead of you as you drive. It automatically stays at one hundred and fifty feet in front of you, acts as a scout of sorts, and feeds the video to your tablet?"

"Yes. The infrared will show us heat signatures of people ahead of us."

"Is the drone armed?"

"I wish," Michi said with a grin as she climbed into the driver's seat. She fired up the engine and yelled out over its noise. "We didn't have time to figure that part out." Looking at the USS Bataan team, she shouted, "Thanks for everything, you guys. We'll see you back on the boat!" The Marines saluted the ladies as they slowly pulled away.

Moving up the tunnel, Jasmine held the drone in the air, turned it on, and when she felt it tugging, let it go, just as Justin had briefed her. The little quadcopter lifted up and scurried to its scouting position, one hundred and fifty feet in front of them. At the same time, the video feed sprung to life on Michi's tablet screen. On the top half was the thermal imaging. On the bottom half was the video feed. There was nothing but blackness, with the occasional flash of light from the ATV's headlights.

Michi was steering and slowly accelerating with her right hand, as her left hand unclicked the tablet from its holder. She handed it over her shoulder to Jasmine. "Keep your eyes on this. If you see any thermal activity at all, tell me immediately, and we'll stop."

"Okay!"

A few Marines stayed in the tunnel area to lock it down, while the rest of them gathered outside the garage door. A number of three-lettered agencies would be coming at random intervals over the next few nights to process the crime scene and glean any information they could about the disappearance of the jet.

For LaunchPad, the nervous wait for the field operations had begun. Trey, Bruce, and Tank were on their way to the Egyptian border. Michi and Jasmine were on their own, advancing through the deep lurid trafficking tunnels of Muammar Gaddafi.

THEODORE RANDALL BAKER and three private jet-loads of wealthy American parents had touched down in Rome and were headed to the swanky Waldorf Cavalieri to check-in and meet their German counterparts. With its array of three Michelin-star rated restaurants and cafes, divinely opulent spas, a private art collection that rivaled most museums, a million-dollar wine cellar, and breathtaking views of the Eternal City, this luxurious hotel had no equal anywhere on the planet.

On arrival, the parents had been graciously ushered to their accommodations by the hotel's impeccably professional staff.

Their luggage had already been delivered to their rooms and discretely unpacked for them. The clothes that Helen Baker had ordered for her and Monica Brown had already been shopped for, cleaned and hung in their respective closets. It was suggested to all the parents that they spend a few hours settling in. Once it was ready, they'd all be texted to gather in one of the hotel's lavish conference rooms which the Secret Service was turning into a state-of-the-art meeting area they'd named The Pulse. Consistent with the rest of the hotel, the room was beautifully appointed. Floor-to-ceiling windows on the far side offered sweeping views of the fabled houses and hills of Rome. Against the windows, there were clusters of opulent couches, chairs, and smaller tables with seating for small groups. In the middle of the room sat two long tables made of impressive raw-edged ebony slabs, presented in a strikingly modern design that it seemed only Italian designers could create. Each table could comfortably seat twenty people in posh Italian leather swivel chairs. Opposite the windows, the Secret Service had created a tech area. A few of the agents were at their laptops setting up information-feeds they'd use to keep the group informed.

DAVID WAS ready to pay Mohammad a visit again, let him use the facilities, bring him some food and coffee, and take him back to the interrogation room.

Hirsch walked in and closed the door behind him. "Good news on your son. He'll survive. I'll let you see each other if you tell me what we need to know about The Lynx."

Serwabi wiped his mouth with a napkin and took a sip of water. "He's very connected."

"So is everyone else, thanks to Facebook."

Serwabi rolled his eyes. "Are we going to be serious, or do we joke around?"

"We know he's connected," David stated point-blank. "Stop acting like you're an Egyptian godfather in a low-budget movie and tell us actionable intel." Hirsch stood up and began collecting the dishes.

"If you give me a piece of paper and a pen, I'll write down names," the MEO said quietly, "Islamic terrorists, Russian bureaucrats, Chinese Triads. I've been watching him for a long time."

David walked out with the dishes and handed them to Ashley, who was outside the door waiting for him.

"Can I get you anything," she asked.

"A pen and paper?"

She ran to find what he needed and brought it right back. "I'll go to the conference room with the others. Is that okay?"

He nodded, turned around, and opened the door.

"Not just names, but how he was connected to them," stated David as he handed the prisoner the pad.

Serwabi was about to start writing, but then he looked up at Hirsch. "You

have to understand how he operates to comprehend his connections."

"Enlighten me."

"The best way to put it is that he's an arms dealer, for the most part," he said, laying his pen down. "What makes him unique and very hard to trace is the currency he uses."

"We had a hard time tracking some of his financials. Does he use diamonds or something?"

Serwabi shook his head. "People. Usually boys and girls."

David was immediately repulsed. "How does that work?"

"He makes a list of the weapons he needs, and they provide him with a list of the people they want."

"Was Jee Hye on that list?"

"Several times. She ... was an amazing girl."

Hirsch resisted the temptation to break Serwabi's jaw.

"The weapons suppliers are ..."

"Russian, Chinese, North Korean."

"How are the children delivered?"

"At big parties. Conferences. Large international events where there are a lot of drunk and high, but powerful, people."

"Like the World Cup."

"Sure. Or the Olympics. Rock concerts. High-end raves."

"Where do his weapons go?"

"Everywhere." He stared up at the ceiling: "Somalia, Syria, Libya, Qatar, Yemen, Bahrain, Jordan. Hell, there's a pretty long list of places that want to kill Westerners."

David's phone buzzed. He checked it and read a text from Leonard Stone.

Bora discovered first meet. Fundraiser nine years ago. Kuta.

Hirsch put his phone back in his pocket and looked at the CIA's MEO. "Tell me about the Ahmaadi family." A speck of fear entered Serwabi's eyes. David was watching it. "We find it kind of interesting that when Fawwaz and Ghalib hold fundraisers for their foundation, The Lynx shows up. You must've noticed that, too."

The Central Intelligence Agency's Middle East Operative was conflicted. Everyone in the conference room watching him could attest to it.

"Like in Kuta, for instance."

Serwabi sat like a stone.

"Mind if I smoke a cigar?" David asked, producing a pouch from his right coat pocket and a glass ashtray from his left. He put them on the table.

"Here? In a government building?"

"Sure. Why not? There are no rules. I'm in charge here." Hirsch could make cigar-lighting a lengthy art in times like these. He carefully opened his bag and lay three cigar options on the table, meticulously looking over each one. He smelled them for sweetness, pinched them to check their humidity levels, ran his forefinger and opposing thumb over the creases to make sure they were tight. Finally, he made his selection, an Arturo Fuente Don Carlos Beliscoso.

Putting away the other two cigars, he pulled out a handsome 24-karat gold Havana punch from his pocket. "The thing is, and you know this, Serwabi. We … are … going … to … find … out … everything." Like a nurse inserting a needle to draw blood, he poked the recessed tip into the cigar and carefully drew out a plug of tobacco from the cigar head. Tapping it lightly on the table, he examined the little bit of tobacco that fell out from the punch tube.

Satisfied, David began to prepare his cedar strips for lighting – two of them, stacked. "I'm only going to offer you this once. After that, the deal is off the table. We'll feed you to the wolves. You know the wolves I'm talking about, right? The ones on every side you've been playing. The ones in England, in Egypt, in Libya, in Washington. And in Malaysia." With deep inner satisfaction, Hirsch noted a tremor in Serwabi's chest.

Leo's friend took out some long wooden matches and lit the cedar sticks. "If I were sitting where you're sitting, it would be clear to me by now that the game was over." He took a long draw on his cigar and blew the smoke into the air. "I'd have two concerns. My life would be one. The lives of my kids would be the other." Then he looked intently at Serwabi. "I'm sorry about your wife. I heard about her car accident."

The MEO was silent.

"Mine died too. She was murdered in her sleep while I was saving America. It took me a long time to get over that."

Everyone outside in the conference room looked at Leo. He nodded. "It's true. She was an amazing lady. She was killed less than a year after they got married."

David looked at the glowing orange butt of his cigar, happy to see it lit up well and was burning consistently, then he continued, "Revenge wasn't as sweet as I thought it would be. But as far as I was concerned, it needed to be done." He took another drag from his cigar. "I never found another. For me, there was only her. There was simply no one else."

Serwabi's face expressed he identified with the grief in David.

"Look. I told you before. We're not terrorists. I'm not going to kill your kids and perch their heads on poles in the middle of town. I'd actually like to bring your kids here and let you explain a few things to them, in person. The reality is, you're not giving me a thing that's new."

"I thought my son was here somewhere. Bleeding like a stuck pig."

"That was earlier. He might still be here. He might not. What is true is that he's not dead."

Serwabi's face turned a slight red as he worked hard to suppress his rage at David's dismissive attitude. But instead of exploding in a tirade his training had taught him to respond in the opposite spirit. He took another few seconds to calm down and then responded thoughtfully. "When I was a kid, I watched Israelis murdering the parents of my Palestinian friends. Then, one day, I remember standing in Jaffa square and watching a kill-team of Palestinians spring out of a van and knife a Jewish man standing right in front of me. When my father got transferred, we ended up living in Nigeria, where Muslims were slaughtering Christians every day." The MEO leaned back. "Wherever I've lived since those years, people were slaughtering people. Blood triggered wars like a sprung beartrap triggers pain. I don't have allegiance to any country. I'm a survivor. That's what I've done all my life. Maybe I'll tell you what you want to know. But when I'm done, I'll survive. Like I always do. There are people above your pay grade who will ensure that."

"You assume that there actually is anyone 'above my pay grade.' Your survival might be out of your control this time."

"I need to talk to my son. And what about my daughter? Where is she?"

David shrugged and blew smoke into the air.

Serwabi sat up and looking directly at Hirsch. He spoke softly, as if confiding. "Jee Hye heard something one night while servicing VIP Muslim clients."

"Do you know who those clients were?"

"She was so scared that she deemed it too dangerous to tell me over the phone."

"Who was there that night?"

"I'm telling you. I don't know. She told me all of the key players were in her book."

"What did she hear?"

"An A-list group of girls in exchange for a Stingray."

Everyone in the conference room felt a chill over their bodies.

"A Stingray?" David asked for clarification. "I'm guessing you're not talking about a Corvette?"

"No. The real deal. Fully trained and pissed off at America."

Leo's friend had to think for a minute. The Stingray members were a dark-world hacker group. They were extremely dangerous and could bring almost any computer system to a complete halt if they wanted to. Four years ago, talented Russian hackers that had been hired by the Kremlin managed to identify a hack that could've crashed thirty planes over the airport in Moscow. A Stingray had left his untraceable imprint on it: a series of numbers that when run through a CIA-designed code-cracker spelled *stngry*.

The MEO stroked his mustache a few times, "When I got that news, I began to comb through my network to find out who could be orchestrating something like that. My conclusion was that it would've had to have been The Lynx – or someone very connected to him."

"Any idea who he'd be delivering the hacker to?"

"No."

"Do you know where he'd find someone like that?"

"Sana'a."

"Yemen?"

"There are a few living there. I don't know where all the others are. They're global. You know that."

"Did you report this through Company channels?"

"The CIA?" Serwabi spat out. His anger seemed to be building out of his control. "To whom in the CIA? Our director had just gotten killed. And when Pearlman stepped in, he was immediately overwhelmed – still is. Cyberwarfare is raging against our nation on so many levels that if the American public knew what was going on, they'd all crawl into caves and live like brutish Neanderthals. *Kol Khara!* No! I did not report this to the CIA. I needed to figure it out on my own."

David looked at what was left of his cigar, ignoring the Arabic curse words. Serwabi obviously didn't really know much about Americans. They weren't the kind of people to go hide in caves when things got tough.

"I needed Jee Hye to tell me specifically who was involved," the MEO insisted. "Whenever I'd try, she'd get so fearful she'd just clam up. She wouldn't send me her black book, so I tried to find a time to see her and get her to talk, but ..." he shrugged, "they got to her before I did."

"You mean in Koreatown."

Serwabi nodded. "I was tracking her phone to an alley, but the killer got away. We managed to follow him to a Walmart on Crenshaw. By the time I got there, he'd escaped."

David knew Jun was not the killer. Serwabi was either misinformed or lying. Leonard's friend thought about that poor girl, caught in so many crosshairs and running for her life. His face turned steely. "You didn't consider getting her out?"

"Why? She was valuable where she was."

"And you didn't think she deserved protection?"

"At the end of the day, although she was intelligent and beautiful, she was unusable in any other capacity. You know what I mean. A hooker like her doesn't shed her skin." He cocked his head to one side, "She was definitely a favorite. Somewhat of a legend. If you hadn't rented her for two weeks, you weren't really in the upper class. Know what I mean? But no. If I tried to protect her, which could have blown up many black operations, then what the hell would she do with her life?"

David stood up, pushing his chair back. He collected the blank pad and pen and pocketed them. Then he placed his cigar butt in the ashtray and picked it up. Still silent, he turned and placed his hand on the door handle. In front of him, he could see Serwabi's image reflecting in the glass slat of the door.

"I feel the same way about your daughter, Meagan."

In a sudden burst of rage, Serwabi exploded up! He pushed the heavy table as hard as his restraints allowed. It was enough to pin Hirsch against the door. David's ashtray fell out of his hand and shattered on the concrete floor. He pushed back with all of his might and was just able to turn around. In a moment of sheer adrenalin, he flipped the table on top of the MEO's head, knocking him down. The table top was lying on top of his upper chest and his hands were pinned awkwardly against it. David reached down and muscled it off Mohammed just as Justin opened the door.

"You guys do anything to her, and I'll clam up," the MEO gasped, his elbow pressed into his bruised side.

David chuckled. "Clam up? You think so? You won't be able to clam up, Mohammad Al Serwabi. I have every tool I need to make you talk. I know you've been trained to resist waterboarding so don't worry, we won't go there unless we just want to be entertained. We'll just go straight to an IV and inject fire into your veins," he said as he and Jee-Hye's cousin reset the table. "It will be like the worst acid trip you've ever taken, you'll start to tremble … froth at the mouth … feel like your throat is being ripped open with razors. And as your eyes are bulging out of your head and your sweat turns to blood, your mind will completely lose its power to resist. You'll talk like a four-year-old after a visit to the zoo. You'll tell us everything we want to know."

"Been there. Done that," he spat back defiantly. "I have nothing to hide. My assignment has been well-documented."

"We'll see, Scumbag. We will see."

Justin walked around the table and shoved Serwabi's chair into the back of his legs as hard as he could, forcefully sitting him down. He took zip-ties out of his pocket and tightly snugged the MEO's legs to his chair-supports. He then pulled Serwabi's chain tight and locked it into an iron cleat on the floor that had been bolted to the concrete for just such a purpose. The man was completely immobilized.

"Jee Hye Park deserved better," David said matter-of-factly, once the securing operation was complete. "Your problem now is not even figuring out your loyalties. Your problem is that you're still scrambling to find your inner bearings. You don't know what your best play is here because long before we got to you, you lost your moral compass. You're just a groveling slave to your masters. You're a failure as a human being on every level. Your daughter probably agrees with me."

He followed Justin out of the room and slammed the door behind him just as Serwabi's spit hit the glass window.

CHAPTER THIRTY-TWO

TREY, BRUCE, AND TANK PULLED THEIR JEEP INTO SOME BUSHES next to a tree. They took time to carefully camouflage it with a desert tarp and some native plants. Located half a mile from where Casey Baker's tracking device had pinged, they'd decided to proceed the rest of the way on foot.

"We'll hump it over this dune," Tank said, pointing straight ahead. He looked at his compass and compared it with the red dot on his tablet's map. "If I've got it right, when we crest the peak we should have a good vantage point down to where our primary was."

The sun was rising over the Libyan desert, lighting up the sky in dramatic hues of orange, light blue, and pale purple. In front of them were giant sand dunes. To their left, the flat sands stretched all the way to the Egyptian border. It was a spectacular region known as the White Desert, or the Sahara el Beyda, one of Egypt's lesser-known national treasures.

The three checked their comms with Saara, then reviewed their plan with Leonard.

"Your audio is coming in loud and clear," Justin said. Everyone in LaunchPad was in the conference room.

"Copy that," Trey acknowledged.

"I've got you plotted on the grid," confirmed Saara, bringing up the screen with three little blue dots. She tapped a few keystrokes on her keyboard, and their names materialized over each dot.

"You're the Blue Team, gentlemen," Leo announced.

"Copy that."

"I think you're ready to go."

Justin raised his hand, "Tank, there are two smaller kits in yours. Did you find them?" He had packed two separate black backpacks into Tatanka's duffle bag with weapons and field gear marked *Howell* and *Kennedy*.

"Copy that," Tank responded.

"We've got the palm print and fingerprints off the image that was uploaded from Ground Zero. Lark's dead. You can leave his kit behind."

Justin was depending on Trey's photographic memory to recall that *Lark* was John F. Kennedy's secret service code name. He quickly understood that Agent Miles Howell was the only security detail still alive with the girls. Kennedy was dead.

"Okay, Blue Team," Leo commanded. "Green light."

The three agents took final swigs of water, tightened their packs, did a final weapons-check and broke into formation to crouch run up the dune, with Tank leading the way.

While the Blue Team was on the move, Trey's father muted the Launch Pad's comms with them, and he took a few minutes to get everyone who'd been sleeping up to speed.

"Okay, here's what we know," he informed them. "Jee Hye Park was involved in an escort ring that serviced very high-end Arab clients. We don't know how she got involved with them in particular, but Bora is researching that one for us. Among them was The Lynx, himself. We've found out that he traffics children in trade for weapons that he distributes to radical elements throughout nations that hate us. There are no money links that we can find at this time. It's either a straight trade or there are cash transactions taking place that we don't know about yet. Then he takes the weapons from those trades to supply select anti-American militant groups with whatever they request."

"Where would he get the children from?" Ashley asked.

"I'm looking into that," Bora answered. "But right now, it's all a little murky. He's very slick. Most of them are Asian, so probably Thailand, Vietnam, and Cambodia."

"My guess is that's not the first time he's used Gadhafi's tunnels," commented David. "We may not know the real people behind all of this, but Bora and Jennifer linked The Lynx with the twin brothers, Fawwaz and Ghalib Ahmaadi." He took a second to send their pictures from his tablet to the LED table screen. "One of them runs their philanthropic foundation. The other owns a European soccer club. These guys are high-rollers, well insulated, and they have a web of connections that's spread across continents in a head-spinning matrix. It's hard to imagine they'd get their hands this dirty. But today, nothing surprises me. The fundraising events they host for their foundation are unrestrained parties where the drugs, prostitutes, and cash flow like a river of degeneracy. We've put calls out to try and trace the fruit back to the roots. Maybe we'll get the connections we need."

Bora had a question.

"When David was interrogating him, Serwabi brought up something that we didn't find in the black book, that I'm aware of."

"Stingray?" Bora queried.

Leo nodded. "I want you to go over it very carefully again. She mentioned *Baker,* and I think we all know what that was about, now. But we have to find if she mentioned the hacker group."

"What would the alternative be?" Justin asked. "That he made it all up?"

"I don't know," David responded. "He seemed pretty convinced of the story. But this would be the first time we hear of The Lynx trading for a weapon that's cyber-related."

Bora was making notes. "I'll go through it and let you know what I find."

"Okay," said Leo nodding. "Some of you might not know that I re-routed Boyd and Fox to London to pay the twins a visit. We'll start with Ghalib."

Ashley looked down trying not to show her fear.

David put his hand on her shoulder. She needed some reassurance. "Fox will be back soon, sweetheart, don't worry."

"Michi and Jasmine are off comms," Trey's father continued. "Saara predicted it, once they got into those tunnels, they'd go dark. They'll connect as soon as they're able."

"The CIA, NSA, FBI and probably a few others, will be arriving at the plane site in Libya within the next twelve hours," David announced. "Saara has sent them our video feed from when

Michi and Jasmine first arrived. They're relatively caught up. Marines from the USS Bataan will stay in place, coordinating ground activity and providing security once everyone gets there."

"Have they informed the Libyan government?" Justin asked.

"Negative. The Libyan government won't know about this until everything's wrapped up ... or maybe never."

"Our responsibility for Ground Zero has officially passed on then," Leo concluded. "We have two objectives right now: The primary one is to pursue The Lynx and get those girls back to Rome, starting with Casey Baker. Running concurrently is the objective of finding those responsible, bringing them to justice, and sinking their networks into the abyss, where they belong."

Saara looked down at the LED table screen and tapped a few times to finalize her inputs. Then she announced, "Okay. When we communicate with Michi and Jasmine, they'll be the Red Team. Fox and Boyd will be the White Team."

Everyone nodded. The update appeared on their tablets.

Leonard Stone sat back, "Saara, I need you to be on Blue Team at all times. If you need to rack out, just tap someone to take your place. You'll be working in the office area."

She nodded.

"Ashley, would you think ahead about possible medical scenarios? Coordinate with the doctors on board the USS Bataan. Make a list of friendlies in Egypt that we could call, should the need arise. Then figure out medevac plans to Rome, should we require them. We'll need to have all of that ready to go."

Ashley nodded. It was going to be a lot to coordinate. "I'll just work from the medical clinic for now."

"Great," Dr. Stone said. Turning to Bora, he suggested, "Why don't you do your research from there too? That way she's not by herself."

"Sure, Dr. Stone," the young law student answered.

"If you need anybody's contact info or Company connections for anything, just message Saara. She'll know how to connect you."

"Okay." Bora took a quick breath, then paused, as if unsure about speaking.

Leo noticed. "What's on your mind?"

"When we were watching David and the MEO, two things stuck out to me."

Everyone was paying attention, and Leo nodded. "Please, speak up at any time. What were they?"

"There was something about the way he said, 'If you didn't rent her for two weeks, you weren't really in the upper class.' I wonder what she did for them, that she didn't do for the others who obtained her services for a shorter period of time."

"That's an interesting thought, Bora," David agreed. "Make a list of anyone that had her for two or more weeks and see if anything jumps out at you."

"What was the second thing?" asked Leo.

"Do we know where his daughter is?"

Nobody did.

"I never really thought about her," confessed Trey's dad.

David agreed again. "Yeah, I was thinking about that too, Bora. We need to lock her down. I'll find somebody in SoCal who can do that for us."

"Great insights. Don't hold back, okay?" Leo said. "I'll tell you this. From my experience. The biggest regrets in my life are from when I didn't speak up when I had the chance. There are a handful of those moments in my life. Some of them could've made a real difference. So trust your gut and get it out into the open when you can. Because sometimes, you don't get another chance."

"Okay, Dr. Stone. I will."

Trey's dad turned to her husband, "Justin, you did a great job coordinating with the USS Bataan and kitting our teams out. Impressive work, as always."

"Thank you, sir."

"You'll have to switch gears now and be in the office with Saara. You're going to be coordinating with the Red and White teams while she focusses on Blue. My suggestion is that you set it all up and then get some sleep. We'll wake you up when they start checking in."

"Yes, sir."

"David and I will be coordinating everything from the conference room. When your team starts rolling, we want situation reports every sixty minutes, starting on the hour. You can call them in, text them in, email them in, or personally drop by. But we need to hear from all of you. It's critical to stay abreast of everything and communicate clearly and decisively, okay? Dismissed."

As everyone disappeared, David turned to Leo. "What should we do with Serwabi?"

"Leave him where he is."

CHAPTER THIRTY-THREE

UNITED AIRLINES' FLIGHT 915 SAFELY TOUCHED DOWN ON 19C, one of the more popular runways at Dulles International Airport. As the chief flight attendant welcomed passengers to the capitol city of the United States of America, some excited tourists clapped and cheered while the Americans whipped out their cell phones to check any notifications they'd missed, and others started texting their friends and families, letting them know they'd made it home safely from Europe.

Boa Zhen pulled out her phone from her bag and turned it on. She'd received one text message, and as she read it, her face drained of its color. She scanned it again, to make sure she wasn't imagining anything. Her hand started to tremble.

Noticing her daughter's change in disposition, Lin Lin Ma was instantly alert. "What is it, Dear?"

Trey's wife turned her phone around. Her mother read her son-in-law's text message.

Tried to reach you, but you had no reception. You've probably just touched down. Go straight to LP. We'll be arriving later than anticipated. On assignment. Dad will update you. I love you.

"Call Leonard, Honey."

"We can't, Mom," Bao Zhen answered. "If they're out on assignment, they've probably already taken the batteries out of their cell phones until this thing is over. It was part of David's security protocol updates."

"How are you supposed to communicate?"

"Through rooted comms and secure tablets."

"What are those?"

"Communications set up by Saara or Justin. They've been sanitized and are virtually impossible to penetrate. But I'm not on comms yet. It takes a special earpiece. And it's usually only for operators."

"Try Ashley."

Bao Zhen shook her head. "Let's do what he says. We'll go to LaunchPad and get the updated face-to-face from Leonard."

"And where's Jasmine?"

"I don't know, Mom."

"Trey wouldn't have taken her along?"

"On assignment? Of course not!" As the words crossed Bao Zhen's lips, she could feel deep anxiety oozing out from the recesses of her heart. She knew that Trey might not have had a choice. As she was thinking about it all, her phone buzzed. It was a message from David.

*Welcome back! Proceed to limo stand. Look for a white Cadillac
Escalade. Driver is Jun. Do not reply to this message. Phones are off.
See you soon.*

The door to the plane of the giant 777 opened and the passengers began to funnel out. Some scurried to their connecting
flights, others walked quickly to restrooms or baggage claim.
The two women didn't have checked luggage, so they headed
straight for the area where limousines would pull up and wait.

A shiny new white Cadillac Escalade sat beside the curb with
the back door open and a handsome Asian chauffeur standing
alongside it.

"Excuse me," Bao Zhen said, "What is your name?"

"Jun."

"You're here for us."

Justin's cousin smiled broadly. "Thanks for coming to me. I
honestly didn't know whom I was waiting for."

"That sounds like David."

He chuckled. "I'm still learning how he rolls."

"How do you know each other?" asked Lin Lin, suspiciously.

"I'm Justin Park's cousin."

"Do you know the pass-phrase for my daughter?"

"It all started on a warm evening of jazz …"

Trey's wife nodded. Their pass phrase expressed the evening she
met her husband at a jazz club in Kuala Lumpur, Malaysia. She
would never forget that night. For just a moment, it took her
back and made her smile. Then she took her mother's arm,
helping her up into one of the Escalade's swanky leather

captain's seats. Jun had chilled water in the cup holders and a bowl of fruit and roasted almonds on the middle console.

"Thank you, Jun, for picking us up," Lin Lin said graciously.

"You're welcome," Jun answered, smiling. He closed the door for the ladies and hurried around to the driver's side to hop in. Reaching down to his right, he grasped a little black pouch. "Mrs. Stone, Saara sent a secure comms-set for you so you could connect with Leo and David. Just pinch the earpiece until the little green light comes on, and then put it in your right ear. It'll alert whoever is monitoring at LaunchPad, and they'll put you through."

"Thanks, Jun," Bao Zhen said, amazed at Saara's forethought. "Are you from the Company?"

"No," he said, shaking his head and slowly accelerating into traffic. "My sister was murdered in Los Angeles a few days ago, and I turned to Justin for help. I guess it started some kind of chain reaction."

Lin Lin Ma looked at Bao Zhen. Both women could immediately identify with his grief. "I'm so sorry, Jun. That's awful."

Trey's wife nodded, "It was good that Justin was able to help you. He has a new bride now. I've heard that she's amazing, too."

"They're both great," agreed Jun. "My assignment is to drop you off and then I'll be heading to Philadelphia to house-sit for Mr. Hirsch and help out at his bar."

"That sounds like a great opportunity to reset," Bao Zhen responded gently, pinching the earpiece until the little LED light turned green.

"Yes, Ma'am. It will be."

"SOMETHING'S UP AHEAD!" Jasmine shouted over the roar of the Yamaha Banshee, echoing off the tunnel walls. "No heat signatures. But it looks like a big cave."

Michi downshifted a few times and then applied the brakes as they coasted into a large cavern. On the left of the tracks was solid rock wall. To the right was a platform that extended beyond the scope of their headlights and into the darkness. "Let's switch to night vision. Can you black out the tablet screen?"

Jasmine set the drone to hover mode and the software to notify her if there was movement. Then, she pressed the button at the top of the tablet. The screen went dark. Switching off her headlamp, she lowered her night vision goggles to her eyes and turned them on. "Should we get off and check it out?"

Michi nodded, reaching to her right thigh and unpinning a Glock 19 nine-millimeter. Measuring just under seven inches, her weapon had a fifteen-round magazine capacity and a hexagonal barrel rifling. It was compact, accurate and only thirty ounces, fully loaded. On her right bicep sleeve, a pair of throwing knives were tucked away.

Carefully they climbed off their four-wheeler and pulled themselves up on to the platform. Michi reached over her shoulder with her right arm and pulled an oblong cylinder from her backpack. She depressed the *power* button on the top and saw a tiny light turn blue at the bottom. Then she put the tube on the platform floor and checked her smart-watch. Pointing to her wrist, she held up her right hand, indicating a two and a zero. They would spend no more than twenty minutes here. Jasmine fell in behind her, and the two snuck along the platform until they arrived at the far right wall of the giant cave. Moving forward slowly, they came to a wooden door. Michi scanned the black stone for video cameras but didn't see any. She gently tried the door handle, and it was unlocked, so she jerked the door open and pointed her weapon into the darkness. It was a little bathroom, and nobody was in it.

She turned around, stepped back outside, and continued right, along the wall. In front of them was nothing but more wall, and to their left, was grainy green-lit darkness. Just as Agent Imada began to move forward, she felt a tap on her left shoulder. She turned back to look.

Jasmine was pointing across the darkness and making a running motion with her index and middle finger. Michi nodded and knelt down to provide cover as Trey's daughter skirted across the cavern floor to the left side. In less than ten seconds, a quick pencil light flashed two times. It was a call sign that indicated everything was clear and Jazzy wanted Michi to come and look at something.

Imada pulled out a scope attachment for her night vision goggles and looked into the darkness, past where Jasmine was squatting down. She didn't see anything, so she sprinted over to Trey's daughter. When she arrived, she could see why she'd been called over. There was a little cut-out in the cave wall that led to a heavy door, gridded with wrought iron bars. Above the door frame, a small painted graphic of an emerald wasp welcomed visitants. Beside the sign were two pegs. On one was a larger key, probably for the door, and on the other one was a set of smaller keys.

Handcuff keys, Michi noted.

Jasmine moved forward and gently tested the door. It opened easily. She was about to slip inside, but Michi tapped her on the shoulder and shook her head, pointing behind her.

With Jazzy on her six, Imada crept into the room, pistol raised, with her red-dot laser-activated. The overpowering stench of dried urine, vomit, feces, and sweat filled her nostrils. Michi cleared the room from right to left and motioned for Trey's daughter to enter. All along the lower parts of the walls, about two feet off the ground, were solid steel rings about half a meter apart, embedded into the rock. On each ring hung a pair of handcuffs with one end locked around the ring and the other hanging open. Jasmine counted them as they crept past. One hundred and sixty rings with handcuffs.

Michi motioned for them to walk on and they continued scrutinizing the cave. As far as she could tell, there were no cameras or any kind of electronic equipment. They cleared three more holding cells, identical to the first one, before coming to the end of the rock hallway. Directly in front of them was another door. It was made of solid steel but was wide open.

Imada signaled for Jasmine to remain outside and keep eyes in the direction they'd just come from. With someone guarding her six, Michi snuck in to clear the room. It had five sets of metal bunk beds and some wooden chairs scattered around a small rectangle table in the middle of the room. There was a bathroom in the back-left corner, a wooden desk in the far-right corner with a large, old-school bank vault door behind it. She crept over to the safe and looked it over. The plaque on the outside read, Diebold. Michi guessed it was originally made in the late 1800s. She knelt down, pulled a stethoscope out from her backpack, and snapped a magnetic rim into place, designed for this exact purpose. Working as fast as possible, she used her right hand to turn the giant combination lock-face and placed her left hand on the safe door to feel the change in pressure from when a gate in the mechanism's set of wheels would line up with its contact point. When all three were in place, she heard the magnified click of the falling pin as it dropped into the fence and sprung the lock bolt open. Quickly Michi put all of her gear away, turned on her video camera, and switched it from *recording to device*, to recording onto an internal memory card. She spun the handle clockwise until the screw bolt released the door. It swung open to reveal a small room about the size of an average walk-in closet. Inside, was a set of five rusty metal shelves filled with stacks of dinar – mostly in denominations of tens and twenties. On the bottom shelf were three bars of shining gold.

Agent Imada closed the safe, locked it, and then turned to rifle through the desk's drawers. They were empty with the exception of an old stack of photos. She pulled them out, slipped them into a zip lock bag, and stuck it into her backpack. She looked at her watch. They'd been at this train stop for eighteen minutes.

Leaving the room, she knelt beside Jasmine. "It's crazy here. Good call on stopping."

"Find anything?"

"It's a bunk room, office, bathroom, and has a bank vault with Libyan cash and a few gold bars."

"Seriously?"

Michi grinned, "Yes, I got video of it all."

"You didn't take the gold?"

"No. It's heavy. Besides, it's something we wouldn't want to get caught with."

Jasmine nodded, "That's very true. Ready to go?"

"Definitely."

The pair jogged down the creepy side-tunnel and back into the open cavern. Jasmine wondered why Michi hadn't paused to make sure it was still clear but got her answer a few seconds later. "What's that?" she asked, watching Michi turn off the black cylinder and guide it back into her backpack.

"It's a motion detector and camera that's linked to my smart-watch. Even if a rat would've walked by, it would have notified me, and I could've viewed it on my smart-watch."

"That's great."

"Justin's a genius," Michi agreed. "By the way, I'm really impressed with how well we communicated back there. Your dad's done a good job of training you."

"We've had a lot of downtime."

Imada smiled. "You've certainly made good use of it. Let's get out of here!"

Jasmine changed the mode of the drone and re-paired it with her tablet. Then she climbed on the back of the Yamaha Banshee and gave Michi a thumb up. The machine's engine chattered to life, and slowly they started to speed up, resuming their journey down the trafficking tunnel, that had been taken over by The Lynx and his Emerald Wasps.

CHAPTER THIRTY-FOUR

THIS PARTICULAR FIFTY-MILLION-DOLLAR DASSAULT FALCON 7X was on loan through David Hirsch's relationship with the CFO of a charter jet company in London. It just so happened that the jet was slated to return to England empty, and David had some friends who needed to hitch a ride. The plush interior had four comfortable seats which were followed by a narrow hallway with sliding doors on each side that opened up into two small bedrooms. Past those was a full, very stylish, and high-end bathroom. With a bright white ceiling, white walls that ran down to the raintree chair rails, white-bleached ostrich-leather chairs that were strikingly contrasted by Grecian-blue pillows, and white flooring, the modern interior of the plane was airy and cheerful.

Fox was sprawled out across the bed in the left bedroom, and Boyd was face down in the feathery pillows of the right bedroom. They'd spent the first few hours of the flight going through their kits from Justin, making plans for their operation in London, and doing some inflight workouts. After a quick meal and showers, they collapsed into their respective beds. At this point, catching a few hours of sleep was critical to the success of their mission.

BLUE TEAM WAS JUST MAKING it to the crest of the giant sand dune in front of them, but before they slithered over, they sat down to look at where they'd come from, rehydrate, and do a weapons check.

"Can't see the jeep at all," Trey commented, satisfied with its camouflage. He pulled out his CheyTac M200 Intervention Sniper Rifle, attached his favorite Raptor scope, and packed and loaded a magazine.

The other two had completed their routine prep and were ready to go.

"I'll take a look," Tank said, switching on his camera.

Trey sidled up to Bruce who had just pulled out his tablet and turned up the brightness.

"You should be getting my camera feed in a few seconds."

Bruce nodded and gave a thumb up. "Go check it out."

Tank slithered up to the very crest, looked at his smartwatch to check the bearings in comparison to Casey Baker's ping, put his tablet in the sand in front of him so he could see the same video feed everyone else was seeing, and then slowly raised his arm so that the camera was just getting over the ridge.

"Holy Moly!! You guys see this?"

Trey and Bruce were blown away.

"Can you zoom in?" Leo asked, from LaunchPad, standing beside Saara and looking at the flat screen that had just lit up with the live feed.

Tank used the nail from his thumb to toggle a switch and zoom in, bracing his arm in the sand to stabilize the picture.

At the base of their dune was a large flat surface surrounded by giant dunes on all sides – it looked like it might have been a small lake bed, thousands of years ago. In its center stood an enormous manmade structure that resembled a warehouse with no walls. It was supported by giant steel pillars, had a concrete floor, and a roof that matched the desert sand perfectly. In fact, as Tank looked at it closely, it seemed like its final coating might have been the sand itself. Under the roof were two rows of barracks, a handful of Humvees, about six transport trucks of various sizes and three fifteen-passenger vans that looked like they'd been converted into four-wheel-drive.

"What are we looking at, LP?" Trey asked his father.

"My guess is that it's a distribution center. Possibly a terrorist training camp. There are dozens of them in that nation," responded Leo.

"Hard to tell how many hostiles there would be. Can we get a thermal scan from overwatch?"

"I'm working on it now," Saara answered. "It seems like that roofing material is pretty sophisticated. It might even have some kind of thermal shield."

"Will the scanner in my kit work?" asked Bruce.

Justin came on comms, "Negative. Not from that distance."

Trey and Bruce crept up the dune to be beside Tank.

"Everyone is staying under the roof's cover," noted Leo. "Can you zoom back out, Tank?"

As the parameters widened, the only thing visible outside of the structure were multiple tire tracks on the east side. They left the warehouse and ran between two large dunes, towards the Egyptian border, only a few miles away.

"My guess is that they do everything at night, under cover of darkness."

"Copy that," Tank acknowledged.

"Anything from Red Team?" asked Trey.

"Negative," Justin answered. "I'm ready to roll, though."

"Copy that."

"Blue Team, hold comms," Leonard said, asking them to refrain from talking for a moment so they could listen in on deliberations.

"Roger, that. Proceed."

"David?"

"Well, we know that our target pinged from that location," Hirsch responded. "She hasn't indicated anything since then, so I assume she's still there."

"I agree," Leo said, nodding.

"These guys are trained, but they aren't trained like our boys. We should go in there and take them all out."

"Justin, are they kitted up for that?"

"Absolutely, sir. Yes. They are."

"Okay, Blue Team. Your input?"

"So, we're to shut off the lights?" Trey asked, confirming that they were getting kill authority.

"Go in hard and fast," David advised.

"Copy that," responded Bruce. "We'll figure it out. Then we'll clear the plan with you in fifteen."

"Roger all," replied Leonard Stone. They were out.

Saara shut down the comms. "I can't believe what we were just looking at," she commented, tapping furiously on her laptop. "There's absolutely no intel on that location. Take a look."

Leonard, Justin, and David looked at the flat screen she'd mirrored with hers.

"These are high-resolution images from Company birds. If you look closely, you can see those track marks that Tank was filming for us. There are actually quite a few of them. But the structure itself is pretty much invisible."

"You sound upset," Justin observed.

"I am, I guess! Frustrated," Saara answered, pulling up something else on the flat-screen next to the one they were using. It was a webpage with a black background and an ominous-looking crest of a person holding a flashlight on a rainy night. "This is a black software program the CIA has worked on for a long time. I helped with it for a while until I got pulled onto something else. It's supposed to help find places like this terrorist camp."

"I've heard of it," Leo commented. "Luminus, right?"

Saara looked at him. "You're right, Dr. Stone. Were you involved with it, too?"

"Only conceptually."

Well, then you know. We've put some satellites in the air that over the entire world with high definition image capturing. Those things are constantly transmitting images every few seconds to one of our company's supercomputers. The computer then stores them in hard drives that have hundreds of petabytes of storage."

"For what purpose?" asked David.

"Well, that's part of the challenge. We were storing all of these images, but they were ridiculously hard to catalog and access. So, two computer programs were being developed when I left. One was Luminus, which was to meant to analyze regular patterns in images and match them against a grid of what is normal or abnormal." Saara turned her chair around to face the three men. "Let's say, for instance, that we are getting shots of a ferry going back and forth from Vancouver to Vancouver Island. The computer would categorize those images as a regular pattern. But one day, the ferry is hijacked by terrorists who have vehicles on board, loaded with explosives. Suddenly, the ship diverts from Victoria, where it would normally go, and keeps on sailing south towards Seattle. The software would recognize this as an abnormal pattern and send an alert to the appropriate agencies."

"Wow!" Justin responded, impressed.

"Pretty sophisticated," Saara agreed. "The second software project was even crazier. It set out to transdimensionalize the images."

"Turn them from two-dimensional images to three-dimensional ones?"

She nodded, "That's right."

"I'm assuming the goal was that one day in the future, those programs would come together."

"That project was blacker than black. But it was the one I got pulled into when I left Luminus."

"So, you're frustrated because ..."

"Luminus should be pointed at Libya. It should be identifying multiplying tire tracks in the middle of the White Desert that go from the Egyptian border and end abruptly in nothing. That is why the program was developed, to begin with. It was supposed to single out these kinds of anomalies."

Leonard Stone could see her point. "Do you think it's a software glitch or something more sinister."

"It's just a developmental failure. I once suggested that we target our enemies first, thinking that any intel we could gain on nations like North Korea, Russia, Libya, Syria, or Iran, would be helpful."

"People opposed you?" David asked, incredulously.

Saara nodded. "It's one of the reasons I had no problem joining LaunchPad. Leonard knows this part."

"Why were you shut down?"

Dr. Stone answered for her. "Because people higher in the food chain thought that rather than targeting our enemies, we should shit all over the constitutional right to privacy and train the eyes of Luminus on the United States of America."

"But, isn't it designed to help protect the nation?" Justin asked.

"That's one way to look at it. That's the way lots of people want to see it. But the problem is that twenty-four hours, seven days a week, thousands of hackers around the world are trying to get into our satellites and hack the transmission of data." Leonard pulled a chair over and sat down. "Eventually, they'll get through. It will be the equivalent of owning a bank and handing over blueprints, biometrics, schedules, and content inventories to a group of known thieves."

"But aren't we spying on other nations?"

"Yes. And they're welcome to spy on us. That's why you read an article in the news every once in a while, about the United States blowing some satellite out of the air. It's because we caught them. But spying on our own people? Not only is that against our right to privacy, but it's also collecting information that will make it a lot easier for our enemies, should they figure out how to steal it."

A loud bellowing noise across the intercom from the interrogation cells interrupted their conversation, and everyone started to chuckle.

"Serwabi needs to use the restroom," David guessed. "I'll take him for a walk."

"Just bring him a bucket," Leo instructed. "I don't want him out of that room until we get what we want."

CHAPTER THIRTY-FIVE

"WHAT ARE YOU THINKING, BRUCE?" AGENT STONE ASKED HIS friend.

"Tank moves left from here and digs down in a spot that covers the east exit of the structure to make sure nobody drives off. I'll steal around to the south, between this dune and the one next to it," he said, pointing it out on his tablet. "As we both start lighting up the building, people will come running for safety to the North, towards you, and the West. You'll have buried down and can take them out with sniper cover."

"Tank?"

"Works for me. They'll think the attacks are coming from the East and the South. We'll press them towards you."

"Can we squeeze them North and still have Bruce beside me?"

"Sure," Tank answered. "When it's dark, Bruce and I could go over to the south side and plant some noisy charges."

"Circle back here before blowing them up?"

"Right. People will think the attack is coming from that side and pull back into our direction. You and Bruce ambush them. I'll cover the road."

Trey nodded. "I like that idea. While the two of you are planting, I'll work my way down the other side of the dune we're on now until I have a clear line of sight through the entire structure. Then, I'll burrow down and get set up."

"When you're ready, we'll blow about half the charges. I'll secure the near right corner of the structure – the Northwest corner," Bruce said, pointing it out on his tablet. "Tank, you'll be on the left – the Northwest corner. We'll move through in formation. About twenty percent of the way through, we'll blow the rest of the charges on the south side to make them think that we've got more guys out there."

"Any chance we get help?" Tank asked.

"No chance. We're in pretty hostile territory, uninvited, and killing people. This is strictly a ghost operation. We were never here."

"Set the second wave of charges to be on a timer. Eight minutes after the first explosions. That way, you can stay focused on clearing the structure."

"Copy that. You saw the activity," Bruce said, turning to Tank. "What's your count?"

"Maybe twenty visible hostiles. If this really is where the train stopped, they might have more people underground."

"That's what I thought, too. I figured those temporary barracks house about twenty people, each."

"Remember," Trey advised, "Clearing this structure is only a means to an end. Our primary objective is to find Casey Baker and extract her to the Jeep. Tank, you'll be the one to take her to safety and wait with her. Bruce and I will rescue whoever we can and meet you back at the Jeep.

Tank and Bruce nodded.

"Okay. You two get busy. Prep your charges now, and when it's dark, get planting. At 0130, we go boom. I'll link up with LaunchPad and brief them, then I'm going to prep for sniper cover."

———

THE PARENTS HAD CHECKED into their rooms, dined, and were called together for the first meeting in The Pulse. The mood was tense, despite the surrounding opulence of the Waldorf in Rome.

George Baker sat behind his large snake-wood desk with the vast mountains of the Telluride region sprawled out behind him, easily visible through his floor to ceiling home-office windows. He watched the parents on his monitor and prepared himself to be introduced via video conferencing.

A nondescript secret service agent stood up and took a microphone into her hands, clearing her throat to get everyone's attention. "Ladies and gentlemen, the former President of the United States of America, President George Baker."

It wasn't a rousing introduction, but President Baker realized it was an appropriate one. This wasn't the time to get everyone springing to their feet and clapping with excitement, as if at a political rally. This was a solemn moment. He waited until the light turned green on his teleprompter software and then began to read the pre-written words as they appeared right below the eye of the camera built into his computer.

"Thank you," he responded. There were subtle nuances of compassion and concern in Baker's voice mixed with authority and sulfites of revenge. "I appreciate the introduction. But today, I'm just George. I'm Ted's father and Casey's grandfather. Just like you, I'm in great distress. I've gone down the full gauntlet of emotions, as have you. I've cried, I've screamed, I've sat … stunned … not wanting to believe that this could really happen. And I've prayed. I've done a lot of praying. Just like you." He looked down, effectively, and then back at the camera. "I appreciate all of you flying to Rome on such short notice and trust that your accommodations there will suffice. As I promised those of you who were in my home, less than twelve hours ago, we'll keep you updated on everything as it happens. Right now, I can tell you that we have the best people our nation has to offer, working tirelessly to bring back our girls."

Someone's hand shot up.

"Yes," the president acknowledged, a little surprised to be interrupted, but knowing he needed to listen. He tapped the spacebar on his computer to pause the scrolling teleprompter software.

"I'm sorry," a German father confessed. "But I did not come to Rome to hear you say that you have some of the best people doing this and you might have a lead that you're pursuing … I want to know details. Please. I think we deserve that."

Baker pursed his lips. He nodded. "Okay, then." He looked into the camera. "If anyone in this room leaks what I'm about to tell you, you will be putting not only your daughter but everyone else's children also at enormous risk. I hope you are all wise enough to recognize that." He cleared his throat. "We have our nation's very best covert operator leading a carefully selected team to a location where we believe the girls are being held. Neither German nor American military is allowed to be in that nation. It makes the ongoing situation enormously delicate. Off the coast, and at full-alert, is a combat-ready amphibious assault ship from the United States Navy. We have members of the NSA, the CIA, the FBI, and the Secret Service heading to the target as we speak."

Another hand went up.

"Do you have proof of life?" a mother demanded.

"Not yet."

"When will they arrive at the location?"

"Within the next twelve hours," the President said, hoping he was buying Trey enough time.

CHAPTER THIRTY-SIX

GHALIB AHMAADI STOOD LIKE A STATUE, HIS DARK EYES AS HARD as black diamonds as he stared out the window of his luxurious top-floor corner office in London's West End. He'd just touched his Bluetooth earpiece to hang up on a call from India where he'd learned that three important links in the chain of his trade had just been erased. It was bothering him. Not that they were dead, although that in itself would complicate things, it was how they had died that concerned him. To blow up a Knight armored SUV from the inside, at a moment in time that wiped out three top-tier criminals, took the kind of meticulous planning and brazen courage that only a handful of people in the world possessed. There was the money issue, too. He hadn't been paid yet, and all three of those bosses had owed him. He thought about what he needed to do – steal it, obviously. He'd have to hire that hacker from Eastern Europe. She was the best.

His iPhone buzzed, and he walked over to his glass desk, admiring the 24-karat gold trim he'd just had added to its corners and edges. He picked up his phone and saw the notification was regarding a message that could only be opened by a specific app on a burner phone he kept in a locked safe-drawer in his desk. He used a thumb-print to open it, took out the phone, and tapped the app. Next, he answered a series of security questions he'd created, and then picked the red truck from a collection of images. The two measures activated his phone's camera and allowed it to do an iris scan of his left eye. With security passed, the red truck dissolved into a short communication. It was from his brother, letting him know that things were running on schedule. He carefully put the phone back in his desk drawer and locked it with his right thumb.

Ghalib reached into the pocket of his navy blue, tonal striped suit, designed personally by Stefano Ricci, and pulled out a thin notepad neatly protected in Arctic fox leather. His father had taught him to always keep his darkest secrets closest to his breast. He still relished writing things down without any kind of a digital trace. He opened his jotter for the notes from the private meditation he'd had in the early morning hours. Extracting the gold pen from its holder, he made a mark in the margin of his notes. It was time to call Prince Faisal Bin Abdulaziz al Saud to let him know that his prize would be arriving in sixteen hours. The birthday present would solidify their relationship, perhaps even for generations to come.

With business items finished, he decided to change into his athletic gear and go for a workout and a light protein snack.

THE MODIFIED YAMAHA BANSHEE had automatically switched to its third and final tank of gas. Glancing down at the trip-o-meter of kilometers they'd traveled, Michi knew something would be coming up soon. They were less than twenty minutes away from where Casey Baker's embedded transponder had pinged. She eased up on the throttle and began to downshift.

"What's going on?" asked Jasmine.

"We'll be arriving soon. Let's hydrate, eat something, and go over our plan."

As the modified four-wheeler came to a stop, the two women climbed off, shut down their night vision goggles and flicked on their headlamps. Jasmine put the drone into sleep mode, which meant it would lower itself to the ground and partially shut down. The cameras would stay active. She tapped the drone's battery icon on her tablet's screen. It had almost cycled through four of its six custom-designed battery packs.

"This tunnel is by far the creepiest place I've ever been," Trey's daughter expressed.

Michi nodded, "For me, too, Jasmine. I have to fight to keep my emotions under control. I keep thinking about all the people that have been trafficked through here. And I've had this other thought: What if we broke down?"

Jazzy had been pondering the same things.

"Your dad taught me to isolate my thinking from what I can't change, and just focus on the task at hand," Michi said, handing Jasmine a water canteen.

"Yeah, he told me that too. It's a lot harder to do than I thought, though."

"Well if it's any encouragement, I think you're doing great."

Jasmine gulped down some water, "Thanks."

The two women opened their duffle bags and found some MRE's packed in separate compartments from their weaponry.

"Have you had the *Meal Ready-to-Eat's* before?" Michi asked.

Jasmine nodded. "Dad would bring some leftover ones home sometimes. My brother and I would watch in amazement at how food would come out of the bag hot, without anything to warm it." She started looking through the self-contained field rations in her bag.

Michi picked one that had tuna, tortillas, dried peaches, and cookies. "I don't think I can eat hot food right now," she said, putting the tortillas back, "I'll have something light."

"Me, too. Here's one that says: Havarti cheese, wheat snack bread, dried fruit, and a chocolate banana muffin top," Jazzy responded, I'll skip the beef stew. I'm a sucker for chocolate ... even in this God-forsaken place."

They ate quickly, loaded their things, and got themselves ready. Michi checked her Glock 19 and then pulled out a Tavor TAR-21 assault rifle that was developed in Israel. Because of the constant threat of its neighbors, Israel had become recognized worldwide for its development of small arms. She attached a MOR red dot laser scope and then a 40mm grenade launcher.

Jasmine did some stretching to get her blood flowing and then checked her own weapon of choice from the same Middle Eastern nation. It was a pistol her father had thought would work for her. She loved it. With its polymer frame and compact size, the Jericho 941 FB was easy to handle, exceptionally accurate and extremely durable. She checked her knife-set and strapped it to her waist with some extra mags. Turning her headlamp off, she switched on her night vision goggles and woke up the drone.

"Ready?" Michiko Imada asked as she loaded her bag on the modified Banshee.

"I'm so nervous," Jasmine admitted.

"Your main job is to stay alive. Mine is to deal with whatever comes. Remember that. You don't have to be a hero. Just protect yourself and lay low. We're going to drive forward for about ten more minutes and then advance on foot."

"Okay, Michi."

CHAPTER THIRTY-SEVEN

BRUCE AND TANK WERE POURING OVER HIGH-RESOLUTION IMAGES on their tablets, deciding where the best place for charges would be.

"We'll be ready in thirty," Bruce said.

Tank nodded and then remarked, thoughtfully, "This is a little trickier than clearing and holding a building with walls."

"In some ways, that's true ... because of the potential to be tagged by friendly fire, right?"

"Exactly."

"I think that's why Trey wanted us on the same side of the warehouse as him before moving forward. We'll move in from opposite corners to divide their attention. The charges should help, too."

"Is he really as good as people say?"

Bruce smiled, "Trey?"

Tank nodded.

"Better."

While the two operatives were finalizing their strategy, Agent Stone had updated the crew back at LaunchPad and was now preparing for a dry run. He'd emptied out his duffle bag and filled it with sand. Then he'd taken the rope out that he'd gone back to the Jeep to recover and created a shoulder harness of sorts at one end, tying the other to the handles of his sack. He decided to run some tests. Scrambling down the hill, he towed his bag of sand behind him. It worked perfectly. He was able to get into position, dig out a little bunker for himself, place his bag full of sand in front of him as a stable, protective buffer and then settle into a kneeling sniper pose. He imagined he was in position and looking at the giant warehouse-like structure with no walls. Digging his boots into the sand, he spread them in a way that would anchor the rest of his body. He propped up on his arms and relaxed, making sure his gun was comfortably and securely in his hands.

With his body position figured out, Trey began to take mental snapshots of himself, remembering how each part of his figure felt. He looked at his feet, his knees, his waist, his hands, and his elbows. Then, he lowered his head and made a note of where his gun was in relation to his jaw and nose. He knew that when the time came, the relationship between his eye and the rear of his scope would be very important. Each time he'd have to aim, he would settle his jaw and nose into the exact same spot, increasing accuracy and consistency. With the night vision scope turned on and the tricky shadows, if he didn't know where his eye should be, he'd waste a lot of precious seconds finding the optimal field of view and chasing images rather than leading them.

He opened his mouth to breathe quietly. Relaxed his pulse. Cleared his mind. Then he imagined squeezing off a round, re-sighting a new target, squeezing off another round, re-sighting and shooting. As he imagined each shot, he continued to breathe consistently, as if he were about to fall asleep. If he were to forget and hold his breath when he'd finally have to breathe again, his body would start to shake, and his aim would become unpredictable. By now, all of these techniques came second nature to him, but he was unapologetically obsessive about practicing and preparing. Emptying the sand out of his duffle bag so that he wouldn't have to exhaust himself dragging it back up the dune, he climbed up to just below the crest, where he refilled his bag and checked his gear one last time. Finally, Trey sat down to overlook the sandy region of eastern Libya.

The air was cooling down as the sun disappeared over the horizon and early stars studded the sky. He rehydrated from his canteen and devoured some beef jerky. Darkness was slowly spreading across the night sky, pushing the dusk away. By now, Tank and Bruce should be in position to start planting charges.

"Hemlock," he said, touching his throat mic. He decided to use a call sign he'd first gotten when he was a kid at the CIA high school in Japan and learning about stealth kills. Many different types of the plant have fatally toxic roots, that when absorbed in low quantities, cause death.

"In position," answered Bruce.

"In position," echoed Tank.

"Plant seeds in five."

"Roger that. Five mikes."

Trey shouldered his gear. He slipped the rope harness over his shoulders and across his chest. Very slowly he snaked over the crest of the dune and began to slither down the hill, dragging his duffle bag full of sand behind him. His eyes were darting back and forth, tracking every movement within his vision. So far, he'd counted ten hostiles. None of them had even turned in his direction or seen him. Four were sitting at a table playing cards and drinking something stronger than water. Three hostiles were standing close to one of the lifted fifteen-passenger vans. One of them was sitting in a chair staring at his mobile phone and tapping it intermittently as if he were playing a game of some sort. The other two were standing guard, more or less. They had guns ready and were leaning against the front hood of a Humvee, looking straight out toward Trey's left, where the tire tracks in the sand indicated that vehicles frequently came in and out.

Trey was careful to go very slow, keeping his bag from rolling down the hill and over him, but quick enough to get into position in a timely manner. When he'd come down the hill far enough to have a clear line of sight from his side to the opposite side, under the roof of the huge structure, he stopped. He checked behind him. As he'd planned, the dragged bag had covered up any impressions in the sand that he'd made with his elbows and knees. He created his bunker, just like he'd practiced. Placing his bag in front of him for protection, he dug until he was satisfied. Then he locked his body into position and placed his jaw and nose exactly where they were supposed to go. Instantly, his eye locked on the men below, as he looked through his scope.

"In position."

"Oscar Mike," said Bruce, acknowledging that they were on the move and planting charges.

Trey's breathing was calmly rhythmic now, and his mind completely focused on the task at hand. He slowly moved his rifle back and forth, looking through the structure to the dune on the opposite side and searching for Bruce and Tank through his scope. A one-time pencil-light flash drew his attention. He clicked his tongue slowly twice against the roof of his mouth, indicating that he'd seen them, but not wanting to make any other noise at this time. He watched their barely visible shadows as they planted charges in the sand opposite of him. One of them stopped. The other snuck further down the hill while staying in the shadows getting as close as possible to the building. Trey saw him get within about fifty feet of the structure, stoop down, and place a charge on the ground. He slowly backed out of the area, and as he did, Agent Stone got a glimpse of his ponytail. It had been Tank. He continued to creep up the dune and back to where Bruce was waiting.

"Mission complete."

"Roger that. Return to nest," Trey said softly, instructing them to go back over their dune and hoof it around to his position.

As he watched them climb up, he kept an eye on any movement in the structure that would indicate they'd been noticed. A few minutes later, they crested the dune and slipped over the top edge. Stone set his scope back on the hostiles again, moving his rifle from one to the other, simulating the movements he'd make as he took them out.

All of a sudden, the four men stopped their card game and stood up. They each grabbed a chair and picked up their table, moving it about thirty feet further from Trey. The guards were on one knee now, looking alert and peering into the darkness. Agent Stone slowly tilted his head to the left, looking out East. There were no headlights or signs of an oncoming vehicle.

The three who had been by the van split up. One walked around to the driver's side, opened the door and started up the engine. The other stayed by the table, and the third guy walked over to one of the smaller transport trucks, reached in through the open window and pulled something out that had been sitting on the dashboard. Trey zoomed in to see him fiddling with a pack of cigarettes. He watched, as the man lit one and reached back into the truck to put his pack back onto the dashboard.

"We have movement," Trey whispered hoarsely. "I'm not sure what's going on, but the hornets are stirring."

Stone zoomed back out and observed the four card-players walking over to a pile of large chains. They split into two teams and worked together to drag the heavy links over to enormous loops of steel that had been sticking out of the ground. He followed the chains to their other ends. They were in some kind of mechanical pulley wheel. Agent Stone suddenly realized what they were doing, and his heart sank. With all the chains in place, one of the men walked over to a support post and pressed a large red button. A diesel generator fired up, and the pulley began to reel in the links. As they tightened, they pulled on the steel loops. After a few minutes, the chains were lifting a large iron lid that was on giant hinges – an enormous trap door, of sorts. The lid must have weighed a couple of tons. As it slowly raised, sand poured off it. The whole thing was now blocking a good portion of Trey's line of sight. He couldn't see any of the action on the other side of the hole's covering.

"LP, we have a large hole that just opened up in the middle of the floor of the structure," he informed LaunchPad. "The trap door is screening my view."

"Copy that, Hemlock. Stay in position," Leo said.

"Vegas, what's your eta?" Trey demanded, sharply, using Bruce's codename.

"Fifteen."

"Make it five." He could hear Tank grunt and knew the two men would be in full sprint now.

Trey's well-trained mind began to calculate the options when all of a sudden, he heard voices. They were definitely male voices yelling directions. It was at the same time he heard the screaming and crying of thirteen-year-old girls being marched somewhere. Everything in him wanted to start shooting now, but he didn't want to endanger the lives of the girls. He didn't know if these crazies would start to panic and execute them. Agent Stone decided to stay in place. His scope had a digital camera feature, and so he started snapping photos. He'd upload them to LaunchPad when it was safe.

The guy in the van had pulled forward a bit and then backed up beside the large iron hatch cover, screening Trey's view even more. The guards were still facing the desert road that led out into the darkness. But the guy who had been playing games on his cell phone jumped up from where he was and disappeared behind the large iron door. The four card players were gone now. Either they were behind the raised cover, just standing on the other side, or they'd gone down the large hatch.

"On your six," Bruce wheezed. "Just coming over the hill."

A few minutes later, Tank was on Trey's left, and Bruce was on his right, both panting like Saint Bernards trying to cool themselves

"Nice view," Trey's friend, commented sarcastically.

"Can't see a thing," Stone complained in a whisper. "You can see this giant iron hatch cover. But I don't know if there are a group of people standing over there or if they all went down into the tunnel."

"Yeah. This won't work," Tank said, stating the obvious. "I'll go down there to see what's going on."

Trey nodded. "I'll cover you. Go to the Northeastern corner."

The Lakota Native took a swig of water, replaced his canteen, and checked his gun. Then he started down the sand dune.

"I'm headed down, too."

"Copy that," answered Trey, his eye fastened to his scope.

It was really dark now, and surprisingly, there were no lights in the structure. Trey figured they didn't have electricity, or if they did, they were paranoid about remaining stealth. He could make Tank out, slithering down the hill on his way to the corner post. Stone looked to his right and saw Bruce, too, was making great time.

Back at LaunchPad, David and Leonard had come out of the conference room. Ashley and Bora had left the medical clinic. Everyone was gathered with Saara and Justin in the office to watch the three blue dots moving around on the map.

Trey focused his scope back onto the hostiles that weren't screened by the giant door. The man in the van had gotten out and was standing in front of it. Cigarette-man was still over by the little transport truck. He might've lit up another tobacco stick. The two guards were still peering into the darkness. *Were they expecting someone to come?*

Suddenly, a massive roar of engines filled the air! Trey had never heard anything like it. The two guards turned around in the direction of the giant hatch and started motioning as if signaling someone to come to them. Cigarette-man dropped his butt and put it out with his shoe. He started walking towards the hatch.

"What's going on?" Bruce shouted into his throat mic.

Nobody needed to answer. Apparently, the hatch wasn't covering a ladder or a set of stairs, it was the lid for a huge tunnel ramp. Unlike any vehicle Trey had ever seen, a large truck surged out of from the hole on the other side of the giant lid like a killer whale breaking the ocean's surface. It was painted flat black and resembled a giant mining dump truck one would see in a rock quarry. It had huge seven-foot-tall black tires with thick treads, a flat front with a massive grill, and a ten-foot ladder that led up to an enclosed cage where the driver and one passenger sat. The modified rear of the truck didn't dump chunks of granite but had been retrofitted to transport goods. Trey knew what these goods were ... people. Young girls, to be exact!

"Take everybody out!" Bruce shouted, pulling out his Glock 17 and carefully threading his way through parked vehicles towards the tunnel opening.

Trey had already taken a shot, using the roaring engine noise to cover up the cracking bursts from his sniper rifle.

The guard on the right was confused. He saw his pal's head explode like a watermelon on a target range. The man who had been standing in front of the van had his head burst too. The remaining guard had no time to react. His head suffered the same fate.

Another giant truck, exactly like the first one, roared up the tunnel. It burst out of the opening, bouncing as it caught a bit of air and then landed heavily. Trey fired off a shot at the driver's side window. The bullet made a clean hole in the glass but didn't have the angle to hit the driver.

"I'm going to follow them!" Tank yelled, running towards a nearby Humvee. The guy by the transport truck spotted him and grabbed a rifle from his cab. He raised it to shoot, but Trey dropped him with his fourth consecutive headshot. Suddenly, a man appeared from behind the steel curtain of the trap door's lid. He had a combat knife in his hand and raced towards Tank.

Five headshots.

Ponytail threw his kit into the passenger's seat, jumped behind the wheel, and searched desperately for a set of keys. He found them in a cup holder and fired up the engine of the Humvee. It roared to life, and he took off, behind the second truck.

Bruce had gotten to the edge of the hatch to look down at the ramp below. There were four guys standing with weapons single-point-strapped to their backs, unaware of all the shooting that had happened on the deck above them. A third truck was firing up its engine, and the noise below was deafening. Agent Locke's left hand reached to his waist and unstrapped a stun grenade. He knew it wouldn't kill anyone, but it would temporarily disorient the men with a blinding flash that would trigger all the photoreceptor cells in their eyes and make vision impossible for a few seconds. The penetratingly loud bang of the grenade, at over one hundred and seventy decibels, would cause temporary loss of hearing, even over the noise of the trucks.

From the other side of the hole, someone was in full sprint towards Bruce. Trey saw him just in time. The figure was preparing to plunge his jambiya into the base of Bruce's skull. It had a curved blade, sharp enough to cut through the bone of a camel, but Trey's sixth headshot sent the attacker flying over Bruce into the tunnel entrance at the same time as the giant third truck began to move forward.

The Lynx screamed with rage. A body with a mutilated head bounced off the window of the cage he was in. "Who the hell was that?" he fulminated at the driver beside him. The blood on the windshield told him the fall was not an accident. His green eyes flashed with fury, "Drive! Drive! Drive!"

It only took Bruce a millisecond to process what must have happened. He stayed focused and pulled the pin from his grenade. As he let it go, two figures in black darted behind the huge truck and latched onto the gigantic bumper. They had black backpacks on them, and their faces were covered with dark camo-paint. He watched the grenade bounce to the four men and knew the magnesium-based pyrotechnic charge was about to detonate. The figures on the truck screamed as the truck surged forward. The hostiles below tried to cover their ears, but it was too late. The stun grenade set off a noise like a sonic boom in the tunnel. Holstering his pistol with his right hand while his left arm swung over his head, Bruce pulled out his personally customized and fully automatic AA-12 from his back strap. The weapon known as the Atchisson Assault Shotgun was a 12-gauge that could unload 300 rounds per minute, making it possible to fire one round at a time with brief trigger pulls. He squeezed the trigger four times. Each of the men dropped to the ground like a sack of potatoes.

Bruce whipped his head around to fire at the back of the truck, but a furiously blinking red light caught his eye. "Holy crap!" he exclaimed, "I almost killed Michi and Jasmine!"

Hearing his friend on the comms, Trey dumped his sniper rifle and tore down the dune like a lion released. He whipped out his handgun and fired useless shots at the side of the truck as it roared forward. Reaching the compound, he could barely make out the two dark shadows holding on to the bumper for dear life.

"Let's go!" he screamed, looking around for a good vehicle to commandeer.

Bruce jogged up beside him. "We've got to secure this site."

"A team from the ship can do it. We have to follow them. Now!"

"Okay. But go back and get our full kits, first. Let's not be stupid." Bruce spotted a gray Toyota Tacoma. "Trey, we'll take that," he said, pointing to it. "You know we can catch up to those beasts in a matter of minutes. They won't be hard to track, and they're slow as hell."

Trey had calmed down. "Are you sure that was Jasmine?"

Both guys winced as their earpieces cackled loudly and their global comms sprang to life.

"Dad?" Jasmine's voice shouted, "Dad, was that you?"

"Jazzy! Yes, that was us. Is Michi with you?"

"She's having some trouble with her comms," his daughter answered. "We're hanging on to the back of the third truck!"

"Okay, Sweetie. Don't let go. We'll be there soon, okay?"

"Dad, we're with the some of the American team. The first truck has the rest of them. The middle truck has the German girls."

Trey was so proud of his daughter! She could actually zero in on what was important in the moment. "Okay, Jasmine! Do you know where Casey Baker is?"

"No. I'm not sure. There are bodies down on the platform that we didn't take the time to identify. We had to make a quick call, so we jumped on the truck." She paused for a second. "Someone tossed something into the tunnel that deafened us. Michi yelled to close my eyes, or I would have been blind. I just hung on with all my might."

"Glad you're okay now," Trey replied calmly reassuring her, "That was a stun grenade. Listen, Honey, we need to get off these comms for now, alright?"

"Okay. Michi says to tell you we'll stay with this truck wherever it goes."

"Roger that," Trey acknowledged and disconnected. He turned to Bruce, "Clear the tunnel, finger-scan everyone and meet me back here. I'll get our kits."

Trey jogged up to where his modified bunker was, emptied the sand out of his duffle bag, grabbed his rifle, and sprinted up over the crest of the dune. He stuffed all of his gear back into his bag and grabbed Bruce's kit. As he was about to race back his father's voice filtered through his earpiece.

"LP to Hemlock."

"Go ahead."

"We suggest you use the Jeep. It has three gas tanks."

"Copy that. Good thinking."

He slid down the dune, jogged over to the Jeep, tore off the camo, tossed all the gear in the back and jumped into the driver's seat. He drove around the huge dune and into the wall-less warehouse. Bruce came running up the tunnel. He was carrying black duffle bags. "Pull it up next to the vans," he yelled. "Let's siphon the gas."

Trey nodded, restarting the engine and repositioning the Jeep by the vans. "Those our bags?"

"Red Team's. Looks like they took what they needed, though." Bruce threw the bags into the back.

"All clear down there?"

"I put down one more hostile, but there's some really bad news."
He pulled out his camera and a cable. Then he hitched it to the
Wolfe system of the Jeep. Tapping the screen a few times, he
said, "LP, I'm uploading the finger-scan images now as well as
some other shots I snapped."

"Copy that, Vegas," Saara answered, choosing to follow Trey's
lead, and using Bruce's code name.

David asked the obvious question. "What's the bad news?"

"It looks like all of the adults on the train were shot. Execution
style to the back of their heads."

"My God. Howell, too?"

"Affirmative. Every single one of them."

CHAPTER THIRTY-EIGHT

THE ROAD IN THE DESERT WAS TRICKY; IN THE STRAIGHTAWAYS, blinding sand was spitting out from the large tires. Tank was constantly correcting the wheel. If he stayed on the tire tracks, he could hang with the large vehicles, but if he got off of them, he could easily get bogged down. Then he'd have to slam the Hummer into four-wheel drive and bore out of it like an angry badger.

His earpiece made a noise, "LP."

"Kinda busy!"

"You're two mikes out from the Egyptian border, but it looks like it's ungoverned space," David continued. "Rebel fighter patrols are definitely going to be in that area. Keep your eyes peeled."

"Are the patrols good or bad?" demanded Tank, as he started drifting through a long-left turn.

"Very bad. Rebels have taken over everything outside of government control. These guys are mostly jihadists. They're into everything you can imagine." Hirsch paused for a second. "They're well-armed, kid; don't underestimate them."

"What happens if we cross into Egypt?"

"Stay with them. We're working on it. Don't let any authority tell you otherwise."

"Copy that!" shouted Tank. He came out of the long corner and into a straightaway. The ground was changing. It was still brown and barren, but the sand was compacted. Just for a second, Agent Tatanka Ptecila remembered camping on that kind of ground on the floor of the Grand Canyon with his family. The Hummer was keeping up just fine, but the bouncing up and down was starting to get annoying.

Saara had identified the sobering images sent from Bruce's camera and forwarded the list of confirmed executed adults to everyone's tablets: Dr. Helmut Donnerwetter, the German team physician; Hans Schmidt, the handsome soccer coach; Herr and Frau Dietrich and Paulina Lowe, a set of parents from Germany; Herr and Frau Bruno and Helga Schmidt, the other set of German parents; Mr. and Mrs. David and Elisabeth Jackson, Savannah's mother and father; Dr. and Mrs. Andrew and Tracey Taylor, Amber's mother and father; Secret Service Agent Miles Howell, the security detail assigned to guard the girls; and Neil Murray, the well-loved soccer coach of the American girls' team. All were confirmed dead.

The tall Finn began to download footage of the entire night's event from Trey's headcam and scope camera. At the same time, footage from Michi's camera started to automatically download on her computer, too.

Leonard Stone was in the conference room on a split-screen video conference, briefing President Baker and his son, while monitoring the ongoing action.

"Mr. President, the lid is going to come off. The Jackson's and the Taylor's are prominent couples. Agent Howell has deep ties to the Army and the Secret Service. And Coach Murray was extensively networked into his local community. It's only a matter of time before relatives and friends wonder why they can't reach these people. Those are the Americans we lost. I'm sure that the German side is just as ready to hit the public. We've got to open the scope of our response."

The elder Baker looked unconvinced.

"Look, George," Trey's father said, carefully using the President's name. "First, you need to open a channel with the press. Nothing concrete. Just prep some allies in the media who can move this forward when the time is right. Second, you'll need to understand that it's one thing for our small team to be running around in the Wild West in Libya. But it's a whole different animal entering Egypt. They're our most dependable allies in the Arab region. They'll have to know from you that we're in their jurisdiction and we need their help."

"I understand what you're saying, Leonard, but we simply cannot trust anyone on the ground there. That nation is a perfect storm of anger and idiocy right now. People are turning against their own brothers and sisters over there, never mind a group from America."

"Certainly, you have people in the area, don't you, Dad?" Ted argued with his father, taking sides with Leo. "Dr. Stone is saying that his people are spread dangerously thin right now."

"We have informants and moderate assets, Son, not a team of weaponized ass-kickers."

The conversation went silent. Leo sat back in his chair and stared at the ceiling. The Lynx was very smart to divide up the girls. "Have you at least brought in the German chancellor?"

"I will, now that these deaths have been confirmed."

"And have you canceled German and American involvement with the tournament leadership in Botswana?"

"Yes," answered Ted. "We have deeply apologized that due to unforeseen circumstances beyond our control, the American and the German teams would not be able to participate."

"No blowback?"

"Nothing that we won't handle."

"Tank to LP!"

Leonard Stone looked through the glass conference room wall at the group gathered in the office area. David was motioning for him to join them.

"Gentlemen, I have to go." He leaned his face very close to the camera and growled, "Mr. President, if you want to see Casey again, then either get support from Egypt or deploy some support to Egypt!" He tapped the red dot to end the call and rushed to the office area. "What is it?"

Justin answered, "It's not good. They are now officially in Egypt. Tank just contacted us to get our attention. He turned on his camera. That's the feed on the right. It doesn't match his GPS signal, though."

As he was speaking, Tank's video feed looked like it was being filmed by a three-year-old. It started jerking up and down, and the image would freeze intermittently.

"Saara, what's going on?" Leo asked clearly puzzled with a slight degree of irritation.

The tech genius shook her head, unsure.

"I know!" exclaimed Justin. "He's driving with his left hand and filming with his right, but he's zoomed in, so it's super jerky."

"Zoomed into what?" asked David.

"I think he's sending us images!" Justin shouted excitedly. "Give me a minute."

A few moments later, the camera was pointing in front of Tank again, and the image had zoomed out and stabilized.

"Tank?" Leo asked. There was no answer. "LP to Tank."

The atmosphere was intensifying in the office area as Tank remained unresponsive.

"Tank?" tried Saara.

"Got it!" Justin cried. "Check this out. I took the first of those moments where we thought the video froze and assumed he was taking a picture instead. I ran it through my software to clean up the images ... but I'm not sure what I'm looking at."

He slid the image from his tablet up onto one of the hanging flat screens.

"That black color matches the paint from the truck he was following," Saara said, tilting her head to the side.

"Okay. Is that a bomb on there?" asked Leo.

"You mean that gray thing?" responded David. "No, I don't think so ... but it does look like something taped together ... duct tape? Did you pack some of that stuff in his kit, Justin?"

"Yes, it's in everybody's kit."

"There seems to be something hanging down from it ... a black wire or something."

"I've got the next image coming through," Justin said, sending it up on the screen as soon as it finished rendering.

"I know what he's done," Leonard Stone said, gravely. "The video feed doesn't match the GPS coordinates because the two trucks have split up. He created a sticky device with duct tape, wrapped his comms package in it and stuck it onto that truck as he drove by."

"Why?" asked Ashley.

"Of course!" Justin said, shaking his head in amazement. "It's the only way to track the truck. His comms have the GPS transponder in it, so he threw it onto there."

David whistled softly. "That was smart."

"Except we can't communicate with him," Saara pointed out worriedly.

"Right," Leonard agreed. "But we can track the second truck, now. Jazzy said it had the German team on it. I'll call President Baker with the location. Can we set up a live feed for the FIS if they want one?"

"The Federal Intelligence Service?" Saara asked, raising her eyebrows. "Sure."

"But we don't want Germany's equivalent of the CIA tracing the originating data to LaunchPad. They won't be able to, will they?"

"No. We're hacked into CIA feed. Any tracing they do would lead them to Company countermeasures. They'll be expecting CIA involvement, under the circumstances."

"Okay. Send the information to my tablet, and I'll relay it to the president." He stood up, "Saara, we'll have to keep up with the video feed from Tank's camera and sync it with satellite mapping imagery to figure out where he is. Would you do that?"

"I'll get to work on it right away."

"Where are Bruce and Trey?" asked David.

She pointed to the screen on the far right. "All we've got are the blue dots, but since they're moving together, I assume they're chasing down the third truck."

"Can you rename Tank's transponder German Team or something like that?"

She nodded, tapping away on her computer. "I sent the tracking info to you, Dr. Stone. Just give that exact link and password to President Baker so he can pass it on to the Bundesnachrichtendienst." She raised her arms to stretch. "I'll get to work on syncing Tank's video with mapping software."

CHAPTER THIRTY-NINE

THE PLANE WAS DESCENDING RAPIDLY THROUGH THE TYPICALLY opacus clouds of England. Boyd Carter was ready to get the show going. She'd logged enough air-time over the last forty-eight hours to last her for a long while. As usual, with the jet about to land, the upcoming task started to roll around in the theater of her mind. She looked over at Fox, staring out the window of the luxury jet, "So. Just to review. You're still thinking we should just walk up to Ghalib Ahmaadi's most-likely uber-secured house and ring the doorbell?"

"Do you have a better idea?" asked Fox, with a slight grin and turning towards her. "I've always thought that people like him appreciate the art of face-to-face conversations."

"What are you going to say to get us inside?"

"I thought about having you give a demonstration."

"I'm not going to flirt with the doorman."

Fox laughed. "I was thinking of you presenting *how to immobilize a security detail in a few easy steps*, but then, that might scare him off."

Boyd chuckled.

"Probably we'll just need to tell him that we'd like to talk about the problem with his German and American shipments."

"And what if he doesn't like what we tell him and he gets all amped on us?"

"... then you might have to make that demonstration after all."

Boyd looked out of her window as they broke through the clouds. She looked out over London as the plane lurched in the wind.

"Damn it!" Fox exclaimed.

"Not used to turbulence?"

"I just remembered something."

She looked over and could tell he was serious.

He touched his earpiece. "Fox to Justin."

"LP," Park answered.

"I forgot something in my backpack."

"I'm listening."

"It's lying on my cot. If you open it, you'll see a wooden box. Make sure David gets it."

"Oka-a-ay."

"It's important, but I completely forgot about it until now."

"No problem. We're all multi-tasking. Just don't let it happen again."

Fox knew Justin was joking, but inwardly the big agent agreed with him. It was a sloppy mistake.

"You okay?" Boyd asked, catching on to everything from listening to one side of the conversation.

"Yeah. Just such a rookie mistake," answered Fox as the plane touched down.

"Nobody's perfect."

"No. But we have to be, on this mission. There's too much at stake."

The two agents got off the airplane, not looking like agents at all. Fox was dressed in dark, fitted Gucci jeans and a black Armani suit jacket with a blue shirt that matched his eyes. The bright white tee-shirt peeping out from under his chin dared anyone to suggest he needed a tie. His wrist was styled with an 18K gold Baume & Mercier wristwatch on a leather band; his eyes were hidden behind a pair of stylish Ray-Ban aviators. Completing his outfit with sophistication, were his leather Berluti shoes. He shouldered his duffle bag as his blond surfer hair cut got mussed in the wind.

"I'm glad it's not raining," Boyd stated. Her dark blue long-sleeved top was right on-trend with Euro styling. The color highlighted her red hair but also spoke of sophistication and command. Her black leather pants screamed money and matched a tight choker around her neck. Her eyes were also hidden behind a set of white Ray-Ban Clubmaster's.

"This is definitely the fanciest I've ever been dressed," Fox grumbled. "Where'd Justin get all this crap?"

Boyd smiled. "I told you he's the most prepared person I've ever met."

"I like your look."

"It matches all my choices in weapons, too."

"I bet," Fox said, picking up her duffle bag. "Hopefully we won't have to use them."

They walked through the arrival area for private planes and picked up their passports from the gate agent who had already cleared them. "Mr. Middleton-Fox and Miss Carter, welcome to England," she said with a pleasant smile and a beautifully-scored British accent. "I believe your driver is just outside. Would you like help with your bags?"

"Thank you, we're fine," Fox said, nodding in appreciation as they turned and walked away.

"You certainly are," the gate agent mumbled, watching Fox with admiration.

The driver was a Company man, but Leo had advised them against any talk in the vehicle about their mission. Instead, Boyd and Fox chatted about whether the Chicago Cubs would ever win another World Series in the modern baseball era and how Saturday Night Live was no longer funny.

As the car raced along the M4, Boyd thought of all the historic sites along this road. From the Cheswick House and Gardens to the palaces of Kensington and from St. James to Buckingham.

As if reading her mind, the driver stated, "Belgravia is very close to Buckingham Palace. If you want to shop at Harrods, it's fairly close by, too."

"I'll remember that thank you," Fox replied, elbowing Boyd.

The driver pulled up to a substantial townhouse. Carter could tell it would have superb views over Eaton Square and would probably fetch eight or nine digits were it to be available on the real estate market. The chauffeur got out and opened Boyd's door first. "I have instructions to wait for you with the engine running."

"Is this thing bulletproof?" Fox asked about the rare V12-powered Mercedes S600.

"Yes."

"Good," the big agent replied. "We'll leave our duffle bags in the trunk. Are you carrying?"

The driver hesitated and then decided to answer honestly. "I am."

"Keep it handy, we might come out hot."

"Seriously?"

Boyd looked at the driver, coolly, and nodded.

Fox's idea to just walk up and ring the doorbell, wasn't destined to happen as planned. The property was managed by the Qatar Group, an arrogant collection of hoteliers that had invested in British properties in the mid-seventies and then re-invested wisely over the decades to position themselves into about a fifth of London's most expensive real estate. It seemed like everyone the two agents encountered, were security personnel doubling as a concierge, bellman, front desk clerk, or whatever other jobs this building needed.

"I'm sorry, sir, but we're not at liberty to talk about who lives here and who doesn't," the gentleman at the front desk said with a smile that Fox wanted to affix to the wall.

Boyd looked around at the stunning receiving lobby, noting how much inlaid gold guilded almost every nook and cranny. She turned to the clerk, carefully removed her sunglasses, and placed them on the counter. "Tell Mr. Ghalib Ahmaadi that we are here and that we need to speak to him. Immediately." Her eyes turned steely as she added, "We know he's here. You know he's here. So, stop screwing around and take us up to him."

The desk clerk was completely unfazed. "I don't know what to tell you," he answered with a dismissing shrug. "You've wasted your time."

What happened next could only be figured out when it was replayed in the security office a few hours later on a super slow-motioned video. Fox's hands moved so fast that by the time the clerk's face bounced off of the peach marble countertop, they were back at rest by his sides. Stunned, the desk man wondered why his forehead was pounding like it had just been sledgehammered and blood was streaming down the front of his clothes from a broken nose. His face wrinkled in confusion and pain. He slipped onto the floor behind the desk, causing a slight uproar.

The doorman raced over to the front desk in a rage, demanding to know what had happened. From across the lobby, a maid sprinted off to call for help. The chief steward jogged over to help the clerk try to stand back up – a useless endeavor...

"I have no idea what just happened," Fox stated. "He was just telling me that Mr. Ahmaadi would see us immediately. The next thing I know his head hit the marble slab, and he fell over."

"You have an appointment with Master Ahmaadi?" the steward asked suspiciously.

"No, but he'd like to see us."

"It's highly unusual for people to drop in for a visit. But let's say that he would like to see you, whom shall I say is waiting for him?"

"It's unusual because the problem he has is unique and delicate," Boyd responded. "Just tell him there's been a hitch with his German and American shipments. We'd like to discuss the issues privately with him."

By now the maid had returned with a few other men who stared at Fox and Boyd suspiciously. Fox could see they were packing heat. The desk clerk was still disoriented on the ground and asking where he was.

"Please," the steward said, "follow me."

He ushered the two agents out of the lobby and up a set of stairs into a large ornate receiving room. With the giant gold-plated walnut French doors carefully closed behind him, he looked the agents over. He gestured towards the two leather wingback chairs centered in front of the large viewing window over the front garden.

"You may wait here. I'll check with Master Ahmaadi."

Boyd nodded and sat down. Fox continued standing as the steward walked by, "Shukran, my friend. Thank you. Please tell him it's of utmost urgency and we won't take more than five minutes of his time."

"Of course."

The man disappeared through another door at the far end of the room.

"Nice work, Fox."

"What do you mean?"

"I saw what you did."

"What?" asked Fox with a smirk.

"I thought your watch was a little on the fancy side."

"My watch?" Fox broke into a smile and turned the rim of his timepiece to the right and then the left. A little click sounded as the tiny bolt slid out of the locking hole and allowed the entire face to open up, exposing a digital interface underneath. "LP, are you getting this? I put a GPS sticker on the steward."

"Yes, I got it, Razor," answered Justin. "I'm overlapping it against building schematics and will let you know where he ends up."

"Hey, why don't I have one of those gadgets?" Boyd asked.

"Women's watches are too small," Fox explained. "That tag has very little battery life. Actually, it can't broadcast the signal much further than where we're standing right now. So, the sticker sends the signal to the watch, which retransmits using cell phone frequencies."

"Razor?" Boyd asked with a smirk.

"Just call me Fox."

"How about Blade or Edgy?"

"Very funny. What's your call sign from back in the day?"

"Have we never talked about this?"

"No. I'd have remembered. I guess Carrot-top would've been too obvious."

Justin interrupted, just as Boyd was about to launch her fist into Fox's side. "Sorry to break up the party. He's standing in one place right now. I'm guessing he's chatting with our target. They are … on the third floor of the Southwest corner of the building."

"So, do we just wait here and see if we're allowed to see him?" asked Fox.

Leonard came on, having wrapped up his conversation with President Baker. "Let's preempt all that. Hellcat, slip up to that floor already get a lay of the land. Razor, stay put, and make sure she's not followed."

"Yes, sir," Fox and Boyd both responded.

"Hellcat?"

"It's a long story," Boyd answered, slipping out of the room.

CHAPTER FORTY

CASEY BAKER HAD ALWAYS WONDERED WHAT IT WAS LIKE FOR people who went through really difficult times in their lives. She remembered hearing the story of an Olympic athlete from Rwanda who'd lost her parents to the genocide, had gotten raped and beaten repeatedly and left for dead. A missionary couple took her in and nursed her back to health. Then, they discovered she had a passion for running, so they found a coach for her. Eventually, she became a national hero, winning the gold medal in her sport. It was so inspiring at the time Casey had seen the story air on television in the United States. But now, she realized how terrifying the whole ordeal must have been for that woman.

She thought about the girls on her team. Savannah and Amber were inconsolable. There was nothing to say. *What was a person to say to someone whose parents had just been murdered right in front of them? And why would anyone want to murder a decent, loving, generous, polite and encouraging soccer coach?* She remembered that evil emerald wasp cage! She felt trapped. It was as if the creature was laying its egg on her body. It symbolized The Lynx perfectly. He was grotesque and awful. *Casey, don't go there.*

As she steered her thinking away from dismembering The Lynx, a sudden picture came to mind. After an influential history teacher had turned her on to an article in the New York Times, she'd gotten into a heated argument with her grandfather about why the United States always felt it had the right to interfere with the business of other nations and even supply weapons to one group of people over another. She pointed out that American policies often pressured dictators in countries that were thousands of miles away and generally assumed the position of being the world police.

Her grandfather had been patient but, in her opinion at the time, very stubborn. "It's not that we're the world police, Casey," he'd said to her. "As a nation, we believe all people are created equal and have the right to worship God as they please and pursue a better life for themselves." She remembered rolling her eyes, but it hadn't deterred him. He'd went on to tell her, "I know it's hard for you to understand, but there really are people who make it their life ambition to do evil things rather than doing something wonderful for this world. They don't care about things like *good* and *bad*. They love the adrenaline rush of breaking the laws of human decency. It's just how they're wired. That's why we have police, isn't it? There are thieves who love to steal, or killers who love to murder, or dealers who love to supply drugs, or even if they don't love those things, there's something evil that they love more than not doing them. The police identify those people and try to protect our society from their wickedness. I'm not naïve enough to think we can stop them all, but maybe we can mess up a few of their plans and give folks the chance to rise up for themselves."

At the time, she had disagreed. "Our government should take care of America and stop involving ourselves in nations where the battle isn't ours, to begin with."

"If you walk past a sick, homeless woman on the street asking for help, and you had the ability to help her, wouldn't you stop and try?"

"I guess."

"If a friend of yours is being beaten up on a date and you had the power to intervene, would you?"

"I guess."

"Why?"

"Probably because I can. I should."

"Why can you?"

"Because I see the problem, I guess ... I'd be concerned about her. If I called an ambulance or something, she might turn out to be okay."

"Would it be any different for people in an oppressed nation? Maybe we're not the world police, but we have a responsibility to be an ambulance of sorts."

Casey Baker remembered getting even angrier. She hadn't been able to put it into words, but she'd hated how her grandpa seemed to have all the right answers. She hadn't really believed there would be people who loved darkness rather than light. Wouldn't everyone, given a chance, want to spread love, kindness, peace, and happiness, instead of fear, revenge, anxiety, and discouragement?

Now, she finally understood where her grandfather was coming from. She had seen evil in The Lynx and in Laila. They were not open to reason or negotiation. They thrived on oppression. And profited from it.

The back of the large transport truck was completely dark, but there were a few cracks of light in the doorframe where the sun was starting to stream through. For the first time on this entire trip, there were no adults with the young girls. Each one had been strapped in an uncomfortable wooden seat. Although the cargo bed of the vehicle seated about sixty on a bare wooden bench that ran around the perimeter of the inside, this time it only held six girls. There were times they would whimper or groan, but for the most part, they found some sort of solace in finally talking quietly with each other. Every once in a while, the tinkling of a moving chain could be heard as a girl would shift position, and the iron links attached to her handcuffs would knock against each other. Casey wondered if the other girls were killed, or if they'd been put in a different truck. She figured it was the latter because when they were loaded up, she'd seen that there were three trucks in the tunnel.

How many times had she rubbed her shoulder to activate her transponder? She wondered if the thing even worked. It had worked fine in Germany, but they were somewhere else now. There were probably no cell phone towers close by. Is that even how the thing worked? Did they use cell phone towers? She didn't know, really. Casey wondered about trying to activate it again but then decided to wait she was sure the truck had arrived at its final destination.

"Hey! Hey everybody! There's somebody following us!"

President Baker's granddaughter jerked her head around to look at Abril Fuentes. She was closest to the door. She was leaning as close to the brightly lit crack around its frame as possible. "What do you mean?"

"It's hard to see because we're bouncing around so much. But, there's a guy in a Hummer following us. I don't think I've ever seen him before."

Casey could tell the girls were uncertain as to whether this was a good thing or a bad thing. She felt the same way.

"Oh, my God! Oh, my God!! Oh my Go-o-o-o-od!!" Abril squealed. "He just stuck his hand out of his window and held up an American flag! He's waving it around. I think he's trying to signal to us."

The six girls stared at each other! Not wanting to jinx the possibility of hope, they sat in complete silence.

ALL THE PARENTS had been summoned to The Pulse, again. They sat in stunned silence as Ted Baker and a German translator read the list of those who had been killed, ending with Coach Murray. Knowing how difficult this horror must be for their daughters, many of the mothers were sobbing.

"Ted, we've got to get them out now!" Mr. Fuentes exploded, jumping to his feet. "You might have connections, but so do we all. We're not paupers, for crying out loud. I'm going to call in some favors from Mexico and get those girls out!" The translator quickly translated what he said for the German parents in the room. Many of them agreed. One of the mothers stood up, too. The translator flipped his talents and went seamlessly from German to English.

"This whole thing is ridiculous," she spat out. "We appreciate you bringing us here, but certainly we can pool our resources and get our daughters back. Have the kidnappers contacted you? How much do they want? Whatever it is, it's no problem!"

Theodor Baker waited for the translation to finish and then continued speaking. "Thank you. Both of you. Please ... take your seat." As he spoke, he realized these parents needed to do something more than just sitting around and wringing their hands. They were not a passive type of people. Almost all of them were problem-solvers who ran successful international businesses.

He looked down at his notes and began to speak again. "Here's the latest update from the headquarters of a private defense team that we're using. The girls have been smuggled through a Libyan tunnel system that's been used in the past to traffic everything from weapons to children." With his laptop hooked up to a projector via Bluetooth, he projected a map of the North African nation onto a large white screen that descended from the ceiling at the touch of a button. "They've been transferred into three large transport trucks that are probably going to cross into Egypt. We're following them with a tactical ops team, so we hope to get news to you very soon. But we've also discovered the person orchestrating everything is this guy." The map changed into a photo of The Lynx.

Baker looked at the screen for a few seconds and then asked. "Does anyone recognize him?" All the parents shook their heads. "This is Sa'im Kashif Zafar. Most people just know him as The Lynx." He reached over and grabbed his tablet, tapping on it a few times. "I've just sent his name and image to all of you." Taking a few seconds to collect his thoughts, Ted stepped to his left, reached for two black leather bar stools, and pulled them over to where he'd been standing. He sat down and motioned for the interpreter to sit, too. Then he continued, respectfully pausing for the translation. "Listen to me carefully. I realize you're all leaders in your field. You're used to being at the top of the food chain, commanding people around, managing accounts, solving problems, and being recognized for excellence and success. This is extremely difficult for you. Not just because your daughters are involved, although that's the worst part of all of this, but also because you are confident it can be solved with influence and money." Ted used a few seconds of silence for dramatic emphasis. "I will tell you right now ... it cannot. The Lynx is not susceptible to being bought off. No. They have not contacted us. They won't." He tapped a few more keystrokes on his computer, and a video started playing on the screen. He explained to the parents what they were looking at. It was footage filmed by the Marines from the USS Bataan and featured the gruesome scene on the plane, the dead doctor against the wall down by the train tracks, and finally, the emerald wasp enclosure at ground zero. As they watched the American cockroaches getting mummified, Theodore Baker explained how the wasps worked.

When the video ended, and the screen went blank, a couple of the moms rushed off to the nearest powder room to throw up. The rest of the group were silent, staring straight ahead. Ted was satisfied with the effect. He needed the parents to understand that this was not something that could go away with diplomacy or negotiation. He didn't want them using their considerable resources to activate black ops teams from contracted defense firms, creating a deadly shootout at the O.K. Corral.

"We're going to take a fifteen-minute break. When we reconvene, I'd like to explain how you can help. Be prepared to roll up your sleeves. Many of you have companies to run. We've set up a business center room for you on the fourth floor. It's furnished with desks, flat screens, dedicated and secure wireless internet services, landlines with private voicemails, and everything else you might need for a comfortable, albeit temporary, working environment. Feel free to make use of it yourself or fly your assistants over and place them there."

CHAPTER FORTY-ONE

"Dr. Stone, the second truck's not going to Egypt," Saara pointed out. "Look."

The little blue dot that bore the label *German Team* was heading off on a southern route along the nation's border, but not crossing over.

"What's over there?"

Bora had completed a massive amount of research in a short time and was prepared for questions. "There are a few things I need to give a report on. But since this is what we're focused on, here's what I've discovered about this particular area."

Leo and David glanced at each other.

She looked up, unsure as to what their glances had meant. "I mean, I wasn't sure where these trucks would go, you know ... so ... after I finished up what I was supposed to be working on and ... I mean ... is that okay?"

"Of course!" Leonard said. "We're glad you're with us, Bora. Show us what you've found."

She blushed when Justin cracked, "Isn't she amazing?"

Bora quickly organized the information on her laptop and detached the display portion, creating a tablet. She sent the information to a hanging flat screen on the far left that wasn't being used. "Most likely they're going into the mountains north of Al-Jawf. A few known terrorist camps are located there in that region, but the most dangerous one is right here." Bora used a stylus to draw a red circle around a spot in the mountainous area on the projected satellite map.

"What makes one terrorist camp worse than another?" asked Ashley.

"I'm sure they are all horrible, but I measured them on whether or not they had actual success in the real world, or if they were just more of an inbred cult-center type of place."

"Okay. So, what has this one done?"

"They successfully pulled off six bombings in various places around the world that add up to hundreds of deaths, thousands of injuries, and millions of dollars in damage. I listed them here. The downing of SA203 over the Atlantic Ocean a few years ago. Remember that? It was the South African Airways flight from Johannesburg to New York."

Everyone nodded.

"They claimed responsibility for an attack on American soil. The bombing of the Greyhound bus outside Houston that killed all thirty-four passengers on board."

"I haven't forgotten," David said. "Greyhound has finally recovered their image, but they almost went down."

"You can see … bombings in France and Spain." Bora continued as she flashed news reports up on the screen. "They trained two of the men that were connected to 9/11."

"Wow. They're big-time," Leo agreed.

"There's one more thing. They're connected to the Free Egyptian Militia."

"I thought the FEM didn't exist."

"The government of Egypt is working hard to convince people that they don't. At the same time, Egyptian intelligence has confirmed knowledge of a terrorist cell operating close to the Egyptian border in Libya. Apparently, this group has collected tons of explosives, surface-to-air missiles, armored vehicles, and tanks. They're working on creating an explosive belt that is undetectable by scanners in Europe."

"Why Europe?" Ashley asked.

"I guess they want to destabilize everything over there."

"Do you think that's why the truck of Germans is headed there?" David asked, turning to Leo.

"Probably," his friend concurred. "It could be where a lot of the weaponry went that was traded for children."

Bora continued, "I was combing through some intelligence left-over from the Blackwater era in Iraq. They had interesting information on Libyan terrorist camps in this region. They reported that these cells specialized in brainwashing techniques and in the training of child soldiers. The methods they use … I won't get into them. They're appalling."

"Okay," Leo concluded, "just having a GPS signal stuck on the truck isn't enough. We need to call in a team." He turned to Bora. "Is there anything else about this region?"

"Yes," she nodded. "The FEM is rumored to have multiplied, south. The western desert area is here," she said, pulling up a map to show them. "It's a smugglers' gateway into the habitually misruled African heartland. After Gadhafi died, Libya's arsenal of weapons provided an unending feast for smugglers. It seems no intelligence group knows who the person is at the head of everything. Maybe there isn't one. But these cells are devoted to creating chaos and fear."

"Radicalized Muslims."

"Absolutely."

"What were you thinking, Leo?" asked David.

"We've got to get to that second truck before it disappears in the mountains. Should there still be multiple terrorist camps in that region that have even half of what the Egyptian intelligence community is saying they have, then those girls would be lost forever."

"Sir?" Bora spoke again.

Leo turned to her.

"I went back over the journal like you asked me to. And I found something. Is now a good time to bring this up?"

David was learning to trust her instincts and caught Leo's eye. "Now's as good a time as any, Bora. What did you find?"

"I really wish I could've known Jee Hye. She was really smart. Nothing came up until Fox gave me the physical journal and I re-photographed the pages in HD and blew each image up. Then I printed them out and hung them up on the wall in the medical clinic. I didn't see it until I stepped back and took them all in. Check this out." Bora put it on-screen for everyone to see. "There were three Korean letters that had first been written in a very light red pen and then over-written in black."

"Wow," Saara gasped. "Wow."

"The Korean letters spell out *gaoli*. In English, the transliteration is five letters, but in Korean, it's only three."

"Stingray," Justin said, astonished.

"That's right."

Leo was clearly flabbergasted. "Why those three letters, Bora?"

"Good question. Those three letters could've been from any of the words in her journal, but they're embedded in three names of people."

"She's telling us the names of the men who were trading children for the hacker from Stingray."

"That's what I think. And two of those three names were men who contracted her services for two weeks or more."

"That's incredible work, Bora. Forget practicing law," David said, "you're not going anywhere. Send those names to Jennifer."

"Okay. I'll do that."

"When Saara's got some time, we'll run them through our database, too."

"We need to ask Serwabi about them," stated Leo.

"Dr. Stone?" Justin called.

Trey's dad nodded.

"Tank is chasing the first truck, and Trey and Bruce are chasing the third truck, right?"

"With Michi and Jasmine on it."

"There's a team of Force Recon Marines from the USS Bataan babysitting a plane in the middle of the Libyan desert. Let's get them to that second truck."

Everyone stared at Justin in surprise.

"Do we have comms set up for them?" Trey's dad asked.

"Yes, sir. I told Michi to give them her spare set. Of course, that might not have been such a great idea, now that she's having problems with hers."

"It was a great idea, kid," David said. "Leo, I think it's worth a shot. Get them on the horn. We need them to drop a sniper team in the area and coordinate an attack with jets from the Eisenhower. It's in the Mediterranean. I think involving the Germans was a positive gesture, but from what Bora is reporting, they won't get there in time. We have ninety minutes. Tops."

"Okay. Get Colonel Strobe on the phone and transfer it to the conference room, Justin. David and I will take it in there. Interrupt us when Fox and Boyd have their chat with Ghalib."

CHAPTER FORTY-TWO

GEORGE BAKER COULD HARDLY BELIEVE WHAT HE WAS HEARING. "How did they find out about it?" he raged at the current President of the United States.

Most people in America agreed that Tucker Webb was a moron, but felt they had nobody else to vote for. He was outspoken at all the wrong times, had the credibility of a used car salesman, burned more bridges than he'd built, and had zero foreign policy experience. What he did have, was millions of adoring teens and twenty-somethings who thought the world should be free. Why shouldn't the rich share with those who looked at work as a bothersome part of life? More importantly, why shouldn't college be free? It was a clear fact that Webb had pandered his way into office by buying votes with college loan forgiveness promises. The fact that he hadn't delivered on those promises and couldn't deliver on them hadn't really caused his base of young people to lose faith with him. Yet.

Webb's whiney voice, responded, "The report on my desk reads that a reporter discovered a website stating, President Baker's granddaughter and the rest of the American team have withdrawn from the International Football Tournament for Goodwill and have thereby turned their backs on Botswana itself."

"Tell me you're on top of this Tucker."

"On top of it ... how do you mean?"

President Baker rolled his eyes, glad that the phone call wasn't a video chat. "Let me tell you something. If my granddaughter ends up dead because of a press leak that caused the kidnappers to panic, I'm going to personally walk into the White House, wrap my hands around your damned throat and choke you to death. You can report my threat to the Secret Service, too. They'd probably be happy to help me. Get on top of this now!" He was roaring with the loudest his voice could get, to make his point.

Webb was silent. Finally, he asked, "What should I do, George? How would you suggest I *get on top of it?*"

"Who's the reporter?"

"Rain Martin."

Baker chuckled. "Is Rain a girl's name or a guy's name?"

"She's an internet reporter from Denver with a YouTube channel that has over seven million subscribers. Her Instagram is swelling with followers. I'm just saying, large media outlets will be all over this story within the hour."

"Well, then you need to activate a barrage of communications that gets the word out there. Casey Baker was honored to have the opportunity to play in an international soccer tournament in the spectacular nation of Botswana. And you can quote me as having said, *"We were all very proud of her accomplishments in making the national team and wished Casey and her teammates well."* President Baker continued. *"Unfortunately, due to security concerns, the team from the United States as well as a team from Germany could not make the trip this year, but they look forward to participating in the next tournament when better security protocols are in place."*

Whiney Webb replied, "I don't know, George. The press will smell a story in the making. You know how they are. They would expect Casey to make this announcement herself."

"Just do what I've suggested, Mr. President. And tell this Rain girl to contact my office. I'll take care of her."

"Okay."

"One more thing. We don't need all the three-lettered agencies in the world stumbling over each other, trying to win the prize and following us around. Keep them in Libya. There's enough there to keep them busy for a year. I have a surgical effort going on, and that's all I want. You can take all the credit in the end, if we're successful – I don't give a damn. But stay the hell out of my way. If I need something from you, I'll let you know." Leo's voice turned ice cold. "And if anybody tries to politicize this afterward, I will take them down. I will end their careers. They won't be able to get a job as a manure consultant for FarmTV. They won't be able to get a job flipping burgers at a diner. That's how dead their career path will be. Am I clear?"

"… yeah."

He hung up on Webb for the final effect.

———————

THERE AREN'T a lot of ways to sneak down a hallway and go up the only staircase in the house. So, Boyd decided to own her movements and walk with confidence. It was the only way that Ghalib's security team, watching the closed-circuit camera footage, would think she had permission to do what she was doing. The downfall was that her gun was neatly situated in the custom pocket of her Prada purse – not safe in her hand. Strutting down the hallway, she mounted up to the third floor, pausing at the top with a feigned interest in an original art piece. It was a framed poem, handwritten by Mahmoud Darwish, the famous Palestinian poet. In actuality, she was listening for any sound that might indicate people were approaching her. Everything was quiet. Boyd turned the corner and calmly walked down the hall toward the Master Suite. Getting within twenty feet of the bedroom's entrance, she suddenly froze. There were multiple voices coming from inside, not just two.

"Razor. Multiple targets."

"Copy that, Hellcat."

"Plan B."

"Roger that. Plan B. Oscar Mike."

As the big blond agent left the reception room and headed up the stairs, Boyd was thinking things through. If this were any kind of a business meeting, it wouldn't be occurring in the Master Suite. Perhaps the toilet was leaking, and this was a group of plumbers, but she doubted it. This had to be a security meeting of some kind. It had to be a response to her and Fox being in the building.

She pulled out a make-up compact from her purse and was about to get a read on how many people there were when a man walked around the corner and almost stepped on her. Before the chief steward could make a sound, she sprung to her feet and simultaneously thrust her open hand into his windpipe with such force that it knocked his breath out of him. She slipped her arm around his neck in a firm hold and put direct pressure on the carotid of his neck, just under his jawline. The blood immediately stopped flowing to his brain, and he started to kick and squirm. Just as he was about to stomp his heel into her toes, she lifted her feet off the floor, adding her body weight to his list of problems. As he started to breathe again, Boyd increased the pressure, so he'd get dizzy. She swung her legs up and pushed against the nearest wall. He struggled to keep his balance. Ten seconds later, he was out. She was just letting go, not wanting to cause unnecessary brain damage, when Fox clicked his tongue twice to let her know he was approaching. He already had zip ties in his hand as he caught the steward's body and laid him down quietly. He listened for a moment. The conversations in the bedroom seemed to be getting more heated.

"I'll tie him up and put him in there," he whispered tersely, nodding his head to a room across the hall. "How many hostiles?"

"I was about to find out," Boyd answered, picking her little compact up off the floor. She cracked the lid open and revealed a small LED screen. Where the mirror would have been, and where the make-up would usually sit, was a thin black tube with a camera and a focused microphone on the end. She unwound the tube and bent it to a ninety-degree angle. Getting on one knee, she carefully sneaked the camera/mic around the baseboard corner and pointed it in the direction of the bedroom suite. Ghalib Ahmaadi was standing about forty feet away, having some kind of a heated discussion. She watched for a few seconds, widened the view of the lens, adjusted the angle of the camera, and then let out a short gasp. His brother was there too!

Deliberately Boyd touched her throat mic three successive times, signaling Fox to hurry up.

"Just a sec."

Boyd Carter moved the camera again, trying to get a headcount … there were three!

"What is it?" Fox asked, getting back from hiding the steward's body in a bedroom closet.

"Are they triplets?"

"Who?"

"The Ahmaadi brothers."

"I don't think so," the big agent answered, getting into a position to see over her shoulder. "What on earth?" he queried as an identical fourth Ahmaadi came into the picture.

Fox retreated a few steps to summon Justin. "We're not transmitting, so you can't see this, but we have eyes on four identical targets."

"Come again," Justin said, sounding a little confused.

"We are looking at our target. There are four of them, and they look exactly the same."

There were a few moments of silence, then David jumped on. "Copy that. Four targets."

Justin came back on. "Hellcat, take off your comms' battery pack. There's a thin red cord at the bottom. You can plug that into your compact. Then we'll get audio."

Boyd looked at Fox and shook her head at Justin's genius. "Copy that. I'm off comms for a minute." She quickly plugged in the red cable, as Justin had instructed.

"Perfect," confirmed David, motioning Saara over to him, away from where she was tracking the Blue Team.

"White Team," she said quickly, understanding Arabic from her undercover days as a doctor in that region of the world, "I suggest you abort the mission. None of those men is your target. They're talking about which one of them should go meet you downstairs and exactly which shipment you're referring to. I think they're all body doubles. Your real target's not even there."

Boyd quickly reeled in her camera/mic, unplugged the comms from the compact, tucked everything into place, and stood up. "Copy that," she nodded.

Fox seemed to be thinking about something.

Boyd shot her eyebrows up at him. "Can we go now?"

"What if we just went in there and took them?"

"What for?"

"Well, are we going to chase this guy around the world, or should we just bring him to us?"

"Can we at least have this conversation in the guest bedroom before some dimwit comes up the stairs and sees us?"

Fox nodded. He withdrew to the room with the closeted steward.

Boyd followed him in. She crossed her arms. "What are you thinking of doing, Razor?"

"These body doubles have a direct way of contacting Ghalib, right?"

She nodded.

"So, let's get them to pass on a message for us."

"Only with a clear plan for extraction."

"Run, jump, and shoot? Maybe not in that order?" Fox suggested.

Boyd shook her head.

"It's an idea. Can you think of something better?"

"White Team," said Leonard Stone, coming online. "It's time for a full-court press. Put some heat on those bastards. Get them to connect you with our target. I'll get to work on Daylight and get him to spill more beans. We need to pick up the pace."

ON THE JEEP, Trey was putting the Wolfe technologies through its paces. Bruce had entered all the pertinent information into the system, including the moving location of Jasmine and Michi. Now the guidance system was taking them on the most drivable route. All four tires were churning through sand as the transmission groaned, squealed and ground through its gears. Sometimes, he was ripping a straight line over hardened soil, creating a cloud of dust behind him that hung in the air hundreds of feet. Other times, he was crawling up steep dunes in four-wheel-drive.

"Hold on!" shouted Trey as the Jeep screamed over the top of a dune and caught air on the other side. It landed on the two left wheels, bouncing onto the two right wheels and then quickly stabilized as they tore down the slope.

"Looks like we're getting close!" Bruce exclaimed, pointing to a cloud of dust about a mile ahead of them.

"Yup. That's got to be them."

As if on cue, Saara came on comms. "Blue Team, you're closing on your target."

"Copy that, LP!" Agent Locke responded, giving Trey a thumb's up. "We have visual."

The desolate landscape was changing. Small, wiry shrubs were poking through the cracked ground. A bright sun started to beat down on them. Bruce pulled out his digital spotting scope. It was a custom-made job by some brains in the Company with powerful, bright optics, a 20x80x magnification, and an 80mm objective lens diameter. Equipped with a Leupold MilDot reticle for range estimation and tactical collaboration, it also featured a digital camera and a Bluetooth uplink to the powerful Wolfe guidance system. As Bruce had described to Jasmine, hanging out on the USS Bataan, it allowed him to zoom in on a fire ant half a mile away, snap a picture of its antennae and upload the photo to her grandfather.

"What do you see?"

"Pull over for a sec. It's too bouncy."

Trey downshifted and braked, thinking about the term *pull over*, when they were off-roading in the middle of a barren desert in North Africa.

"Here, check it out," Bruce said, hopping out and handing the scope to his friend as he came around the front of the jeep. "It looks like they're still on the back of the truck."

Trey tapped his throat mic to isolate comms with Jazzy. "Hey Sweetie!" he shouted, hearing the competing noise from the large truck. Signaling for Bruce to take over at the wheel, he jumped into the passenger's seat.

Jazz's voice was tight with emotion "We're still hanging on!"

"I know! I can see you!"

"You can see us?!" she squealed, "Where are you?"

"About a mile behind you. But we're using the scope."

"Awesome!"

Bruce glanced at Trey.

"Listen, we can't go too fast now," Jazz's dad continued. "We don't want to attract attention to our dust trail. Just know we're close. Okay?"

"Got it!"

"Make sure you both stay hydrated. Super important!"

"We will."

Agent Stone disconnected comms and reached into the back of the Jeep to grab his kit. It was time to gear up.

CHAPTER FORTY-THREE

LEONARD STONE IMAGINED HOW TERRIFIED THE GIRLS FROM THE soccer teams must be. He could smell their fear. He could feel the agony of the girls whose parents had been so shockingly executed. With fury, distress, and grief in his head, he strode into Serwabi's interrogation room and slammed the door. Clearly, he'd just woken the MEO up.

"We're through screwing around with you," Dr. Stone spat out. "Look at me. You've seen people like me. You know I'm speaking from experience when I say that I could flay you like a trout and get the information we want. I've done it before for lesser slime than you. I'm just hoping I won't have to get out my toolbox. You know what I mean."

"I've told you everything you need to know."

"A bunch of names? Connect them to the top of the pile."

Serwabi shrugged, indifferently. "Ask me what you want to know. I'll decide if I can answer. A lot of what I do is classified at the highest level."

Leo looked down at his tablet at all the information he and Bora had gone over just before he'd walked in. "The Arab names you gave us are connected to Jee Hye and The Lynx. The Chinese names you gave us are connected to The Red Flag Commerce and Development Company. We know them. They traffic Southeast Asian kids and cover it all up with legitimate shipping enterprises. We've been watching them for a while. The Russian names you wrote down are connected to financial institutions in the motherland."

"Sounds like you've done some homework."

Leo didn't bother looking up. "You told David that The Lynx trades children for weapons, is that right?"

Serwabi nodded.

"Then he distributes these weapons to people who want to kill Americans."

Again, the MEO nodded. "Right."

"Does he give them away for free?" Leonard asked, with an edge of sarcasm. "Whoever wants a weapon can have one?" Stone slowly looked up and locked his gaze. His piercing blue eyes were crystal clear.

Serwabi stayed quiet.

"See the problem is that nothing that you've told us completes the circle." Leonard leaned forward. He whispered hoarsely, "I know you're hiding something." Suddenly his right hand flew across the table to grab the MEO's neck. He squeezed the windpipe with such a vicious power that it nearly shattered. Serwabi choked, in shock. His zip-tied hands reached vainly from behind the chair, but Stone had let go.

As the Arab sputtered and gasped, the pallor returned to his face. "How dare you!" he hissed. "I am an agent of the Central Intelligence Agency, and you're doing this to me on American soil? I'll bury you! I'll take you out!" He tried rubbing his throat and glared at Trey's father.

Leo sat back. Serwabi's eyes betrayed him, and Trey's father saw it as clearly as if it had been written down in ink. The MEO completed the circle. He was profiting from the selling of children in exchange for weaponry. He was linked to the money from trafficked weapons, just as Bora had speculated.

"I'm going to say three names, and you're going to tell me when and how you delivered a very specific weapon to them."

"Me? Deliver a weapon? Are you out of your mind? Get the hell out of here!"

"Aasil Muhammed Abdullah Al-Abbasi."

Serwabi froze.

"Omar Hasan Mohammed Zahran."

The MEO's breathing quickened.

"Amir Wassim Essam Al-Khattab."

His jaw started flexing involuntarily.

"You know, Mohammad Al Serwabi, as good as you are, you're falling apart here."

"You're imagining things."

"Shortness of breath. Sweat on your forehead. Jaw twitching like a snake caught in a trap. Your eyes darting around for help." Leonard Stone moved in for the kill. "Tell me, traitor, who paid you the money for a Stingray? Where is that hacker right now?"

MICHI HAD CONSTRUCTED a harness that used her backpack-straps as something she could leverage her body weight against. Jasmine copied her, and the two had been fastened onto the back of the truck for almost two hours.

"How much further, do you think?" Jasmine yelled out over the roar of the truck noise.

"No idea. Why?" Agent Imada replied.

"I mean ... this is a huge truck, right?"

"Yes."

"It must use a lot of fuel."

The Japanese CIA agent connected the dots. "Of course! I can't believe we didn't think of that earlier."

Jasmine nodded. "Could we cut something or cause a leak?"

"I think there's a hose I can cut. I'll take a look."

She slipped her right arm into a solid iron towing ring that was welded onto the back of the huge vehicle. Then she used her left hand to undo the harness straps and brought them up to her right arm. Tying the end to the ring, she used the straps as a sort of rope and leaned to the right side of the back of the truck. Using every inch of length, she could, she peeked around the corner of the truck and then quickly pulled herself back, hoping nobody had seen her in the dusty side-view mirror. Just as she'd thought, the wheels had no kind of a well or cover and were spitting mad amounts of sand, dirt, and rock into the air. On the other side of the giant tires were the gas tanks. There would most likely be one on each side of the truck. But ... with the flying debris, it would be too dangerous to approach the gas tanks by crawling over the spinning tires. She could slide under the truck and make her way forward. Michi didn't like that option either. Her body could get torn to shreds by passing rocks, cacti, and bushes. Only one other alternative was left. She would have to shoot the tanks from where she was.

Imada knew that popping a hole in the giant black cylinders would not cause them to explode. Those detonations would need both oxygen and a spark. Her copper-jacketed steel bullets would do. The fuel these types of machines used would most likely be classified as low explosive level.

"I'm going to need your help."

Jasmine nodded.

"Tie this to your left wrist. Make sure it's tight," instructed Michi as she handed Jasmine the opposite end of her improvised rope attached to the iron ring. "Hang on to my right ankle as I hang upside down. Don't let go."

"What?"

"I'm going to have to shoot the tank."

"Upside down?"

Michi nodded grimly.

She hooked a carabiner onto her backpack and hung it from the iron ring. Then she reached inside, took out her Glock 19 and chambered a round as the truck careened harshly, demolishing a dry creek bed and rumbling on. Raising her leg, she placed her ankle in Jasmine's waiting hands. "All you have to do is hold on. If you're losing me, just tell me. I'll pull myself up, and we'll try again."

Trey's daughter was so nervous she could only move her head up and down.

With amazing agility, Agent Imada rotated her body and lowered herself down until she was hanging from her ankle. She had a clear view of the diesel tank. With all the jostling, it looked like it was going to be a difficult shot. Michi took a few moments to calm down her adrenalin. Then, with the speed of lightning, she pointed her pistol and fired at the tank on the right. Amazingly, it broke the plane of the metal shell and created a neat hole. But no fuel came out. *Was it used up?* She'd have to shoot the other one.

With the same technique, she took another shot at the tank on the left. The bullet glanced off the mark, ricocheted from a steel structural plate, and boomeranged back, missing agent Imada's head! It flew past her and dug into the desert sand. Jasmine shrieked. Michi couldn't think about that near miss. The blood was flowing into her head and causing temporary dizziness. With her right arm, she braced herself as the truck kept bouncing along.

"Are you okay Jasmine?!"

"Hurry!"

"One more try," muttered the Agent, lifting her gun and shooting again. This time, the bullet penetrated the lower half of the metal tank. The fuel started spewing out. Quickly she swung her body up and grasped Jasmine's sleeve. With the shift of weight, Jasmine's grip slipped! Michi tumbled off the back of the truck and hit the sand with a thud.

"Michi!!" Trey's daughter screamed with all her might. She could only watch in horror as one of her favorite people on the planet rolled down a steep hill like a sack of potatoes that spilled off a pickup truck.

Everything shifted into in slow motion now for Jasmine Stone. Later, she would remember that she'd even heard her own breathing. She tossed her backpack to the ground, scooted over to unhook Michi's bag and untied her make-shift rope. Then she vaulted from the back of the truck and dived into the bushes for cover.

It took a few seconds for her world to stop spinning. She lay unmoving until the noise of the truck engine was barely discernable. Jazzy touched her push-to-talk button on her throat mic to connect with her father.

"Hemlock ... we ... jumped off the truck."

She was amazed at how calm her dad's voice was. "Copy that. We're seven minutes from your location."

"Okay. Please hurry."

Jasmine sat up. Could she spot Agent Imada in the shrubs and rocks down there?

"Michiko!" she yelled at the top of her lungs. "Mi-chi-ko!"

No response. Jasmine gingerly struggled to her feet. She needed to retrace their tracks and pick up the gear she'd ditched. She found the makeshift rope and wobbling on, located Michi's backpack. Walking a little further, over a hill surrounded by tall brush, she spotted her own mini-kit. She went and took out her gun, did a quick mag check, and zipped her pack closed. Everything was collected now. She would keep searching for Agent Imada. Just as she shouldered her backpack to keep moving, chills started to crawl up and down her spine.

She was not alone.

Standing off to her left, was a man dressed in a dirty blue robe with a white turban on his head. His arm was wrapped around Michi, and he was pressing a pistol barrel against her right temple. Glaring coldly at Jasmine, he barked something at her in Arabic.

"I don't understand you," Jazzy responded, trying to turn towards him slightly, wondering if he'd seen the gun in her right hand.

He spoke again more animated this time.

"Do you speak English?" Trey's daughter asked, suddenly noticing movement on her right. As she turned slowly towards it, she found herself face to face with a boy – he couldn't have been more than twelve years old, and his eyes were loaded with a hatred that went back generations. He was carrying an AK-74 with the business end pointed at her chest. Trey had taught Jasmine about weapons. This gun was the standard-issue assault rifle of the Russian military and all their surrogates. She guessed that the recoil might be enough to knock him over.

He screamed something in Arabic and motioned to her gun.

"Michi?"

"You should probably drop it, Jasmine."

Trey's daughter nodded at the boy. "Okay, okay ... I'll put it down. I'm laying the gun down, okay?" She slowly bent down and placed her gun in the sand. "Alright, just relax."

As she stood up, the boy got a look on his face that almost made Jasmine's heart stop. He grabbed his shirt and tugged on it, indicating he wanted her to take hers off.

At that moment, Jasmine Stone heard a sound. It was the whining engine of an approaching Jeep. The boy jumped back and started chattering to the would-be kidnapper. Jazzy used the distraction and in one fluid motion, bent down, scooped up her gun and slammed the barrel into the boy's temple. Imada, too, crashed her elbow into the captor's gut with such force, that it knocked the wind out of him. She sunk her teeth into his arm and as he shook her off, his grip on her loosened enough for her to spin around with a wheelhouse kick to his jaw. He hit the ground like a felled tree and Michi retrieved his weapon. Before she could do anything with it, the rat-a-tat-tat of a lighter Russian-made weapon cracked through the air and bullets whizzed past her head.

"Get down!" Michi yelled. But Jasmine was slamming the boy's face into her knee. His body rolled into the sand with blood spurting through the hand covering his face.

More shots rang out. They were of the heavier American variety. Michi spun around again. Three Muslim men tumbled forward, their right shoulders bleeding. Whirling around, she realized the Jeep was almost on top of them. She rolled behind a bush and pointed her weapon.

"Michi, don't!" yelled Jasmine. "It's Dad!"

Suddenly everything computed. Michi lowered her gun as the loaded Jeep came ripping into view. Sand was flying in every direction. Bruce was driving. Trey was in the back with one knee on the seat. He had been stabilizing himself with roll bars, and his gun was still searching.

"Get in!" he shouted as Bruce slowed down.

"I've got your backpack, Michi," Jasmine hollered. She jumped into the back, next to her father.

Michi flew into the passenger seat next to Bruce. She tugged the door closed, noticing the window was rolled down. Pointing the Arab's weapon out through the space where the glass would have been, she squeezed off a test round and got ready to shoot anyone else that might appear.

"Go! Go!" shouted Trey. The powerful wheels spun furiously, gaining the needed traction, and propelling the vehicle forward.

Blood was still flowing from his broken nose, but the boy was on his feet now. He'd found his gun and pointed it at the fleeing Jeep. Trey whirled around and squeezed his trigger. The bullet raced out from the barrel into the fleshy side of the kid's left shin, right where Stone had intended it to go. The boy screamed in pain and doubled over, dropping his gun and grabbing his leg.

Bruce was driving like a manic. He slammed through shrubs, gassed his way up the slopes, caught air on the other sides and skidded down. Finally, they were at a safe distance. He just kept speeding along.

"Those guys are going to alert the truck. I guarantee it. What happened?" he asked, watching Trey and Jasmine embrace in his rearview mirror.

"Jasmine Stone is amazing. That's what happened," Michi replied loudly.

"So-o sorry I dropped you!" Jazzy was still shaken.

"Are you kidding? You were great. We did it! That truck is spewing out diesel. If it hasn't already stopped, it will soon."

"You shot the tank?" Trey asked, impressed.

"Dad, Michi was awesome!" his daughter squealed "She was hanging upside down and shooting the tank. I was holding on to her ankle. But after her third shot, I couldn't hold on anymore, and she fell off the truck."

"Your daughter did all the right things, Trey. She collected our stuff and jumped off. I'm sure glad she did." She smiled at the two in the back and then turned around to face the front. "There seem to be rebels everywhere!"

"More than we realized, that's for sure," Bruce answered gravely. "We're gonna have to assume that the truck, if it's run out of gas, will be very well protected, soon."

Trey agreed. "It seems there are terrorist training camps sprinkled throughout this region. We'll really have to watch ourselves." He tapped Bruce on the shoulder, "Are you still following the truck tracks?"

"Yeah ... they're pretty clear. Let's all keep our eyes open for the truck so we can stop in time. We need to think through our approach before we race headlong into an armed hornet's nest."

CHAPTER FORTY-FOUR

It was moments like these when Tank wished he could communicate with LaunchPad. He hoped his rudimentary duct-tape-comms-unit-sticky-thing was still transmitting from the other truck. Tucking the American flag he'd been waving back into his boot, he continued to tail the giant black vehicle in front of him. A while ago, he'd disconnected his helmet cam to hook it up to the USB charger he'd stuck into the old cigarette lighter, but now he thought it was a good time to send the group at LP a few more minutes of live footage. He unplugged it, turned it on, and had just stuck it back onto his helmet when his eyes caught a bright flash of fire from the hills to his right.

RPG!

His response wasn't cerebral. It was an instant reaction – a manifestation of years of war and training. His leg jammed on the brake pedal as his arms jerked the steering wheel to the left, rocketing the Humvee down a small slope. The Rocket Propelled Grenade was already halfway to its target!

It would've detonated on impact as the crushed piezoelectric fuse in its tip transmitted to the missile's charge. But because of his evasive maneuver, the point didn't make direct contact with the hummer. It glanced off its hood, speeding into the desert, where the HE round exploded into thousands of deadly fragments.

The RPG-7's force, coupled with the momentum of the hummer skidding down the short slope was enough to flip Tank's vehicle upside down. The roof slammed into the left wrist of his arm as it instinctively protected his head. The American's neck twisted with the impact and his body strained against the seat harness, testing its limits. Impatiently waiting until everything had stopped moving, Tank fumbled with the belt's buckles until he could carefully lower himself down.

Back at LaunchPad, Justin was staring at the screen in front of him in shock. "Dr. Stone! David! I think Tank's just been hit with an RPG."

Leonard came running out of the conference room with David right behind him. Justin threw the live footage on one screen and played the video from the beginning in super slow motion on another screen.

"There it is," David muttered. "And for some reason, he turned his camera on just in time."

Saara spoke up, "That explains why they didn't take him out earlier. They must be coordinating with rebel groups in the region."

"Right. That makes sense. My guess is they probably have a schedule to keep, and these rebel groups are going to help them through if they need to."

"Why didn't Tank try to take the truck?"

"Too dangerous. Those girls could be wired to explosives for all we know."

By now, everyone had gathered around the screens and were watching the action.

"Smart kid," Leonard commented as they watched Tank's hands, from his point of view. He was setting charges in the hummer.

Trey's father turned to Justin. "Did you finish arranging what we'd talked about?"

Agent Park nodded. "There's a black team from Benghazi that can get to an extraction zone within sixty minutes. I've got them on standby."

"Get them there before he's target practice for a dozen rebel groups."

Justin put on a headset with a small boom mic. "I'll get them online right away."

"But how will we communicate with him?" Ashley asked.

Leonard turned to Saara. "Any ideas?"

"I've been thinking about it ever since he stuck his comms onto the truck with the German girls on it."

"Let's hear it."

"His tablet has live camera feed from his headcam. But it also has a multi-cam function that comes on automatically if a base is coordinating the cameras."

"Brilliant," David responded. "So, if we hook up a headcam here and he looks at his tablet, he should be able to see our live feed alongside his own."

"Exactly."

"Okay," Leonard said, thinking out loud. "Those cameras don't have audio, right?"

"You're correct. But we could transmit a still-shot of a short message."

"Of course, you're right. The only thing we need him to see is the EZ and a time."

"I've got the extraction zone right here," Justin said, taking off his headset. "The Company team from Benghazi is scrambling and will be airborne in five."

"David and Justin work on getting the message to Tank."

David hurried to the conference room to create a still-shot of the EZ while Justin dug a spare headcam out of his work area and tested it out.

The rest of the group was glued to Tank's live feed. He belly-crawled onto the scratchy hardened sand, grabbed his kit, and was moving along the base of the little slope he'd flipped down. He set two claymores that he could trigger-detonate from a safe distance and then began to leave the scene, making sure that he was melting into the wilderness shrubbery.

Tank was confident in his ability to cover his tracks. He was just wondering how to get out of this God-forsaken desert. He'd be up against people who knew the land in ways he never would.

Shouldering his kit, he suddenly decided it would be better to keep moving, then to get pinned down in a thorny shrub. He looked at his compass and took off, crouch running, and trying to carve a path that took advantage of any bushes that were taller than waist-high. He'd been on the move for about ten minutes when he remembered his headcam and wondered if it had caught the footage of the RPG. If he slowed it down, he might be able to see exactly where it came from. He didn't even know if he could rewind live footage, but he thought he'd give it a shot. Kneeling down, he pulled out his tablet.

"I just sent you the image," reported Justin, racing out of the conference room and back to the hanging flat screen with the live footage from Tank's camera.

"He's pulling out his tablet!" Bora exclaimed.

Everyone in LaunchPad cheered as they watched Tank looking down at his tablet and seeing two live feeds at the same time – his own, and theirs.

Tank read the message. It had satellite coordinates and the words EZ in sixty minutes. Excited cheers filled the room again as they saw the native Lakota agent stretch his arm out and signal a thumb up.

Suddenly, Tank threw his tablet back in his bag, and the headcam jerked up. He'd spotted movement back at the Hummer. About seven people had gathered around it and were searching for its driver. Tank zoomed in on them with his head cam and snapped a few still shots. Then he pressed a button, powering the camera down to save its battery, and stuck it in his pocket. It was time for him to blow some things up.

He looked to his right and saw about thirty armed hostiles on foot, following the tracks made by the huge black truck and eyeing the flipped hummer, just ahead of them.

Tank guessed he was pretty near to the distance-limit of his triggers, so he decided to blow up the claymore closest to the group that was walking along the road before they'd be right on top of it. He didn't see the need to kill everyone, just the immediate threats. Getting into a position that would allow him to slowly move out after the explosions, he squeezed his hand together and heard the click of the trigger, letting him know the signal had engaged. The bang had no canyon walls that would've created an impressive echo, nor was it part of a visually stimulating plan to implode a building. Instead, from Tank's distance, it was a relatively unimpressive popping noise, with a burst of flame and a cloud of smoke. But he knew that for the group on the road, it would have been deafeningly terrifying as the two pounds of C4 created a small earthquake under their feet.

Several from the group went flying with the force of the explosion, others were on their knees and clutching their ears to stop the ringing. The more experienced fighters fumbled with their weapons trying to locate where an American could be hiding in the wilderness. Those around the hummer left the vehicle and dashed up the little knoll to see what had happened. It seemed like a good time to blow up the vehicle. Tank moved the toggle on his switch and detonated the charges. He watched as a tiny wisp of smoke threaded through the inside of the military vehicle, looking for a fraction of a second like a seat had caught on fire. Suddenly a large ball of smoke appeared, screening the windows, followed by a giant boom that filled the air as debris scattered like a bursting firework on the Fourth of July. The hood shot straight up in the air, doors flew off the sides, engine parts looked like they were raining up instead of down. Three of the tires shot backward while one raced forward. The men who had just left the hummer were yelling hysterically and trying to organize themselves towards a target they couldn't see.

Slowly, but methodically Tank slipped away, detonating his final claymore to complete the distraction.

FOX CHECKED on the steward in the closet. He was awake and alert, but his zip ties were holding, and the duct tape was still over his mouth.

"I'll be standing right outside. If I hear a noise from you, I'll come in and finish you," the huge agent growled. "Do you understand?"

The steward nodded.

Closing the door behind him as he left, Fox quietly joined Boyd in the hallway.

"So far, I haven't found any cameras on this floor," she said.

"You won't find any. My guess is that Ghalib doesn't want any evidence of who he's bringing into his bedroom."

"You're probably right."

The two agents crept back down the hallway to stack up by the entrance of the master bedroom. Boyd pulled out a small black canister with a steel ball on the end labeled CTS Model 9590M Sting-Ball. She squeezed the handle, pulled the pin, and tossed it into the master bedroom. The first stage of the device was a loud set of clicks, just enough to get everyone's attention, then it was suddenly followed by a muted explosion severe enough to stun each person for several minutes. By the time their heads had stopped throbbing, their eyes had dried up, and the ringing in their ears had faded to background noise, Fox and Boyd had zip-tied and muzzled the four look-alikes. They were all in a row and on their knees.

Carter cleared the bathroom, closets, and attic crawlspace, while Fox waited by the doorway with his weapon drawn to see if the muted bang had alerted anybody. With the area cleared, the big agent pulled out his tablet and put Saara on speaker-phone as he began to work over the four men.

"I don't care to torture you to get the information we need, so I'll make this simple," he said. "I'm going to drag each of you into the closet and shoot you until one of you talks. If I have to shoot all four of you, then we'll torture the steward to find out what we want. He's in a closet down the hall. Do you understand?"

The four men nodded after hearing Saara's translation but didn't seem eager to cooperate.

"We need to know how many look-alikes Ghalib uses and where he is right now."

The men all shook their head, so Fox picked up the guy nearest him and threw the wriggling, protesting man over his shoulder. When the others saw this, they started to panic. The big agent and his trophy disappeared out of view into one of the two large master bedroom closets. Muffled screams could be heard and then the sound of a silenced pistol firing two rounds. There was a loud thud of a falling body. Then silence.

A few minutes later, Fox came walking around the corner with a picture on his phone. It was the body of the man he supposedly shot. In actuality, he'd used one of the fake blood packs that Justin had packed in his kit and tried to make it look like the man had been shot in the chest.

He held up the phone to the other three, so they could see the image he'd just taken. It had the desired effect. "LP, they're looking at one of the men I just killed. Ask them if they're going to talk now or if I should shoot another one."

The three men's heads were bobbing up and down like boggle heads on a stick; all of them were eager to talk. Boyd stepped over to the guy closest to her and ripped the tape off his mouth. He started chattering away, but Fox held up his hand to create space for Saara to translate.

"He's begging for his life," she said.

"Tell him to answer the questions," Fox snarled.

"He says if he answers them, he'll be dead."

"He's got that wrong. If he doesn't answer them, he'll be dead."

"He's saying that Ghalib will kill him."

"Tell him to answer the questions and then go home to his family and get them to someplace safe. We'll take care of Ghalib."

The man was silent for a few seconds, and then he turned and looked at the other two men. They were nodding vigorously. He drew a deep breath and spoke while the tall Finn at LaunchPad translated.

"There were six of them earlier this year, but now there are only four."

"Where are the other two?" asked Fox.

"They were executed for getting too fat."

Fox nodded, "Okay. So where is Ghalib now?"

There was a pause while Saara and the man spoke back and forth a few times.

"He says he can't be sure. Most likely, he is at his office to meet some clients for tonight's party."

"What's going on at tonight's party?"

As the man answered, Saara explained, "He usually meets the top donors at his office in the afternoon, and then they go with him to the event. Tonight is a fundraiser for his foundation. The four look-alikes need to start getting ready because they need to be available for his beck and call during times like these."

Boyd instantly thought of something. "LP, ask him if they've been to these foundation fundraisers before."

Saara translated, and the man nodded his head.

"Have they seen things that could incriminate Ghalib?"

The man was totally silent, and the two agents could see fear crawling over them like a cloud.

Fox and Boyd realized the three men were not going to talk. Not now, anyway.

"LP, are you alone?" Carter asked.

"No," Leonard Stone answered. "We're all here."

"These guys are suddenly very important. We need to take them somewhere safe."

"You make the call," Leo answered. "You're on the ground. You'll know whether it's even possible. But if that's the move, we'll find a green zone for you."

"Copy that."

"You need to understand something, though. Your hot priority is to get to your target before he leaves for the party. Otherwise, there would be just too many moving parts to intercept him." Leonard paused. He continued with urgency in his voice, "Attempts to recover our primary are not going well. We need to get to Ghalib and apply immense pressure on him."

"Roger, all," Fox replied grimly. "Translate this for them. Tell them that we are going to get them out of here and to a safe place. I'm sorry about their dead friend, but if any of them try to escape or warn anyone of our presence, I'll shoot them on the spot."

Saara translated what Fox had said. The men began to protest, but the big agent pulled out his gun and reached for the man closest to him. The bluff worked.

"I'd bet that Ghalib has a secret way in and out of his bedroom, doesn't he?" Fox asked.

After hearing the translation, the men nodded and pointed to the closet opposite the one their friend was lying in.

"LP, contact our driver and tell him to meet us on the north side of the building," Boyd said. "We'll need that green zone."

CHAPTER FORTY-FIVE

IT HAD BEEN JUST OVER THREE HOURS SINCE THEY'D LEFT THE underground rail station and the mood in the back was one of utter hopelessness. Abril had reported to the group that the American following them had been blown up by a missile. It was a disappointment that dissolved their former optimism with a sickening black ooze of fear. Everyone was silenced by its finality. Casey had debated many times whether or not she should tell her teammates about her beacon, knowing it would lift their spirits, but decided against it. If the other girls were ever interrogated and tortured, they'd probably cough up the truth pretty quickly. *Then what chances of being found would they have?*

She watched Savannah Jackson and Amber Taylor. They'd just lost their parents. They were completely broken. Their grief was raw. She knew they were being emotionally destroyed. Even before her parents were killed, Savannah had been sitting closest to Jason Kennedy, she had experienced him being shot and killed on the plane. Casey wondered how people could even recover from experiences like these. Savannah had told Casey a little bit about her mom when they had stayed up late one night during training camp. From her daughter's formerly resentful perspective, Mrs. Jackson had been a hyper-controlling woman that was very hard to please. Now that she was gone, Casey supposed Savannah would be full of guilt and shame. She'd probably have a hard time making her own decisions since they'd always been made for her. She wondered what thoughts were going through her new friend's mind – if any. Savannah's face was hidden from everyone under her long brown hair. She was leaning against the side of the truck. Her body was being jostled with every bump and turn.

"I'm so sore …" Amber groaned as her head dropped forward again onto her chest. Like Savannah, she was one of the team's two strikers and known as the most accurate shooter on the team. A classic finisher, she had the natural talent to adjust her body in mid-air to almost any incoming cross and guide the ball into the nylon. Of course, soccer was the last thing on her mind, now. She was psychologically vacant. The sounds she made were almost like reflex noises instead of cognizant communications. Her reddish-blond hair stuck to her sweaty face. Her normally bright blue eyes had transformed themselves into dull, lifeless orifices.

President Baker's granddaughter stretched to her left as far as she could. She was able to touch Amber's hand. It was cold, despite the fact that the truck was heating up like an oven. "Amber. Don't give up." She tried to massage some circulation with the back of her hand. "Listen. We're all here together. You're not alone." Then she spoke louder, "That goes for all of us." She looked around at the five other girls.

Abril was still peering out the crack of light that framed the door. In her mind, if there had been one person out there to help, there might still be others. Shelly Brown was just staring at

Casey. Then, she held up her handcuffed hands and made a little heart formation with her fingers. Baker returned the signal, pursing her lips together and nodding. Savannah was unchanged. Was she asleep? Or watching everything from behind her hair veil?

Sally Mei was the only girl in the back of the truck whom Casey didn't know at all – although some rumors about her family had gone around the team. Apparently, her father was a communications tycoon from Hong Kong but had left the city for New York, after the region had been handed back to the Chinese by the British in 1997. Even though he'd divorced her mom and had remarried twice, he'd stayed in a random pattern of contact with his daughter. Sally had grown up in Portland, Oregon, where her mother had won full custody of her daughter. Her mother had also remarried. Sally's stepfather was an accountant for the Daktronics Corporation – a company that manufactured analog circuitry. One thing that Casey had noticed about Sally was that she had mastered the generally pissed off about everything look. Baker had a hard time reading her. Deep down, Casey would have loved to connect with her to find out more about who she was. Right now, her Asian eyes were boring a hole through her, wondering what else Casey was about to say.

"Listen to me," Casey went on, "we're in the middle of a terrible moment in our lives. But it is just a moment! My dad always tells me when we're in a tough situation, we need to remember that it won't last forever."

"At least you have a dad!" Savannah suddenly snapped at her from behind her hair.

Casey Baker could have been intimidated and allowed another tsunami of grief to overtake the girls, but she replied, lovingly and gently. "You're right, Savannah. The stuff we're going through is unbelievable. You and Amber have had it the hardest.

But we're still here with you, okay? You're not alone! No matter what happens, we have each other. We're going to fight to the very end. We're fighters, y'all. That's who we are. We're fighters. And we're winners. We're going to make it through this and get Oprah to do an interview of us."

The last line brought a slight smile to some. But just then, the truck lurched and jerked, starting to downshift. Their faces betrayed their inner fears.

"What's happening?" Shelly asked, panicking.

"We'll find out," Casey responded. "Let's stay calm. Let's stay together."

The truck came to a stop, and for about five minutes, they sat in silence. Their noses had become immune to their stench, but as Abril looked around, she knew the truck must reek. She could see the sweat dripping off their faces, the urine on the floor under their wooden seats, the dried puke on their clothes. She pulled her heavy chain onto her lap and raised her arms to fix her hair. Combing her fingers through it and pulling it back into her trademark high ponytail, she kind of smiled as Sally finally broke the silence and snidely asked her if she was going on a date.

"I've decided there must be more Americans on their way, so I'm going to look my best for them," she said, trying hard to smile.

"Even if you smell like road kill?"

"Yes. Even if I smell like that," she answered, trying not to cry. Then she shrieked in shock as the back doors flew open. The girls blinked and squinted trying to adjust to the sudden sunlight.

Glaring up at them with a sinister scowl on her face, was Laila and standing beside her with his evil smirk was The Lynx.

THE JEEP WAS ABOUT to crest a hill when Trey motioned with his hand for Bruce to bring it to a halt. He climbed out and carefully walked forward to check things out. Down in the valley below, he could see the big black truck. It had stopped. It was exactly where he hoped it would be – in the middle of the sandy desert with no protection. He squatted down and motioned for the others to join him.

Trey asked, "How far's the shot?"

Bruce pulled out his scope. "Guess."

"Under 2000 meters. I'd say 1880."

"1876."

"Keep an eye on it," Agent Stone replied, sliding back and away from the crest. He jogged to the Jeep to grab his kit.

"Blue Team to LP," Bruce called in.

The response was almost impossible to understand.

"Michi, shoot Saara a text. Tell her that we have eyes on the target. Tell her we're moving in. Our signal is too weak here, so I'm not going to waste time trying to figure out what they're saying."

Agent Imada slipped back to the Jeep where Trey was doing a final weapons check and checking his Kestrel 4000 Pocket Weather Tracker. The device had a remarkably sensitive fan that would move, even with the lightest of breezes, and digitally measure wind speeds, chills, and directions. Using the information it collected, the tracker would report air temperature, humidity levels, barometric pressure, sun directions, and other weather-related data that affected a sniper bullet's flight.

He crawled back to Bruce.

"Drive the Jeep down this slope honking like a madman. We want to get their attention. I'm guessing the driver's inside calling for help."

"Okay ... so, if he gets out to see the commotion?"

"I'll take him out."

"Do I keep going?"

"All the way. Jasmine stays with me."

Michi had finished updating LaunchPad and rejoined the group. "Once we get in range, we should be able to turn on the Wolfe's thermal imaging function."

"Great idea," said Trey, turning to her, "You focus on that, while Bruce drives. Keep your head down at all times. Hopefully, our connection with LP will improve, and they can give us over-watch, but if not, we've got this anyway."

"Copy that," she said, with a quick bow. "Are you going to stay here?"

"No. You see that little hill down there?" he asked, pointing it out. "We'll ride with you and then jump out of the Jeep and scramble to the top where those shrubs are. It's probably eight hundred meters closer. That's a big difference."

Bruce nodded. "Okay, let's roll."

"One more thing," Trey added, "If you get into trouble of some sort, make sure that you run to the west side of the truck, so I can get a clear shot. Taking cover on the east side will leave you exposed."

"Copy that."

The group scrambled backward and climbed into the Jeep. While Bruce and Michi checked their kits and got everything together for easy access, Trey and Jasmine prepared their gear and got in place to jump out.

"Comms check," Trey announced, making sure all of their earpieces were working.

"Check," Jasmine said, giving a thumbs up.

"Check," Michiko expressed.

"Five by five," answered Bruce, "Check this out, Michi." He depressed a rectangle button located just under the Wolfe screen. It clicked and released from the dash with an attached trail of wires that could easily extend several feet.

"Wow!" she exclaimed. "That's great! I'll sit down on the floor here and fire this up." She reached back and put Bruce's kit on the passenger's seat, next to hers, and then sat down on the floor.

The engine sprang to life, and Bruce raced forward. They sped down the hill, spewing sand like snow from a snowblower.

"Go words are Gold Star!" Trey shouted over the Jeep's noise.

"Copy that, Hemlock," Bruce said, giving a thumbs up. "Gold Star!"

Just as they reached the bottom of Trey's hill, Bruce eased up slightly. Jasmine tossed her dad's kit out the back, followed by hers.

"See you in a few!" Agent Stone hollered as he fell off the back of the Jeep, keeping his sniper rifle up in the air and rolling along in the sand. Jasmine was right with him.

"That's the second time I've jumped from a vehicle today, Dad," Jasmine bragged as the Jeep roared down what was left of the hill and tore into the flat sand of the valley floor. "It's more fun with you."

"I bet," Trey said, springing to his feet and grabbing the handles of his kit with his free arm. "Let's move, Sweetie."

"On your six."

He grinned at her growing use of military jargon and scrambled up the hill. Pulling a folded shovel from his kit, he began to dig furiously and speak to his daughter at the same time. "Jazzy, pull out one of the smaller shrubs up here and go down to where our footprints begin. Brush them over and camouflage them as much as possible. It doesn't have to be perfect, just try to blend them in. You've got two minutes."

She scurried down the hill and did as she was told. By the time she got back up to the top, Trey had dug two holes – one for her to sit in and one for him.

"Okay, Jazzy. No talking. I have to concentrate. What I do need you to do, though, is sit in this hole, pull some shrubs around you and face the hill we just came down. Your job is to make sure that nobody sneaks up on us from any angle so pretend your head is on a slow-moving swivel. I'll be looking straight ahead. Most of the time, it will be through my scope."

"Got it."

"If you see anything, call it out right away, using the numbers on the clock for directions, okay? The truck is twelve. So, three will be to my right, and nine will be to my left. If a vehicle comes over the hill, freeze. People's eyes are attracted to movement. Bruce and Michi will be doing plenty of movement, so we don't want to distract from them at all."

"Okay, Dad," she said as she stepped forward and pecked him on the cheek. "I love you."

"I love you too, Jazzy. Let's get in position and do our part to free those girls."

CHAPTER FORTY-SIX

FOR JUST OVER FORTY-FIVE MINUTES, TANK HAD BEEN CAREFULLY moving forward to the extraction zone. He'd been vigilantly rationing his water, but the sun was starting to annoy him, and he knew he needed to stave off dehydration with some Drip-Drop, a powdered product that activates the sodium-glucose co-transport system in his body. It would literally draw water from his gut and hydrate his body. He took a moment to hide in a thicket of bushes on a small knoll and then added some of the lemon-flavored concentrate to whatever was left in his canteen. Checking his tablet for a few seconds, he saw he was about ten minutes from where he needed to end up, so he stuck everything back in his pack, shouldered it, and checked his weapon. That's when his heart skipped a beat, and his breathing stopped. There was movement about five hundred meters away on the desert floor. He watched for a few minutes as the large group spread out in an organized search pattern and continued moving in his direction. That wasn't the problem; Tank felt like something else wasn't quite right.

Some people called it his spidey senses, while others attributed it to his genetics. He felt the latter was true. Legends had been passed down from generation to generation among the Lakota people of scouts in his family lineage who had saved many a village in times of inter-tribal battles. He was proud to have had family members that had served in every war during modern times, too. They'd always provided valuable intel on the field. Tatanka Ptecila waited, in complete silence, frozen to the shrubbery like he was its fruit.

Time seemed to slow down. Then he heard a crunch, just to his right. It would've been inaudible to the average human, but to Tank, the shifting of hard sand under the pressure of a rubber boot was like a thunderclap. His right hand was holding his gas-operated carbine HK416 A5. The worst enemy of many guns is sand and grit, but this weapon was battle-tested and could be pulled out of mud, sand, or water and still fire accurately. His left hand was moving very slowly to the combat knife on his belt. Out of the periphery of his right eye he saw two figures moving forward with the stealth of snakes.

The wind warned him of the danger on his left, carrying him the scent of a human. It wasn't just his foreign body odor, or the sweat-drenched clothes he was wearing, or the shawarma sauce on his breath. Tank smelled adrenalin. Too much of it. He knew the man on his left would be prone to make a mistake in the excitement of his death. The breeze blew again, confirming his observations, just as his left hand was closing around the handle of his Kampfmesser 3000. The spear-tipped blade was made from German spring steel, and the handle was of a sand-colored slip-proof grip with an end that was hard enough to shatter thick glass. Some warriors had knife sheaths that buttoned closed, others had a new quick-release technology that made a loud clicking sound, but Tank's was a custom-made magnetic strap. His thumb silently lifted it out of the way and inched the knife out, so it was free and clear.

Little Bull, as his Lakota name translated, was about to become Raging Bull. He knew he needed to act quickly before the larger group he'd spotted on the desert floor made it up the hill to his position. That team was the designed distraction; they were meant to draw Tatanka out from the brush. These three men were the real killers. Skilled assassins.

Tank figured they didn't know exactly where he was, or they'd have shot at him already. There was no mercy, no hesitation, in this part of the world. They were good. He'd give them that. He decided they must've caught glimpses of him but didn't have enough of a bead for a clear shot. They didn't want to miss and alert him to their coming, so the slayers crept towards him. Now? Here they were. At the top of this knoll. The two men on his right were still about fifteen feet away and probably couldn't see him, hidden around the thick bush. The man on his left, though, was close enough for Tank to hear his breathing. His eyes slid left, and he could see the mass of the person, although not clearly defined. He was large – almost the size of Fox.

Tank decided he'd take advantage of the elements of surprise and height. In one fluid motion, he dropped to a crouching posi-tion and then threw up his left arm, driving his combat knife into the man's right kidney. As the hostile bent over in surprise, the Lakota native extracted his blade and whipped it across his enemy's throat, just below his hyoid bone. It sliced through the thyroid cartilage, ripped the trachea and even cut into his nerve cord. As the giant fell like Goliath before David, Tank dropped his left shoulder, let his backpack slide to the dust. He ducked around the backside of the bush, making it harder for the two that had been on his right to see exactly what was going on.

The remaining assassins were better trained than he expected. They didn't panic when their third hit the ground and began making unnatural sounds from his dying body. Instead, they calmly split up and began to move around either side of the thick bush. Tank immediately knew he couldn't allow them to both converge on him at the same time, so he picked the one on his right. Taking one long, but powerful, stride, he launched himself into the air and threw his body into a position horizontal to the ground. As his head came around the bush, his eyes locked on his target. The hostile was completely surprised at the attack, and by the time he focused his weapon on his attacker, Tank's rounds were pounding through his heart, ripping his vital organ to shreds.

Twisting in the air so he'd land facing the final hostile, Little Bull rolled into the sand and let his left shoulder bear the brunt of his fall. The guy came ripping around the shrub, firing, but he wasn't expecting Tank to be on the ground. His bullet path was four feet too high, and the armor-piercers spun harmlessly over the agent's head. Tatanka, on the other hand, was expecting his mark to be right where he was. The headshot wasn't pretty, but it was final.

Already hearing the shouts of the approaching rebel group and figuring they were less than four hundred meters away; Tank didn't have time to collect any intel. He wiped his blade on his pants, glad that the knife was coated with liquid-resistant protection, sheathed it, and raced back around the bush to scoop up his kit and tear down the knoll in the direction of the extraction zone – on the opposite slope from the approaching gang. It was going to be a very close race. He guessed he was faster than most of the guys chasing him, but they weren't carrying all the gear he had, and he didn't want to ditch his pack. Justin's forethought had proved the kit's weight in gold. If for some reason the extraction team wasn't there, he'd have to make use of almost everything in his bag.

Tank raced across the sand as fast as he could go. He hoped he remembered everything properly as he saw the hill in front of him and anticipated a chopper or something on the other side. About halfway up the slope, he heard the snapping reports of assault rifles, instinctively zig-zagged and saw bullets kicking into the sand around him. Then the sound he was dreading the most. The report of a sniper rifle. Fortunately, the guy wasn't a great shot. He was probably breathing hard, sweaty, and trying to calm a pounding heart. He missed somewhere to Tanks left. Suddenly a human form rose up from a bush directly in front of him and grabbed his left arm!

"This way!"

With no time to think, he just followed the guy's lead. They ran behind a large boulder and Tank immediately recognized two Hayes M1030 diesel dirt bikes. These amazing machines have 670cc, four-stroke engine that can ford two feet of water and go hundreds of miles before refueling. He threw his weapon into his bag, climbed on the one closest to him, and sighed with relief as their engines sprang to life.

"On my six!" the Company man shouted as his wheels spun out of the sand.

The rebels were advancing dangerously close as the two men tore out from behind the rock and crested the hill. There was no helicopter in sight, but Tank knew this plan was better. They would outrun the enemy and then board a chopper inside a safe zone.

CHAPTER FORTY-SEVEN

IN A PERFECT WORLD, FOX AND BOYD WOULD'VE TROTTED OUT OF
Ghalib's mansion with their three new friends, climbed into the
waiting car and driven off to a nearby Starbucks for a civil
conversation about lugubrious fundraising parties for a famous,
and most likely, corrupt foundation. Instead, they crept through
a maze of secret passageways and finally arrived at a door to the
outside that triggered a silent alarm when it was opened.

The sun was blinding, and the two agents whipped on their
sunglasses to counteract the effect. Their driver was waiting
about two hundred feet away, at the curb on the other side of an
opened tall cast-iron gate flanked by high rock walls. As
instructed, his car doors were open, and the engine was
running.

Not knowing the alarm had been triggered, Fox gave a nonchalant thumb up and pointed the driver out to the three men.
"We're getting in that car."

The gunshot was predicated by some shouts of anger from
security people who were leaking out of the house onto the

property. Fox felt the bullet tear through the tail of his black Armani suit jacket but didn't have time to think about how he nearly got a bullet lodged in his buttocks. Instead, he pushed the men forward, herding them towards the gate. "Run!"

The chauffeur sprung out of the car, whipped out his Glock 17 and began laying covering fire. Boyd pointed the men into the back seat and then squeezed herself in and rolled down her window. She began shooting and yelling for the chauffeur to pull back. He raced around the car and jumped into his seat, just as Fox climbed into the front passenger's chair. The Mercedes engine roared as the tires squealed, and the driver expertly drove like a bat out of hell.

"Where are we going?" he yelled.

"Ghalib's office."

He shook his head. "You guys are crazy."

"You'll drop us off and take these men to a safe house."

"LP to White Team."

Boyd tilted her head and pressed her right hand to her earpiece, so she could hear better. "Come in LP."

"Your target has left his office in a hurry," Justin informed her. "He's driving a midnight blue Ferrari F60 America. I'm uploading two sets of coordinates to your driver's heads-up display. The first one is the drop-off. The second is your target."

"Copy that," Boyd answered, rolling her eyes and looking at Fox. "We need to intercept one of the fastest road cars in the world."

The driver viewed her in his rearview mirror. "Regardless of what you drive, cars here are only as fast as the traffic." He looked back and saw the information appear on his windshield's display. "Hang on. The drop-off point is about a kilometer away," he said as he punched the gas and flew through a red light.

Fox was impressed with their driver's skills. He weaved in and out of cars with inches to spare and left a trail of honking horns but was always in control. The Mercedes was crowded in the back seat, and Boyd was getting irritable, being reminded of her seats on planes from India. She tried to focus on something else and began to grill Justin about where they were going to leave their passengers.

"So, who are we handing these guys off to?"

"He's a Company guy," Park reassured her.

"What does he look like?"

"I'll send you an image, now."

"Where is he going to take them?"

"He'll babysit them until we can get them out."

"Will someone be there to interrogate them?"

"I'm working on that."

"How will we know that the intel they gather will get relayed to us with no interference?"

"We'll set up a live video feed. No intermediaries."

"They have someone who speaks Arabic on the ground and available?"

"Yes, your contact point speaks Arabic."

Boyd looked out her open window at a group of people that had been waiting at a bus stop but scattered noisily as the Mercedes roared by. She wasn't feeling the peace she needed to. "I don't like it."

"Don't like what?" Justin asked.

"The whole thing. I think I should stay with them."

Leonard came on comms. "Out of the question, Carter. We need you in the field."

"These guys can identify everyone, Dr. Stone. They can identify people that were at parties. They know who is regularly in the lives of these twins. And they can identify us. We need them buttoned down. It might take months to fully debrief them. Do you personally know our contact point?"

"No. I don't."

"Someone needs to stay with these guys. Our target is a very influential person."

Back in the LaunchPad conference room, David stood up and looked at Leonard. "She's right, Leo. God only knows how many influential Londoners have been to his foundation fundraisers and have compromised themselves. He'll do anything to protect them, and they'll do anything they must to protect him. Our agents are in danger. We have no idea who Ghalib might leverage in this situation."

"We can't keep them in the car and pick him up," Leonard argued. "If he sees them, every one of their family members will be dead."

"They're families are already in peril. But I'm working on that." David leaned forward, placing his palms on the table to brace his weight. "One of ours needs to stay with them."

Leonard looked at Justin. "Which one has the best skill set for each situation?"

"Without a doubt," Park responded, "Fox stays with them, and Boyd gets to Ghalib."

"That's what I thought too," David agreed.

"Okay," Leo said, relinking with Boyd. "Razor stays with the cargo. Hellcat goes after the target."

Boyd was surprised. She looked at Fox and said, "Repeat last."

"You go after the target," Trey's dad repeated. "Razor stays with the cargo."

"Roger that," Fox acknowledged, voicing for the first time in this discussion.

"Razor, you'll be dropped off at an old Company safe house," David said. "Consider this VIP protection. We'll work on an extraction plan to get you all out quickly and safely. Your operational protocols are lethal."

"Copy that," the big agent answered, understanding that he had kill authority if they were attacked.

Moments later, the driver slammed on the brakes and pulled up to the right curb. A young scrawny-looking kid who couldn't have been drinking age in the United States was waiving at Boyd.

Agent Carter looked at her tablet and saw that the picture Justin had sent matched the kid in front of her. "Dr. Stone," she said, "you definitely made the right call here. This kid's barely out of high school."

"I'm Spider," the kid said, sticking his head in her window. "I'm your contact point."

Fox got out of the car, grabbed his kit from the trunk, and motioned for the three men to join him. When they looked confused, Spider barked at them in Arabic and urged them to hurry. The last one had barely stepped out of the car when the driver took off, the back-door slamming shut with the momentum of the accelerating Mercedes.

It was time to hunt down Ghalib Ahmaadi.

Fox, Spider, and the triplets walked half a block down a street that could've been anywhere in London. They passed an Indian restaurant, a fish and chips joint that boasted over a century of service for the British palate, an old bookstore, and a small pipe tobacco shop. The next building had a wooden door with a sign above it that read, *The North American Research Group for Middle Eastern Affairs.* Fox chuckled. Nothing said CIA like a nebulous title in a foreign country.

Spider led them down a hallway and up a set of stairs to another wooden door that had the ridiculous acronym TNARGFMEA stenciled on a frosted glass insert. They entered a room that was bare, even by CIA standards. It had four wooden desks in one room, each with an uncomfortable oak chair.

"Home sweet home," the kid said, motioning to the desks. "Make yourselves comfortable. I'll get some tea." He repeated the same thing in Arabic and went into an adjoining kitchen.

Fox surveyed the place, trying to figure out how to make it safe. He watched as the three men each took a chair and then walked into the kitchenette. There weren't any windows, and the only door was ajar, displaying a small bathroom. "Is this everything?"

Spider nodded. "There's wireless internet if you need to check your email."

"I'm good."

"It's secure."

"I haven't checked email in weeks."

The kid shrugged, "You want some tea, too?"

"No thanks," the big agent said, going back into the desk-room. He walked over to the only window and looked down into the street. A few people were walking by – business types on their way to finance the world – and then a young couple, deeply in love or high on something. There was a man stepping out of a corner pub. He lit a cigarette and then leaned against a lamp post and pulled out his phone. Fox backed away from the windows and drew the curtains. Although a sniper shot from across the street was highly unlikely, he felt more comfortable with the curtains closed.

Spider served the three men tea, and Fox could tell that it was the right move; the men were deeply appreciative.

"Razor to LP."

"Go ahead," Justin answered.

"All clear here. Just waiting for extract. The specs on this place aren't ideal. I feel like I'm trapped in a concrete box."

"Copy that. That's the best we can do right now. Make yourself at home; it might be a while."

The men were starting to relax. One of them seemed to be more in charge than the others. He leaned in and started talking with the other two.

Fox opened up his kit and found a cylinder similar to the one Michi had used in the tunnels. It was a motion detector and camera. He went outside of the office and placed it in a strategic location on the stairway, activating the video function. He set up a remotely detonated stun grenade by the door as he backed back into the room. He got out the battery kit that Justin had packed and quickly replaced the batteries in his comms. Rebooting them, he checked in with LaunchPad. "I just traded out my batteries. How copy?"

"Loud and clear," Justin answered.

"Setting up a perimeter. Did I already say that I don't like it here?"

"We're working on getting you out."

The large agent turned to Spider. "If we get breached," he explained, waiting for the translation, "then everyone falls back into the kitchen. If you hear me yell, America, then close your eyes, because I'm about to activate the stun grenade."

The three men nodded when they understood the translation.

"As soon as you hear that thing go off," Fox continued, "open your eyes and follow me out of here."

The three men nodded, sipping their tea, and acting like this was just another day in their life. Spider, on the other hand, was super excited.

"Who are these guys?" he asked.

Fox smiled. "Just some triplets we need to protect."

The young kid wasn't quite satisfied with the answer.

"Are they famous?"

Fox looked him over. "You're in the big leagues now, kid."

His truck was just leaving the desert floor and about to start the climb into the Libyan mountain range where the German girls would be delivered to the *Hands of Allah* terrorist group, one of the many Libyan-based cells connected to the *Free Egyptian Militia*. But, the evil flight attendant with the million-dollar smile needed to pee. The large black machine jerked as he downshifted and applied the brakes, pulling over to the side of the road. He explained what he was doing to the man sitting beside him who, as it turned out, also needed to relieve himself.

No thought was given to how the girls in the back were doing. Neither man cared, really. They were doing their job, getting paid very well, and then moving on to the next assignment. He climbed down from the cab and motioned to his coworker to urinate at the back of the truck while he walked around the front to do his business. As the flight attendant urinated, he thought about sampling the product. This time, The Lynx wasn't here to stop him, and he'd always been curious to see what a western girl would really be like. He already knew the girl he wanted to ravage, and his heartbeat quickened as he thought about her.

Neither man saw the dark shapes of two thirty-eight-million-dollar Boeing F/A-18E Super Hornets from the USS Dwight D. Eisenhower fly over them. Nor did they see the release of two satellite-guided air-to-surface AGM-65 Maverick missiles. By the time the thunderous noise from the Hornets' engines almost deafened the men, the pair of fighter jets were already turning back towards the Nimitz class nuclear-powered aircraft carrier they called home and their missiles were blasting craters the size of inverted Egyptian pyramids on either end of the truck.

His smile was gone. In fact, the flight attendant was completely terrified! He scurried under the large truck and began to scream like a four-year-old girl getting barked at by a half-starved Pitbull. His body was shaking uncontrollably, and by the time he finally stopped, he realized someone was shouting his name. It was his partner.

"I'm coming," he said, as he scrambled out from underneath the truck.

"I found something."

"What is it?"

"I don't know," the man said. "A bomb?"

The flight attendant shook his head, "It doesn't seem like one."

His hands were still shaking from fear as he took the duct-taped package into his hands and looked at it curiously. Then he pulled out his Swiss Army knife and began to cut away the sticky gray wrapping. Inside was Tank's ear-comms unit and battery pack. Terror set into the flight attendant's face as he turned to his partner. "They've been tracking us."

"Who?"

"The Americans, you fool," he hissed.

Those were his last words. Sniper bullets sizzled through both men's heads at exactly the same time, spattering their blood across the back of the big black truck. The Force Recon Marine snipers fist-bumped and the rest of their team moved in formation to set up a perimeter around the area, waiting for extraction orders. The truck sat on a neatly formed bridge, with about thirty feet of dirt showing on the front and back ends.

CHAPTER FORTY-EIGHT

THE PARENTS HAD BEEN ORDERED TO RENDEZVOUS IN THE PULSE immediately, and within ten minutes they were all present. If he could've allowed himself to be vulnerable, Ted Baker would've probably shared that he was emotionally compromised. On the one hand, he couldn't wait to deliver the news to the German parents that their daughters were being evacuated by a stealth landing team of brave men and women from the USS Bataan. He'd just gotten more detailed intel, that a medical team from their German counterparts in Cairo were arriving on the scene to travel back with the group to the American warship. But on the other hand, he was deeply worried about his own child. He had a strong feeling, the kind he just couldn't shake, a gut sense that he'd learned to depend on over the years, that she was on the truck that Tank had lost and the chances of finding her were dissolving with every passing minute.

"Thank you all for coming," he said as parents scurried to their seats. "We promised transparency, and so here we go." The German translator started speaking as he walked up to the front and joined President Baker's son. "I'm just going to get right to the point. The soccer team from Germany has been found, rescued, and is at this very moment being safely evacuated."

Loud cheers erupted from the team's parents, and the Americans did their best to seem happy as they watched the Germans break into ecstatic hugs and emotional tears of joy. For several minutes they celebrated the news and the relief it brought them. One by one, they sat back down, husbands took their wives hands, and many were wiping tears from their faces.

Ted continued, "Through the amazing work of a squad of U.S. Marines and a parallel effort from a German medical team from Cairo, the girls are in safe hands and will be transported to an American navy vessel in the Mediterranean. It is equipped with the latest in medical technologies, and we will make sure that your daughters are well-treated and gently cared for. They will be debriefed to glean any important information they might be able to share and will, of course, undergo basic medical evaluations. We are so grateful and pleased to share that we were able to find and rescue the entire team. Not one of the girls was lost."

More cheers erupted.

"Each one of you will get an immediate medical and psychological opinion both from the German medical team and from our Navy doctors. It will help prepare you for their arrival. We also have a special team of psychologists on their way to coach you on how to receive the girls. We expect them to join us here within the next twenty-four hours."

The German parents were clearly surprised at how quickly things were moving and could hardly wait to embrace their daughters.

"As for the Americans," Mr. Baker continued, "We're praying that they, too, will be rescued and evacuated."

Many of the Germans turned and looked at the American parents as the realization of what was going on hit them.

"What does that mean, Ted?" an American mother shouted, angrily. Her voice was emotionally raw and painfully expressive.

"It means that we have a special ops team moving in on some of the American girls as we speak. But there are a lot of moving parts."

"*Some of the American girls?*" a man demanded, angrily. "Which ones? And what about the others?"

"We're still locating the others," Ted admitted.

A few of the parents were incensed. "What do you mean by that, Baker?" one of them yelled. "You don't know where all of them are?"

Ted looked down at his notes for a few minutes and then addressed the group with a quiet and somber exposure. "My own daughter is among them. And yes, I don't know where she is. One of our most highly-skilled agents was trailing one of the transport vehicles that we know is holding some of our daughters, but he was attacked and driven off the pursuit by a rebel group from one of the nearby terrorist camps. He only just managed to escape death himself after a prolonged running battle with at least fifty well-armed rebels."

The room grew very quiet as a few of the women covered their mouths in shock.

"He's been safely evacuated – thanks for asking," Baker said not without a hint of sarcasm. "We'll know more about the girls within a few hours. Listen, people, the situation is very serious. I hope you're praying as hard as I am that they'll all be found safely and rescued. Thank you again for being here. You're all free to go for now. We'll notify you the moment we have any further information."

LIKE NEARLY SEVENTY percent of the people living in Colorado, Rain Martin was physically fit and dressed in work-out clothes. Sporting a bright yellow vintage hoodie on the top half of her body and black leggings on the bottom half, she looked like she'd just climbed Pike's Peak and was ready to run a marathon for fun. Her short dirty-blonde hair was carefully spiked in various directions and dominated by large, round, fashionably red, thick-rimmed glasses that had become her signature look on the internet.

When the blades of President Baker's helicopter stopped spinning, she opened the door, climbed down, and was instantly met by his security people who'd been instructed to make her entrance a big deal.

"I'm sorry, ma'am, no cell phones," the biggest agent said, holding a black cloth bag open for her to deposit hers into.

"Are you kidding?" Rain answered insolently. "I'm a reporter."

"And we're the Secret Service."

Martin rolled her eyes. "Is this how it's going to be?"

"Clearly, you've never met with a president before, ma'am. Nobody gets a pass."

With a big sigh, she put her phone in the bag. "I'm not telling you the password," she stated defiantly.

"No, ma'am. We wouldn't need it."

Rain followed the big agent with the black Faraday bag off the helipad, down the stairs, and through the bridge-tunnel that led up the hill to the giant Telluride mansion. Reaching a side-door to the home, he stepped forward and tapped twice. Turning to her, he paused and said, "I'm headed back to the chopper. Someone will be with you shortly." He handed Rain the bag, and then turned and disappeared back the way they'd come.

He'd just gone from view when a female agent opened the door. She pulled out a bright orange wand and said, "Good afternoon, Miss Martin. I'm Agent Burke. Please come inside and then raise your hands, I need to do a quick search."

Rain rolled her eyes again and followed her into a large austere concrete, windowless room.

"I'll take that, thanks," the agent said, taking the Faraday bag with Rain's phone.

"Is this really necessary?" asked the reporter

The rod searched her front and her legs but lit up and beeped loudly when it scanned her back. "Apparently it is. Could you please lift your hoodie? I'm getting an unauthorized digital signature."

Martin was busted. She lifted her hoodie, as instructed, and exposed a thin black wire that ran from just below her collar line to a small black patch on her lower back. The female agent took out a pair of scissors and snipped the cord, rendering the little mic useless.

"I just wanted to record our conversation, that's all," Rain confessed, embarrassed.

"Without permission."

"It's not illegal."

Burke didn't say anything but pointed to a tall cylinder-looking object with an open sliding door. "Please step into there while I run a weapons search."

"Are you kidding me?"

"Please hurry, Miss Martin. President Baker has a schedule to keep."

Rain stepped into the cylinder, and the door closed behind her. There was a flash of light and a whirring sound, like a group of hummingbirds in a spring garden. Then it stopped, and the door opened again.

"Right this way, ma'am," the agent said, leading the way out of the room and up a set of concrete stairs. At the top, there was another agent. This one was clearly into weight training and maintaining his impeccably good looks. His beautiful brown eyes and genuine smile melted Rain's animosity.

"Agent Graham, this is Rain Martin."

"Miss Martin. It's a pleasure to meet you. I'm a big fan of yours."

"Really? You've seen my channel?"

"Everything you've ever posted," he said with a winning smile, not letting on that it was his job.

"Wow. That's cool."

"Thank you, Agent Burke," he said, "I'll take her to the President."

They parted ways with the female agent, and *Mr. Cool* led Rain through the spectacular home to the President's reception room where George Baker himself greeted her.

"Rain," he said, turning from the view window to walk over to her. Smiling warmly, he shook her hand with both of his. "Thank you so much for coming on such short notice."

"Mr. President, it's such an honor to meet you," she responded, trying to calm her adrenalin.

Mr. Cool excused himself and disappeared.

President Baker motioned to one of the four Arthur Old World Chesterfield Style brown leather wingbacks in front of the large picture window.

"Would you like something to drink?" George asked.

Rain shook her head. "I'm fine, thank you."

The President waited for her to take her seat and then sat down across from her. "Miss Martin, you stumbled onto a website that we've taken down and ground into an internet shredder. It's now completely untraceable."

"I noticed."

"I've been informed that you saved the page on your computer."

Rain Martin froze. "You accessed my computer?"

"I didn't. But you have to understand that there are many people who are tasked with keeping the President, and all former Presidents, safe."

"So, they hack into people's computers?"

"I have no idea how they get the information they acquire, Miss Martin, but they do their job very well." He looked out the window with a thoughtful gaze. Then he said, "But you and I have our own jobs to do, right?"

She nodded.

"You want to create a whirlwind of trending news, boost your viewership, and then pay your rent."

Rain smiled at the way he'd put it, but he was basically right.

"I hope that happens for you. I really do," the former leader of the free world said, as he turned to face her. "I just want to make sure that everything comes out truthfully and in a way that won't get anyone killed." With the steady expression that had won him tens of millions of votes across the country, he said, "The veracity of the story is something I can help you with. The lives or deaths of innocent people is your responsibility."

There were a few seconds of heavy silence as what he said registered with Miss Martin. But she hadn't become a popular journalistic icon of her generation for nothing. Her reflexive snark and rejection of authority kicked in immediately.

"Wait. Uh, Mr. President. You've just laid the fate of people's lives on me?"

"Words have power, Rain. How you decide to use yours will kill people or keep them alive."

"What's happening, Mr. President?"

Over the next thirty minutes, George Baker worked the type of negotiating magic that had made him one of America's best presidents. He knew nothing was more important to a reporter than being first on a story – for many of them, it was more important than the truth. By the time Rain retrieved her phone and climbed back on the helicopter, she knew most of the story and had agreed to sit on it for forty-eight hours in exchange for an exclusive interview with Ted, Helen, and hopefully their daughter, Casey. It would launch her blog into stratospheric numbers of followers, and she was smart enough to know a life-changing opportunity when she saw one. She wasn't going to blow it.

President Baker watched her climb into the chopper and then walked over to his liquor cabinet to pour himself a glass of whiskey. He tiredly settled into his favorite chair, toyed with the cigar cutter in his drink-free hand, and stared into the fire in his fireplace, deep in thought.

CHAPTER FORTY-NINE

Trey was in position and waiting for someone to make an appearance down by the truck. He glanced down at his weather tracker and computed some numbers in his head while calculating the distances. Then he slowly reached his hand up to the top of his gun and made an adjustment.

"Um, dad?" Jasmine called out, uncertainly. "There is a hummer coming over the ridge of the hill behind us."

Agent Stone didn't move. "Is it following Bruce's Jeep tracks?"

"Uh-huh."

"Okay, don't move, whatever you do."

"Dad?"

"Yes, Jazzy."

"There's another truck coming after it."

"Describe it, Sweetie."

"It's dark gray and has big tires. There's a cab with two people in the front. The back is kind of high and has canvas over it – like the wagons pioneers used to travel in."

Trey didn't like the sounds of that – a troop transport truck. "Okay, Jasmine. Is it just the two vehicles?" he asked while keeping his sniper scope trained on the truck.

"Yes. They're coming down the dune's face, just like we did. But they're moving a lot slower."

"How long before they pass us, honey?"

"About four minutes, I think."

"Let me know when they're thirty seconds away, okay?"

"Alright."

Trey called out to Bruce. "Hemlock to Vegas."

"Loud and clear."

"You've got company and nowhere to hide."

Bruce jerked his head around for a second and could see the vehicles snaking their way down the slope, about ten minutes away from his current position. He faced the front and guessed he was about five minutes from reaching the giant fuel-less truck, ahead of them. "Is *Wolfe* running, yet?"

"Almost," Michi answered. "Got it!"

"What do you see?"

"There are ..." she paused to count the infrared images on her screen from the truck the girls were in. "Sixteen in the back and ... two in the front."

"Uh ... dad?" Jasmine said again.

"Yes."

"There's a third one. It's a big truck with a water tank on the back."

"Fuel tank?"

"Right. That makes sense. A fuel tank."

Leonard Stone's voice crackled on comms. "Blue Team. Acknowledge. We boosted the signal. Do you copy?"

"Ninety percent," Michi responded.

Saara spoke, "We have thermal imaging from Overwatch."

"Roger that, LP!" Bruce shouted over the noise of the engine as a continuous cloud of sand sprayed out from behind his Jeep. "Great timing!"

"Hemlock. The first vehicle has four hostiles."

"Copy that. Four in the Hummer."

"There are two in the cab of the transport truck and twelve in the back."

"Copy that. Two and twelve."

"There are two in the third truck."

"Copy that. Two in the fuel truck."

"There's no help coming. You're on your own. A team from the ship is Oscar Mike but won't make it in time."

"Roger that!" answered Bruce.

"The drone is bingo fuel, returning to base." Trey's dad said, meaning that it had just enough fuel left to make it to the nearest refueling field.

"Copy that."

"LP, out."

Trey hoped the shrubs around them would provide enough camouflage from the vehicles that were about to race by and was glad that he'd dug the holes, so their profiles wouldn't be seen laying on the sand.

"Alright, everybody. We're Gold Star!" Trey called out, signaling that their plan of action was completely in play now.

"Copy that. Gold Star!" Michi answered.

Bruce began to honk and flash his lights like a crazed drunk. He stuck his left arm out of the driver's side window and waived hysterically. It took a minute, but Trey saw a man emerge and begin climbing down the ladder on the passenger's side of the truck. He had a pair of binoculars in one hand and an assault rifle of some sort in the other.

This is why Trey was one of the top operators in the world. His brain was furiously crunching the numbers that most spotters would do in situations like these – something his superiors had known was a very special talent. He breathed in and then out – in and then out. His index finger straightened out along the trigger guard, then gently curled into position around the trigger. With a final exhale, he softly squeezed the trigger back towards him, making sure that his finger followed all the way through the shot. The gun recoiled straight back into him and then settled back into position, ready for another shot. The three seconds it took for the bullet to reach its target seemed like an eternity, but then Trey saw a splotch of red on the target's chest, saw him drop his weapon and fall back to the ground. Agent Stone was ready for a second shot, but the guy wasn't moving.

"Passenger from primary target eliminated," he reported to Bruce and Michi.

"Copy that," answered Agent Locke. He quickly downshifted and then played the pedals, so he was spraying even more sand from the tires than usual. Then he slammed on his brakes while a swirling cloud of fine sandy dust engulfed them. Michi grabbed her weapon, opened the door, and rolled out. Blasting into gear again, Bruce showered her with sand and dirt and raced forward towards his target.

"Yata!" Michi exclaimed, a Japanese phrase of excitement. She rolled off the road and burrowed into the sand – about a hundred meters from the truck.

"Well done," Trey responded. "Vegas, divert left. Draw the driver out."

"On it!"

Bruce swerved to the left, heading into open desert and was finally at an angle where he could see the driver's side of the truck. The man was just loading something into a tube-like mechanism!

Agent Locke jammed on his brakes. "Bazooka!"

He grabbed his kit from off the passenger seat, opened the door and dove out, the Jeep's momentum carrying on without him. A few seconds later, the distinct swooshing sound of a bazooka shot was followed by the Jeep bursting into hundreds of parts. The explosives that Justin had put into Michi's kit, as well as ammo from the mini-kits made for Jason Kennedy and Miles Howell, were lighting up like backpack bombs. Bruce lay flat on his stomach with his legs spread out and his hands over his ears. He could feel the detonations lift him a few inches off the ground but knew he'd be safe.

It was a race now. Bruce saw the man loading up another round while agent Locke ripped open his pack from Justin. The first weapon he saw was the Atchisson Assault Shotgun he'd used back at the train station. He didn't know how many slugs were left in the 32-shell magazine nor whether it would reach the hostile, but he'd have to risk it. He sprang up to his feet and sprinted forward, firing off rounds like he was in target practice.

His gun had the reach.

By the time Bruce arrived at the truck, and his gun ran empty, the hostile had had more lead pumped into him than you'd see on most fishing boats.

"Driver eliminated," Bruce announced as he raced around to the passenger's side to make sure the hostile Trey shot was dead. "Truck is secure. I repeat truck is secure."

"Roger that," Trey said, as the first two vehicles roared past him. All their eyes were on the ball of fire that had been the Jeep. "Vegas, get into position to intercept the lead vehicle. I'm going to take out the tanker." He recalled Michi's nickname. It tapped into her amazing talent to be able to disguise herself and blend in. "Gisō, cover the transport truck, but don't fire on them unless absolutely necessary."

Michi answered from beneath the sand, "Copy that."

"Roger," Bruce said, scrambling to get under the giant black truck and then belly-crawling towards the back, rear tire where he settled down and switched his shotgun out for an M4 carbine – the newer and lighter variant of the American-made M16. Not taking his eyes off the oncoming caravan, he reached into his pack and pulled out an M203 grenade launcher, attaching it to his rifle. Then he felt around for the type of round he needed and selected the M433 – a high explosive munition that can penetrate steel armor and cause a lot of radial damage.

Trey watched as the tanker truck went speeding past, displacing enormous amounts of sand into the air.

"Stay where you are, Jazzy. There might be more coming, and I don't want any surprises."

"Okay, dad."

Agent Stone checked his weather tracker again and peered through his scope, measuring the distance to the tanker. He zoomed in on the make of the vehicle and saw that it was a Chinese-made Beiben 4x4 Fuel Tanker truck. Trey figured that it weighed around twenty tons if it was full and had a tank that was most likely made from carbon steel. Fixing his scope on the right front tire, he followed it, then moved his scope a few meters in front of it and rehearsed squeezing the trigger at the perfect moment. After a few more trial runs, he squeezed the trigger as if still practicing. The tire splintered into hard rubber strips and fell apart.

Trey lined up the back-left tire and skipped the rehearsal. The rubber peeled off like an old tricycle tire on gravel. Suddenly, the frame of the vehicle began to twist with the stress of perpendicular momentum and the tanker section shifted loudly as the steel threatened to disengage from its anchors. As if in slow motion now, the truck bent unnaturally and then being too top-heavy to stay on its chassis, it slowly flopped over, landing heavily in the sand and skidding to a stop.

The brake lights of the troop transport truck lit up, and the vehicle would've screeched to a halt, had it been on asphalt. A dozen militants streamed out of the back and raced towards the tanker setting up a loose perimeter and trying to figure out what happened. The driver and the man in the passenger's seat had broken the windshield and were trying to climb out. One of them was on what appeared to be a satellite phone. Trey slowly moved his rifle scope around and found the barrel-end of Michi's gun sticking out of the sand, about ten feet off the right of the dusty roadway and nearly twenty feet ahead of where the truck had stopped.

Stone located the hummer in his scope and saw that it hadn't stopped. It was barreling down towards the big black truck.

"Vegas, I could disable the hummer. But it might expose my position."

"Negative, Hemlock. Do not expose," Bruce directed. "I've got these guys."

"Roger that. Gisō, don't take out the transport truck. We might need it."

"Copy."

Trey refocused on the troops around the tanker. Four of them were busy trying to help the driver and passenger out while the rest were scanning the area for combatants. But Agent Stone wasn't just watching the action, he was calculating every shot – preparing for an all-out sniper assault.

"Jazzy?"

"Yeah, dad."

"I need you to reach into my bag and pull out the HK UMP45. Set it for three-round bursts."

"Okay. I'm on it."

"Keep an eye out for more vehicles, too. Ok?"

"Copy that, Dad."

Trey knew that if they were rushed and pinned down, he'd have to switch from his sniper rifle to a submachine gun. The UMP that Justin had selected for him was a blowback-operated, magazine-fed weapon that fired from a closed bolt, meaning it was less susceptible to things like sand that could cause it to jam. It was a little jumpy at times, but Trey had figured it out a long time ago.

"Hemlock, I'm about to go boom," Bruce informed his sniper friend.

"Copy that. I'm ready. Gisō?"

"Ready."

A few seconds after Trey had answered, Bruce launched his M203 at the oncoming hummer. The grenade performed beautifully as it arced, spun through the air, and lodged into the only place on the Humvee that was truly vulnerable – right between the grill spaces on the front. Tremendous explosive energy blew through the grate and into the engine block. The radial blast confirmed something Bruce had suspected: these tires were not United States Military issue. They weren't lined with steel belts to withstand IEDs – instead, they were made from cheap third-grade rubber and blew off the rims like a hat in a hurricane.

The driver and passenger were dead instantly, but the two in the back of the vehicle stumbled out and stupidly rushed Bruce. He calmly reloaded the grenade launcher and took them both out with one shot.

As Bruce fired his grenades, Trey started taking out the rebel forces that were around the tanker truck. He started with the guy on his phone. All hell was breaking loose on the desert floor. Some were racing towards Bruce but found themselves dying from Trey's sniper bullets. A few others were beginning to rush towards Trey and Jasmine, but Michi was picking them off from under her sandy dugout. Then there was the group, now frantically, trying to pull out the driver and passenger from the flipped truck. Trey left them until last and then took them out one by one.

Everything went quiet.

"Hemlock to LP."

Leonard came on comms. "Go ahead."

"Gold Star was a success."

The relief in Trey's father's voice was easily heard. "Copy that, Hemlock. Gold Star's a wrap." Blue Team could hear LaunchPad cheering in the background.

By the time Trey and Jasmine picked up their gear and slid down the knoll that had been their fort, Michi pulled up in the transport truck with a big smile on her face. The Stone's climbed in front with her, but as they were passing the fuel truck, Trey motioned for her to stop.

He hopped down, ran over to the bodies, and quickly, but methodically, searched them for their phones. He ran back and hoisted himself up and into the cab. "Good to go."

When they arrived at the black truck, Bruce was standing patiently by. "I thought you'd all want to be here for this," he said.

The four looked at each other with deep satisfaction and excitement. Trey looked at his daughter.

"Honey, you open the door, okay?"

Jasmine didn't need to be told again. She hopped up the ladder on the back of the truck, slid the guard bolts out of place, and swung the heavy steel door wide open.

CHAPTER FIFTY

"SIR, IT'S FOR YOU," THE COMPANY MAN SAID, HANDING TANK A secure phone as they boarded the CIA chopper.

"Hello?"

Leonard Stone's voice conveyed concern. "How are you, kid?"

"I'm fine, sir."

"No broken bones?"

"No, just a few bruises. My shoulder could use a hot tub, but I'm ready to keep going."

"Are you hydrated?"

"Yes, they've been taking good care of me."

"Hey, Tank?" David came on.

"Sir?"

"Your quick-thinking got the German team rescued. Sticking your comms on that truck was brilliant."

The Lakota scout felt a surge of relief. "Great news! That's awesome!" The native scout felt emotions well up. "Wow. Thank you, sir. I'm glad it worked."

Leonard came back on. "Trey and his team have secured our Beta objective and will be transitioning them to a team of Marines. If you're good to go, we're going to keep you on the trail."

"I'm fine, sir."

"Okay," said David. "You're not going to the safe house in Benghazi. We want you to catch up with the Blue Team in Cairo at the U.S. Embassy."

"Copy that, sir. I'm guessing we're about two hours out?"

"Hopefully a little less. Put our Company friend back on the phone for me, would you?"

"And kid?" Leonard came back on. "Try to get some sleep on the way."

"Roger that," Tank said, handing the phone back to the CIA agent.

THE MERCEDES WAS within half a mile from the Ferrari, and Boyd was hugging the headrest in front of her trying not to slide from side to side. Her kit lay open on the floor under her feet, and she'd packed a smaller backpack that was strapped to her body. Agent Carter's right hand darted up to her earpiece and pressed it against her ear to hear better. "Give me some good news."

"Target's seven hundred yards ahead of you," Justin advised, calmly. "He just left the A4 and is in standstill traffic on the M4 right above the Chiswick Roundabout area. There's an accident ahead of him ... right around Carville Hall Park."

"Copy that," Boyd replied. She looked ahead into the driver's rearview mirror. "There's an accident on the M4, and he's stuck in that traffic. When we get close, I'm getting out and chasing him on foot."

"Do you want me to come with you? I can park on the shoulder."

"No. I'll be fine. But I need you to have an escape route ready. I'll bring him back to you, and we'll need to move out fast."

"Okay. I'll come up with something."

When the Mercedes hit the traffic jam, Boyd sprung out of the car and tore through the stopped traffic. Her arms were pumping like a sprinter in the Olympics, and her backpack was furiously swinging back and forth.

"Four hundred yards," Justin's voice was mechanical and still relaxed. "He's in the far-right lane. FYI. Your driver is reversing, and it looks like his plan is to park on the off-ramp about two hundred yards west of where he dropped you off."

"Copy that," Boyd said, stretching her legs in a full run. She hadn't pulled out a weapon yet, she wanted to get close, first.

"He's still stopped. In another hundred and fifty yards, slow down ... catch your breath."

Boyd did exactly that. As she eased up into a jog, she let her backpack slide down and then slowed to a walk. There was a large yellow semi-truck with *Wittle Movers Group* splashed on the side in bold black font.

"When you pass that truck, you should have a visual."

As Agent Carter spotted the blue Ferrari, some male drivers were getting out of their vehicles or leaning out of their windows and whistling at her. A few were asking if she needed a ride. But nothing shouts *uninterested* like pulling out a gun. When she'd pulled out hers, they shrunk back like frightened turtles and rolled up their windows. Her Rock Island Armory Ultra FS 9mm had bright red grips on it, customized by Justin, but was a classic looking gun with historic appeal. Carter loved it but realized the hecklers were now pulling out cell phones and turning on their camera apps.

Justin was silent on comms. He watched as her driver was getting off the highway and going somewhere but couldn't tell Carter about it. Not right this minute, anyway. It was time to let Boyd do her thing. She snuck up to within three car lengths of the target, over one lane to the left, and then broke towards the car, shooting out the back-left tire. The Michelin Sports Cup 2 depressurized so quickly, the driver felt a severe jolt and opened the car door in a rage, just as Boyd shot out the back window.

It was an Asian woman about Boyd's size.

Her eyes bulged when she saw Carter's weapon. "You are shooting me?!" she yelled before unleashing a string of obscenities.

"LP, we have a problem. The driver's not our target. There's no passenger."

"Who's driving?"

"I'll text you an image."

The lady was frozen in fear.

"Move, and I'll shoot you," Boyd said authoritatively.

"Who are you?"

"We'll talk later." Boyd held her gun steady, shouldered her backpack, dug her phone out of her left pocket, and snapped a picture. Launch Pad's secure app automatically sent any picture the phone took.

The lady glared angrily as Boyd walked to the back of the car and snapped a photo of the license plate while keeping her weapon trained on the lady. Traffic was starting to crawl forward, but phone cameras were still documenting every moment.

A car from the opposite direction, on the other side of the steel highway barrier, was honking obnoxiously. Boyd glanced over. It was her driver and the sleek Mercedes! He hopped out, with his gun drawn.

"Lady, get in my car!" he commanded the Asian. He looked at Boyd and said, "Get her purse, phone ... and whatever else. Then let's get out of here."

"You heard him," Boyd growled. "Get into his car. Now."

"Are you crazy? I'm not going to do that!"

Boyd wasn't messing around. She fired a round into the concrete, two feet in front of the woman. The lady jumped and hurried over to the median, climbed over, and got into the back of the car, pouting like an enraged three-year-old. The chauffeur kept his gun trained on her until Boyd joined them and got into the back seat, next to the target. Holstering his gun, the driver took his seat and tore away from the scene.

Boyd jammed her weapon into the lady's face, making sure the safety was on. "Who are you?"

The lady just stared straight ahead as police sirens were heard racing to the disabled sports car.

"Hellcat, that's his car," Justin said, having checked out the license plate. "And we made sure we followed it when it left his building. It didn't make any stops."

"Why are you driving Ghalib Ahmaadi's Ferrari?"

No answer.

Boyd calmly laid her gun on the floor and then with lightning speed drove her hand under the lady's chin and began to squeeze. "There are dozens of lives at stake, and I'm not messing around! You might think that by keeping quiet, you're safer. But you're not safe. Not in this car. Not with me! I'll rip you apart, starting with your throat."

The lady began to choke and sputter – then started nodding her head vigorously. Carter released her grip and picked up her gun, casually holding it in her hand.

Gasping for air and rubbing her chest vigorously, she spat out, "I'm just an executive assistant for Mr. Ahmaadi. I was told to drive to the airport and await instructions."

"By whom?"

"Mr. Ahmaadi."

"When did he send you?"

"Around noon, after his workout, the lady said, still sputtering.

"Where'd he go after that?"

"He said he was going home."

FOX WAS IN THE BATHROOM, just off the kitchen, swapping his brand-name outfit for his usual attire. Suddenly an alarm sounded from his tablet on the table. He dropped his shirt on the floor and almost ripped the door off, wearing only his belted black combat pants and his boots. The tablet was flashing red, and the screen was displaying video from his motion detector. One of the body doubles was disappearing down the stairwell and had triggered the motion sensor! Spider was in the kitchen drying the teacups he'd just collected and washed. He whirled around as Fox came storming out of the bathroom and raced out of the kitchen.

The door to the CIA safe house was open. But, just the big agent was about to tear after the escaping triplet, Spider yelled, "Stop! Look!!" He had the tablet in his hand. Fox spun around and saw what Spider was looking at. The small screen showed five armed men creeping up the stairs.

The big agent's comms sprang to life!

"Razor?" Boyd sounded concerned.

"Danger close!" Fox whispered curtly. "One of the triplets escaped, and I've got five hostiles approaching up the staircase."

Carter computed everything instantly. "He wasn't a double! He was the real deal. That's our target."

Fox raced back to the kitchen and grabbed a stun grenade he'd put on the counter. Then he spun around, pulling the pin, and with the throw of a baseball pitcher, he rocketed it through the open front door yelling, "America!"

The two remaining body doubles stayed where they were.

"Get in the kitchen," he yelled as Spider translated behind him.

At that moment, the large agent realized the remaining doubles were in on it all along. And now they weren't moving because they were committed to sacrificing their lives. Ghalib must have promised to protect their families. "Get them in the kitchen! Force them if you have to," he shouted as he covered the door with his custom-designed Fusion Tactical pistol, wishing that he'd grabbed his automatic rifle from out of his kit in the bathroom.

The grenade could be heard skipping down the stairs, and then it seemed to pause for a second before a window-shattering pop. Fox turned his head just in time to close his eyes for the flash and charged into the stairwell with his gun ready. Four of the five gunmen were still stacked on the staircase moaning and rubbing their eyes vigorously. It was like shooting fish in a barrel and four loud bangs later, their threat was neutralized.

"Grenades!" Spider sounded panicked as the noise of shattering glass registered in Fox's head.

A rapid series of explosions ripped through The North American Research Group for Middle Eastern Affairs, rattling the building with such a sudden force that the giant agent found himself tumbling down the steps over the bodies he'd just shot.

Boyd was about a kilometer away when she saw the wisp of smoke. She caught the driver's eye in the rearview mirror. "We need to get there now!"

"Flashing blue lights," he responded, checking his side-view mirror. "They'll be on us in minutes."

"Great."

"I'll have to pull over."

"Negative. Hours of red tape."

"I'll have to lose them."

Boyd calculated that it'd take about ninety seconds to run the distance with her gear. "Drop me off, then take them on a ride."

Agent Carter's backpack was still on and she grabbed her kit from off the floorboard as the driver came to a sudden halt. She sprung out and the driver tore off. When the police had a clear view of him, he drifted through a sudden left turn. Boyd shouldered her kit, front-strapped her backpack to it, and walked casually until the cops screamed past her. Then she took off running, keeping her gun-arm glued to her thigh.

"Hellcat!" Justin's voice was pressing.

"What's going on!"

"Razor's dark."

"Sixty seconds out."

"At least one hostile's in the area. Come in hot."

"Copy that." Boyd was in full sprint but slowed to a jog as she got closer.

People were starting to walk towards where the explosion had happened, sirens were beginning to crescendo from a few miles away. She was just wondering how to proceed when she passed someone on foot headed the opposite direction. She spun around and watched him for a second. There was something familiar about him. *And why was he walking away from everything when everyone else seemed to be standing still or following their curiosity?* She quickly crept up behind him and buried her weapon into his back. "Stop."

The man froze. Then he attempted to whirl around and grab Carter's weapon. It wasn't a great move. She drove her boot into the front of his left knee with such force that it overextended.

"Nice try," he grunted, reaching for a knife that was front-sheathed.

"Where's Ahmaadi?" Boyd demanded as her right hand sailed into the air, and his eyes followed it, unsure as to what to expect. It was a distraction. This time, she leaped into the air, crunching her core and landed by thrusting both legs into the man's other knee, forcing pressure on it from the inside out. It sounded like a giant stick of celery as the patella tendon stretched, tore, and then separated from his tibia. The man twisted to the ground as his support system crumpled and his face became clearly visible. She did know this guy! The side of his head was still bruised from when she'd bashed it into the side of a baggage claim carousel at the airport in Baltimore.

"You?!" he hissed as the pallor drained from his face, and the torn ultrastructure of sensory nerve endings in his knee-joint capsule began to burn.

In one motion, Carter spun her gun around and handle-whipped him in the same bruise she'd created on his head earlier. He went unconscious, and she knew he'd be out for a while. Agent Carter needed to get to Fox!

JASMINE KNEW she would never forget the moment she opened the door to the back of the big black truck. It seemed like a thousand thoughts ran through her head in seconds. She felt a wave of heat like she'd opened an oven door. The stench was almost overpowering. And Trey's daughter clearly witnessed the physical manifestation of helplessness. Each girl there had come to the place of despair. They knew they were just meat in a trade. Nobody was going to see them for their imagination or intelligence. Any dream or vision they had of their future had been violently shredded in their hearts. Their slave traders were only interested in the moving and selling of product, and the reality of someone being dominated and abused the way these girls had been, hit Jazzy hard. Something in her gut twisted. She knew it was her own memories, but she refused to let them surface. Suddenly a voice flashed through her mind. It was that of her brother's. He was screaming as he was being tortured. She blinked and drew in a breath. The girls came back into focus, and she forced a smile.

They were turning their heads and rubbing their eyes, blinded by the sudden light. Then they looked towards the door, expecting one of their evil captors. Disbelief registered on their faces when they saw the confident face of Trey's daughter as she climbed up into the truck. Then confusion.

"Hi, girls. My name is Jasmine Stone. We're going to get you out of here and back to your parents. They're waiting for you in Rome and can't wait to see you. You're safe. But we have to hurry and get out of here."

At first, her words didn't register.

"Girls, the nightmare is over. Let's get out of here."

Michi hiked up the ladder of the giant machine and stepped inside, standing beside her. "Hi, everyone. My name is Michiko Imada. The people who took you are dead. We've killed all of them." Then she saw the chains and realized, the girls couldn't move. "I'll get some bolt cutters and let's break those off of you."

She jumped off the truck and tapped her comms. "Come in LP."

"Go ahead," responded Saara.

"Confirming a negative on our primary target."

"Copy that. Primary target is not in this truck." The team at LaunchPad overheard her. Casey Baker was not on board.

Trey was going through the corpses and stripping them of phones and identification. Michi and Jasmine were working on setting the girls free from their restraints, giving them what little vitamin water and beef jerky they had in their packs, and attending to cuts and minor medical needs. While they worked, they gently asked the girls questions, trying to uncover where the last remaining truck with their team-mates could be headed. Bruce had rigged up a makeshift hose-apparatus and was using it to siphon fuel from the tanker to fill the troop transport truck.

Off in the distance, and to the west, four black specks in the sky were getting larger and larger just as Saara's voice came through Trey's comms.

"LP to Blue Team"

"Yes?" Trey replied.

"Birds from the USS Bataan are in the air and should be visible."

"Copy that. I've got visual."

"We need all our assets to get to Cairo ASAP. We're dissolving the Red Team, and you'll all be the Blue Team. One of the birds is for you. Converge at the U.S. Embassy and Tank will meet you there."

"Confirm. We're to leave the girls?"

"Our Marines will do their job. We've got to get our primary target."

"I don't think we should take a chopper," Bruce said, walking up to Trey.

David Hirsch spoke up. "Why not?"

"We need to track these people. Let's stay on the ground and trace their steps as much as we can."

"They'll end up in Cairo."

"Can you guarantee that?"

David and Leo looked at each other. Bruce was right.

"Tank can set up in Cairo," Trey suggested. "We'll work our way to him if that's where the truck of girls ends up."

"Okay. We're concurring. Take the transport truck to the border. We'll work on what will happen there and get you transportation that you can use without drawing attention."

"Copy that."

CHAPTER FIFTY-ONE

THE GERMAN PARENTS HAD BEEN DISMISSED, AND TED BAKER HAD asked the American parents to stay close by. But now, he was convening them again in the meeting room with the large table. No longer needing a translator, he spoke to the parents directly.

"I've just received news that rescue of the second truck of girls has been successful. They'll be joining the German team on one of our navy ships and will arrive here at the same time." A collective gasp of gratitude passed over the parents.

He paused to look down at his list. "Six girls were not among them, and we're actively pursuing them into Egypt."

The parents waited, anxiously.

"Abril Fuentes, Amber Taylor, Sally Mei, Savannah Jackson, Shelly Brown ..." he paused and flexed his jaw muscles, "... and Casey Baker ... have not yet been rescued."

It was déjà vu. Some parents started weeping with joy while others wept with worry.

"If I did not call your daughter's name, she is safe and is being escorted by some of our best Marines. They deserve a lot of thanks. I really appreciate how some of you have asked about Amber and Savannah, both of whom have lost their parents. Mr. Mei has graciously offered to fly their grandparents and other close relatives over here, and we are looking into where they live and how that could work. We are arranging counseling for them on the Navy ship. It will be a long haul, that's for sure. Thanks for your concerns. When we get all our girls back, those two will need some very special attention."

Mr. Fuentes raised his hand, and Ted acknowledged him.

"Mr. Baker, where's Abril and those other girls, now?"

"We don't know. I'm just being straight with you. It's a guess at this point, but we have reason to believe they're being taken to Cairo."

"Why?"

"Well, we don't have much to go on. But some of the people involved have done business there before."

"I have business connections in Egypt. I have a night club in Cairo."

"I'm sure we could use those right away. Does anyone else know people there?"

Nobody raised their hands.

"We'll inform all of you if we have any new information. You're dismissed," said Ted, motioning for Abril's father to follow him out the door.

The two of them sat down in a set of elegant plaid wing-backed chairs that were set on either side of a small bistro table and perched by a window with a clear view of the city.

"Our team is in Libya, and we need immediate help," the President's son confessed.

"Crossing the border?"

Ted nodded.

"Where do they need to cross?"

"Just north of the White Desert."

"There's a trail about two miles south of the Patrol Road. It's littered with trucks and tanks that the Egyptians have blown up over the years, but there are no border guards there."

"If it's littered with vehicles the Egyptians have blown up, doesn't that mean it's under Egyptian surveillance?"

"One guy. Not *Egyptian surveillance*. There's one guy watching everything, and I know how to get money to him, so he'll look the other way."

President Baker's son gave him a long piercing stare.

"The girls were in the tunnels, weren't they?"

"How do you know about those?"

"Egypt was one of the first clubs we opened outside of North America. I've heard a lot about them, and Gadhafi wasn't the only one using those tunnels. He leased them to cartel organizations. It was very profitable for him."

"And you're connected to organized crime?"

Fuentes shook his head. "No. But I've been invited to be. Many times. I know that area pretty well. Nightclubs attract a certain clientele."

"You're just telling me this now?"

"I didn't know they were going to Egypt until you just told us."

Ted felt his temper rising but kept his emotions under control. "They'll be driving a troop transport truck that they commandeered from a local terrorist cell."

"Doesn't it have Libyan plates? They can't drive that around in Egypt. They need to ditch it on the Libyan side of the border and hike about two miles. I'll have someone meet them on the Egyptian side."

"Someone you trust?"

"As much as you can trust someone in that area of the world. He's a tour guide in Beni Suef at the Medom Pyramid, but he's in the Siwa Oasis right now leading a group of archaeologists through the Temple of the Oracle of Amun."

Ted looked unconvinced.

"The tourists he guides aren't really tourists."

"I'm not sure I want to know more."

Abril's father nodded his head. "How big is the spec ops team?"

Baker picked up his phone and started to dial Leonard Stone's number. "Four. Two males. Two females." He paused dialing and looked at Fuentes. "Any idea where these girls are headed?"

"Most of the smugglers in the region go through Beni Suef and then on to Cairo.""

"Why Beni Suef?"

"They use the Nile to go North."

LEONARD STONE and David Hirsch were in the conference room by themselves. They'd just hung up the phone and needed to piece some things together.

"Boyd and Fox are on the roof. It's the only place they could escape without drawing attention," Trey's dad said, looking at a brief that Saara had just sent them. We'll get their driver to bail them out of there when everything's calmed down. He won the police chase."

"Spider's dead and so are the other two body doubles," David stated, reading what was in front of him and shaking his head. "Boyd said that Serwabi has a man there. She recognized him from the airport here in Baltimore and clobbered him with her gun. Unfortunately, the police picked him up and are holding him as a person of interest in the bombing. Otherwise, he'd be up on the roof with Carter and Fox spilling his guts."

"What's your thoughts on him?" Hirsch asked his friend.

"He must've been the one who threw the grenades through the window and killed three men."

"Maybe," David said, nodding. "But maybe not. Obviously, he's tied to Serwabi, but what if he's one of our guys? What if he's an operator in the MEO's classified mission?"

"I've dug around. I can't find anyone who has authorized Serwabi to do anything. Not officially anyway."

"Okay, Leonard. We'll let the police in London do their jobs, but I'll call a buddy of mine and tell him to keep an eye on things. If he gets released for any reason, we'll pick him up."

Leonard leaned back in his chair. "Is it time to apply more than just verbal pressure on Serwabi?"

"Not yet. We have a lot of information that makes him nervous, but I still don't think we've hit the key to making him talk. If he's telling the truth ... well ... we have to be very careful. He may have permission to do what he's doing from some young punk up the food chain that you and I don't know."

"The Nile sounds like a nightmare. There are literally hundreds of locations along that river where they could offload the girls."

David agreed and was about to say something when the door to the conference room opened. Bora was holding her laptop open and looked like she'd just seen a ghost.

"Can I come in?"

"Of course," answered Leo. "What's wrong?"

She came in and sat down, putting the laptop on the table and turning it so the two men could see the screen.

"I'd contacted Jennifer about an hour ago and told her to go deeper into the financials of all the parents."

Leo looked at David, then back at Bora. "The parents? Why?"

"Just checking off all the boxes." She brightened the screen of her laptop. "Wu just called me back. Look at what she just found."

Stone read it out loud. "It looks like a donation of $250,000 to Ahmadi's foundation. But who is Platinum Liquors?"

"It's the liquor company that's owned by Abril's father. It supplies all the booze to his nightclubs."

Leo gasped and looked up as David jumped out of his seat! "Oh, no!"

"Dr. Stone?" Justin's wife pressed.

"I don't believe what I'm hearing."

"Dr. Stone, whose idea was our involvement in this tournament?"

"I'm not sure, Bora," Leonard responded.

"I think we need to find out."

David was pacing impatiently. "Get President Baker on the line now."

FOX WAS JUST COMING TO, and in a lot of pain, but he was grateful that he hadn't broken any bones. His head was still groggy from the explosions, and his right shoulder and arm felt like he'd tried to tackle a telephone pole. He was laying down, and Boyd was sitting next to him, weapon in hand and ready, should the door from the stairwell open. The two operatives were hidden in the shadows of the only thing of size on the roof, a large water tank that resembled a giant horizontally positioned egg. "I don't know how you got me up three flights of stairs."

"You need to lose a foot of height and eighty pounds," Boyd answered with a grin.

"Seriously. How'd you do it?"

"Fireman's Carry."

"Nobody saw you?"

"I went into the building next door and found a connecting point to this building. Crossed over and went downstairs to get you. They had you on a stretcher on the stair landing. So, I popped smoke."

Fox shook his head in amazement.

"I tossed it down the steps, and when it went off, the people investigating the scene started freaking out. I added a flash grenade in the middle of the smoke. Dude, they couldn't get out of the building fast enough and left you behind. I think they were waiting for another explosion. So, I had a few minutes to race through the safe house and confirm what I'd suspected. Spider's dead. So are two of the triplets."

It took a minute to register with the big agent. "He was a good kid."

"Seemed like it," she said sadly. "Nerdy, but in a good way."

"He was excited to be part of something big. Good kid," Fox repeated thickly.

"Then I picked you up and put you down, right where you are now."

"You think they'll check up here?"

"I think they already did before I came up here because they haven't been up here since. It's why I've got my eye on the door, though. They might check again, eventually, but they won't think to do it right away. They're immersed in the crime scene downstairs."

Fox knew Boyd was talented. They'd been through some tight situations before, in Ghana. But what she had just accomplished was very impressive. He turned to face her. "You're pretty amazing, Hellcat. Thanks."

"It's what we do, isn't it?" she said, nodding appreciatively. "But, yeah ... you're welcome."

"We have instructions?"

"Wait for evac."

"You didn't happen to see my kit when you checked out the crime scene, did you?"

Boyd grinned, again. "I'm no rookie, Razor. I even checked the bathroom. Plus, I thought you'd need to put a shirt on."

Fox willed himself into a sitting position and spotted his kit next to hers.

"I put your tablet inside."

"Geez, Boyd. Did you grab a double espresso, too? I could use one."

"No," she answered with a sly smirk, "But I snagged some energy drinks from the plane before we landed and put them in my kit. You want one?"

"Absolutely." Fox waited while Boyd retrieved the liquid vigor, then he unscrewed the lid and drank it shot-style. "Thanks." He shook his head like a dog shaking off water, then raised his eyebrows. "So, H..e..ll..c..a..t."

"Ra..z..or?"

"How'd you get your nickname?"

"We were under attack at BIAP, and I used an RPG to disable a tank that was about to fry our whole unit."

"Baghdad International Airport. That was like a portal to hell on some days."

Carter nodded, turning to him. "You've been there."

Kurt Middleton-Fox nodded.

"Well, don't expect me to make that RPG shot today. It was a one-time fluke. Probably couldn't do it again if I tried."

Fox chuckled, "So the legends of Boyd Carter are true. You took out a tank with a Glock," then he winced as his neck reminded him it was a little tweaked.

Carter smiled. "RPG. Little more powerful." She looked down as if remembering the experience for a moment, and then back up at the rooftop door. "A World War II buff on my team christened me with the name. He told me Hellcats were the most effective tank destroyers in the U.S. arsenal back in the day. Small and lightweight, but super-fast because they were outfitted with the same radial engine that Sherman tanks had."

"He was right. They were game-changers. I like it."

"Thanks. Where'd you get your knife skills?"

"Some kids play basketball in their driveways. I'd practice with knives in my backyard every day. Don't really know why. I'd make my own mannequin out of hay and then knife the thing until it was a pile of straw at my feet."

"Seriously?"

Fox chuckled. "Yeah."

"Did you ever seek psychiatric help?" Boyd asked, and they both started to laugh.

"My parents probably figured that as long as I wasn't doing drugs or sowing my wild oats, everything was cool."

The two quieted down and sat in silence for a few minutes, and then Fox stood up and gingerly stretched. He walked over to his kit to pull out his black long-sleeved shirt and his weapon. "Why don't I watch the door for a bit, and you can change out of your high-end designer outfit?"

"Truly. That's a fantastic idea. I'm ready to get into some tactical clothes."

WITH THE GIRLS safely in the air and on their way to the USS Bataan, Trey, Bruce, Michi and Jasmine climbed into the transport truck and headed East. The vehicle was obviously built for this terrain, and they were making good time. Agent Imada guessed they were less than twenty minutes from the Egyptian border. Stone and his daughter were in the back, facing each other on benches, and the other two were up front.

"Dad, I'll never forget what just happened. I know you do this kind of thing all the time, but ..." her emotions were starting to bubble up as the adrenaline was wearing off. "The looks on those girls' faces.

"It was pretty sobering."

"Will they ever recover from something like this?"

Trey thought about it for a few minutes and then nodded. "I think about what we've been through as a family. There's something that Dr. Messerman told us when we first met with him. He said that people were created to heal. Those girls will need help finding the path forward, and it will definitely take some time and lots of counseling, but they have a long life ahead of them. I think they'll be fine."

"I remember reading that in India, there are fifteen million women and children who are slaves. I just wonder, 'Who will rescue them?'"

"LP to Blue Team," Saara interrupted.

"Go ahead, LP," Michi responded for the everyone. The transmission started to get lost, and nobody could make out what the Finnish agent at LaunchPad was saying.

She shouted into her comms, "Repeat! Did not transmit. You did not transmit! Over?"

Again, everything was jumbled, and then suddenly Saara's voice came through. "You're ... ... from the border. Park, disable the vehicle, and proceed on foot."

"Copy that. Park. Disable. And proceed on foot."

There was more static and garbled talk.

"Say again!" shouted Agent Imada over the noise of the truck engine. "Repeat last."

More static. "... proceed ... on foot. Sending coordinates." The static sounded like a radio station that was fading out of range. "... a perimeter. Exfil in ninety-minutes." More annoying electrical disturbance. "... Blue Land Rover ... Siwa Oasis. Hakiim."

"Copy that," Imada said, figuring she got most of it. There was a short burst of static, and she assumed Saara was saying something like, "Good luck" or "Over and out."

Trey had pulled out a set of binoculars and was scanning out the back of the truck. "It's time for us to focus."

PRESIDENT BAKER'S face came up on David's tablet. "Please tell me you have good news."

"We're putting some puzzle pieces together," Leo responded. "I have a few questions for you."

"Go ahead."

"Did you send any of your Secret Service detail over with Ted?"

"I did."

"Who'd you send?" asked David.

"My best man. Vince Graham."

"What's he best at?"

"Everything. He's the real deal. Why?"

Leonard sat forward and looked into the tablet's camera, "Before I answer, George, whose idea was it to be part of this tournament?"

The President paused, recalling. "Well, the tournament was an official FIFA-sponsored goodwill event – so I guess they got the ball rolling."

"But the United States isn't a big soccer nation. Who was the impetus at our end?"

"If I remember correctly, I think one of the parents reached out to Ted."

"Felipe Fuentes?"

"Yes! I think it was … Fuentes," the President nodded. "The nightclub owner."

"Just a second, Mr. President," Leo said, hitting the mute button on the tablet. He looked at David. "Do we think Ted's part of this?"

"No, Leonard. I don't. I've thought about that. He's put up a lot of his own money to get these girls back. He's given us full freedom to do whatever we need. I think he's clean." He turned to Bora. "Did anything ping when you investigated Ted Baker's financials?"

"No, sir. Nothing. He runs a great company, and although the politically-motivated IRS has tried their best to find something on him, they haven't been able to. His records are current and transparent. He keeps almost all of his charitable donations stateside, so they're easy to trace." She shrugged. "Everything was clean."

Leo nodded, unmuted the tablet, and proceeded to fill in the retired President of the United States.

CHAPTER FIFTY-TWO

TED BAKER HAD JUST CALLED LAUNCHPAD AND INFORMED THEM of where Trey and his team could be picked up and taken further into Egypt when his phone buzzed with a text message. It was from his father.

Fuentes dirty. Take him to your room. Vince Graham has questions.

"I don't know about you," the President's son said casually, "I could use a stiff drink."

"I'm in," Fuentes said with a smile. "Should we go down to the bar?"

"I brought a few of my favorite scotches. Let's break one open in my suite and wait for news from Egypt."

The two men got up and headed over to the elevator.

"This whole ordeal is such a disaster," the nightclub owner said as the doors closed, and the lift began to climb.

"It's a nightmare. No doubt about that."

When they arrived at his suite, Baker put his thumb on the scanner, and the door's lock clicked open. He held the door and motioned his guest inside. In one smooth motion, Vince Graham stepped out of the bathroom behind Fuentes and then stuck a gun barrel into his left side!

"What the hell?" Fuentes shouted.

"Move slowly and walk straight ahead," commanded the Secret Service agent.

"Are you out of your mind??"

Vince jabbed the gun harder into Felipe's rib cage. Fuentes started walking into the living room. "Stand beside that wooden chair. I'm going to frisk you. Try anything, and I'll put a bullet in your head." A quick pat-down revealed a Trejo machine pistol, the smallest fully automatic weapon ever made and a throwback to the Mexican Dirty War – a civil conflict between the U.S. backed PRI-ruled government and the left-wing student and guerrilla groups in the 1960s and 1970s. Those dark days left rumors of the systematic torturing and illegal executions of over 1200 people.

Baker noticed the infamous apple logo on the side of the gun's slide when Graham handed it to him. It was a reference to the town of its origin, famous for its apple cider. "You're a piece of garbage!" he spat.

"What are you talking about?" raged Fuentes. "Have you gone crazy? And who are you?" he demanded, looking at Graham.

"Sit down," the agent responded menacingly, duct-taping Felipe's hands behind his back and then wrapping his ankles to the chair legs when he'd sat. "You want to know who I am?" Vince hissed, standing up. "I'm the guy that's going to make you squeal like a pig."

"Me? What have I done? I'm supporting Ted! I've been working with him! Ask him. Have I not been helping you?" Abril's dad's eyes were bulging, and his face was red as he desperately looked at the President's son.

Baker sat down on the couch, perched across from the wooden chair, propped his legs up on a coffee table and texted his father back.

Q&A started. If you're right, TS and team are in imminent danger!

BLUE TEAM HAD DITCHED the truck, wiped anything they'd touched and let the air out of the tires. Now they were hoofing it on foot to the coordinates that Saara had texted them. Their comms were still down, and even texting LaunchPad wasn't working. Bruce and Michi were leading the formation with Jasmine in the middle and Trey at the back. They were proceeding along a dusty road with dunes on either side. The hills had light shrubbery and a few cacti, but no trees. It was just like Fuentes had predicted. Along the way were shells of cars, rusted truck frames, and even a few old tanks, that littered the road – vehicles that had been torched by Egyptian forces who had been protecting the border from Libyan insurgents for many years.

Bruce put up his hand and stopped the advance. "Trey, we're about three hundred meters out. Our rendezvous point should be just around the corner."

"Okay," Agent Stone nodded, kneeling down and opening up his kit. He moved the sniper rifle he'd been carrying over his shoulder, so it was double-point-strapped to his body and pulled out his HK UMP45. It was still set to three-round bursts, from when Jasmine had set it back at their sniper burrow. "I'll sneak up and scout it out. Michi, you protect our six. Bruce, watch the ledge on the right and Jasmine, you watch the hilltops to our left. Give me five minutes and then proceed forward. If the coast isn't clear, I'll come back to you, and we'll regroup." The team nodded, and Trey moved forward quickly, carefully checking every junk metal skeleton and anywhere there might be an ambush. He crept around the corner of the hill that had been in front of them and to their left and knelt down beside a shot-out 1983 Toyota Landcruiser. Everything was quiet. He pulled out his binoculars and carefully searched the terrain. There was nobody around, although he noted that the metal skeletons had thinned out. There were only a few burned-out vehicles ahead of him. He guessed that he must've just crossed the border into Egypt. He burrowed down beside an old tank and waited in a position that gave him the full view of everything in front of him.

A few minutes passed, and then he saw a quarter-sized stone bounce past him. He didn't need to turn around. Bruce was letting him know that they were approaching. He heard their footsteps and jostling gear as they got closer. Then he felt Michi's pat on his shoulder.

"Pretty quiet," Bruce noted.

"It's kind of eerie," said Jasmine. The group waited in place for a few more minutes. "How much further?"

Michi looked at her smartphone. "It's where that old Mercedes taxi cab is. Straight ahead."

Trey looked at Bruce. "We still don't have comms. But the last thing Saara told us was to set up a perimeter."

Agent Locke nodded.

"I'm thinking Jasmine and I fall back about fifty meters and climb halfway up the dune on our left. Michi sets up here. And Bruce, you go across from the Mercedes and find a spot on the dune to the right."

"We're waiting for a blue Land Rover from the Siwa Oasis. And some guy named *Hakiim* is our contact point, right?"

Trey nodded.

"I don't like this."

"It is what it is. Let's just be ready for anything. We'll take a few minutes to fully kit up. Grenades, smoke, combat knives, ankle weapons. Be on full alert."

"If Hakiim is on time, he should be here in about fifty minutes," Michi advised everyone.

The three operatives and Jasmine got ready and then broke to their various positions.

"Jazzy, just like last time. You're watching our back and checking the hilltops behind us. I'll be looking forward through my sniper scope. Michi will be looking up, on the right and left, watching the tops of the dunes in front of us. Bruce will have the big picture, checking everything."

"Okay, dad. Should we dig holes again?"

"Not this time. Just get close to a bush and kneel down. It's not a perfect cover, but it's better than being in an area of open sand."

Trey got prone and had a good view of the road ahead while Jasmine knelt in position and began to systematically check the areas she was responsible for. The tension in the air was palpable, and the team was on edge. They all desperately needed rest.

Trey took the time to pull up the map of Egypt in his head. He pictured Cairo and worked his way down the Nile. Siwa Oasis wasn't there. He browsed to the East and then again to the West. Bingo. It was close to the Libyan border. *Why was the Land Rover coming from Siwa Oasis?* It certainly was an odd place to have an asset.

In the bottom of his scope-view, was Michi and it didn't seem that long before he noted that she had her hand up with her fingers and thumb spread wide.

"Five minutes," Trey said out loud.

Jasmine responded. "Copy that. Five minutes."

Agent Stone was doing the math, checking the wind and humidity, and imagining various scenarios. He redirected his scope to the tops of the dunes, calculating what shots in those directions would entail. Then he'd refocus down the road, doing more computations. Slowly breathing in and out, now, he was sending his body and mind a practiced message. He was ready.

"I DON'T like waiting like this."

"What are you thinking?"

Fox was feeling better. He'd taken an opioid that Justin had included in his kit, and with the changed perception of pain running through his spinal cord and central nervous system, the soreness in his body was hiding. "I think we need to find a way off this roof and make ourselves useful."

"I'm ready if you are."

"We could sneak down the stairs and shoot anybody that looks at us strangely."

"I thought about that. Probably not the best option."

"We could jump off the building and hope to fly."

"Also, not good."

"Okay, Hellcat, what's your plan?" Fox asked, knowing that she had one.

"We cross over to the next-door building the way I came. It's super easy," Boyd said, standing up.

Her big counterpart got to his feet too, and stretched, then zipped up his kit. "Super easy," he repeated with a dubious tone.

"Yeah. We'll go back to the stairwell and down a floor. I found a unit that's under construction in the building across from this one. They had some 4"x6" planks. So, I extended one over here and walked across. These structures are close together. Old-style, you know? About five feet. We'll just extend the plank again, walk across and return it to where it came from." She grinned. "Easy."

"You're kidding, right?" asked Fox, but Boyd was already by the door to the stairwell, carrying her kit. "I'm not much of a tightrope walker," he commented, continuing his protest. "Maybe we should just wait up here."

Boyd grinned and held the door open for him. "Maybe I should change your nickname from Razor to Plank."

"Or Splat."

CHAPTER FIFTY-THREE

THE TRUCK HAD FINALLY COME TO A STOP, AND CASEY BAKER felt like she was about to throw up – like she'd been violently sea-sick and was now back on land. She looked around at the faces of the other girls. Almost every one was a physical manifestation of terror and dread. Sally Mei locked eyes with her. Neither girl said a word. The President's daughter was starting to feel fear creep through her body. Amber Taylor started crying, reliving the murder of her parents. Shelly Brown, too, was terrified. She buried her head in her hands and began to shake uncontrollably.

When the door swung open, all the girls jumped, startled.

A giant man hopped into the truck and wrinkled his nose at the smell. They'd never seen him before. He wore a pair of khakis and a white polo shirt with short-sleeves that strained around his bulging biceps. His face was a mess of skin problems, a nose that had been broken in more fights than he could count, and beady eyes that made people look the other way. What hair he had left, he'd colored an odd orange. Perhaps it was a bleach job gone bad. "Welcome to Egypt. I will uncuff you, and you will get out of the truck," he stated matter-of-factly.

"We're in Egypt?" Amber Taylor gasped.

Savannah Jackson began to whimper. "What's going to happen to us? Who are you?" Her cries grew louder. "What are you going to do to us?"

"Just do what you're told to do," the big man hissed.

Leila climbed up on the bumper and peered in, her dark eyes flashing. "Come girls. Get out of the truck, walk through the gate, and line up against the wall in the courtyard."

Casey got up and led the way. One by one, each girl followed, walking gingerly and groaning as their sore limbs unfolded out of the truck. Baker spotted The Lynx. He was a few hundred feet away, barking into his phone, and pacing back and forth. She looked around at the compound they'd just stepped into. It was very typically and distinctively Egyptian. The sandy-colored limestone building was probably around 10,000 square feet of living space set into a tall one-story structure that was built via the post and lintel method of construction. It had strong, elegant vertical pillars that drew people's gaze up towards the thick, stone horizontal headers. Probably over half a century old, each column had etchings of papyrus plants in the walls that faced into the courtyard. In some ways, the home felt like a giant Mexican hacienda. If the situation wasn't so awful, Casey thought she would enjoy living in a place like this. "I'm a sucker for courtyards," she admitted to herself. A slightly inappropriate water feature in the middle featured three naked boys with their backs to each other, peeing off the top level of the three-level-fountain. Despite its beauty, Ted's daughter decided there was a dark, insidious feel to the place. She stood against a wall as instructed, with the girls from her team to her right.

The big man with the oddly colored orange hair walked up and down the line, inspecting the girls and striking fear in them at the same time by standing a little too close for comfort. As he did, Casey noticed The Lynx was getting more and more animated. He'd followed them into the courtyard and now stood in the middle, trying to speak over the fountain noise. She strained to hear what he was saying while not to appear conspicuous, but then realized she couldn't understand him. He was speaking Arabic. Finally, he shouted some things that everyone in the building probably heard. Casey figured they were obscenities mixed with threats and curses, and then he hung up, glaring at everyone.

"Girls," Leila said. "It's time for you to get clean. I'm going to take you to shower, and we have clothes for you to put on afterward. Decent clothes. You'll see. We have everything you need. It's very nice."

Shelly Brown thought about asking where they were going and why they had to look nice but bit her tongue. It was the first time Leila didn't appear like she wanted to rip their throats out, so Casey's friend decided not to upset the mood. Walking single file across the courtyard, she followed the rest of the girls and Leila. They walked through a door and into a clean hallway lit with Egyptian spun-brass pear pendant lighting that was inset into the walls, casting off an orangish grid pattern across the ceilings and floors.

After passing a few heavy wooden doors, Leila stopped at one and opened it. "Go in," she urged the girls. It was a large all-tiled room with locker-room style showers. White towels on hooks hung along the wall to their right, across from the shower-heads and taps.

"There's no way you'll escape this place without being shot," Leila stated matter-of-factly as she leaned against some sinks to their left, across from some more showers. "Even if you did make it out, nobody here speaks English. And you should know we have eyes everywhere." She nodded, satisfied that she had made her point. "There is body wash and shampoo by each shower. Wait until all of you are done showering, wrap your towels around you, and open the door to the left of this one. You will find hairdryers, brushes, hair oil and whatever else you might need. Your clothes are hanging on hooks with your name just above them. I will give you sixty minutes to shower and dress, then I'll come get you from the dressing room. I know you might not know how to properly put on a hijab. When I come and get you, I'll show you." She turned and walked out, clearly implying that she would not answer any questions, but then she stopped in the doorway and rotated around to face the girls. "Tonight, you are going on beautiful cruise up the Nile River to Cairo. It's what every tourist here dreams of doing. You will love it. And later, you'll meet your husbands."

BAO ZHEN and Lin Lin Ma were awake. Jun had dropped them off and continued to drive over to Philadelphia to meet Rocco and see Hirsch's iconic cigar bar for the first time. After debriefing with Leonard, the mother and daughter had slept for several hours and were now making coffee and toasting bread while they chatted quietly with each other.

David slipped out of the conference room and joined them. "I'm sorry that Jasmine and Trey are not on their way here. This interruption to your outing wasn't anticipated or planned."

"I understand," Lin Lin said graciously, although her voice betrayed some nervous tension.

463

Hirsch sat down at the table close to the kitchen area and put his tablet on the table. "They've rescued the second group of girls, while you were asleep."

"That's great to hear!" expressed Ma. "Really wonderful."

"Has President Baker's daughter been rescued?" Bao Zhen wondered.

Hirsch shook his head. "She wasn't in that group."

"So, where's the final group of girls, David?" Trey's wife asked, taking a seat at the table.

"We're not sure."

She waited for him to continue.

"Jasmine, Trey, Michi, and Bruce are on the Libyan border right now, about to cross into Egypt. We think the girls traveled through the same spot about five hours before them and are headed towards a town on the Nile River."

Lin Lin Ma nodded, walking over to the fridge to find some cream for her coffee.

Bao Zhen could spot a liar a mile away. Hirsch wasn't one. But, he wasn't telling her everything, she was sure. "You know, David, when Koa was ten years old, I remember asking him if he'd finished his homework. He said he had." She paused, remembering. "I trusted he was telling the truth, but I sensed there was more to his answer. Well, the next day, his teacher called me, telling me that he hadn't finished his math. It turns out he'd forgotten it at school the night before." She took a sip of coffee. "So, he'd finished the homework. That was true. But he'd only finished the homework he had brought home with him. He hadn't finished everything that he needed to do."

David fixed his gaze on her, but now he looked away.

"What aren't you telling us?"

He decided not to hold anything back. "They're waiting for an asset who will provide transportation to them in Egypt. But we have credible intel that the whole situation could go south. The person who set it up is compromised. Their transportation could be, too. They might be stepping into an ambush."

Trey's wife didn't say anything.

"We can't warn them. Comms are sketchy at best."

She still didn't speak.

"The compromised informant is a father to one of the girls."

"Oh, my God! No!"

David nodded. "We think he's part of all of this but haven't quite connected the dots."

"Who's working on that?"

"Bora. She's very good."

"Leonard told me he's been impressed by her research abilities," Bao Zhen agreed. "I want to work with her."

Cocking his head to the side, David asked, "Are you sure?"

"Yes. I'll go crazy here if I don't do something."

"I think that's an excellent idea." Lin Lin chimed in, joining the other two at the table. "I'll help, too. Leonard told us that Red Flag is involved. I'd like to look into that a bit more."

"That's fine with me, if you feel you're up to it," David responded to the ladies.

"Who is that?" Trey's mother-in-law asked suddenly, seeing a photo on David's tablet.

"That's Serwabi. The CIA's Middle East Operative that's caught up in all of this. We're holding him in an interrogation room here. Why?"

"He looks vaguely familiar somehow," she said thoughtfully. Then she chuckled, "I don't know. At my age, everyone looks familiar!"

"I know what you mean," David said.

CHAPTER FIFTY-FOUR

"I'VE GOT MOVEMENT," TREY SAID TO JASMINE, ADJUSTING HIS scope to focus. With a quick hand motion, he signaled Bruce, who was keeping an eye on him, knowing that comms were down.

"Vehicle approaching," Locke interpreted to himself. Using his green-dot laser, he got Michi's attention. She understood.

Abruptly the chain of communication was reversed. Agent Imada indicated to everyone that there was movement on the left ridge, in front of them. Three hostiles.

"Dad?"

"Yes, Sweetie."

"There's a beige and green camo jeep headed our way from behind us. I'd say it's two miles away."

"Take the binoculars and see if you can see how many people are in it. Move slowly, okay?"

"Copy that."

Bruce was now signaling the team. He could see another group of armed militias trailing the blue Land Rover by about half a mile. They looked to be driving a big black SUV.

Trey had a lot going on in his head, and one of them was whether or not the new SUV was an ambush or extra protection for their ride to Cairo.

"Jazzy?"

"Four."

"Armed?"

"I can't really tell."

Bruce was looking back at Trey and signaling something. A funny face, like a drunken clown, and then two fingers forward, like a horizontal peace sign. Agent Stone had one eye in his scope and his other eye watching his friend. He slowly took his trigger hand off his rifle and made the same sign with his hand.

About five years after they'd first met, the two agents had gotten sent to the northern Philippines to do a VIP escort from Tagaytay, safely back to Manilla. It seemed harmless enough. They'd been instructed to "not look like armed guards," but more like "brown-nosing bank employees that were tagging along to help." The Director's words exactly. "And no guns," again the Director's words. What their fearless CIA leader forgot to mention, was that the Swiss-German Chief Executive Officer of one of the most powerful banks in Western Europe had a bladder that filled up faster than a Junior High boy in his lunchroom on Pizza Day. Every ten to fifteen minutes, they had to pull over to let the dignitary empty his bouncing organ.

"I guess the good news is that I'm not dehydrated," the *King* joked as he'd climbed back into the black Ford Bronco II and wedged himself between the agents. "If I was, I wouldn't have to keep stopping."

Trey burst out laughing with a pretty believable fake laugh, and Bruce shook his head in marvel. The Filipino chauffeur and his friend up front beamed as well. "You're absolutely correct," Locke agreed. "That is good news. You're very hydrated."

The dutiful yes-men sitting on either side of Herr Vatever-his-name-vas had to exit the vehicle every time and pretend like it was no big deal when actually it was stressfully part of their job.

It's a good thing they were there. On one of the many stops, where the CEO had insisted they pull over so he could pee into the Poblacion River and look at the beautiful Laguna Lake at the same time, Trey and Bruce noticed gunmen approaching in an amateur-hour, but armed-and-dangerous, kind of pattern. It wasn't their guns that had given them away, although the way their fingers were resting on their triggers as they moved forward screamed a lack of training. But it looked like they'd all gotten their sunglasses at the same night market. The lenses weren't constructed for a stealth attack; they were reflecting sunlight like flashing fireflies on a warm summer evening.

Bruce's brilliant idea was that he'd dart out onto the street and draw fire. His thinking was that if these weren't hostiles, they wouldn't really pay attention to him. And if they were hostiles, then the sudden distraction would surprise them, and at least a few of the amateurs would fire on him, most likely missing their target because it looked like they had more experience on their Sony Playstations than they did in actual combat. He could see their VIP was about to zip up, so he didn't have time to explain what he was doing to Trey, but as soon as he executed his kind-of-a-plan, the talented Agent Stone figured it out.

Bruce's tactic had worked. He'd drawn fire like the only remaining person on an opposing dodgeball team. Bullets flew all around him as Trey sprang into action and literally threw the half-zipped CEO into the back seat of the Jeep. Stone dragged the driver onto the street, since he wasn't that good, stole his weapon, and while Bruce replaced the guy in the passenger's seat, he fired up the engine, and they took off. When agent Locke looked into the back seat, the CEO was lying with his legs frozen in place like scissor blades that were jammed open, and he was still trying to zip up.

The remaining ninety-minute drive to Manilla took about fifty minutes with Trey at the wheel, and once he'd gotten sorted out, the poor VIP was so shaken up that he forgot to pee for the rest of the trip.

A week later, as the two friends met up for a beer at *David's*, they decided to name Bruce's tactical plan and devise a clever call signal. The horizontal peace sign with the forefinger and middle finger – complete with the thumb wedged in between – was an homage to the dear CEO. The name of the Bruce-draws-attention-while-Trey-figures-things-out plan was *The Laguna*.

Agent Locke waited for about three more minutes after he'd gotten the thumbs up from Trey. Then he jumped up and ran into the dusty road, speeding up and stopping in a jerky-run. He ran from where he was, to a disabled and very rusty Datsun 620. The truck had been new in the 1970s but had probably died on the Libyan border few decades later.

The Laguna worked, yet again. It was the hostiles on the ridge who started firing first. They hadn't seen Michi. She took them out with three short bursts and then looked back at Trey. He made a signal with his hand while keeping still and very focused on the oncoming vehicles. One of them was a blue Land Rover.

Michi read his command and stealthily, but quickly, repositioned herself, so she had a clear line of sight to the camo Jeep approaching on their six.

Trey was torn between shooting through the windshield and taking out the hostiles in the Land Rover or waiting until they came into their web. Even if this was an ambush, which it looked like it was, Blue Team would need a vehicle in Egypt, and preferably one without a shot-out windshield. He checked the vehicle that was trailing the first vehicle. It was pulling closer to the lead car. Agent Stone held very still and squinted into his scope. An American-made Suburban.

Michi's gun gave off another burst of noisy bullets.

"The Jeep's front tire exploded, Dad!" Jasmine Stone reported excitedly.

"Great! Keep me informed."

Trey decided he couldn't risk the blue Land Rover getting any closer. His daughter was a potential target, and he'd rather walk to Cairo then let something happen to her. He was just about to take out the driver when he saw the rear window of the Suburban roll all the way down. A human form leaned out of it, and then a weapon emerged. Stone watched the automatic weapon launch a grenade into the rear window of the Range Rover. A few seconds later, it exploded into a ball of fire!

Bruce quizzically looked back at Trey, but Stone shook his head, wondering what had just happened. He kept his gun sighted on the big black vehicle.

"The Jeep has stopped."

"Copy that."

"They're getting out, Dad."

"Are they going to shoot at Michi?"

She paused. "No. They're running away. One of them has something white he's waving in the air. An undershirt maybe?"

"Probably a good idea."

Jasmine was right. The four hostiles realized that someone who could shoot out their tire from a significant distance could most likely take their heads off, too. There was no shame in wanting to stay alive.

Trey had his eyes on the back window of the Suburban. It was still rolled down. As he watched it, a little American flag emerged. Bruce had his binoculars up and saw the same thing. He knew Trey well enough to know that whoever was in that vehicle could've sung the *Star-Spangled Banner* from a bullhorn and recited the *Pledge of Allegiance* backward at the same time; Stone wouldn't lower his guard.

Michi watched the hostiles in the camo Jeep abscond. She didn't blame them and didn't take them out. They were running back to their homes; their spouses; their children; and yes, their terrorist camps where they'd been summoned from, but they weren't a high priority target. As a matter of fact, they were a very low priority target. She made sure they were definitely gone and then crouch-ran up the dune to Jasmine and Trey. "Our six is clear."

"Copy that," acknowledged Trey.

"Great shooting," Jasmine expressed, admiringly.

The Japanese agent smiled, "Thanks. What's going on with the Suburban?"

Trey answered. "It could be friendlies. They took out the blue Rover and waived an American flag."

"Wasn't the Land Rover our friendly?"

"That's what we were told."

The Suburban was driving passed the smoking wreckage and then slowed down as if the people inside were checking their work carefully. Then stopped completely. Trey watched as back the back window rolled up, and the door opened. Someone stepped out, most likely the person who shot the grenade. Trey chuckled, seeing a man with a now-familiar ponytail in his crosshairs waving his arms desperately, not wanting to get shot by one of the CIA's top snipers.

"NOTHING PERSONAL. You're a lot of fun. But I never want to do that with you again."

Boyd grinned. "I thought that plank was going to break. It's a good thing I made two trips to carry our kits over. When you stepped on that thing ..." she chuckled. "I'm just saying. A little more weight and you would've ... I mean ... did you see how much that wood plank was bending??"

"Yeah. I get the picture. So now what?" Fox asked, shouldering his pack and looking down the alley behind the building they'd just exited.

"We either have to find the guy that I recognized from the airport in Baltimore, or we need to track down Ahmaadi."

"Is there a reason we're not using comms?"

"Batteries are dead."

"Why didn't you recharge them?"

"We're in England. They use Type G power plugs and sockets. Our American chargers won't work in them, and I don't have an adapter."

"I thought Justin included a multi-adapter in my kit."

Boyd squinted at Fox and furrowed her eyebrows. "I don't think so."

Fox slid his pack off his shoulders, put it on the ground, unzipped it and began to dig around. "I really hate it when I'm right," he smirked as he held up the multi-charger like he'd just discovered gold.

"Great," Agent Carter acknowledged, rolling her eyes. "We could've spent all this time charging our gear."

Fox put his pack back on. "We need to connect with LaunchPad right away and let them know we're mobile. They'll want to cancel our rescue from the rooftop."

"You're right. But let's figure out what we're going to do, first. My guess is that local law enforcement has Serwabi's man. We need to hunt down Ghalib Ahmaadi."

The big blond agent nodded. "I agree. Do we go back to his house or to his office?"

"Do we look for his assistant? I wonder what happened to her."

"I don't think he's going to call her. Too obvious a play. If he did, he'd probably be doing it to throw us off his trail. I wouldn't trust anything she says to us."

"What would you do if you were in his shoes?"

"I'd have had plans in place for a situation like this ..."

Boyd nodded supportively.

"Different routes out of here. Car. Bus. Train. Helicoptor. Plane."

"Depending on ..."

"Depending on where I need to go and what I need to avoid."

"He doesn't need to avoid local law enforcement," Carter surmised. "Chances are that he owns them or at the very least has well-positioned informants."

"Right," Fox agreed. He rubbed his chin, thinking things through. "His big problem is that he's pretty recognizable in Europe. Everyone knows soccer, and everyone knows these twins."

"That pretty much rules out public transportation. But I'd think he'd want to get out of Europe until things calm down a little bit. Or at least until he thinks we've moved on to something else."

"That would involve a plan by water or by air."

"He's got all the money to do either. Yacht or private jet?"

"If he took the yacht, it would mean that he wasn't in a super hurry to get somewhere ... he could take a few days to cruise around. Literally."

Boyd nodded. "But there's the shipment coming from Libya. He's going to want to connect with them as soon as possible."

"If it wasn't a play for Baker's granddaughter, I'd disagree with you," Fox stated, thinking out loud. "I'd say that he'd let it go and regroup. It's too dangerous to resurface."

"But with her still in their hands, all the big investors are going to want to get close?"

"Exactly. Casey Baker is too big a catch. Whoever financed this, and/or planned it, will want to be very hands-on. You get what you *inspect*, not what you *expect*."

"Private jet," concluded Boyd.

Fox nodded. "Private jet."

"We need to get back to the airport right away. Justin didn't include a car charger for our comms, did he?"

"He did."

"Let's hail a cab and charge a set while we drive. As soon as it has some juice, we'll check in with LP."

Lɪɴ Lɪɴ and her daughter walked to the Medical Center, where Ashley had set up space for Bora's team to work.

"Hello, Ms. Ma," Bora said, bowing ever so slightly, in the Chinese tradition.

"Good afternoon," Lin Lin answered, returning the bow. "Thank you so much for letting us join you."

"Of course," said Ashley, happy to have the two ladies in the Medical Center.

"Will we actually be of help to you?" Boa Zhen asked.

"Absolutely."

"Tell us what you're working on."

Bora pointed to her computer screen. "I sent Jennifer Wu all the names of the people in Jee Hye's black book, and she pulled up their last ten years of financials and sent them to us. So now, I'm trying to find any financial connections with The Lynx, the

Foundation that Ghalib manages, Red Flag, or anything else that we might find interesting."

"What have you found so far?"

"Not much. We matched a few people with donations to the foundation. But other than that, there's not much connection. So, we focused on The Lynx. He doesn't connect to anyone financially, and we haven't been able to connect him to the twins, directly, or to Red Flag. I really don't know who he's working for."

"I'll help you with this," said Trey's wife.

Lin Lin looked at her daughter. "I need to try and find something. It might take a long time."

"What is it?"

"I brought my laptop and my external hard drives in my carry-on. I need to go through them and try to find a picture."

"Of Serwabi?"

Lin Lin nodded.

"It's not just your age?"

Ms. Ma smiled. "No. I really think that I know him from somewhere."

"Okay, mom. Which part of your life do you think he's from?"

"I'm pretty sure I saw him when I was working for the United Nations in Geneva."

"Is it a positive memory or a negative one?"

"I'm not sure."

"Well, you work on that, then. I'll help Bora. Ashley, what are you working on?"

"I've been putting together an evacuation team in Cairo. We've got a plane standing by that will have a small medical staff on board, some security detail and a psychologist. They'll take the girls straight to Rome, to meet up with their parents – at least that's the hope, anyway. I also have a different plane on standby. It's set up to fly their bodies directly to the United States, should that be the awful scenario."

CHAPTER FIFTY-FIVE

TED BAKER HAD LEFT FUENTES IN THE CAPABLE HANDS OF AGENT
Graham and was back in The Pulse with all the American
parents – those whose girls had been found and those who were
still waiting for good news. He divided them up into small
groups of two couples per group and gave them instructions to
meet with the professionals at each station and then wait for a
signal to rotate to the next station.

The first, had a team of two trauma psychologists who were
going over what the parents might expect when they reunited
with their daughters. They would cover things like what questions to ask and which to avoid as well as the importance of
establishing every space they are in as a safe place and reassuring their daughters that it was safe. The next station had an
expert in Post-Traumatic Stress Disorders. She was informing
the parents about behaviors to look out for as the children
experienced the long-term effects of what they'd gone through.
From the fear of reconnecting with people to a variety of obsessive-compulsive behaviors, spotting symptoms early could
make a huge difference in recovery. An investigative unit made

up of officers from the CIA and the FBI were at the next station. They'd been carefully selected by President Baker, had to sign a strict non-disclosure agreement, and were going through lists of questions they'd created to try and understand how these particular girls had become a target. The fourth station was set up with an administrative team from Ted's company who were making themselves available to help with practical details that needed to be covered. From new clothes for the girls, to travel arrangements home, they were making sure that nothing fell through the cracks.

As the younger Baker watched parents rotate stations, it suddenly dawned on him that he needed to sit in on the group sessions, too. It wasn't wise for him to assume he could handle everything or that he instinctively knew what his daughter would need when she got back. He looked for his wife, Helen, and spotted her at the station with the psychologists. Grabbing a chair, Ted walked over and sat down beside her. The facial expression of gratitude she flashed him made him relieved that he'd thought of it.

" ... so that's something to be very aware of," the older psychologist agreed, looking over at President Baker's son and giving him a nod. "Welcome. We were just talking about how Casey and the other girls have probably witnessed several trauma-inducing scenarios, not just one."

Ted nodded, reaching out to take his wife's hand.

"There's the descent of the plane, the abduction, the murders of the adults, and who knows what other traumatic events they've dealt with. Just one of these things is quite an ordeal. When you put them all together, each girl will need a lot of love and reassurance. In my experience, complete recovery could take years. The memories will never disappear, but over time, hopefully, the pain and other emotional consequences of their ordeal will fade."

He couldn't do it. Ted couldn't sit in a therapy group while his daughter was still suffering. "I'm sorry," he blurted out. He turned to his wife. "I'm sorry, honey. I can't just sit here. I wanted to, but I ... I ..." He stood up abruptly and strode out of the room towards the elevators. Vince Graham had better have extrapolated some new information from Mr. Fuentes otherwise Baker would take over, and with his simmering rage, things could escalate very quickly.

***

BRUCE WAS DRIVING. Tank was in the passenger's seat. And Michi, Jasmine, and Trey were in the middle row. The back row had been folded down to provide enough room for everyone's kits. It made quite the collection of weaponry. As the Blue Team rumbled along in the black Suburban, Tank filled everyone in on what had happened to him.

"So, after you were picked up, LaunchPad diverted your helicopter to Cairo and then again, to where?" asked Bruce.

"Siwa Oasis."

"Why?" Trey questioned.

"We had a contact point from Beni Suef who was leading a tour group in Siwa Oasis. But then we found out he was compromised." Tank went on to fill in the team about Abril's father and the intel that Vince Graham had extracted.

"Do we know for sure that Fuentes is involved?" asked Michi.

"I don't have many details on that. I just know that he's being questioned, and he provided the contact that was in the Land Rover."

"There were a few others that tried to attack us. Amateurs, most likely from a local terrorist group."

"I don't know if he had anything to do with them, but he could have. The more likely scenario is that the guy in the Land Rover contacted them for backup."

"That would make sense," Bruce thought out loud.

Abruptly, the team's comms sprang to life!

"LP to Blue Team," Saara said, her voice in autopilot – like she'd been trying to reach them for hours.

"Copy that, LP. Blue Team plus one, standing by," confirmed Trey.

"Thank God!! That's great news! Let me tell the others that you're back in range."

Jasmine smiled. "I guess they've been worried."

"Sounds that way," agreed her dad.

"Blue Team!" David Hirsch said joyfully. "Welcome back."

"Copy that," Trey said. "We're glad to be back."

"What was the issue?"

"No reception. Either a signal-scrambler along the border or just a dead zone."

"Sitrep?"

"We're intact. Had to take down a few hostiles. The Land Rover was completely disabled."

"Copy that. *Completely.*"

"Confirmed. We're with Ponytail headed to the oasis."

"Okay. Sounds good. Just so you know. We're all one happy family here."

Trey breathed a giant sigh of relief. His wife and mother-in-law were safely at LaunchPad. He noted that Michi was telling Jasmine what David had meant and looked over to catch his daughter's big smile. "That's great news. Let everyone know that we're safe and sound."

"So, what's next?" Bruce asked.

"We're sure the primary target is either at the oasis or was moved through there very recently. Go pick up the scent."

"Okay. We're Oscar Mike."

"Refresh your tablets. Saara uploaded some important information."

GHALIB AAMADI WAS STARTING to get upset. His older twin brother didn't seem to appreciate how close he'd been to death. As the private jet climbed into the air, his face was turning deeper shades of red. "Fawwaz," he growled, "I'm telling you. I was kidnapped. I was about to be interrogated by very qualified people. High-level people. Americans. Very talented at what they do. Thanks-be-Allah, I escaped. But what do they want? All of a sudden, they come after me? They came to my house, they get past all my security?"

"How do I not know of this?"

"Now you know."

"When did this happen?"

"Today! Just a few hours ago. I fled and got on my plane."

"This is not good, Ghalib. There's more to what is happening. It's why I was trying to get a hold of you."

"Well you have *a hold of me*," the younger brother retorted, annoyed that his older brother wasn't being more sympathetic to his plight. "We're talking. Tell me what is soooo important."

The plane banked steeply to its left and then began to straighten out.

"That damn psychopath couldn't resist exploiting the information we gave him. You remember what we told him. One girl. THE girl. The only girl that matters."

"Of course, I remember."

"He took the entire American team."

The younger twin was stunned. Speechless.

"He took their parents, their coaches, their doctors, even their security people ..." Fawwaz stopped.

"How do you know this?" his brother exploded, angry that there was something more important than what he'd just been through.

"That's not all."

"That's *not all*?"

"He took an entire German team, as well. They were on the same plane."

"A German team? From Germany? What the ... how ..." Ghalib was dazed with rage.

"He … he … took their whole plane."

"He hijacked a plane?"

"The whole thing."

"And now the German special forces are involved, every agency in America, the United States Navy … it's very bad."

"But how could he do this?"

"I don't know."

"Is he still in Botswana?"

"Their plane never made it. I don't know where it landed exactly."

"*Al'ama!*" Ghalib swore in Arabic. "Where is that rat bastard now?"

"I received a message. Didn't you get it?"

"I got a message saying everything was on schedule."

"No. After that one."

"Of course, I didn't get it. I was running for my life, Fawwaz! I left that phone in my office. I'm going to kill him."

"*Ehdha, ehdha,*" the older brother said, trying to calm his twin down. "He's bringing everyone to the rendezvous point. You're still headed there, right?"

"I am," Ghalib confirmed. "I had to move my departure forward, obviously. I'll get to Cairo a few hours early."

"Good. I'll be about four hours behind you. I'm headed to the airport now."

"Fawwaz. Now what?"

"Just get her. We don't give a damn about any of the others."

"Okay."

"If there's a few that you think would be good, then bring them, too. But you need to be able to handle whatever you bring back."

"Okay."

"Wait, Ghalib. What about that Mexican's daughter?"

"Get her, too."

BOYD AND FOX were in the taxi and almost at the airport. Agent Carter unplugged her comms from the car charger and booted them up.

"Hellcat to LP."

"Come in, Hellcat!" exclaimed Justin relieved. He'd been sitting in the conference room with Dr. Stone, nervously monitoring any incoming communications.

"We extracted ourselves and are in a taxi, heading back to the airport."

"Good news," Leonard said. "That's the right move. Great thinking."

"Anything from Blue Team?"

"On the scent, but nothing yet. They're in Egypt and traveling up from the border. Justin's updating your tablet."

"Okay. We're out of battery on all our devices except this set of comms."

"Any news on your target?"

"No. But we figured that with the high-profile product he's moving, he's already on his way to a rendezvous point. We thought we'd like to be there."

"I totally agree."

Justin chimed in. "The plane you took is already in the air. It wasn't ours. But I was able to organize a larger one for you, thanks to Maverick. I'll have the pilots file the flight plan. They've been on standby and should have the jet fueled and ready to go. You can charge your devices up on the plane, obviously."

"Copy that," Boyd stated, glad to hear that Ted Baker was able to help get them a plane. "Is there any way to trace private jets that have left Heathrow in the last few hours?"

"Great idea. I'll see what I can find out."

"Do we have any assets in Cairo that can get to the airport to put eyes on arriving planes?" Leonard asked David Hirsch, who had just walked in.

"I'll find someone," his friend responded. "How are you both?"

"Razor has some bumps and bruises, but nothing is broken. I'm fine. We're starving and tired, but we'll use the flight time to refresh."

"Copy that. You both did good work. There's plenty of food on the plane. Eat and then get some rest. LP out."

Justin shut off the communications and turned to Leo. "I'll see if I can access flight plans from private jets in England that are headed to Cairo."

"Sounds good," Stone said, yawning. "I think I need to lay down for a bit."

"This is probably a good time for that," David said. "I'll do the same. I'm waiting for a call from my contact in London. He was going to try and find out more about the guy that Boyd identified who is being held by the local police in connection with the explosion. After I hear from him, I might have some new questions for Serwabi."

"How's the MEO doing?"

"He's fine. Ashley just fed him. He's grumpy, for sure. But I don't give a damn."

"What about his son?"

"Boyd put a tracker on his cell phone when they intercepted him in Baltimore. He's back in California and seems to be behaving."

"Okay," Leo said, standing up. "I'm headed to bed."

"Right behind you. You should get rest too, kid," David suggested, gently touching Justin's shoulder. "Now that we've heard from Boyd and Fox, you can put your mind at ease."

"I will. I'm just going to trace the departing jets from London and wait until White Team's safely in the air."

"Alright. I'm going to tell Bora and Saara to get some rest, too. Bao Zhen and Lin Lin will probably want to stay up. They're jet lagging anyway. I'll brief them on how to monitor the comms. If something comes in, they can wake us up."

CHAPTER FIFTY-SIX

As they neared the Siwa Oasis, Trey was running through what his brain had photographed about the region. He recalled that it was a small settlement lodged between the Qattara Depression and the Great Sand Sea in the Western Desert of Egypt, about thirty miles east of the Libyan border and three hundred and fifty miles southwest of Cairo. The isolated group of homes and shops is populated with around 30,000 people, mostly Berbers. Their Siwi language is as different from Arabic as their culture is from the rest of Egypt. Famous as the home of a mystical oracle from the god Ammon, the ancient ruins have always been a popular attraction for modern tourists, and history books report that the region used to be part of Ancient Libya.

Agent Stone remembered that Ammon was mentioned in the Bible when God spoke to the Jeremiah, recorded in the twenty-fifth verse of the forty-sixth chapter of the prophet's book. The Lord said, "Behold, I am bringing punishment upon Ammon of Thebes, and Pharaoh and Egypt and her gods and her kings, upon Pharaoh and those who trust in him." Trey made a mental note to find out why God felt punishment was necessary and what that ended up being.

Although tourism is a rigorous part of the economy and several hotels support the industry, agriculture is still the main activity of modern Siwa. Stone remembered reading that the harvest of dates and olives get distributed throughout the Arab world and that the local uniquely hand-crafted basketry, pottery, silverwork, and embroidery is famous.

"You okay?" Bruce asked his friend.

"Yeah, fine. Just thinking about this place and what our strategy should be."

"Let's throw out some options."

"We could drive around the whole oasis and see if we recognize anyone," Jasmine thought out loud.

"That's not a bad idea," agreed Bruce, "... scout out the land."

"We could be tourists," stated Michi. "Get rooms in a few different hotels that we base from and then divide and conquer. Of course, we won't be spending the night, but we could set up safely in a few different locations."

"This is a small place, right?" asked Tank.

"It's a little tricky," Trey answered. "It has just over 30,000 people, so ... not that big, but it's quite spread out. The oasis itself is about fifty miles long and twelve miles wide. There are hotels and villas all around it."

"Do you think that's where they would've brought the girls? To a hotel?" Jasmine asked.

"I doubt it," responded Bruce. "Too public. What are the villas like?"

"Some of them are quite spectacular," Trey answered. "Think mud-brick walls and date-palm ceilings with fountains, pools, natural hot springs, and an almost *hacienda* feel."

The group was silent for a few minutes, and then Jasmine spoke up again. "We haven't had a ping from Casey's transponder in a long time."

"Either they haven't gotten to what she thinks is a final location, or her battery has died," Michi surmised.

Stone leaned forward and put his hand on Tank's shoulder. "My thought, Tatanka Ptecila, is that this is where you shine. I think the best thing to do is to let you go off on your own for twenty minutes, or maybe with Bruce, and explore. My suggestion is that Jasmine, Michi and I will fuel up the car and maybe find a café or hookah lounge in the most popular part of town. Those are always good places to ask a few questions. With Jasmine's Asian features, people will just think we're a family. I don't think we have time to get hotel rooms. We have to be ready to roll it all up immediately."

"Okay. I agree," said Michi. "Are you thinking the girls are still here?"

"I'm not sure."

"No," answered Tank, suddenly.

Trey furrowed his brow. "Really? You don't?"

"I feel they were on this route. The same as we are. I also feel like they were at the oasis, but I don't sense their presence there anymore."

Stone sat back and leaned his head against his headrest, looking up at the ceiling of the Suburban. It would be smart to make sure that the girls were no longer in the vicinity of the oasis. On the other hand, time was really of the essence, and he deeply respected the Lakota *spidey sense* that Tank possessed.

"Looking at what Saara sent us on our tablets," Jasmine spoke up, looking down at hers, "the contact in the blue Land Rover that was going to meet us at the border, was from Beni Suef. If they've already left the oasis, maybe they're already on their way there."

"That would make sense," acknowledged Trey. "It's on the Nile, and they could take that all the way to Cairo."

"It's also more populous, so they wouldn't draw as much attention. Saara noted that the population is just over 200,000 people."

"Tank, it's your call. We're about ten minutes away from the Siwa Oasis. We'll need to stop and gas up anyway. What would you like us to do?"

"It makes sense that they'd move through. Let's just stop for fuel and power on."

CHAPTER FIFTY-SEVEN

FOX COULD HEAR THE ALARM AND BOYD CALLING HIS NAME, BUT he didn't want to believe it was actually happening.

"Thirty minutes to landing, big guy."

He groaned and shifted in his seat.

"Come on. Early bird gets the worm. Rise and shine, Sunshine. Let's go, Sleeping Beauty. Wakey, wakey. One, two, good morning to you! Three, four, I love you more!"

"Oh, good grief," Fox responded. Forcing his eyes to open and gratefully seeing Boyd standing there with a cup of black coffee. "I'd better get up before you start throwing ice on me."

"That was phase two. We have thirty-two minutes. Not much time. We have to eat, go through our kits and check our gear, and then come up with a POA."

"My *plan of action* was to sleep for twelve more hours on the plane at the airport in Egypt."

Boyd grinned. "That's a great idea. You do that while I go save Casey by myself."

"Can't do that. Can't let you get the credit. Not after all I've been through."

"Spare me the misery index."

Fox was awake now. "Alright, Hellcat. Plan of action. When did you wake up?"

"About five minutes ago," Boyd answered, reaching for her tablet and unplugging it from the plane's outlet. "Fully charged," she said, booting it up. "All of our stuff should be ready to go."

Fox reached in front of him and unplugged his comms. He turned them on and tucked the earpiece into his ear and then stood up and stretched. "Razor to LP."

David was surprised to hear Fox's voice in his earpiece and woke up right away. "Hi, Razor. In Egypt already?"

"No, sir. About twenty-five minutes out."

"Okay, great. Did you get some rest?"

"Yes, sir."

Hirsch checked his tablet and saw that he'd gotten a message in the short few hours he'd been sleeping. "My contact at the airport in Cairo sent a message. He has eyes on your target."

"Copy that!" Boyd exclaimed excitedly, looking over to Fox. "Looks like we made the right call."

"You did. My guy's going to tail him. As soon as you arrive, I'll connect you to his location. Do not, for any reason, engage with our asset. It's important that he not be compromised in any way. He's important to the company in this region, and they were pretty reluctant to lend him out."

"Copy that," replied Fox. "We'll be discreet and just make a smooth hand-off."

David rolled over and went back to sleep. *Just for a few more minutes*, he thought.

THE SUN WAS BEGINNING to set, and the hot desert temperature was beginning to cool as the Suburban roared past a *Welcome to Siwa Oasis* sign in several languages and a handful of donkey-pulled carts. Bruce eased up on the accelerator and gradually slowed down as they got into the heart of the town. It was beautiful; a very simple place with a mixture of mud-houses and two or three-story buildings. But it's not the stereotypical tiny oasis that's seen in movies or imagined by mirages in the desert. Expansive and surrounded by miles of palm trees, the area is marked by being one of the most lusciously green areas in Egypt. It wasn't nearly as commercialized as Cairo or Alexandria and the heart of the town was the markets. The oasis is considered to be the easternmost extension to the North African indigenous Amazigh culture, deeply rooted in Berber history.

As they drove down the dusty road, Trey thought about how Siwa was always an importantly traveled trade route. As a result, it presented a historical cross-section of cultures, but with all the coming and going, the locals worked hard to retain the core of their conservative culture and kept a language that's a local version of Tamazight mixed with Arabic.

The team found a place to fuel up and use the restrooms, then they got back into the black Suburban. As they proceeded through the town, they were quiet, each thinking a mixture of thoughts. Jasmine was pondering about Casey Baker and what she and the girls were experiencing. Trey was lost in the history of where they were, Bruce was mentally going through his kit and what weapons he might need, visualizing different scenarios. And Michi was wondering how Boyd and Fox were doing. Tank was just trying to feel the moment when everyone's thoughts were suddenly interrupted by Bruce.

"What on earth?"

Trey instinctively reached for his gun.

There, just off to the left side of the road, parked against a high brick wall, sat the giant mining truck used to transport the girls. It was as out of place as the pyramids in the middle of the desert. The passenger door was open, and so was the back door leading to where the girls had been held.

"Abandoned?" Trey asked.

"Well, they couldn't take it much further. The thing sucks fuel like no other vehicle," answered Bruce.

"We need to find out what's behind this wall. Bruce, you're with me. We'll take a look around. Michi, you stay here with Jasmine. Tank, you check out the truck and figure out what they're driving now."

Bruce popped the back window of the vehicle and quickly got out to get some things from his kit.

"Don't walk on anything around the truck. Tank will need to read the signs accurately."

"Copy that." Bruce tossed a grappling hook over the wall and climbed against it. "No cameras that I can see. It's a villa on the water." He dropped down the other side and waited for Trey. The tall sandy-colored limestone structure was empty. They walked through the courtyard, passed the weird fountain with the three naked boys. The water was off, and whatever was in the catchments was evaporating quickly.

Bruce and Trey would stack up outside every heavy wooden door and clear each room. They discovered bedrooms, a hookah bar, bathrooms and then found themselves in an elegantly appointed office with a six-foot-tall gold, Egyptian cheetah sitting proudly in the far corner away from the window. Next to it was a golden King Tutankhamen throne chair. On the right side under the window was a black and gold lounge chaise with the markings of Cleopatra. And in the middle stood a solitary desk with a glass top, supported by four colorful Egyptian Renenutet cobra goddesses.

"I'm going to search this room," Trey said to his friend. "Are you okay clearing the rest of the building?"

Bruce nodded, "No problem."

Agent Stone decided to start with a giant cabinet directly to his right, against the wall. It has been hand-crafted to look like an ancient altar. On the front, was the image of Tenenit, surrounded by genuine leather side-panels that had brushed gold handles - cabinet doors. Under the doors were two rows of six generously apportioned storage drawers. The top of the unit was adorned with a horizontally lying braided gold scepter.

He opened each drawer, quickly rifling through the contents. Then he checked the cabinet doors and discovered a flat-screen television. Underneath was a built-in stacked unit that housed the normal electronics you'd link to a tv. Under those, was a wooden drawer that had a lock built into it. Trey set out to look for the key.

It wasn't inside the cabinet; he hadn't seen it in the drawers. The desktop was completely clear of any items, but he walked over to check it out anyway. He sat in an olive-green, natural leather

Chesterfield desk chair and looked around the room. He glanced down to his left.

Bingo! A small silver key hung from the forked tongue of the supporting cobra-goddess.

When he unlocked the drawer, he knew he'd found an important piece. A gold-colored MacBook Air. He slipped it into his pack, locked the drawer and returned the key.

"Hemlock."

"Where are you?"

"About three rooms to your right."

"Copy that."

Trey left the office and walked down the hallway with the Egyptian spun-brass pear pendant lighting that Casey Baker and the girls had passed, just a few hours before. He spotted Bruce standing by the doorway. "Got something?"

Bruce held the door open to the shower room. "They were here."

"How do you know?"

"Go through that door on the left."

Trey did and entered the changing room with the mirrors, hairdryers, brushes, and hair oil. In the corner of the room were three white canvas clothes hamper-carts. They were filled with the clothes the girls had worn. Stained from piss and reeking of puke, the smell overwhelmed the room. He turned to his friend and could tell that both of them were having a hard time containing the rage they felt. "Let's get the hell out of here," he growled.

"Hold on, Trey. We need to search a little more thoroughly. This is the first place that I think they might've had a chance to leave a clue."

For the next ten minutes, the two of them searched the room carefully. They checked all the clothes, they checked the mirrors, toilet paper rolls, examined the sink cabinets, under the benches that provided a locker-room style seating.

"Nothing here," Bruce finally admitted.

"Let's get help and search the whole place."

"Vegas to Gisō."

"Loud and clear."

"We need two of you here."

"Copy that."

A few minutes later, Jasmine and Michi joined Bruce and Trey at the fountain in the center of the courtyard. Agent Locke outlined the plan, and they split up to search the entire place. After fifteen minutes, they converged in the courtyard.

Michi looked around. "I didn't find anything helpful. What about you, Jasmine?"

"There was one thing that I noticed. I was in the dining room. On the wall are a number of pictures of girls in graduation regalia. They're standing in front of a school called *Wasta Preparatory Academy for Girls*. I looked it up on my tablet, and it's just passed Beni Suef. What stuck out to me was how close it was to the Nile."

"What are you thinking?" her dad asked.

"Well then, in the kitchen, by the phone, there was a notepad with the school on it and pinned to the wall above it was the school calendar. I noticed that it's summer break here in Egypt, so the school is probably empty."

"That's interesting," Bruce said, thoughtfully. "I saw a bookshelf in one of the bedrooms that had a year-book for that school.."

Trey thought for a few seconds. "That seems like it might be a good place for them to go. We should probably check it out. Let's get back to the Suburban and see what Tank has found."

"What about you, Trey? Did you find anything?"

His friend nodded. "A laptop that was under lock and key in an office drawer."

"Jackpot."

"I hope so."

Ponytail had slowly moved around the area. He got to the back of the big mining truck and climbed up and into it. A few minutes later, he came out and deliberately walked a lap around the entire vehicle. Then, he got on his hands and knees, unhurriedly moving into the dusty road. He picked up the dirt and held it to his nose, taking a deep whiff. Then he crawled forward like a cat about to pounce on prey. Stopping after about five paces, he lowered his head and bent his ear to the ground. He got up onto his knees, kneeling in the sand, then slowly bent and held his hand to the road, as if measuring something. Suddenly, he stood to his feet, bent his head back, and looked up at the sky. Hearing the others coming back, he jogged back to the Suburban just as they all dropped back over the wall.

"Success?" asked Agent Locke.

Tank nodded as they all got back into the large black vehicle and as Bruce started the engine, Trey briefed him on what they'd found. Then he asked, "What about you, Tank?"

"The good news is that we're not that far behind. I'd say less than thirty minutes. The bad news is they divided into two vehicles. Judging by the span between the tire treads and the types of tires they used, I'd say that they put the girls in two 2002 Lexus LX 470s. One of them is significantly heavier than the other. I'd say over four hundred pounds."

"Meaning ..."

"My guess is that there are six or seven people in the first Lexus, and four in the second one."

"The Lynx is smart, always dividing them up."

"We're going to need another vehicle," Michi observed.

"Yes, we are."

"Let's roll," Bruce said, putting the Suburban into gear. "We don't have any time to lose. What do you think, Tank?" Bruce asked.

"It feels right to me."

"Michi, how much cash did Justin put in your kit for the team?"

"$7500."

"When we get to Beni Suef, let's buy a truck. I'm thinking of something that can blend in really well. Maybe a 4x4 taxi? The average taxi driver makes $2300 a year. We should be able to buy one for around $2000. Just need to make sure it runs well."

"Good idea," agreed Trey. "I'm guessing the second Lexus has Casey Baker in it. They've separated her from the group and have her with the smaller group. That's what I would've done. Bruce and Michi, you'll take the Suburban. Tank, you'll drive Jasmine and me in the taxi. We'll go after Baker. The two of you go find the others."

"Sounds good," Tank answered, and the others agreed. "I just have to say something. This is the most professional and respectful team I've ever worked with."

Bruce looked over at him and then focused back on the road. "Thanks, man. That was some pretty amazing work you did back there."

CASEY BAKER WAS TERRIFIED. She'd been the strong leader, the girl to keep up morale. There was an instinct that she had, more like a responsibility that she felt. The girls needed her. But now they were separated, and she felt physically ill, not knowing what was happening to them. There was also her transponder. She didn't know whether the battery was still working, but she was saving what she had calculated to be her last shoulder-dig for when she'd arrive at their final location. Now, the other four girls had no way of being found. She looked over at Abril, staring out her window. Green was the sacred color of Islam and the color of Miss Fuentes' hijab. It looked strange to see her free-wheeling friend completely covered, with only the frame of her face visible for the world to see. She wondered what she looked like. The blue she was wearing matched her eye-color, but she was thinking about her overall appearance. It felt foreign to be dressed the way she was. The Lynx was in the passenger seat, and some man she didn't know was driving. Leila and the big ox were with the other girls.

"Where are you taking us," Abril asked, suddenly.

"You are going to be greatly honored, girls," The Lynx said, with a sadistic smile. "Both of you are to be married to a prince."

Fuentes didn't respond. Neither did Casey. What was there to say? Life as they knew it was over.

CHAPTER FIFTY-EIGHT

Fox and Boyd had arrived in Cairo and got into the rental car that David had organized for them. It was a dark blue Toyota Tundra with a twin cab, four doors, and was probably more than a decade old.

"This brings back memories, doesn't it Hellcat?"

"Ghana. We were driving a Tundra just like this."

"You get to sit up front, this time."

"Hopefully the roads will be in better condition," Boyd said wryly. "That was some crazy action." Fox didn't say anything, and Boyd didn't want to press him. It seemed neither one wanted to talk about the slave castle in Cape Coast or the demented things they experienced there. "Our tablet just pinged," Agent Carter informed her partner, glad for the change in subject. "Okay, we have a map. We're the blue dot, and we need to catch up to the red dot. Just follow the instructions and put some heat on it."

Fox immediately sped up, knowing he'd have to make up the difference by speeding and going through red lights.

"When we get there, we're looking for a White 2002 Mercedes-Benz ML 320. The Cairo license plate has a blue stripe on the top and under the Arabic numerals are the numbers 299 BTM."

"Copy that. Our biggest challenge is that Ghalib knows our faces."

"True. He knows you better, and it's hard to disguise your body and stature. Let's see where he ends up, though. I have some things in my kit that can help hide my face. I'll just put those on – dark sunglasses, black baseball cap, that kind of thing."

"Didn't Justin pack a black burka?"

"He did. Should I wear that?"

"You could pose as my wife and pack weapons under that thing."

"I'll think about it," Boyd answered. "You know, the red dot has been stopped for a while. Oh … here's a text from David. They've stopped in Maadi."

"The embassy district?" Fox asked.

"On the east bank of the Nile. And it looks like they've checked into a hotel called the Villa Belle Époque. It's not right on the river. About a twenty to thirty-minute walk, or seven minutes by car."

"Alright. Shouldn't be too hard. Obviously, David will get us a room there."

"He can't," stated Agent Carter, reading her incoming messages. "Ghalib has booked the whole hotel for three days. There are no available rooms."

"The entire hotel?"

"It only has thirty-three guest rooms, apparently."

"Is there a hotel next door?"

"No, but there's the Maadi Police Department just down the street. The Embassy of Namibia's on one side and the German Embassy is on the other."

"Sounds like the perfect choice. Off the main drag, they take over the hotel, pay employees to look the other way, and bring in diplomats from the embassies. Right under the nose of the cops, too. Typical."

"The hotel's been in business for over one hundred years.," Boyd noted. "I'm going to text David that we need to look into who owns the place."

"So is the blue dot our target-vehicle or our asset's?"

"It's our asset. He has the target vehicle in sight and followed them into the hotel to try and secure a room. That's how we found out that the whole place is booked and on lockdown."

"Okay, we're getting close," Fox reported. "Text David that we just turned onto the 216. We're six minutes away."

Boyd tapped in the information. A few minutes later, she got a responding text. "Our asset is parallel parked on the street on the right side, a block past the hotel. When he sees us, he'll pull out, and we're to take his place."

"Copy that. Does the hotel have restaurants that are open to the public?"

"Not sure."

Fox turned off the 216 and onto Port Said, now entering the world of international embassies, Egyptian government buildings, and the stores, cafés, and restaurants that serve them. The buildings were large, expensive and gated. Tall leafy trees lined the streets like three-hundred-year-old sentries. When he got to Street 13, he turned left by the Republic of Namibia's Embassy and spotted the asset's vehicle right away. There was an empty parking spot behind the white Mercedes, so he pulled in there and as soon as he did, the asset began to pull forward, turn left and blend into traffic, leaving behind a black duffle bag in the center of his parking spot. Fox made sure his wheels missed it as he pulled forward and parked on top of it.

"I'm guessing that's not a bomb," Boyd said, half-sure.

"Makes me a little nervous too."

"I'll get it since there's nobody on the sidewalk and it will draw less attention then if you got out of the driver's side to crawl underneath."

Fox nodded and looked into his side mirror. There was a steady flow of traffic, and it was dark enough where people had to turn on their headlights. Boyd opened her door, slipped under the Toyota Tundra, grabbed the bag and tossed it to Fox as she climbed back into the truck. The big agent took a deep breath and tugged on the zipper.

WHEN TED BAKER walked into his suite, he could barely recognize Abril's father. His body was straining against the restraints of the heavy wooden chair, and if the zip ties hadn't been there, the seat would've pitched forward slamming his head into the coffee table. His shoulders were going from side to side and then bobbing up and down – trying desperately not to pass out. Blood was all over his body. Most of it was caked and dried, but obviously, he'd lost a lot of blood. His nose looked crooked, most likely broken, and he had deep cuts in his arms and legs.

His eyes were both swollen and whenever he moved sounds came from his throat, but none of them were discernible. It was obvious that Vince Graham had pulled out all the stops. The Secret Service agent was sitting comfortably in the kitchen, munching on a sandwich and reading a book.

He looked up as Ted came in. "Hey, Chief."

"Vince."

"I've got a few things to tell you. Is this a good time?"

Ted nodded. "Go ahead."

Agent Graham folded the corner of the page he was reading, closed his book, and went to the fridge. "Beer?"

"Please. Are there still some Bitburgers in there?"

"Yes, sir."

The President's son popped the top and handed the agent the opener that had been lying on the counter. "What did you find out? Did he break?"

"Yeah, he broke. It took some encouragement, for sure, but he did."

Ted took a sip of his beer, knowing that Agent Graham was thinking through all the evidence and categorizing it in his head.

"Probably the most important things are that it was never supposed to be the whole team, the plane was never supposed to be hijacked, and he doesn't know who's really calling the shots."

"I'm sure you recorded everything?"

Vince nodded. "He reported to some guy named Ghalib."

"Why did he feed them the information, to begin with?"

"Ghalib had paid him for a big event in Ibiza, but he spent the money before it happened and then didn't have the capital to pull it off. Rather than lose face over the event not happening, Ghalib worked out a deal with Fuentes. He'd cover the event, by basically paying for it twice, if Abril's father would work with Ghalib's brother to organize an international soccer competition in Botswana."

"How did they know Fuentes could pull off the tournament?"

"He'd been blabbing to them about how great a soccer player his daughter was, and one time, after a lot of drinking, he told Ghalib that she even got to play with Casey Baker."

Ted thought about everything for a few minutes as he tossed his empty bottle into the trash and pulled a second one out of the fridge. "Why was he hanging out with Ghalib?"

"He said that after Ibiza, they did several events together."

"What would he do for these events?"

"Supply the alcohol. And not just a bunch of light beers in a cooler. We're talking super high-end stuff … Suntory Yamazaki 1960 Whiskey … that kind of thing. $90,000 a bottle. Sometimes he'd sell cases of the stuff."

"So, if it wasn't the whole team, he must be worried about his daughter. Did you pick that up from him?"

Graham nodded. "Definitely. He's terrified of what could happen to her. But, at the same time, he seems to think that Ghalib would protect her."

"He doesn't think Ghalib is behind everything?"

"He said he didn't know. I believe him, sir."

"Great work, Vince. Stay here with Fuentes. When you're finished eating, take him to the master bathroom, clean him up, and let him rest. Handcuffed of course. I may contact you with more questions to ask him if I think of any. You think he'd answer them?"

"Yes, sir. He would."

Ted drained the rest of his bottle and put it on the counter. It was time to contact his dad and the folks at LaunchPad to compare notes.

ASHLEY WAS STILL RESTING, but Bora had woken up and found Lin Lin and Jasmine in the conference room, where David had left them to work and monitor comms. She listened intently as the ladies filled her in on what they'd discovered.

A few minutes later, David joined them, looking like he would have liked to sleep a little longer. "Leonard will be here in a minute. But I've got President Baker on the line by phone, and we're video conferencing with Ted Baker, his son. I think you need to hear what he's saying."

Saara walked into the conference room, rubbing the sleep out her eyes. She was followed by Leo and Justin.

"Ted, we're all here. Go ahead," David stated.

The young Baker filled everyone in on what Vince had told him. As he was finishing, Bora suddenly whipped out her laptop and started typing furiously. When she'd found what she was searching for, her face paled. She wasn't sure what to do, and since she didn't feel very comfortable speaking up in front of the former President of the United States, she decided to wait until the meeting was over before she told the LaunchPad group.

"Fuentes is saying the team was supposed to land in Botswana," President Baker restated, making sure he understood everything. "His only role was to provide some impetus in launching the international tournament and make sure that Casey would be attending. And he did this to get out of a financial mess that he'd gotten himself into."

"That sums it up," agreed Ted.

"I wondered how he could have involved his daughter," Leonard said. "So, I guess it makes sense that she wasn't supposed to be taken."

"Vince said that the dad seemed legitimately upset about his daughter being snatched."

David then filled in the President and his son with the information they'd received about the possibility of the girls being taken to the girl's school north of Beni Suef. He shared that Blue Team was on the move in that direction. He didn't mention the most recent intel about the girls being separated.

"All right. Let's keep putting things together," George Baker stated, hoping that it wasn't too obvious to everyone else that he needed a drink.

After they'd all disconnected, Leonard looked around the conference room. "I think that was the shortest four hours of sleep I've gotten in a long time."

"I agree," Saara said.

Hirsch spoke up. "Bora, I noticed that look on your face during the meeting. What did you find out?"

"You remember that Serwabi was in Cairo at the same time that Jee Hye was being tortured by that group of men, right?"

Everyone nodded.

"Fuentes was there, too," she said, sending her information to everyone's tablets. "These are pictures of him checking in; here's one with him at the hotel bar; another, with him at the pool. He wasn't listed in Jee Hye's black book, so I didn't think to look him up."

"Wow. Were there any other parents there?" Dr. Stone asked.

Bora shook her head. "No, I just checked."

"So, Fuentes is there on the night that Jee Hye is raped ruthlessly, overhears about the Russians, the Chinese, the name Baker, and then meets Serwabi the next day."

"That's correct."

"Was Abril's father in the room with those men?"

"No. I don't think so. Otherwise he would have been on Jee Hye's list, or at least described. She was meticulous."

CHAPTER FIFTY-NINE

"THERE ARE ALL KINDS OF GOODIES IN HERE," FOX REPORTED, looking into the black duffle bag that Agent Carter plucked from underneath the Tundra. "Snacks, bottles of water, and look!" he exclaimed, handing her a package.

"A disguise kit?" Boyd read out loud as she turned it over to read the bag. "Comes with hair dye, scissors, fake eyelashes, a wig, temporary make-up, sunglasses, and fake contact lenses. Impressive. Have you ever seen one of these? I've always had to put my own together."

"No. But look, I've got one, too."

She looked over at his. "Nice. It looks like you're going from blond to black." He pointed to the diagram on the back of the package, and she grinned. "Nice mustache."

"We need to put this on, I guess. Is there a hotel in walking distance?"

"We passed one about two blocks away on El-Nahda Street."

"Alright. Tell me what you think. Option one, we go to that hotel and get in our disguises then come back here and try to get into this hotel or the restaurant if they have one. Option two, there's a school across the street from the hotel. It seems to have minimum security if any. I could break in and situate on the roof while you go get disguised and monitor things from the ground. Option three ..."

"All of those are good if we're planning on setting up here and wait things out. Is that what we want to do?"

"You're saying we should just go in and get him?"

"We're both good at operating on the fly. He's obviously one of the first people here because it's booked for the next three days and we haven't seen anyone go in or come out. My guess is that he's getting the place ready for everyone else. Would you rather go in now or when there are over thirty rooms of guests?"

"I see your point."

"Come on," Boyd said, looking at Fox incredulously. "Are you being the cautious one? I thought that was my role. You're the fly-by-the-seat-of-your-pants guy."

"I'm with you on one condition. You go in there first. Look around. See what kind of video cameras they have, if you see any security standing around, how many workers are milling around ... things like that. Then we'll make a plan."

"I have a different idea. This place has balconies off the rooms. It's only a two-story building. You hoist me up. I check things out and find out where he's staying. We can skip the lobby and any security if they have any."

The traffic was lightening up as the sky was darkening. People who had been at work were now safely home, and just the occasional car was coming by as the dusk settled into night.

"Okay. But if I don't hear from you in fifteen minutes, I'm going in the front door wielding knives and guns."

Boyd stuck out her hand. "Deal."

Fox shook, and she deftly climbed into the back seat and handed his kit up to him. Then, she pulled hers off the seat and onto the floor-board and unzipped it wide open. The adrenaline was beginning to kick in. She loved the feeling. Boyd knew she was created for these operations and it was showtime.

RACING along at close to eighty miles an hour, Bruce was testing the limits of the Suburban. But thus far, it was performing well enough. It wasn't the speed that was the issue. It was the speed plus the road condition. The shock absorbers were taking a thrashing as the tires bounced in and out of potholes that would have shattered most car axels. The engine was loving the cruelty of what remained of the asphalt road, taking it head-on with the gusto of linebacker in American football saving a game-winning touchdown. The shower of dust, rocks, and pieces of tar their tires spat out behind them was rude to anyone else on the road, but Bruce didn't care.

Over a mile behind him, Tank was flying along, too, but, the 1997 Toyota Land Cruiser wasn't quite a match for the Suburban. They'd paid a little more than they wanted to in Beni Suef, but Trey knew that if they saved Casey, nobody would care about the costs. Somewhere under the mud, grime, and dust was a white paint job. The vehicle had been modified to seat nine people, was furnished with a roof rack that was strong enough to carry an ox, and on the rear spare tire cover were a few remaining letters of what used to read, *Siwa Safari Tours*. Speeding along the Aswan Western Agricultural Road, the trip would normally take fifty minutes. Both drivers were trying to cut that time by a third.

Bruce and Michi flew through the town of Ash Shinnawiyyah, past coffee shops, bars, and shops, angering other drivers and pedestrians with their flashing lights and honking horns. But then they eased up a little through Al Maymum, locally known as a police speed trap. Picking up the pace again on the other side of the town, they reached the outskirts of Zawiyat Al Maslub in record time. They knew they were getting close.

"Kits ready?" Bruce asked Michi who relocated to the back of the big black machine.

"Yes. Is there anything else you want in your backpack from your kit?"

"Yeah. I changed my mind on my Glock. I'm going to use that Desert Eagle Mark XIX instead. It's black, too."

"Found it."

"I just want the extra muzzle energy."

"Okay, then I have your M4, too."

"Perfect. You're using your Tavor and Glock combination?"

"Yes. I have my throwing knives strapped on, too."

"I'm going to pull over here," Bruce said as he turned left from Toason Street and on to Ahmed Oraby Road, parallel parking in front of Eldiaa Market. "Let's suit up, check in with LP and Trey, then we'll move forward on foot. I purposefully didn't drive past the school. Nothing screams *Americans* like this gas-guzzling Suburban."

The two of them had just finished their preparation when Michi whispered tersely, "Bruce! Lexus!"

Both agents instinctively sunk down into their seats as a darkly colored 2002 Lexus LX 470 drove past them.

"What do you think?"

"We have to know. Stay here. Check out the school. I'm going to follow that Lexus!"

Michi reached forward to hand him his Desert Eagle. "The safety's on, but it's ready to fire," she informed him as she grabbed her kit and got out of the Suburban. "Good luck."

Bruce eased back into the streets and turned his headlights on. He could see the Lexus two cars in front of him. The street traffic was fairly heavy. Typical in Egypt, the nightlife could be more crowded than the day time. Some families didn't eat dinner until nine or ten in the evening as they would wait for the heat to lift and the cool night air to take its place. Keeping his eye on the Lexus, he slowed down as a group of people crossed the road in front of him. The vehicle he was following seemed to be in no hurry either.

"Vegas to Hemlock."

Trey answered. "We're three clicks out."

"I've got eyes on possible target."

"Whiskey?" Trey asked, using President Baker's code name.

"Copy that. I left Gisō in location and am in gentle pursuit."

The Lexus passed a local dive called *Pizza Star* and then coasted by the Hayatna Medical Center before driving under a bridge and suddenly turning right.

"Oka-a-ay," Bruce muttered to himself, continuing to drive a block past where the Lexus had just turned before turning right on Yaacoub Street. He parked the car and shouldered his backpack. "They've parked under the Al Menia - Al Wosta Bridge that goes over the Nile River. I've got a bad feeling about this."

"Get eyes on them right away, Vegas," Trey said urgently. "I'll be there in six minutes. Lakota will stay with Gisō, and I'm bringing Sunrise with me."

Sunrise, Bruce thought. *He must have just named Jasmine.*

"Copy that," he answered, jogging towards the Nile.

THE VILLA BELLE Époque was a better-than-average boutique hotel. Quaint, with a well-maintained property, relaxing gardens and a lap pool that was shaded by mature trees and surrounded with colorful flowers, it carried an early 20th-century elegance with style and pride. In the dark, the lights were carefully placed and projected an aura of grace and refinement.

The two agents had snuck in the back of the property, past the pool, and succeeded at being unnoticed by anyone, staying in the shadows and moving with the stealth that only comes from years of experience and practice. There weren't many guests, but they needed to be careful of the staff. When they were sure nobody was looking, they darted forward into position under a second-floor balcony to a random darkened room. Boyd stood on Fox's shoulders and reached up for the floor of the terrace, just able to get a climber's finger-grip on it. She hoisted herself up and swung her right leg over to lock it between the balusters of the railing. Then she pulled her body up, grabbed onto the top horizontal rail and swung her hips over, landing lightly on her feet. Fox handed her pack up to her and then melted back into the thick bushes and trees that surrounded the hotel. She snuck up to the edge of the window and looked in. The room was dark, and as far as she could tell, it was unoccupied. She briefly debated the pros and cons of sneaking in if it wasn't, and decided it was worth the risk. The French door from the room onto the balcony was antique and hinged. Agent Carter thought about smashing one of the little glass panels and reaching through to unlock the door but decided that picking the lock would be importantly discreet.

She unshouldered her backpack, unzipped it, and located the pouch that contained a lock-pick set. Inserting her hook pick into the upper keyhole Boyd felt around and counted five levers. She carefully removed the pick and inserted a tension wrench into the lower keyhole and found the notch in the bolt. Setting the wrench, she began to turn it counterclockwise. The bolt stopped turning, so she used the wrench to hold it in place with moderate tension and, reinserting the pick, she gently pushed upwards on each lever until she found the one that was the hardest to lift. Slowly elevating it until the bolt moved slightly and the lever stopped moving, she completed setting it to the correct height for the bolt to slide through. When she'd repeated this process for each of the remaining levers, she used the tension wrench to turn the bolt and unlock the door with a gentle click.

Carter knelt down and cracked the door open, then waited for any indication of noise from inside. Hearing nothing, she reached up to the comms unit in her ear and tapped on it three times, indicating that she was safely inside. Fox tapped back. Slowly, Boyd opened the door wide enough to slip into the room and then carefully closed it behind her, leaving it unlocked. She turned on her tactical torchlight with adjustable brightness settings and set it on *dim*.

The room was spacious and, as she thought it would be, graciously decorated with large comfortable and elegant furniture from a bygone era. There were a few touches of modern convenience like a fridge, microwave, and flat-screen television, and the room appeared untenanted.

"Razor?"

"Hellcat."

"Start your clock."

"Copy that. Starting countdown."

She put her lock-pick set back in her bag and pulled out her Glock 19, having screwed a silencer onto it earlier while she was prepping in the Toyota Tacoma. Creeping forward, a sudden noise almost caused her to have a coronary! It was the air conditioning unit for the room firing up. The rattling noise was surprisingly loud. She located the thermostat and turned up the temperature. As the air from the room got sucked through the return vents, it passed by the sensor and the coils, comparing the temperature to the new setting, and immediately shut off. Relieved to have silence again, she moved forward to open the door into the hallway. But just as she was reaching for the doorknob, she heard heavy footsteps coming up the stairs and the sound of two men's voices.

"We're honored to have you stay at our hotel, Herr Zeller. Please let us know if there's anything we can do for you."

"*Masha'Allah. Shukran, shukran,*" the other man responded in Arabic. "Thank you."

Agent Carter was horrified to hear the key being inserted into the lock of the door she had been about to open. Looking around the room, there was no good place to hide! The door handle began to move down, and she suddenly realized there was a spot. Throwing her bag under the large four-post bed, she followed after it and curled up in a ball against the wall.

CHAPTER SIXTY

AGENT STONE HAD JUST DROPPED TANK OFF AT THE GIRL'S academy to connect with Michi, and now his mind was in hyper-gear. He was computing probabilities in a way that would astonish any professor of math at MIT and had come to the most likely conclusion. The two Lexus vehicles had driven together from the Oasis and had converged at the school. One group was staying there as collateral – bargaining chips in case anything went wrong. The group that Bruce was following was taking their prized possession and putting her on a boat to sail up to Cairo.

"Hemlock."

"Loud and clear."

"Sitrep?" Asked Trey as he drove through the crowded streets in a way that wouldn't draw attention.

"Target vehicle in sight. No movement from inside."

"Copy that. ETA two minutes."

"What do you want me to do when we get there?" Jasmine asked, her heartbeat speeding up at the thought of action and danger.

"Your primary objective is to stay safe. It's not to get involved in the rescue attempt. Is that clear?"

"Yes, dad."

"Stay armed at all times and be ready to fire at anyone that threatens you. Kill shots. Don't miss. You're trained for this, okay?"

"Got it."

"Keep your comms on at all times. Every once in a while, adjust your setting and update LaunchPad."

"Why don't we all keep our comms on?"

"It can be distracting to other operatives. Michi and Tank, for instance, might need complete radio silence. We can't risk their lives, and they don't want to risk ours. So, your job of reporting needs to be done concisely and sporadically."

"Makes sense. What do I do if you and Bruce get into trouble?"

"We'll find a way out. Don't get involved. Stay alive and report everything. LaunchPad will respond and figure things out, okay? Not your job. Your mission is to stay alive.

"I can do that, dad. Don't worry about me."

He made a right turn off of the main drag onto Yaacoub, the same street that Bruce had turned on, and spotted the only car parked on the road, a big American SUV. On either side of him were low-lying buildings. It looked like one was a government office of sorts, maybe a social services building. The other appeared to be an electronics store. Both were closed, dark and silent. The Suburban was standing at the end of the lane with its back to the Nile – ready for a snappy exit. Agent Stone did a U-turn at the end of the road and parked in front of where Bruce had parked, leaving plenty of room for Locke to dig out if he needed to.

"Alright, Jazzy. You ready?"

She nodded resolutely.

The two got out of the Toyota Land Cruiser, quietly closed their doors and then opened the back hinge-door to retrieve their backpacks.

"Jasmine, just wait here. I'm going to walk up and find a spot for you to hide. When I tell you where to go, move into location, kneel down comfortably and keep your head on a swivel. If you see anyone walking past you or towards where we are, let us know, okay?"

"Okay, dad."

Jasmine crouched close to the ground and glanced down at her Israeli-made Jericho 941 FB she was holding. It was ready, and so was she. Then she looked up just in time to see her father get to the end of the road and stealthily disappear into some bushes. Beyond them, Trey found himself on a dirt walking path that ran parallel to the smooth, quietly-flowing Nile River. He crossed over it and walked through more bushes and trees, towards the water. Once through the foliage, he discovered a long narrow beach of sorts, with skiffs, bass boats, canoes, shad boats, and other river-craft pulled up onto it. Most of them were secured to short wooden pilings with rope. The one closest to him looked like it had been sitting in its same spot for a decade. It was a simple flat-bottomed wooden boat about the size of an Alaskan umiak. Directly across from it was a thicket of bushes. Perfect for hiding.

"Sunrise?"

"Yes ... I mean ... um ... Hemlock," Jasmine stuttered, slightly embarrassed.

Trey explained where he was and instructed Jasmine to set up in the bushes but to be sure that she was comfortably within throwing range of the boat. "If you really get in trouble, then toss a grenade into the boat as a distraction. I'm setting up some smoke along our way. If I tell you to detonate them, you activate the SEFRIS on my mark and the retreat to the Tundra. I'm going to leave the unit for you in this bush."

"Copy that. I'm Oscar Mike."

The Superior Signal Electric Fire - Remote Ignition System or SEFRIS is a privately-made, defense-contractor quality wireless programmable firing system designed to initiate smoke grenades on command from distances as long as 600 feet. It's durable, waterproof, and can withstand extreme weather conditions.

As he looked to his right, about a quarter of a mile in front of him and over a hundred feet in the air, was the giant concrete four-lane bridge with noisy traffic racing by. The giant structure provided almost complete darkness underneath. Trey left the beach and discretely planted a few more smoke grenades in a wide arc pattern that would offer a complete screen if they needed it.

"Hemlock, where are you?" Bruce asked.

"I'm set up. Just south of where you were."

"Keep heading north, more east than west."

"Copy that." Trey understood. The Nile was east of him. Bruce wanted him in the bushes and trees between the river and the path. He snuggly double-point-strapped his CheyTac M200 Intervention Sniper Rifle to his back and reached into his bag to pull out a full-sized 9mm Sig Sauer P226 Tactical Operations Pistol. It featured a stainless-steel slide with a Nitron finish and was designed for a fast trigger return and surgical control during high-speed shooting. The beavertail frame is black hard-anodized lightweight alloy with an integral Picatinny rail and polymer Magwell grips. Justin made sure it came with four 20-round high capacity magazines. Agent Stone attached a suppressor device to its threaded barrel and debated using his night-vision goggles but decided it would be better to let his eyes adjust to the growing darkness when he got closer to the bridge. "Oscar Mike."

"Copy that."

Because it was directly surrounded by mostly closed businesses, the area was surprisingly completely void of people, despite the busy nightlife only a few blocks away. Trey moved through the trees as only he could move. Almost invisibly, had anyone been watching. After about seven hundred feet, he could make out the shape of the Lexus parked under the bridge. He slowly knelt down behind a bush and then got prone, a position he was almost more comfortable with than walking.

With methodical movements, he kept his 9mm in front of him while bringing his sniper rifle off his back and into position. He belly-crawled forward under the bush until he had a clear sight of the Lexus, Trey stopped and adjusted his Raptor scope. He zoomed in on the vehicle, first checking the outside completely, searching for sentries. There were none. Suddenly, he saw a green laser-flash from the top of the concrete slant that led to bridge supports. Bruce was perched up there.

"Got it," Trey acknowledged. "No signs of ghosts."

"Copy that. No action outside of the vehicle. I've got your six."

Trey brought his crosshairs down to the Lexus. He counted four shapes inside. The driver appeared to be male just based on his body mass. He looked to be Fox's size. It was impossible to make out the passenger. He fixed his eyes on the person in the far rear seat and could make out what appeared to be a Muslim head covering. Moving his eyes to the person next to her, behind the driver, he noted that she, too, was wearing a hijab. He waited patiently. And then she turned to look out the window. It was Casey Baker.

EVERYONE AT LAUNCHPAD was awake now and in the conference room. Saara was monitoring the chatter between Bruce and Trey. Justin was following Boyd and Fox. And David was waiting for an update from Tank and Michi. They'd already checked in and confirmed that they'd found each other and were setting out to explore the school. Bora, Lin Lin, and Bao Zhen had returned to the Medical Center to work, but were now coming back to the conference room and were just sitting down. Ashley was making coffee, bagels with cream cheese, and fruit for everyone, and had just entered the room, setting everything on a side table in the corner.

"Thank you," Dr. Stone said. "Help yourself, everyone. It's important to eat." As people filed by the food and took their share back to where they were sitting, Leonard continued speaking, giving some instructions. "It's good for us to be together right now, but if communications start happening at the same time, Saara and David will go to the office, Justin will stay here with me. It will be very important for me to be constantly informed and I'll be making regular rounds to check in with all of you. You can see in the middle of our table here, that Saara has provided us with two maps. This one is tracking what's happening at the Villa Belle Époque and is a satellite view," he said, pointing to it. "The other one is only a map because everything is taking place in a very dark place with greenery and the cover of the bridge. The satellite would be useless there, and besides, we haven't been able to put a bird over that area. You can see the three dots. Jasmine is here. Bruce is over here. And Trey is here. This is also on the flat screens in the office area. Can we put names on the dots?"

"Of course," Saara said. "Hold on."

It only took a few minutes, and all the dots on both maps were labeled.

"Great. That's very helpful. While we're waiting for reports, we need to prioritize extraction plans. Justin, I know you came up with plans A, B, and C for each group. We need to pick the best one and put them into action. Can you work on that and monitor your team's comms at the same time?"

"Yes, sir. I'll just step outside and make some phone calls. People are standing by; they just need to be activated."

"I want them in position and ready. Even if we don't use them, they need to be on high alert. Are you using company assets?"

"Exclusively. They came from President Baker, himself."

"Ashley, did you finish the evac setups at the airport in Cairo?"

"Yes, sir. We're ready for whatever happens."

"Good. And Ted should have everything organized at his end."

"That's, great," Lin Lin said, with visible relief in her voice. Bao Zhen reached over and took her hand. "Is there anything we can do?"

"I think you need to open up some diplomatic channels for immediate evac of our team out of Egypt. The jet that Fox and Boyd used had to leave on another mission. We need a military medical plane. David will give you a contact to call and President Baker's number. Get them into a conference call and tell them what we'll need. I want our whole team out of there discreetly and safely as soon as this is over."

"No problem. I can do that."

"Bao Zhen, can you assist her with setting that up?"

"Sure."

"The two of you can work from the Medical Center. Ashely, you can keep working from there, too."

"Okay, Dr. Stone."

"Bora, I need you to go back and evaluate everything. We need to know who is behind all this and I can't help but think we're missing something. Start with Jee Hye's black book. I just don't think we've exhausted what she created for us. There's still something that makes it so valuable she got killed over it. I know she's given us a lot, but just give it another go. Then put the information we received from Jennifer overtop of all that and the stuff we learned from Fuentes. You can work here, if you'd like, or if it's too distracting, go wherever you're comfortable spreading out."

"I've had the same feeling," Bora responded. "There are some pieces that we're still not connecting. I'll just work here."

Just as she said that the news came from Trey that he had eyes on the team's primary target. It was just the boost of excitement and energy that everyone at LaunchPad needed.

BOYD WAS IN TROUBLE. She didn't want to lie under the bed, letting the minutes tick by, causing Fox to burst into the lobby creating a chaotic rescue mission that wasn't really needed. But she couldn't verbally interact with him in case Herr Zeller overheard her. This would be a test of how well Fox really understood her. She decided to try an almost impossible way of communicating and started tapping on her comms unit.

Tap. Tap tap. / Tap. Tap tap. Tap. Tap tap. / Tap. Tap tap. / Tap. Tap tap.

"Hellcat, what are you doing? That's annoying," complained Fox.

Tap. Tap tap. / Tap. Tap tap. Tap. Tap tap. / Tap. Tap tap. / Tap. Tap tap.

"Hellcat? Is that you?"

Tap.

"Wait. Are you trying to tell me something?"

Tap.

"Okay," the big agent said, figuring it out. "One tap is *yes,* and two taps is *no.* If that's what you're doing, tap once."

Tap.

"Do you need immediate evac?"

Tap tap.

"Okay, that's good. Danger close?"

Tap tap.

Fox thought for a few minutes, trying to put himself in her shoes. After going through a few scenarios, he decided there could be only one thing she was trying to tell him. "Do you need more time?"

Tap.

"Obviously, you can't talk out loud. I've got it. I'm going to give some increments, okay?"

Tap.

"Five to ten minutes from now?"

Tap tap.

"Ten to twenty minutes?"

Tap tap.

"Twenty-five minutes?"

Tap tap.

"Thirty?"

Tap.

"Thirty. Got it. I'll reset my timer."

Boyd shook her head in wonder. Fox was great. She peeked under the bed and could see Herr Zeller was obviously the type of traveler who liked to set up his room right away. She could see the legs of what was most likely a suitcase stand and watched him go back and forth to a chest-of-drawers. Sometimes he'd go over to a wardrobe, and she'd hear its door open and hangers rattling as hung some of his clothes on hangers. It seemed to take forever, but finally the inevitable took place, and Agent Carter was ready; he went to the bathroom.

With cat-like speed, Boyd darted out from under the bed, threw her backpack on, and whipped out her Glock 19. Cracking the door to the room open and seeing nobody in the hall, she slipped into it and shut the door behind her, just as she heard Herr Zeller flushing his toilet. There weren't any cameras in the hall, so Boyd knew she wasn't being watched.

In a perfect situation, she'd have a hand-held thermal imaging scanner and would at least be able to see which rooms were empty, and which had people in them. But she wasn't in a perfect situation, so she decided to knock on doors instead. It wasn't the most tactical way of moving forward, but possibly the most efficient. She looked down at her watch and saw that she had no time to lose, Fox would come charging through the lobby of the hotel in fourteen minutes and that could cause all kinds of problems, the worst of which would be Ghalib getting a pre-warning and escaping.

She decided to start at the far end of the passageway and work her way towards the staircase, but before she did, she dug out the black burka from her pack and slid it on. Standing in front of room 216, she knocked loudly enough for someone in the room to hear, but not so loud that the front desk would hear it. Nobody came to the door, so she knocked again. There was no answer. 215 had the same result. So did 214, 213, 212, and 211. She skipped 210, Herr Zeller's room.

Boyd knocked on the door of room 209 and heard footsteps. The peephole darkened, then the door opened slightly. Boyd Carter was staring straight into the polished face of Ghalib Ahmaadi!

He greeted her with a slightly perplexed look on his face. "As-salāmu ʿalaykum."

In a split second, the American agent kicked the door with such force that it slammed into his forehead, cracking his nose. He stumbled backward, and before he could recover, she pistol-whipped his temple with brutal force. Like a falling tree, he bounced off the bed and landed on the floor unconscious. She darted to the door, hung the *Do Not Disturb* sign on the handle, shut it, and locked the deadbolt.

"Razor?"

"Sitrep."

"Target acquired."

"Copy that. Extraction?"

Boyd looked Ghalib over. She figured she could probably flip him over the balcony rail and pass him down to Fox. Suddenly she remembered something. "Hold on."

Agent Carter pulled out her camera phone and shot his face, making sure to get a clear image. Next, she went through each of his fingers and snapped their prints. They couldn't afford to be duped again. She uploaded them to Justin. "LP please confirm the identity I've sent you."

"Copy that, Hellcat. Five minutes."

"No longer than three. I need it right away."

Boyd looked around the room for intel. The chamber was similar to Herr Zellers but furnished with a few extra touches. It had fresh flowers sitting on the kitchen table and a larger television. She spotted a MacBook Pro on Ghalib's desk and an iPhone next to it. Opening her pack, she stuck them inside. Then she sighted a wallet on top of the microwave with a set of car keys and took the billfold. Checking the closet, she noticed an array of high-end clothes. She went through them all and came across a slim leather book. It looked very expensive, and when she briefly thumbed through it, she knew she'd hit the prize.

"We don't have prints but facial recognition is 97%. Target confirmed."

"Thanks, LP. Out," Boyd responded, nodding satisfyingly. "Razor. Ready for extract." She thought for a second and decided to use the Hawaiian word for *balcony*. "*Lanai*, 209."

Fox left the Tundra and threaded his way through the trees, keeping his eyes open for the staff or more hotel guests. But the only one that had arrived was the Swiss-German guest, and he seemed to be in his room watching the television. As the big blond agent got to the tree line, across from 209, he could see Zeller's blue light from his flat-screen reflecting intermittent flashes off his walls. The long lap pool was to Fox's left. It was lit up beautifully but very empty. Completely still, in fact.

He crouched down and tapped his comms three times. The balcony door opened, and he could see Boyd struggling to drag something heavy. She got close to the rail and motioned for him to come over.

"This is your plan?" he asked.

"Get ready to catch him."

He sprinted across the grassy area just as Boyd propped Ghalib's shoulders against the top of the rail. She lifted his legs up and then rotated his body around so his feet would go down first.

"Ready," Fox said.

Agent Carter locked her arms under the armpits of the younger twin and jerked his body so his feet would go into the air.

Gravity pulled his body down, and as her partner reached up to grab Ghalib's legs, Boyd lowered him in a controlled fall.

"Got him," Fox grunted as he draped the body over his shoulder and hustled into the woods and back to the Tundra.

"I'll be right there."

Boyd dashed back into the room, retrieved her backpack, and then looked around to see if there was anything else she should take. Racing back to the balcony, and with her Krav Maga training fully dialed in, she tossed her bag onto the grass below and vaulted over the railing, landing lightly on her feet and doing a roll. She stepped back, scooped up her kit and raced through the trees to meet up with Fox.

Ghalib was just waking up as the big agent was stuffing his body in the back seat of the four-door Tundra. He was about to scream, so Fox slammed his hand over the younger twin's mouth. With a swift kick to Fox's ribcage, he was able to get his mouth uncovered. "Help me!" he screamed.

The door behind his head flew open, and Boyd smashed her bag into his face. She jumped on top of him and slammed the door shut as Fox closed the opposing door, jumped in front and drove off.

"You didn't zip-tie him or something?" Fox asked.

"I just wanted to get out of there. I didn't think he'd come-to," Boyd answered, shoving her bag onto the floor and drawing out her gun. She pointed it right into Ghalib's face. "Stop kicking and moving."

He froze in fear. Then he wondered if she was bluffing.

"Give me one reason to pull this trigger. I'd happily do it. We'd be out of the country and on a beach in Croatia by the time

they'd find your face-less corpse. You know who I am, Ghalib?"
She leaned forward and whispered into his ear. "Just so you
know I'm not bluffing. Two days ago, I was in New Delhi."

His face darkened, puzzled. Then he recognized what she was
talking about.

Fox glanced back and saw that everything was under control, so
he pulled into a dark parking lot of a hair salon and got some
zip ties and duct tape out from his kit.

CHAPTER SIXTY-ONE

MICHI WAS RELIEVED TO HAVE TANK JOIN HER. "IT'S GOOD TO SEE you," she said, fist-bumping him. This place is dark and not just physically. Did you know that last year, over 3000 girls were surveyed in this area and over fifty-five percent of them had gone through genital mutilation?"

Tank shook his head. "I don't like this area either."

"I've done a quick check of the building. I don't think it's being used right now. I think Jasmine was right. The students are on break. The school is made up of three connected, three-story buildings in a U formation around a courtyard with a large wrought iron gate," Agent Imada reported. "The entire property is fenced off. The Lexus is parked inside on the right side of the courtyard and backed into the corner, so it's facing the gate. I counted seven people exiting the vehicle and going into the school building directly behind it. Four of them were wearing hijabs, and I have to think, they're our girls. We have a problem, though, there are two black Toyota Land Cruisers parked there, too. Eight seaters."

"That's definitely not good," Tank agreed. "Do we need to coordinate our attack with the others? I'm afraid that if we don't, we risk the lives of the girls. All of us have to strike at the same time."

"You're right. But before we connect them and before we can attack, we need more intel," Michi responded. "I think we need to take fifteen minutes and peek inside."

"Okay," the Lakota tribesman said. "I've got some wire cutters. Let's cut out a small part of the fence and go through into the property. I'll take the left part of the structure, and you take the right."

Michi and Tank proceeded to a part of the fence that was clothed in shrubbery and worked on cutting out a square patch and removing it.

"Keep radio contact minimal," Michi suggested after they'd crawled through.

"I will."

The two of them split up, and Agent Imada moved through the front of the courtyard with the stealth of a black cat at midnight. She had her Glock 19 in her hand and had screwed on her suppressor. Hanging on her side was her Tavor TAR-21 assault rifle.

Tank had slowly crept around the left side of the courtyard, making sure to stay in the cover of darkness. He positioned himself under a window and checked it to see if it was locked. It was. Then he briefly shone his flashlight into the room to check the flooring. *Linoleum.* He knew he couldn't just smash the glass. The falling shards would make way too much noise. Tank took a good look at the window and decided to remove the windowpane. It would take longer, but it would be noiseless. He reached into his bag and pulled out a flat-head screwdriver and starting in the bottom right corner, working it into the beading channel. Gently putting pressure onto it, he was able to nudge the beading out of its moorings. He worked his way around the entire frame until all the wooden tracking was loosened and the windowpane was sitting in its frame, on its own, with nothing holding it in place. He slid his knife between the glass pane at the bottom of the window and the wooden frame and then used light leverage to pry it towards him. The glass fell out relatively easily and into his waiting left hand. He gently put it on the ground, dropped his kit into the room, and then lifted himself up and through.

"Inside," he said into his comms.

"Copy that. Me too." She had taken the same strategy as the Lakota native, but instead of having to remove a windowpane, she'd found a window that was unlocked, climbed through, and had been waiting for him to contact her.

"Clear the first floor, then check in."

"Copy that."

Shouldering his pack, he quietly exited the classroom he was in. Tank looked to his right. The hallway turned the corner and led to the middle section of the U-shaped structure. Noticing nothing out of the ordinary, he turned to his left and stealthily moved through the hallway, hearing and seeing no one. The classroom doors were all open and dark. He got to the end and finding a staircase, he crouch-walked up and found himself on the second floor.

"All quiet so far. I just got up the stairs and am on the second floor."

"Copy that. Same here."

The hallway was an exact replica of the first floor and Tank carefully walked through it, finding no one. Retracing his steps, he went back into the staircase, and moved up to the third floor. He heard voices echoing in the hallway but ahead of him was nothing but dark empty classrooms. Like Michi, Tank had a Glock 19 with a silencer screwed onto the end. And like Bruce, he carried a fully automatic AA-12 Atchisson Assault Shotgun on his side. It too was a 12-gauge that unloaded 300 rounds per minute.

"There are some people on the third floor of the middle section."

"I hear them. My floor looks clear, ahead of me."

"Copy that. Same here."

Just as she said that two men came walking around the corner! She melted back into a classroom doorway and knelt down.

"I've got contact," Tank whispered tersely.

"Me too. Take them out."

Like Michi, Tank had retreated into a classroom. He waited for the two men to walk past the doorway and then snuck up behind them. In one fluid motion, he shot the man on the left in the head and then the one on the right. They didn't even know what hit them.

Silencers aren't exactly silent, they just suppress the noise, and Tank acted quickly to guide the bodies to the ground as blood fountained all over the place. He dragged them into the classroom and pulled them around the corner, then quickly repositioned himself to see if anyone had heard the noise.

Michi used a different approach. She let them pass her and then snuck up behind them. With her deadly blades in both hands, she sprung up and reached over their shoulders slicing their throats from their Adam's apples around to their carotid arteries. As they pitched forward, she withdrew her knives and plunged them into their lower back, right into their spinal cords. The gurgling noises and grunts were audible, but not loud. She quickly dragged one body at a time into the classroom behind her, trying not to step in the slippery blood.

With the mission accomplished, she tapped her comms.

"All clear," Tank said quietly. "Two down."

"Make it four."

"I think they were setting up sentries."

"My thoughts, too. We need to contact Trey."

LEONARD WAS PRETTY EXCITED, and Trey could hear it in his dad's voice. "Good work Blue Team. Confirming that you have eyes on the primary target."

"Copy that," his son responded.

"Proceed with extreme caution."

"Vegas," Trey called to Bruce, "we have two hostiles in the front seat and our two targets in the back seat."

"Hemlock, I have no angle on the front players."

Trey was trying to figure out the best way to proceed and running through the odds of every option. It was tricky. He didn't know whether Casey or her team-mate were wired with a bomb or whether the two hostiles in front were talking to anyone who could call in their cavalry. He focused his sniper weapon on the front tire of the Lexus. Certainly, they'd need to disable the vehicle and attack at the same time. It was time to contact Michi.

"Gisō to Hemlock."

"I was just saying we needed to contact you," Trey responded, quietly.

"We have as many as fifteen armed hostiles and four priorities. We just took down four hostiles, but we're going to have to go *boom* to continue."

"Copy that. We're ready for you. We have confirmation of Primary Target and another Priority. Two hostiles. As soon as you go *boom*, we'll take them out."

"Are you in position?"

"Affirmative. Ready when you are."

"Blue Team, this is LP," Leonard's voice came on. "Those two hostiles are sitting under that bridge with our Primary Target for a reason. I think you have to expect hostiles from the river if you don't move very quickly. My guess is that their *rendezvous* is running late."

"Copy that, LP," Bruce acknowledged. "I agree."

Michi started creeping back, away from the middle section of the building and moved towards the last classroom before the staircase. Once inside it, she jogged over to the window and looked down into the courtyard. There were two men standing at the gate. Newly placed guards.

"Lakota, you were right. They're setting up sentries. Two of them are guarding the gate."

"Gisō, toss the *boom* down to them. That should draw out some hostiles. Be ready to take them out. I'll clear the third floor."

"My guess is there are sentries on every floor, now. We can't assume any of the areas we've cleared are still clear."

"I concur."

"Hemlock and Vegas, you have sixty-seconds," Michi updated Trey and Bruce.

"Roger that. Sixty and counting down," Bruce confirmed.

"Sunrise," Trey called to Jasmine urgently. "Are you in position?"

"Copy that," his daughter responded, with a calmness that surprised her father. "I've been monitoring the comms. I'm ready."

"Just make sure you keep covering our six. Keep an eye on the river, too."

"Okay. Got it."

Michi put down her pack and removed her comms from her ears. She pulled out a pair of earplugs, squeezed them and stuck them in. Then she took out three M67 grenades. The U.S. military has been using them since 1968. Each one weighs about fourteen ounces and pack 180 grams of composition B explosive. The primary explosive is fired by the M213 pyrotechnic delay fuse which delays detonation between four and five seconds after the spoon is released. With brutal and deadly force, steel fragments produce an injury radius of about fifty feet with a fatality radius of around sixteen feet. She placed them on a bookshelf and opened the window.

Snaking a knife out of her set, she cut the mosquito netting from the window frame and stuck her head out. She had a clear throw to the sentries by the gate. "That's about a sixty-foot throw," she mumbled to herself. "No problem." Michi jogged back to the classroom door and quietly closed it, noticing that it was solid wood and didn't have a glass slat, like many classroom doors normally have. "It has a lock on the door handle, too" she muttered to herself, kind of surprised. She depressed the lock button. It wasn't a very good deterrent if hostiles breached the classroom, she knew, but it was better than nothing.

She picked up a grenade and removed the safety clip, grasped the pull-ring with her non-throwing hand, and kept a firm grasp on the body of the grenade and most importantly, the safety spoon with her throwing hand. She took a deep breath, then pulled the grenade and pull-ring assembly apart, removing the safety pin from the fuse assembly. The fuse remained unfired because the thumb of her throwing hand was still holding the spoon down.

Agent Imada made sure that she wasn't going to hit the window frame as she threw, looked down at the hostiles again and then launched the grenade in a high arc towards the gate and the two hostiles. It was a textbook throw. The moment her hands released the powerful weapon, the striker spring released the safety lever, allowing it to fly free and the striker hit the cap, igniting the pyrotechnic delayed fuse. The ball didn't strike any obstacles, and the height of her arc took about three-and-a-half seconds. By the fourth second, it was five feet above their heads, and by the time the fuse initiated the grenade's explosive filler, it was right at their knees. The explosion shattered windows, and the deafening sound thundered around the courtyard. Deadly metal fragments raced through the air at phenomenally high velocities, and the two hostiles were obliterated.

CHAPTER SIXTY-TWO

SHOUTS OF RAGE AND CONFUSION PERMEATED THE AIR! FOUR MEN came sprinting out of the front door of the school and then hesitated, wondering what had happened. They were carrying the same guns that the traffickers in Ghaddafi's tunnels had carried: Chinese-made QBZ-95s. Not knowing exactly where the attack had come from, they fell into a diamond formation and moved towards the heavy wrought iron gate which had been blown off its hinges and was awkwardly sitting half-open and half-tilted on its side. Michi speedily readied the second grenade and threw it in almost the exact same location. This time, instead of killing two hostiles, it killed four.

The gate looked even more injured, and Michi realized the vehicles would have a hard time getting out. She didn't need to blow them up. So, she placed the unused grenade into her kit, took out her Glock 19, unplugged her ears and stuck in her comms. Just as she did, Imada heard the unmistakable sound of an AA-12 Atchisson Assault Shotgun. Tank was on the move.

Unlike the deafening noise in the school, Trey was lying in complete silence. He watched the driver's arm go up to his ear, holding what was most likely a phone. The reaction to the news from the school was telling. He didn't start yelling or slamming his fist into the dashboard. He simply nodded and hung up. "He's not in charge," Trey realized. "He's hired."

Suddenly, the air filled with the noise of a roaring engine as the Lexus sprang to life. Trey used the sound as cover and neatly took out the front and back tires. The vehicle lurched sideways as air evacuated the rubber at the same time the driver stepped on the accelerator.

"Vehicle disabled," Agent Stone reported.

"Copy that," Bruce answered.

The Lexus spun in a crazed circle like a mad Pitbull chained to a spiral stake. Then it slammed to a stop, almost exactly in its original position.

The enraged driver burst out of his door, and Trey could see the full size of the man. He was huge. Bigger than Fox. In the glint of reflection off the Nile, Stone couldn't help but notice his weird orange hair. With the door open, Trey sighted the passenger. It was Leila. He put the crosshairs on her head and was about to pull the trigger when Jasmine's voice came through his comms!

"Sunrise to Hemlock. A boat's coming! Fast! It'll reach you in seconds."

In that split moment, Leila had jumped out of the vehicle and jerked the back door open. She held a gun to the head of the girl closest to her and yanked her out. Casey followed.

Trey refocused his rifle on the driver and popped his head wide open. "One down."

544

The big ox fell to the ground in a crumpled, bloody mess as Leila shrieked with shock and rage!

"She knows we're here."

"Copy that," Bruce acknowledged from his perch. "Oscar Mike."

Stone focused on Leila but didn't have a shot. She was crouched down and using the girls as shields as she moved the group towards the Nile. He raised his head from his scope and looked to his left. A custom-painted black 2002 Baja 292 Islander was racing towards the sandy little beach under the bridge. It's 450 horse-power engine, fifty-five mile-per-hour top-speed, and flawless ability to turn sharply made it an ideal covert boat for the Nile. Swooping in, it banked sharply, creating a giant white wave in its wake, and then headed straight for the sandy beach. Trey whipped his gun around and looked through his scope. Three hostiles were in the boat. Two were in front, and one was behind them, in the main section, steering. He wanted to take them out, but with the bobbing up and down of the vessel, it wasn't a high percentage shot. Conserving his bullets, he waited. The boat slowed abruptly and coasted forward, its engine reduced to a soft idle.

"I'll kill them if anyone comes close to us!" Leila screamed, moving as quickly as possible towards the water, tugging at the girls and making sure they were screening her.

"Vegas, I'll disable Leila. Get the boat."

"Copy that. Coming around the Lexus on the north side."

Trey snuck a quick glance and saw Bruce on the near side of the Lexus, crouched down and almost invisible.

One of the hostiles in the front of the boat jumped down into the shallow water and started making their way to Leila, and the two soccer players. The driver was keeping the boat steady, pressing it against the sand with a low-running idle. Whether it was on purpose or not, Casey stumbled forward when they reached the sand, exposing Leila's left thigh. In two shots that would have awed any championship marksman, Trey shot the weapon out of her hand and planted a bullet just to the right of her femoral shaft.

Suddenly, several things happened almost instantaneously. Police sirens could be heard in the distance, making their way to the school. Leila shrieked in pain and fury and fell into the water. The captain of the boat fired up the reverse thrusters. Shot's snapped out of Bruce's M4 carbine, the newer and lighter variant of the American-made M16. The hostile that was headed to collect the girls fell backward with blood spurting out of his chest. Casey and her friend crouched down screaming and covering their ears. More shots fired out of Bruce's weapon. The boat captain's bullet-ridden body pitched over the side of the 2002 Baja 292 Islander. The remaining hostile had ducked down into the bow of the boat and was now raising his hands fearfully, waving his shirt in air.

There was a bizarre silence from the boat and the guns. The only thing making noise was Leila, thrashing around in pain like an injured shark.

"Casey, get behind me, NOW!" Bruce yelled.

The girls looked up, startled to hear an American voice, and the police sirens were getting louder. With the noise from the gunfire, it sounded like they were changing tact and heading for the battle scene under the bridge.

"Casey!" shouted Trey.

"Dad, a police boat!"

Trey jumped up, deftly moved his sniper rifle over his shoulder and picked up his Full-sized 9mm Sig Sauer P226 Tactical Operations Pistol.

Bruce heard Jasmine over his comms, too. He raced forward and grabbed the girls, lifting them up out of the water and shoving them in Trey's direction. "Follow him! This is your only chance!" They stumbled forward, almost falling, and then took off running towards Agent Stone.

Bruce picked up Leila and delivered a knockout punch to her head. He threw her over his shoulder, grunting with the combined weight of his kit and a human body, and took off following his friend as fast as he could. As he took off running, Trey turned and saw the shirtless hostile diving off his vessel and into the Nile. Thirty seconds later, the police boat came roaring into the area, its deafening sound echoing loudly off the bridge concrete. Someone began barking directions in Arabic through a bull horn. The wailing police cars arrived on the scene, and men in local Egyptian police uniforms spilled out, running towards the beach. Some of them saw Bruce and took off after him.

"Sunrise, NOW!" Trey shouted.

Jasmine leaped out of her hiding place. She looked down at the little black box in her hand and extended the antenna on it. Then she slid the black toggle switch on the left from *off* to *arm*, snapped the red switch to down and depressed the button that read *fire*. Little popping noises started sounding from everywhere, and within a few seconds, she could see smoke discharging and starting to spread. She grabbed her Jericho 941 FB and raced back to the white Toyota Land Cruiser. As she was running past the Suburban, she heard the locks pop up. Bruce must have unlocked them! She yanked the driver's door open and the one behind it. Then she ran to the vehicle that Trey had been driving and opened the passenger door. As fast as she could, she ran around the front of the vehicle and got into the driver's seat, starting the engine.

Trey came first, with the girls. He yanked the back door of the Land Cruiser open. "Get in!"

They obeyed.

"Jasmine, get out of here. Drive normally and stay on main roads. Stay off comms until you hear from me or my dad!"

His daughter didn't need to be told twice, she banged the vehicle into *drive* and took off, the passenger door slamming shut with the forward thrust. The two girls were thrown against the back seat.

Trey spun around, just in time to see Bruce stumbling forward with Leila on his back. He ran over and shouted, "Secure her in the back of the Suburban and keep the engine running. I'll be right back!"

"Trey, let's go!" Bruce yelled, but Agent Stone was already racing into the bushes on his way back to the scene. Locke focused on getting to the big black SUV. He opened the back hinge-door and tossed Leila onto the cargo floor. In less than a minute, he had her zip-tied and her mouth duct-taped. He slammed the door shut, and when he looked into the second row, he saw Trey's kit and rifle. *What's he doing?* he wondered as he threw his own pack on the floorboard, hopped into the driver's seat and starting the engine.

The police were completely lost in a cloud of smoke, coughing angrily and shouting obscenities. Two of them almost shot each other when they physically bumped together in the fog.

Trey, too, was in the synthetic fog. He crouched down and waited for a moment as a policeman ran right past him. Now in a bellycrawl, Agent Stone slipped through the thickest part of the confusion. Suddenly, he spotted a man in front of him facing the Nile. He was squatting in a thicket by a large Sycamore tree, frozen in place.

Stone approached him with the stealth of a legendary sniper. Noiseless. Fearless. Senses on the highest alert. The man's hair was soaking wet, and his pants were still dripping from when he dove off the boat. Placing his silenced weapon at the base of the man's skull, Trey said, "What you're feeling is the end of my 9mm Sig Sauer P226 Tactical Operations Pistol. I'm good at using it. You're going to get up, turn around slowly and walk in front of me. I'll tell you exactly what to do. If you don't, I'm going to kill you."

Thinking he could move faster than Trey, The Lynx whirled around attempting a grab at the business end of Trey's gun. The pistol jumped twice in quick succession in Agent Stone's hand. And with that, he removed one of the evilest men he'd ever met from among the living, and sent him to hell.

Trey took out his phone and snapped identifying pictures, just as the smoke started to thin out. A few police spotted them and started yelling. Some even pulled out their weapons. But by the time they got to where Trey had been, he'd vanished. One of them looked down at the corpse lying on its side in front of him, its eyes frozen in lifeless fury. Blood was still running freely out of the two bullet holes. One was in the man's forehead. The other was from a gaping hole in his back. Blood from that hole was oozing down over a giant tattoo of an emerald wasp.

Bruce was getting impatient. He knew the smoke cover would only last another few minutes. Thankfully, there was no breeze to clear the air. He rotated in his seat and saw his friend racing towards the SUV.

"Let's go!" he shouted, running around to the passenger's side, jumping in and slamming the door shut.

Bruce hit the accelerator like he was in a drag race. The tires squealed, bleeding rubber onto the road, and the vehicle shot ahead. "What the hell was that?!"

Stone scrambled into the back and dumped himself into the cargo area. "I killed The Lynx."

Bruce looked into his rearview mirror, the astonishment resonating on his face. "What the hell? What did you just say, Trey?"

"He was on the boat. I didn't know until the cops arrived, and I saw him dive off. I recognized the profile of his face from videos of him at various parties."

"So, you just shot him?"

"I told him to come with me. He went for my weapon. And I plugged him through the head and through a tattoo on his back."

"Incredible."

"Let's get to Michi. They could be in real danger."

"Copy that. Where's Baker?"

"Both girls are with Jasmine."

Agent Stone looked down at Leila in disgust. She looked utterly terrified. She was breathing heavily, and sweat was breaking out on her forehead.

Bruce was driving like it was Sunday morning on Route 66. "Nothing to see here, kids," he said as several police cars went screaming past him. "How much time do you need back there?"

Trey was cutting Leila's black cargo pants off on her left leg, right above where the bullet wound was. There was a First-Aid kit that he'd pulled from his pack sitting next to him.

"Seven minutes."

CHAPTER SIXTY-THREE

THE MOOD AT LAUNCHPAD WAS TENSE. JUSTIN WAS URGENTLY looking for a safe house in Cairo that could handle the discretion of someone of Ghalib's public stature. The first two he'd found had recently been burned and weren't stable. David was in the office area, following the actions of Tank and Michi. From his count, they'd taken out nine hostiles and had ten left. Although he agreed with the call, he hoped their *boom* strategy didn't result in the death of the hostages.

He kept looking up at the flat screens that hung above the desks, hoping for some kind of update to the maps or for a communication and anxiously pacing back and forth. Obviously, all the operators were keeping radio chatter to a minimum. He knew what that was like. Bullets. The smell of death. Fear. Totally focused. In the zone. Things playing out that needed full attention. Debriefs would come later. Second-guessing. The *what-if's* and *if only's*.

Saara was sitting at a desk with David pacing behind her. Not only was she monitoring the situation with Bruce and Trey, but also following Jasmine. The situation wasn't ideal at all. Trey's daughter was driving by herself, in an area with known terrorists, and carrying the most important piece of the entire mission: Casey Baker.

Leonard Stone was in the conference room and on the phone with Captain Daniel F. Jackson, the U.S. Navy's Commanding Officer at the U.S. Naval Medical Research Unit-No. 3 in Cairo. Their mission was to study, monitor, and detect emerging and re-emerging disease threats of military and public health importance, and to develop mitigation strategies in partnership with a lot of acronymed international agencies. President Baker had already communicated to the captain, and Leo was following up, but running smack into a wall of policies and procedures.

"I don't understand," Trey's dad said again, his voice rising. "You just received a phone call from the former President of the United States, whose security clearance is still above yours, telling you about a high-value person that needs to be held somewhere safe for a while and you're being *that guy*? The guy who is in our way? The obstacle?"

"Dr. Stone, we're a laboratory. We're full of infectious diseases that we're studying, we can't possibly bring anyone here who hasn't been vetted."

"You are first and foremost United States Navy. And are you telling me that in your little lab, you don't have a safehouse?"

"Not for the public, no."

"I'm going to give you one more chance to save your job and do what's right here, Captain."

"My job is quite safe, I assure you."

Stone hung up.

The conference room door opened, and Lin Lin Ma walked in.

"Leonard?" she called.

"Yes."

"I know of a place you could take Ghalib."

"Where?"

"A connection of mine owns a second-hand car dealership close to the airport on El-Nozha Street. I've been trying to get a hold of him for hours and finally just reached him. He said it'd be fine."

"How do you know him?"

"He's a supplier."

"Of?"

"Auto parts."

Leo didn't press. With her son-in-law and only grandchild in the field, she wouldn't be recommending this contact if she wasn't rock solid about the guy's trustworthiness. "What's his name?"

She looked down at her phone and tapped around. "I just sent you his contact information. Send it to Fox or Boyd. He's expecting their call."

"Thanks, Lin Lin," Leonard answered. The information popped up on his tablet and he immediately forwarded it to Fox and Boyd. "Hellcat and Razor. I just sent you the address for your safehouse. Take your guy there. We need to know where his brother is and who is in ..."

Dr. Stone was interrupted by an urgent yell!

"Black mamba!" Justin screamed. He was in the glass conference room and pointing outside of it to three, forty-three-inch television screens that were hanging in his section. They were dedicated to the closed-circuit cameras that provided security for Launch Pad. "We're being attacked! Black mamba! Black mamba!"

Six figures in combat fatigues could be seen approaching the building!

Everyone in the conference room immediately understood. The black mamba is the fastest snake in the world and one of the deadliest. Every time it sinks its teeth into its victims, it injects a deadly amount of neurotoxic venom into their bloodstream and humans die in less than thirty minutes. David had picked the code words to infuse speed and lethality into any emergency situation.

Leonard jumped to his feet and started barking orders. "Bora! Get to the medical room and lock the doors! Turn the lights off." Turning to Justin, he growled, "Get us our weapons packs, now!"

"On it!" Justin shouted.

Bora raced out of the conference room and ran to the Medical Center as fast as possible. Justin was right behind her and Leonard was following her. "David," he roared, "black mamba! Black mamba! Saara, switch off our comms to our teams and take them off our monitors. Make sure all of our internal comms are up. Have the emergency EMP ready! Black mamba, people!"

Justin could see the figures stacking outside the building's door, preparing to breach Launch Pad's outer hallway. He held his thumb to a scanner on a locker in his area with a bright red door. It clicked and he slammed it open. He was ready for something like this. He grabbed a stack of lightweight bullet-proof vests, and as David came running up to him, Justin threw him one.

"Put it on. Here's your kit," Justin said, handing it to Hirsch after he'd fastened the Velcro attachments on the vest. "HK MR556 semi-automatic rifle, HK 512 shotgun, HK VP9 9mm, stun grenades, flash bangs, smoke, lots of ammo."

"Got it." David said, racing off to take a tactical location in the kitchen area, facing the door. He unzipped his kit and took out the rifle and the pistol, laying them on the ground behind the island. He carefully removed two smoke grenades and put them there, too. Then he took out the shotgun and retreated twenty steps, laying it on the ground behind where the cabinets ended. It would be his fallback spot. He jogged forward and took up his position.

"Here's your vest. Here's your kit, Dr. Stone. Colt Model 1911 pistol, FN P90 submachine gun with your custom 5.7mm rounds, and the Benelli Black Eagle shotgun. You've got all the ammo you need."

"Thanks, kid. You know where to go?"

"Yes, sir."

Leonard turned to Saara, who was getting her vest put on by Justin while she tapped furiously on her tablet. "Make sure that Serwabi doesn't escape, okay?"

"Yes, sir."

"Saara, you've got four HK G36C's," Justin said, holding her backpack up for her to slip on. "No need to reload in an emergency. Just pick up the next weapon. They're ready to go. If for some reason you expel your ammo, there are more loaded clips in your bag. Safety's are all off!!" he finished, raising his voice as she ran off towards the interrogation rooms. Looking at the monitor, he yelled. "Outer doors are breached! Attack is imminent!" As he spoke, the Launch Pad in-house comms sprang to life.

"In position," David reported from behind the kitchen island.

Leonard responded. "Copy. Me too." He'd dragged the table out of the lounge area, flipped it on its side and set up behind it.

"We're ready," said Ashley from the Medical Center.

Justin grabbed his pack and sprinted across the large room to the little bedrooms. He went in his, wedged the door open, and lay prone behind the door frame where he had a clear and direct view of the only door into the warehouse. Leonard was to his left, about one hundred paces. David was at his two o'clock about two hundred feet in front of him. They'd all agreed the front door would be twelve o'clock. He dropped his bag, unzipped it, pulled out an FNH Scar 17. Then he emptied a pile of packed clips onto the floor next to him. They had seconds, not minutes. He didn't have time to make it all pretty.

In the medical center, as Ashley handed Bao Zhen a Glock 19, she asked the others, "Have either of you been rated on a Glock?"

"I haven't," Bora answered.

Lin Lin shook her head. "Me neither."

"Okay. Let's flip the operating table on its side, just like we practiced. We'll hide in the corner behind it. Hopefully, if they come through here, we'll draw them in. Bao Zhen, you'll be hiding behind the door and shoot them all in the back."

"I'm ready."

"Oh ... my ... God. Oh ... oh ... nooooooo!" Lin Lin said as the others climbed behind the table. She was standing still, as if she'd seen a ghost.

"What? Hurry up." Bora urged. "Get behind the table!"

"What is it Mama?" Boa Zhen asked, crouching in position, behind where the door would open.

"I know where I've seen Serwabi before."

CHAPTER SIXTY-FOUR

"LP?" Fox asked. "Come in LP."

There was no response.

"Hellcat to LP," Boyd tried. "Hell .. cat .. to .. LP!"

"It's weird. Like our comms have been shut down."

"Very strange," Agent Carter agreed, shrugging her shoulders. "Doesn't really matter though. We've got instructions to go to this car repair place. Let's find it, set up, and get to work on this guy. We need to find his brother."

"I agree."

Ghalib was trying to move around, but it was impossible. Zip-tied like a calf in a rodeo and sporting a silvery duct-taped face, it was already hard. But lying behind the front seats of the Tundra on the floor with a blanket over his head and Boyd's heavy kit on his chest, ensured that he had no room to wiggle. He was starting to feel claustrophobic.

Fox punched the address into the GPS on his tablet. "Thirty-two minutes. That's not bad."

JASMINE STONE TOOK a deep breath and let the air out. The shaking was finally stopping. She looked in her rearview mirror. Neither girl had said anything. They just stared at her.

"I'm so sorry. I was just focused on getting out of there. My name is Jasmine Stone."

Silence.

She looked at the blonde. "You must be Casey Baker."

Still nothing.

"And you're Abril Fuentes?"

"How do you know my name?" the teenaged Latino snapped back.

"There's been a group of us searching for all of you girls. Nonstop from the time your plane disappeared."

"Who sent you?"

"Your grandfather, Casey. And your dad. They've been unbelievably amazing in providing whatever we needed to get to you."

"I don't trust you," Baker responded. "You're obviously not special ops. What are you, like sixteen? As old as we are?"

Trey's daughter smiled. "You're good. That's pretty much my age. And you're right. I'm not spec ops or anything like that. My dad is though. He's one of the world's best snipers. We were on vacation in Europe when your grandfather reached out to him. My Dad and his team had no choice but to drag me along."

"So, we're not safe yet, is what you're saying," Casey said, a little meanly.

Jasmine tapped her comms. "Launch Pad?" she hesitated. "Oh, crap. My earpiece is dead." She turned her head. "Casey, can you reach into my bag? It's on the passenger seat here. There's a bright orange charger in there," she said, pulling her earpiece out. "Here, put this into the little unit when you find it. I'll plug it into the cigarette lighter."

President Baker's daughter took the bag and brought it to her back seat to rummage through it. "You have a gun?" she exclaimed, seeing Jasmine's Jericho 941 FB.

"You're safer than you think."

"Do you know how to use this?"

"My dad trained me."

"Where are you taking us?"

Jazzy looked at the fuel gauge. "I'm pretty sure we have enough gas to make it to Cairo. We'll go the American Embassy. I think it's a little under two hours from here," she said, taking the charger unit from Casey's outstretched hand. "Can you find my tablet in there and pull up Google Maps?" She asked, plugging her comms in.

Casey did as she was told and punched in the Embassy. "Where were we?"

"Put in Al Wasta. Two separate words. We're on the Aswan Western Agricultural Road."

Baker input the information. "Yup. We're one hour and fifty-four minutes away."

"Okay, zip up my pack and put it back on the front seat. I think it would be good if you girls got some rest. I'm fine driving with you sleeping."

Casey and Abril made themselves as comfortable as they could.

"Jasmine?" Ted's daughter said.

"Yes."

"Sorry I snapped a bit."

"No prob. I get it."

"Was your dad the one who pulled us out?"

"That was my dad's closest friend, Bruce. My dad was the one you followed to the car."

"Is he going to be okay?"

"I hope so."

"Why did he stay behind?" Abril asked.

"Probably to get to the other girls?"

"Where are they? And what happened to the German team?"

Trey's daughter filled the girls in on everything she knew. Leaving out the part about Abril's dad, of course.

TREY HAD WASHED the bullet hole in Leila's leg. He couldn't ignore the tattoo of an emerald wasp. It was large and detailed, taking up her entire thigh. After the rinse, he extracted the slug with some large tweezers, packed the wound with antibiotics and skin glue, and then wrapped her leg with adhesive tape. It wasn't going to win any medical awards, but it would keep her alive. He'd thought about giving her one of the two morphine shots in his kit but decided against it. Instead, he injected her with thirty milliliters of Clomethiazole. It would keep her asleep for three to five hours.

"Bruce, I can't reach Launch Pad," Agent Stone reported.

"I can't either."

"I've got a bad feeling. Like something's wrong."

Bruce had learned to trust his friend's gut. "We need to switch comms to inter-team only. If something's going down on their end, we can't be heard talking with each other."

"Good idea. I'll take care of it."

CHAPTER SIXTY-FIVE

TANK WAS FOCUSED AND DANGEROUS. STILL ON THE THIRD FLOOR of the structure on the left side of the courtyard, he'd waited patiently for the first *boom*. With the walls still shaking, he stole around the corner, into the middle-building's hallway. Directly in front of him were three hostiles who'd been standing together chatting. With the thunder of the explosion, they whirled around in different directions. None of them were ready for the business end of Tank's gas operated carbine HK416 A5. The first kill was a head shot. The other two were loaded with lead in their chests and backs. Without looking down, he reached around into his pack's side zipper and grasped the 40 mm low velocity GLM/M320 grenade launcher. Clipping it on, he was ready for the four hostiles that came spilling out of the room at the far end of the hall. His timing couldn't have been better. With an *ommph* swishing sound, the grenade sailed down the hall and when it detonated, the fragmentation filler ripped them all to shreds at the same time as he heard Michi's second grenade go off.

He crouch-ran down the hall, clearing each room until he got to the mess he'd created at the end by the staircase. There were two classrooms and he checked the one on his right. It was empty. The one on his left was a science lab. Four girls in Muslim hijabs were cowering in the corner behind the far workstation. They were crying and scared. Some debris from the power of the grenade explosion was hanging from the ceiling. Glass from the blown out windows had scattered on the floor.

"Targets secured. Seven hostiles down. I'm by the stairs."

"Copy that," Michi responded. "That leaves three. I'm coming to you."

"My name is Tank," he said to the hostages. "We're here to rescue you, okay? Stay where you are. I'll be right back." Sneaking out of the classroom, he carefully checked to his right. Except for the bodies at the far end, the corridor was still empty. He passed what remained of the four men he grenaded and snuck around the corner. Michi was coming out of her room at the far end of the hall. She started towards him.

Seeing that she was okay, he went back around the corner just in time to see a head do a quick peep-check at the other end. "We've got company," he reported firing off a few shots of covering fire in the direction of where the head had been.

Michi squeezed his shoulder so he'd know she'd arrived. "I'll get the girls. We have to get out of here."

"Copy that," he acknowledged firing off a few more shots.

Agent Imada went inside the lab. "Amber, Savannah, Sally, and Shelly, right?"

The girls just stared and her, trembling.

"My name is Michiko Imada. Your nightmare is almost over, okay? But you need to come with me. Right now. Hurry."

The four girls' soccer team members just continued to stand in the corner, paralyzed with fear. Michi ran through the lab tables and over to them. She grabbed Sally's arm. "Girls! Now!! We have to go. Stay very close to me. This is our only chance!"

Slowly, the information was making it into their brains.

"Are ... are ... are ... you American?" Shelly asked, uncertainly.

"I'm Japanese, but I'm part of an American special operations team that's been searching for you."

"There was a man with a flag. He got blown up. Was he with you?" Amber asked.

"That was Tank. He's fine. He's right here with us. That was the guy that was just in this room. He was driving a Hummer, right?"

Savannah nodded. "Yes."

"His vehicle got hit with a rocket-propelled grenade?"

All of them nodded.

"He made it out! We can talk about this later. You have to trust me. We're your only hope."

The girls jumped as Tank fired off his weapon. "Hostile down."

The wailing sound of police sirens sailed through the night air.

"NOW!" Michi said, sternly, shaking them all out of their stupor. "Follow me." She turned around and jogged through the lab, to the door. The girls followed.

"I'll take the lead," Tank said. "Girls, follow me in a single file. Don't bunch up. Don't get separated. Stay close."

He backed up to the staircase and glanced down. A hostile was coming up from the second floor and fired off shots from a Chinese-made assault rifle. Tank ducked out of the way, then stepped forward and fired back. None of the bullets were landing. The sirens were getting louder. With a loud Native scream, Tank jumped over the railing, untucking his Kampfmesser 3000! He landed on top of the man, plunging the spear-tipped German-made steel into his neck, ripping it wide open.

"Go, girls!" Michi urged, pushing them down the stairs. The girls screamed as they stumbled down the stairs.

Tank pulled his blade out of the bloody mess, shook it and sheathed it while repositioning his gun. Just in time. A hostile was coming up from the first floor. With another ear-piercing tribal scream, Lakota leaped over the railing and pounded bullets into the crown of the enemy's head. He landed on top of the guy's body, crushing it beneath him. "Clear!"

Michi and the four soccer players hurried down the stairs. The police sirens were about ninety seconds away.

"Hemlock to Gisō!"

"Perfect timing! Where are you?"

"Rear side of the school's middle building cutting the fence."

"Sixty seconds out. There's six of us," Michi responded.

"Copy that. Standing by for extract."

Tank raced ahead, finding a classroom with a window that faced Trey and Bruce. He launched a chair through it with such force that it shattered the glass and shredded the mosquito screen. Using the barrel of his gun, he swept away the shards of glass from around the edges of the frame. "Okay girls. You first," he said to Amber Taylor, taking her gently by the arm.

The police were thirty seconds away.

One by one, Tank helped the girls through the window. Then Michi threw her kit through the other side and followed it with her body. Tank did the same.

"Good work," Trey said. "Girls, follow me."

Bruce led the way, followed by Trey, the four soccer players, Michi, and Tank. They stooped through the fence and jogged to the big, black Suburban parked in the street directly behind the school.

Trey had raised the back seat-bench and moved Leila into the boot compartment in the back. "All four of you get in the back bench please," he directed. "Don't worry about seat belts. Just squeeze in back there. Gisō, in the passenger's seat. Vegas, you drive. Tank and I will sit in the middle-row-captain-chairs." The girls filed into the SUV. "If it's too crowded back there, one of you can sit on the floor space in front of you." With the operative's kits taking up the rest of the real estate, it was crowded, but everyone was safely inside. Bruce kept the headlights off and drove slowly, not wanting to attract attention. Although many of the cops in Egypt were hard-working and reliable, he didn't want to be pulled over by any of them. The red tape and media fallout would be tremendously bothersome. And then there was the fact that some of them were on the take.

When he'd gotten a block away, though, he turned the lights on and drove at a normal speed. Within seconds, cop cars went screaming past them, headed to the school. They'd have plenty of work to keep them occupied.

CHAPTER SIXTY-SIX

THE METAL SECURITY DOOR WAS FIRST. BLOWING OFF ITS HINGES with the force that only explosives can bring, it flew through the air into Launch Pad like a piece of plywood in a tornado. Then came the stun grenades. Two of them in rapid succession. The blinding flash of over seven million candelas with a simultaneous bang that was north of one hundred and seventy decibels crippled Justin, David, and Leonard. For a few seconds, their photoreceptor cells were rendered visionless and the fluid in their ear was severely agitated, causing a total loss of balance.

Two men entered in formation. They were dressed in black combat fatigues and wore dark grey Kevlar ballistics masks with eerie white skulls painted on their faces. One broke left and the other broke right, towards David.

Saara peeked out the glass slat in her door, unaffected by the flash-bang grenades because she'd been in a separate enclosed space. "David, fifty feet out. Your ten o'clock. Another one coming straight for me. A third and fourth one just entered the door and squatted down on either side. Hey! It's a classic snatch and grab formation!"

"They're coming for Serwabi!" Dr. Stone roared, struggling to get to his feet.

David focused hard on picking up a smoke grenade, but his whole body was trying to drag him away from where he was reaching. His head was spinning like he'd played a game of *running in circles until we all fall down*. Finally, gripping the cylinder, he pulled the pin and rolled it to his right. Within seconds, the entire kitchen area began to fill with thick acrid smoke. He'd just knelt down when a shotgun blast ripped through the air, missing him by inches! Hirsch immediately recognized the sound of a Norinco NR87. It was a short, Chinese-made, lever action gun. The smoke was thickening now. David took about ten steps backwards and felt his way to the end of the cabinets. He knelt down, just as another shotgun blast ripped through the silence and splintering the side of the island where he'd just been. Suddenly, a figure crept by him in the fog. Hirsch grabbed a kitchen knife off the counter and drove it through the guy's spine, then he lined up the guy's head with his HK 512 shotgun and pulled the trigger. With the adrenaline overpowering the stupor of the stun grenade, David found his way back to his 9mm and semi-automatic rifle. He knelt down by the shot-up island and decided to wait for the smoke to clear.

Leonard, too, was shaking off the effects. He peeped out from behind the table and saw a man in black fatigues pounding on Serwabi's door. The hostile had broken the thin slat of glass from the interrogation room door, but couldn't risk sticking his hand through the opening. Saara had already fired off a few warning shots. Noting the headgear and bulky black combat suit, Leo realized these guys had body armor that was pretty extensive. He crouched down and aimed his FN P90 at the hostile's feet. The custom-made bullets left his muzzle at over 2300 feet per second and embedded themselves into the assailant's ankles. He bellowed in pain and fell to the ground unable to walk. Suddenly, the two hostiles crouching by the door fired at Leonard. He deftly moved behind the table again.

Justin leaped to his feet and started walking to the front door, firing his FNH Scar 17. He could tell that their chests were protected. Their faces, too. But he kept pummeling them with shots until the momentum was too much for them to take and knocked them over. He shot out the backs of their knees. They fell to the ground. His bullets sliced through their exposed necks.

"Sitrep!" Leo barked.

"One down," David responded.

"Two down," updated Justin.

Saara burst through her door and pointed her weapon at the hostile writhing in the pain of having his ankles hobbled by Leo's bullets. "Move, and I'll put a bullet in your head," the tall Finn said matter-of-factly. The hostile started screaming, swear words in Arabic.

Justin and David met at the door. This time it was Leo's friend who tossed the stun grenade into the hallway. It detonated with vicious energy. The two remaining hostiles were obviously caught by surprise. David and Justin both entered the hallway and fired their weapons relentlessly, making sure the assailants were very dead.

The silence that followed was the same eerie silence that follows any shooting campaign. Gurgling noises from body cavities, the hostile by Saara rolling around in pain. And shouts of instructions.

"Clear!" Leonard announced. "Ashley, bring everyone here to help. Justin, search the bodies for anything. Cell phones. ID.

Take their prints. Face pictures. Saara, stay where you are. We'll talk to this guy in a second. David, come with me."

Hirsch scrambled to keep up with Trey's father as he marched into Serwabi's room.

"You lying sack of shit!" Leonard screamed, the fury boiling over. "How did they know you were here??" he demanded, holding his FN P90 firmly and pointing it at the MEO.

Serwabi sneered, his face contorted with an arrogant evil. "Fuck you!! And you too!" he said, spitting at David. "Rot in hell. American whores for your brainless government."

David Hirsch strode around the table and put his kit on the floor. Stooping over, he took out a knife and walked over to Serwabi. He cut off the zip ties from his wrists and feet. "Stand up!"

The MEO did.

David's knife whipped across Serwabi's chest, slicing his shirt, but not his skin. Hirsch ripped it off, just as Justin was coming into the room. "Check it." He proceeded to rip off Serwabi's wife-beater shirt. There on his back was the tattoo of an emerald wasp. "Take your pants off."

"Go to hell."

"Take them off, or I'll slice them off. And this time, I might carve you up a little bit."

"I don't know your names, but I know who you are. You're all cockroaches. CIA, FBI, Secret Service. All slaves to Jewish money."

"I know your name," a cold voice said from the door. "You're Adiacras Qadir Zafar."

The MEO's head spun around to stare at the speaker.

Lin Lin Ma continued. "Distinguished guest of the United Nations in Geneva at their ridiculous *Multinational Forum for the Liberation of the Palestinian People* conference. I translated for you. I still remember the title of your speech. *Alsawt Alfilastiniu. The Palestinian Voice.* You ended by leading a chant, *We will never give up.*"

Serwabi was stunned but quickly tried to recover with an almost whiney, pathetic voice. "You're crazy, lady. My name is Mohammad Al Serwabi."

"You're Palestinian. But you were born in Libya. Your parents decided to flee North Africa and took their kids to live in the Gaza strip. A few years after they moved there, they were killed in an Israeli airstrike. It was a brutal revenge attack."

"You're lying!!!" Serwabi screamed. "It was murder, not revenge."

David struck the MEO in the kidney and shoved him into his chair. "Not another word."

Trey's mother-in-law continued. "It … was … revenge," she reiterated. "Palestinians had captured a pregnant Israeli mother and gutted her for the world to see. Israel was furious. They carpet-bombed the whole area and killed over eighty people. Zafar's mother and father were killed in that strike." Lin Lin Ma turned to Leonard Stone. "He went on to raise his brother and sister on his own. He taught them everything. Including how to allow hate, rage, and bitterness to govern their lives." She turned back to look at Bao Zhen, who had just appeared at the doorway. "A gut-wrenching story, to be sure. Like many refugee stories around the world, I guess. But his carried an extra dose of hostility and unforgiveness."

Trey's mother-in-law walked over to a chair and sat down. "The name *Adiacras* means *king of the Libyans* and *Qadir* means *able, capable, and powerful.* You made sure everyone understood your destiny," she said, looking straight into Serwabi's twitching face. "A Libyan-born Palestinian knight of sorts commissioned to rescue his people and deliver a death blow to Israel and all of its friends. I remember you well now. Your face. Your eyes. Your voice. The nervous licking of your lips." She shuddered.

Serwabi sneered at Leonard; then back at Ma.

"It was almost thirty years ago. Isn't that something? But I remember it as if it was yesterday." She put a piece of paper on the table. "A few minutes ago, while the gunshots were going off, I was at the Medical Center's computer, searching the United Nations database." She looked at Leo. "I still have access, thanks to Saara. I found this. I knew it existed."

"Who's in the picture?" Leonard asked, needing his reading glasses. He could see that there were three people standing in a room.

David stepped forward. "You lied about living in Nigeria with your father." He picked up the picture and described it to his friend. "Serwabi's in it. Looking very young. He's standing in what looks like a meeting room of sorts. On his right is a very attractive young woman with jet-black hair." Hirsch stared at the girl's dark eyes. Even for her young age, they flashed a dark evil.

The MEO was boiling with rage. Everyone could see it.

"On his left, is a young man."

"You remember this room?" Lin Lin Ma asked the MEO and pointing to the picture as David put it back on the table for all to see. "The white chairs? The front wall? That art piece by

Jacob Sørensen that nobody can make sense of?" She turned to David. "It's an homage to genocidal dictators, titled, *Confused*." She looked back at Adiacras Qadir Zafar. "It's one of the board rooms at the United Nations building in Geneva."

"Wait!" David said, stepping back in shock. "Is that Serwabi with The Lynx and Leila??"

"That's how you know them," Bao Zhen answered, looking at her mom, at the MEO, and then back at David. "That's Adiacras Qadir Zafar standing with his younger brother and sister."

CHAPTER SIXTY-SEVEN

"LP to Hellcat and Razor," Justin called out.

"You're back!" Boyd exclaimed.

"You have new orders."

"Copy that," responded Fox.

"I just sent them to your tablet."

Boyd looked down and read what he'd sent. "Copy that. Are they expecting us?"

"They are."

"Roger that. We'll proceed to the new coordinates."

Justin disengaged the comms and Fox turned to Boyd. "Where are we going?"

"The United States Embassy in Cairo."

"With one of the most famous faces in Europe hog-tied in our vehicle?"

"He said they're expecting us," Boyd said, putting the tablet back into a place where Fox could follow the GPS directions. "It's only about twenty minutes away."

"LP to Hemlock."

It was great to hear Saara's calm voice.

"Hemlock and Vegas," Trey responded. "Did we lose you?"

"We had a black mamba, but everything's fine. We'll update you later. We need a sitrep."

Trey suppressed his desire to shout, *what happened??!!* Instead, he echoed Saara's calm voice. "Mission successful. We have our cargo with us." Then smiled as he heard the cheers in the background.

"Well done, Blue Team. I'm sending the coordinates to where you're supposed to go. You should have it on your tablet. Hemlock, we've been unable to reach Sunrise."

"She hasn't responded to us either. But I know her well. She's got our Primary Objective plus one, and is mobile until she hears from you or me."

Bruce held up his tablet so Trey could see that they needed to get to the Embassy.

"Copy that," Saara said, a little nervously.

Jasmine was driving the speed limit, not wanting any reason to be pulled over. She looked at the sleeping girls in the back seat and then figured her comms had charged up a bit, so she decided to see if they had enough juice to work. Her dad had told her not to use them until she was contacted, but she decided to risk initiating communication. Removing them from the charger, she stuck the little earpiece in her ear and turned it on.

"Um ... Sunrise to LP?"

IT HAD BEEN about twenty minutes since the attack on Launch-Pad. Leonard was talking to President Baker on the phone. Saara had rebooted comms, and all the operators had reported in. Justin had taken the living hostage to the medical facility where the patient was under anesthesia while Ashley worked on his ankles to remove the bullets. Bora was giving her a hand. Lin Lin and Bao Zhen were cleaning up the mess, careful not to move the bodies. And David was on his phone talking to someone he could trust to come and get the corpses and deliver them to the Company.

Dr. Stone hung up his phone and called everyone except Bora and Ashley into the conference room. "President Baker and his son send their congratulations to us all."

"Hold on," Saara said. "Let's patch in the Medical Center." She tapped a few times on her tablet and Ashely, and Bora appeared on her screen. She propped up her tablet on the table and adjusted it so the two could see everyone else. "Just keep working," she said, "I wanted you to be be a part of this meeting though."

"Got it," Ashley said. "Go ahead."

Leonard repeated what he had just said, "President Baker and his son send their congratulations to us all."

"This was intense; I'm not going to lie," David confessed. "I was just crawling around in the smoke and hoping I'd see the attacker before he saw me."

"Let's do a quick sitrep," Leonard said, nodding. "Justin? You had something you wanted to say?"

With his right hand, Bora's husband held up a little square panel of sorts. It was about the size of a quarter, but square, thin, and grey. "This is a low-level transponder. I found it in Serwabi's ... I mean, Adiacras Qadir Zafar's, shirt collar. It's how his men found him. Also, I don't know if you looked at all the bodies. I ripped their shirts open." He tapped on his tablet and the smart-table lit up with pictures. "An emerald wasp is tattooed on all their chests."

"They were Palestinian operators," Leonard said. "Right here in the United States. Well-trained, too. If we weren't as prepared as we were, there's no question they would've extracted him and most likely collected a lot of intel from our computers."

"Bora?" David asked. "You wanted to share something?"

Ashley nodded, "It's okay. Go ahead."

Justin's wife turned to the camera. "Dr. Stone, you'd asked me to go back through Jee Hye's black book. I did. Honey, can you pull it up?"

Justin tapped on his tablet, and another set of pictures came up on the table. They were photographs of Jee Hye's diary.

"I'm sorry I missed it, but I don't think I would have seen it until we had all these pieces in place. This woman was ... unbelievable. I'm so disappointed that I never got to meet her. She was truly brilliant. If you look at how she wrote, you can see that there are individual Korean characters that are slightly elevated in her text. It's subtle, but I drew horizontal lines ... Honey?"

Justin tapped again, and thin red lines appeared in the text.

"See that? I drew those lines."

"Okay," Leonard said. "I see what you mean. Individual characters that are about three millimeters higher than the characters around them. What do they say?"

"Well they're in Korean, but different elevated characters run through the entire book, about two or three of them on each page. When transliterated, they read, *Fuentes, Zafar, Lynx, Leila.*"

"My God," said Dr. Stone. "No wonder Jee Hye was murdered because of this book."

Everyone in the room was stunned.

"You mean …" David couldn't finish; he was so shocked.

"I think all four of them were in the room when she was being raped."

"… and when she heard *Baker*, it's because they were planning the abduction of Casey?" Bao Zhen asked, incredulously.

Bora nodded. "That's what I think."

"And they either witnessed or took part in … in … what happened to her?" Lin Lin asked, covering her mouth in shock.

"Most likely, yes."

CHAPTER SIXTY-EIGHT

The security at the United States Embassy was on the highest alert. When Jasmine pulled up, she was surrounded by guards. She rolled all the windows down in the vehicle.

"Identification?"

"I'm sorry," she answered. "I don't think any of us have any."

"What's your name?"

"Jasmine Stone. The girls in the back are President Baker's granddaughter, Casey, and her friend, Abril Fuentes."

"Turn your engine off, please."

Trey's daughter complied. "I have weapons in my backpack."

"Keep your hands on the steering wheel then, please, Miss Stone."

One of the other guards opened the back door and looked in at the girls in the back seat. "Uncover your heads, please."

Casey and Amber complied, looking like they'd just woken up.

The guard touched his radio. "I have positive recognition of Casey Baker."

The first guard, who stood by Jasmine's door the whole time said, "Miss Stone, turn your engine back on and drive forward very slowly. I'm going to walk in front of your vehicle and lead you to where you need to park."

"Yes, sir," she answered, starting the engine and shifting into *drive*.

The gates opened, and she slowly followed the Marine in front of her. He led them to drive around the corner, and she burst into tears at the sight of Fox and Boyd waiting for her. She parked as directed, still sobbing, and then got out.

"Hi Jazzy," Fox said, as she collapsed into his arms.

"Well done," Boyd said, making it a group hug. "You did so well. We're so proud of you."

Jasmine just couldn't stop crying.

"It's all over," the big blond agent said. "It's all over. Your dad, Bruce, Michi, and Tank are on their way. They're about twenty minutes behind you."

They hugged for a little longer and then Jasmine pushed back. "Fox, Boyd? This is Casey and Abril."

The four exchanged hugs.

"I can't imagine what you've been through," Boyd said compassionately. "But it's all over now. We're in a very secure facility, as you can see, and we're just going to wait for the other girls to join us. Then we'll get out of here."

"They're coming here?" Casey asked, excited, and relieved.

"Yes," Fox said. "They are all safe and on their way."

The Embassy's Marines escorted everyone inside the building to a receiving lounge of sorts. It was a large room, windowless, but beautifully lit, full of tables and couches, a place where visiting dignitaries and their families could relax. There was a bubbling water fountain in the corner that injected a soothing sound into the ambiance, a kitchenette with drinks on the counter, and what Jasmine noticed, beautiful fresh flowers and fruit adorning several side tables.

Trey's daughter had pulled herself together and sat on a couch next to Casey and Abril.

"Ma'am, there are some people who want to say hi to you two," a Marine said, handing the soccer players a tablet.

The faces of President Baker, his son, and Abril's mother came onto the screen.

BACK IN ROME, the American parents were crying with joy at the news they'd received. Several of them were hugging each other. Some were on their knees, thanking God. Ted and his wife were going from couple to couple hugging generously. All of them had gotten a chance to speak to their daughters via video calls and were now just enjoying the relief of the moment. All except one. Felipe Fuentes wasn't in the building anymore. He was already on his way to the airport in cuffs, escorted by Vince Graham, and on his way to prison hell. He would never see a trial or be placed in a normal prison. Because of the intel he still possessed he would disappear into a place that officially didn't even exist.

FAWWAZ AHMAADI WAS MAD. He closed all the windows in the plane and sat down; even the bright sunlight was irritating. His fifteen-million-dollar ERJ 145, made by Embraer, the Brazilian jet company, lowered its landing gear. The older twin hadn't been able to reach his brother for the entire flight. This lack of communication was just the kind of thing that infuriated him. At important times, when he really needed to talk, Ghalib always had somewhere else to go or some deal he was making. It really ticked him off. Fawwaz sat down, wearing a facial expression that was something between a pouting two-year-old and an old drunken tyrant. With a slight bump, the aircraft completed its journey from Italy to Cairo. One more time, he tried calling his brother, but his younger twin's phone went straight to voicemail.

The plane parked and he unbuckled his seatbelt. When the door opened, and the staircase was lowered, he stood, gathered his things, and strode towards the exit.

"Have a good evening, sir," the pilot said.

Fawwaz paused. Even in wrath, he needed to be kind to the help. "*Shukran*, my friend," he said, shaking the pilot's hand. "Thank you."

The air was clean, the sky was blue, and sunshine was filling the nation with light. Holding onto the railing, he descended the short staircase and then straightened up noticing that there were half a dozen dark SUV's parked around the plane. Unexpectedly, their doors flew open, and within seconds, he was swarmed by American operators; his bags were yanked out of his hands; some of them boarded the plane, waiving a warrant at the pilot. The older brother was thrown onto the concrete face down and cuffs were being slapped onto the wrists of the great Fawwaz Ahmaadi. Blood started dripping out of his broken nose.

CHAPTER SIXTY-NINE

A FULL MONTH HAD GONE BY SINCE THE GIRLS HAD BEEN RESCUED. David organized some friends he could trust to clean up and repair the physical damage at LaunchPad. And now, everyone on the team had gathered to celebrate and debrief the experience. Jun had come down from *David's*, and together with Ashley, they laid out quite a buffet. A long table with chairs had been set just outside the doors of the interrogation rooms, and a few people were taking their seats with loaded plates.

"This looks fantastic," David said to Justin.

"It does. I'm starving," the young man responded. Then their eyes met. Just for a moment. And there was a look that passed between them. It's the kind of look two people give each other after they've survived a trauma that no human being should have to go through. David had seen it many times. As had Justin.

"Me too, kid. Me too."

"Did you see Rain's interview with the U.S. soccer team?" Lin Lin asked Bora and Bruce as they stood in line for the food.

"I thought it was really powerful."

"President Baker delivered," Leo chimed in, putting some roast beef on his plate and a spoon of horseradish. "Her viewer ratings are skyrocketing and I hear she's getting calls from major networks that want to interview her."

"I'm glad," Ms. Ma said. "But it was clear to me that the girls still have a long way to go. Especially the ones who lost their parents. All of them experienced so much anguish."

"That's for sure. Their emotions were raw. Parts of it were hard to watch."

Trey had walked over to his wife and daughter, who were getting themselves drinks from the kitchen island. "Hey Jazzy, I have some news," he said, quietly.

Bao Zhen smiled and looked at her daughter.

"What is it, dad?"

"David thinks we should live more normally. We're moving out of hiding."

"Really??"

"Yes, dear," her mom said, smiling.

"Seriously."

"We'll have 24-hour security for a while, but, yes. You need to have a normal life."

"Thank you!" she exclaimed, pulling her parents together. "Thank you so much! I'm so happy!!"

Lin Lin Ma looked over at the three of them and gave her son-in-law a big smile. She knew the news that had just been delivered and was looking forward to being closer to them.

Fox was walking out from his bedroom when all of a sudden, he stumbled and grunted. "Help!" he cried as he pitched forward and fell to the ground!

"Ashley!!" David yelled. "Something's wrong with Fox!"

Everyone that was at the table jumped up and hurried over. Bao Zhen knelt beside him and then Ashley came rushing in, kneeling across from her.

"Fox! What's wrong??"

"My legs. My chest. My ..."

"What? Are they aching? Is it a sharp pain?"

"My hand. Look at my hand."

Ashley checked his right hand. It looked fine. But his left hand was curled up in a tight fist. She grabbed his hand and put everything she had into prying his fingers apart. All of a sudden, it popped open and a ring fell out. White gold. With a beautifully attached princess cut 2-carat diamond. Fox sat up unexpectedly and shifted to one knee.

She started trembling.

"Ashley, I'll never forget the first time I saw you. You took my breath away. We've grown together so much since that time. I would've never dreamed that someone as beautiful as you would become as close a friend as you've become."

Tears began spilling down her cheek. "Fox ... I ... I ..."

"And I've fallen in love with you. I didn't know what to say to you on that first day we met, but I know what to say now."

The trembling increased into sobs.

"Will you marry me?"

David was grinning from ear to ear as everyone else switched from being deeply concerned to jubilation.

"Kurt Middleton-Fox," she answered, pitching forward into his arms. "If you ever do something like this to me again ... I'll ..." and then she completely melted. It surprised and embarrassed her a little bit. She couldn't stop. But everyone understood. It was like a purging from her own grief of losing her fiancé several years back. He'd been on her operating table when he died, and it seemed like in this moment with Fox, she finally forgave herself for believing like she hadn't done enough to save his life. She clung to the giant agent. "Are you sure you want me?"

"I've never been more sure in my life. I just needed some help to realize that," Fox said, looking up at David and then back at her.

"Okay, then," Ashley responded. "Yes!!! I want to marry you and I have for quite a while now."

Everyone broke out in cheers and applause!

The eating and celebrating went on for a few hours. Nobody was in a hurry to go. Justin and Bora talked about their wedding and told some fun stories. Ashley had some hilarious anecdotes about growing up with David as her adopted dad and Trey as her adopted uncle. Jun shared what it was like to be working at *David's*. The group had a lot of fun.

As the evening went on, Jun and Justin started to clean up and were joined by Bora and Ashley. Lin Lin, Bao Zhen, and Jasmine were relishing some tea and talking about what it was like to leave Switzerland and what it would be like to live *normally* again.

David, Leo, Fox, and Trey decided to go to the conference room for cigars and whiskey.

As they sat down, Trey got a big smile on his face. "Congratulations, Fox. Well done." The others echoed the sentiments as they lit up their stogies. Bruce and Boyd decided to join them.

Soon they were swapping stories from the experience they'd just been through and often deferring to moments of silence when there was really nothing to say. But as in any time like this, they also started asking and answering questions.

"Hey, David. Whatever happened to the wooden box I brought from California?" Fox asked.

"We usually use any collected resources to pay for stuff around here. But that box was different. It was Jee Hye's. We're going to use that money to set up Jun and also put his mom through rehab. Haven't told him yet."

"That's a great idea."

"Dad, I heard from some of my Company contacts that they've been able to leverage that guy with the shot-out ankles," Trey said. "Is that true?"

Leonard nodded, "He's given up five Palestinian child-trafficking cells in the United States that were part of the Emerald Wasp network. The MEO was at the top of the food chain. He's going to have a military tribunal and will probably be executed."

"Whatever happened to Adam and his sister?" Fox asked.

"Yeah, were they really his kids?" added Boyd.

"Adam's been detained in L.A. for questioning. Megan is still off-grid somewhere. I suspect she might be in Mexico." Trey's dad shook his head and chuckled, as he looked at his glass. "Yeah, they're his kids."

They took a moment to puff on their cigars or take a sip.

Bruce spoke up. "Does anybody else find it weird that lynxes aren't found in the Middle East? I wonder how that name became famous."

Fox chuckled. "I wondered that, too."

"What about Leila?" Trey asked.

"She's been directly connected with the laptop you found in Egypt. Between that and the computer Boyd got from Ghalib, there's enough evidence to put everyone away forever, including the twins. That little book she discovered in his suit ..." Trey's dad shook his head, "... I mean ... wow. It's hard to believe he'd keep paper records of the stuff they were involved in."

"Yeah. That was surprising," agreed Agent Carter. "We never tracked down the Stingray, did we?"

David looked at her and then at Leonard. "No. We didn't."

"Did we ever find out how Jee Hye got connected to these people?" Bruce asked.

Dr. Stone shook his head. "We may never know."

Trey watched the ash from his cigar fall into the large ashtray in front of him. "I wonder how many Jee Hye's are out there?"

The smokers all sat in silence, thinking about what Agent Stone had just said.

"We did a good job. But we can't say we're done just because we made evil start to limp."

ABOUT THE AUTHOR

Conrad Brasso is an emerging author of CIA thriller novels. This is Conrad's second book.

Get notice of new releases and special deals by following the author at http://www.bookbub.com/authors/conrad-brasso

Join the insiders updates list at www.conradbrasso.com for advance access, insider information, and exclusive free bonuses!

FROM THE NEXT BOOK IN THE TREY STONE SERIES:

Torching The Crimson Flag

CHAPTER ONE

Meticulous. Brilliant. Professional.

Trustworthy. Accurate.

Studious.

Discreet.

Patriot.

Those were just a few of the ways people described the most protected man on the planet. He wasn't the president of the free world, he held no high position in a company, he didn't own a world-changing patent, and he certainly wasn't a social media magnet. He was the opposite of that, whatever it would be called. He had no wife, no kids, and no family. Not even a dog. That was part of the deal. He didn't mind; it actually appealed to his slightly neurotic obsessive-compulsive personality. Nathan

B. Harris liked to lead a simple life, yet the United States government had no limit on the amount of money and resources they devoted to keeping him safe.

Dr. Harris was the Chief White House Translator. He spoke eleven languages fluently and had diplomatic status in all of them. That meant that he could just as easily translate conversations on trade as he could facilitate talks about the effects of Genetically Modified Organisms on corn crops in Argentina. He'd honored four administrations with his skills and had sat in on almost every meeting that those American Presidents had held with foreign dignitaries. He was part of the meeting on nuclear disarmament between President George Baker and the leader of North Korea. He sat next to President Webb at the Euro/America Summit when the United States was embroiled in intense negotiations with Russia. Two years ago, when Japan had experienced provocation from China, he was part of those bilateral meetings, seamlessly moving from English into Japanese and Mandarin, and back to English. He accompanied the American Ambassador to Israel when an Arab-led coalition was questioning the integrity of a newly-negotiated peace process. His official role there had been part of the hospitality team. Only the U.S. Ambassador knew Nathan was fluent in Arabic and harvesting information from the other side while he worked in disguise.

Despite all of his grand accolades, another word to describe Harris would've been *unrecognizable*. As a matter of fact, if anyone saw a picture of him, nobody would know who he was or remember having seen him before. It was one of his most important attributes and, believe it or not, one of the reasons he still held the position over a sexy director from a flashy communications firm in New York who'd matched his linguistic skills and tried to steal his job.

The day he was kidnapped began like every other day in the last thirty years of his life. His alarm started chirping like a bird at 4:30AM, gradually getting louder, until he turned it off six minutes later. He got out of bed and immediately remade it, perfectly. Although Nathan Harris was simple, he'd always purchased quality. And every time he made his bed, he'd run his hand over the uber-soft seamless Dreamsacks silken sheets and think about the importance of being the best. After using the restroom, he'd walk to the kitchen and drink a full glass of water before going downstairs and spending an hour on his Expresso Fitness S3 Novo – an exercise bike that features a 19-inch monitor, an interactive fitness management system, over thirty virtual tours of the world, and the ability to race against other bikers with real-time road conditions. After an ice-shower, fifteen minutes in a steam room, and another ice shower, he'd get dressed in quality but plain clothes, have breakfast, and take ten minutes to read the Bible and center himself in his faith. Then he'd stand by his front door until his security detail pulled up at the curb and said it was okay to step outside.

Tim Michaels was former Secret Service. He wasn't retired. He'd been cherry-picked for this job along with five other highly competent operators. They traveled with Nathan to foreign countries, checked his accommodations, and were on constant protective duty and high alert. Being former SS worked well because they understood how the President's security functioned and were able to seamlessly integrate the translator when he needed to be present.

On this day, the medium gray 2005 Cadillac Escalade with darkly smoked windows pulled up to the curb. This particular vehicle had been custom-designed in Silao, Mexico at the factory. The word *escalade* refers to a siege warfare tactic of scaling fortified walls or ramparts with the aid of ladders or siege towers. From the outside, the bullet-resistant exterior seemed to match any other Cadillac. But inside, the vehicle was battle-ready, equipped with the latest in technology and communications.

Nathan observed four men in dark suits with sunglasses get out. One watched ahead, the other viewed back, the third stood just outside the driver's side door and pivoted his head in multiple directions. Tim was the fourth man. He checked left and right and then calmly walked up the sidewalk to Nathan's front door.

"Dr. Harris."

"Tim."

"Good night?"

"Always," he said, allowing a slight smile to emerge from under his mustache. Checking the angle of his carefully placed brown homburg on his bald head, he tipped the brim and said, "We're living the dream, kid. Living the dream."

The conversation was always the same. It wasn't an accident. If Dr. Nathan B. Harris had been intimidated, threatened, frightened, or was under any other kind of duress during his resttime in his home, he'd have responded differently. He'd have said, "Yes, thank you. I slept great." That would trigger a myriad of prepared responses beginning with him being physically scuttled away. Then, a few members of his team would clear his house, take all of his digital equipment, sweep the place for spying bugs, and that was just the beginning of the protective protocol.

"Package received," Tim informed the others. He waited for Harris to close his front door and make use of the thumb scanner in the center of it to lock and arm the home.

The two men were just turning to walk down the sidewalk when four KTM 250 motorcycles came ripping around the street corners! Two at each end of the short block. They accelerated with tremendous velocity – their riders hunched over to maximize aerodynamics.

Tim pushed the translator forward, "Get into the car, now!!"

It was too late. The bikers had their QBZ-95's ready. By the time Nathan Harris' security detail drew their Glocks, small-caliber, high-velocity, copper-alloy-jacketed hardened steel-cored bullets were ripping their bodies apart.

Harris froze. Terrified.

"Get in the car!" John Grayson yelled, from the driver's seat. "Nathan! Move!"

One of the bikers pulled up beside the Escalade and tossed a black sticky object against the driver's side door. In a short second, the bomb exploded the bullet-proof door and the rider shot Grayson. His blood splattered all over the inside of the half-million dollar vehicle. A white 2004 Ford E Series Van skidded onto the scene with its side door open and screeched to a halt. Two figures hopped off their bikes and threw Dr. Harris to the ground. They zip-tied him like cowboys tying a calf in a rodeo and tossed him into the van.

The whole scene had taken less than a minute and now the street was eerily quiet, except for the noise of death gurgling from the government-provided security personnel. Several neighbors called 9-1-1 to report the gunfire. But there was one house, two houses down and across the street, who had three roommates sharing the space. In the neighborhood, they were known as young Millennial entrepreneurs trying to make it in the digital marketing space. In reality, they were hired by the Secret Service to monitor Nathan's house for just such a moment. They took turns keeping constant watch, monitoring comms and recording every action around his home. Every minute of every hour. Night and day. It was boring and tedious. But not right now. As soon as things began to happen, they scurried together and placed an immediate call to the President directly. It was a short conversation with devastating news.

As the information got reported through secure intelligence channels, dozens of heads of nations from around the world were in full-fledged panic mode.

Dr. Harris knew all their secrets.